PRIMAL BARGAINS

RALEIGH DAVIS

CHAPTER 1

I have no idea Gideon Wolfe's life is as fucked up as rumor says until I see the smashed gate-access box.

I've heard all kinds of things. Whispers about a ruined face, a mind gone totally insane, a company left completely leaderless—all that flashed through my mind when I got the call about installing a new security system at Wolfe's South Bay compound. But I put them out of my mind—at least I tried to, because some of them are *wild*—and focused on the job. A job with a possible payday that could solve all my problems and then some. So I'm going to ignore the rumors and give Wolfe the best security system in the world.

Every single crazy story comes rushing back to me as we pull up to the front gate, all big and wrought iron and imposing, at least several feet higher than the roof of my little work van. I reach out to punch the buttons in the call box...

And where the screen and keypad are supposed to be is just a mess of wires and smashed glass and broken buttons. The post is still standing straight, so it wasn't a car plowing into it that did this. It's very specifically localized to the screen and buttons—the metal box is intact and smooth. It's almost like someone took their fist to the sensitive parts of the box.

Suddenly the darkest rumors I heard don't seem so far-fetched.

I pull my hand back as I swallow hard. I look at Victoria in the passenger seat. She's my coworker and best friend. And my lieutenant once upon a time, back when we were both in the Army. We exchange raised eyebrows.

"What the hell is going on?" I ask.

She bites her lip like she wants to turn around. But she says, "That's why we're here, right? To make this place secure?"

"The dude I talked to didn't say anything about the gate-code box being smashed." I take a quick glance around and lower my voice. "And then there's all the stuff everyone's been saying."

Things like Wolfe's face is completely scarred. That he has burns over ninety percent of his body. That he knew his attacker. That he hasn't been seen by *anyone* since the incident. That he's locked himself in his attic like some mad wife in a book.

Of course, there are also the rumors that he's just fine, that this is a publicity stunt, that he hired the guy who attacked him.

The only thing anyone knows for sure is that Gideon Wolfe, billionaire and inventor of lifesaving, revolutionary medical devices, had something happen at his compound a week ago. Ambulances came, smoke was spotted, the police were there. And he hasn't been seen in public since.

No one knows where the rumors came from, but it doesn't really matter. Once they lit up, it was like a wildfire, racing from person to person. Even if Wolfe did start the rumors, he can't control them now.

The one thing *I* know for certain is that my fledgling security firm was hired yesterday to come out and beef up his security. I was offered an insane amount of money to drop everything to do it, the kind of money that will wipe out my student loans, my parents' mortgage, and my sister's legal debts. My whole family would be debt-free for the first time in… ever. We could actually all take a breath without hundreds of thousands of dollars of worry hanging over us.

It was also a huge coup for my firm, Shield Solutions, to be offered this job. We're small and scrappy, and being hired by one of the most famous men in Silicon Valley would be awesome for our name recognition.

Wolfe might even pass our name on to his billionaire friends. He's got a circle of them, five guys who came up together in the rough-and-tumble tech world. They all started their own companies, and they all got super, super wealthy from them. The rumors about the five of them are even wilder than the rumors about what happened to Wolfe. They belong to the same exclusive sex club. They own a private island—for sex parties, of course. They fly together on their private jet—and have sex parties on it. Oh, and mostly they're photographed together at fancy parties… where they're not having sex. But they probably go to the sex club together after.

When I heard those things, I thought they were funny, like something out of a prestige drama that took itself too seriously. But now that I'm actually going to meet Gideon Wolfe, imagining those stories makes my mouth dry and my heart pound in a way that isn't exactly disapproval.

Victoria blows out a long breath. "We don't know what happened." She looks to the closed gates. "But if we go inside, we can find out."

"Why, Victoria Shepard, are you suggesting we snoop?"

Her cheeks go pink. "No. But we might see something as we're going through the place."

I look up at the gate. "Well, I'm very tempted to do some snooping. But nothing's going to happen until we get through this." I reach for my cell phone. "Let me call the guy and see what's going on."

Right as my hand closes over the phone, the gates start to swing open slowly, silently. Something about the sweep of them reminds me of a bell tolling, which is weird.

"I guess the security cameras weren't smashed then," I say.

But as we drive through the gates, I can't see any cameras. And I know exactly where to look because I install the things. If someone is watching us, I can't see where they're watching from.

The estate is out in the middle of nowhere. Like real nowhere, not the Bay Area version of it. We came in on the 84, passed a few small, charming towns, then had to go south on a dirt road. We turned on another dirt road, then another, until we finally ended up on something called a truck trail. If I hadn't looked up the place on Google Earth, I would have suspected it didn't actually exist after all those dirt roads.

But here it is. The driveway is lined with thick trees that block our view of the rest of the property. I can't see the house yet. The roof on Google Earth looked pretty nice—and pretty massive—though. I've done things for wealthy clients before, but not so wealthy they had a wooded estate. I feel like I could get lost in all this acreage. The forest and shrubs grow thick enough to almost seem like armor for the house.

Victoria is scanning the trees like she expects someone to pop out of them. I wish she'd stop since it's making me nervous, but I know old habits die hard.

Finally the house appears. It's very… linear, like stacks of glass and wood and steel are rising from the earth to make up the two stories of it. A long deck wraps around the south face, a solid wooden fence enclosing it. The entire first floor seems to be nothing but windows, but I wouldn't call it open. Elegant sci-fi fortress is how I'd describe it.

"Wow." Victoria's staring at it with wide eyes.

My eyes are just as wide because it really is something. This is the most extra place we've ever been, and tech titans with money can get pretty extra at times. The fortress-like feeling makes the smashed gate call box that much stranger.

This house is holding secrets, that's for sure.

A man is waiting on the front steps, wearing a dark suit. He's got massive shoulders, a thick neck, and a powerful resting angry face. His expression doesn't flicker as we pull up.

Victoria and I exchange a look. "That's the welcoming committee," I whisper.

"If he flexes too hard, he'll tear that suit apart."

I wink at her. "If we're lucky." I'm mostly joking—this guy's too surly for me—but Victoria rolls her eyes and laughs, which was my goal.

I walk up with my shoulders back, my steps brisk, my spine military straight. Confidence is ninety percent posture, and I'm going to grab for that ninety percent and then some.

"You're Rustem?" I ask, holding out my hand. "I'm Tess Robards with Shield Solutions."

His face relaxes and he shakes my hand with a firm but not punishing grip. "That's me." He's got a faint, hard-to-place accent. "You found it all right?"

"We did."

Rustem shakes Victoria's hand, then motions her aside. The movement is brusque and leaves no room for disagreement.

I grit my teeth and remind myself to keep it cool. Victoria is my employee, but she's also my friend. I feel as responsible for her now as she did for me back when we were in the Army. All this guy did was be kind of rude. And he's the client—or the employee of the client—and they're always right.

Rustem takes something that looks like a phone out of his

pocket and sweeps it over the car and even crouches down to check the undercarriage. He swabs the tires and sticks the testing strip into a slot on the phone. I can't be completely sure, but I think he's checking for explosives. Except I didn't know those machines were phone-sized now.

"You should have done that before we got this close to the house." I can't help offering the suggestion. "If we wanted to blow this place up, we could have detonated by now."

He cuts me a look. "I know. Things are… You'll see. And that's what you're here for." He puts the phone back in his pocket, gestures for us to raise our arms. He takes a wand from behind his back and sweeps us but doesn't pat us down. Again, the wand doesn't look like any type I've seen before, and I know my metal detectors. Maybe this is like the phone, something totally new.

But if Wolfe has access to all these cool security toys, why call us in?

"You're clean," Rustem says once he's satisfied.

A sudden suspicion occurs to me. "Did you just x-ray us?" If the explosives sniffer is pocket-sized, what could they have done with an X-ray scanner?

He says nothing, just motions us forward.

I watch him walk off, and I consider leaving. This is strange, and my gut is not liking it. The job might not be worth whatever is going on here.

But… it really *is* worth it. The amount I was promised is astronomical. Life changing. Not just for me but for my entire family. And for Victoria too.

I exhale sharply and start to follow him.

Victoria leans toward me and drops her voice. "This is like bizarro airport security. The wand, the scanner… He was checking for explosives, right?"

"I think so," I whisper back. "This whole deal is super weird."

"But super well paying."

We walk up the low steps, which are made of slabs of gray slate, and come to a nondescript door. If I wasn't looking closely, I might have missed it. Must be the servants' entrance.

But when we walk into a gorgeous foyer, I realize I was wrong. That was the front door, although nothing about it was welcoming. The foyer itself is large, leading right into a living room with a massive fireplace dividing the space. Other than the fireplace, there are no walls, and with the exterior walls made entirely of glass, there's a sense that the space is never ending. A few tastefully refined pieces of furniture are scattered around but not enough to break up the sense of vastness.

Even though it's all very modern, I'm reminded of a medieval great hall. There should be knights crowded in, waiting to pay tribute to the lord and lady seated before the massive fireplace.

There's an electronics panel set into a far wall, probably some kind of fully integrated climate-control/security/entertainment thing. It's also smashed to bits, wires and glass scattered beneath it.

There's one thing I can immediately fix: if the security system is part of the rest of the control system of the house, that's got to change. I gesture to the broken panel. "Was that the security system? Was it running alongside the other home systems?"

Rustem nods.

"Okay. Well, you should have the security system as a walled garden. Those other systems could be a back door to attack the security." Although they wouldn't be if all the panels were smashed to bits. Maybe that's why they were destroyed—someone got something in through the panels. It's extreme, but effective.

Victoria nods while Rustem stares at the panel. I can't read anything from his expression.

"What happened here?" One smashed security panel could be an accident. Two is deliberate. And if I'm going to be repairing these things, I should know what went down.

Rustem shifts, his massive shoulders rolling under his suit jacket. "Mr. Wolfe will explain everything. I'm taking you through the house first so you can see what you're working with."

Victoria and I share a look. We're going to meet Wolfe. We're going to see what happened to him and hear the full story. The anticipation vibrates under my skin. But we keep our glance brief so Rustem doesn't catch us.

"Great," I say, pressing my tone flat. "I'm looking forward to it."

The rest of the house isn't quite as impressive as what I'm calling the great room, but it's still pretty damn amazing. There's a library filled with books and chairs for reading, a study perfect for long hours of focused work, and a kitchen that a master chef would swoon to use.

And in each and every room, the electronics have been completely destroyed. There was a laptop in the library—smashed. A desktop machine in the study—crashed on the floor.

We eventually come to the garage. There's not one but two Inspiron sedans there. These cars are the rarest things in the world: individually hand built by the company and outfitted with the very latest in technology. Supposedly they're entirely self-driving—and completely emissions-free—but they're so rare nobody knows for sure. Seeing one on the road is like seeing a white elephant.

For all that the cars are so secret, the CEO of the company sure isn't. Axel Beck is model handsome and appears every morning in the gossip section of *Disrupt Dispatch* in an amazing suit and with a beautiful person on his arm—sometimes a man, sometimes a woman. He's certainly savvy about keeping his PR machine running. Right now he's carrying on a fairy-tale romance with a woman he insists is the one, Morgan Nash. She's the genius behind the AI that runs Inspiron cars, and the press is calling them the prince and princess of Silicon Valley.

My hands get shaky as I approach one. It's like getting close to a unicorn. Victoria's eyes are so wide; she must feel the same.

I gasp when I look inside.

The entire instrument and center panel of the car is just… gone. Like someone reached in and tore everything out in great handfuls.

My hands are still shaking, but it's not from excitement anymore. There's probably over a million dollars' worth of damage here, if not more. And it was all done deliberately.

I wet my dry lips. "Is there… is there anything else we need to see?" I'm more than ready to stop this odd tour and meet the man himself. Enough creepy damage.

Rustem shakes his head and ushers us back inside. "That's it," he says, shutting the door on the ruined cars. "Time to speak with Mr. Wolfe."

I hold in my excitement as he leads us to a room we didn't see before. There's nothing in it but an intact TV screen on the wall and some chairs. It reminds me of an interrogation room for some reason.

"He's coming here?" I ask.

Rustem doesn't answer, only gestures me to a seat. "Not you," he says as Victoria goes to sit down. "Her alone. You come with me."

I give Victoria a reassuring look even though I'm not really feeling this. It's not like I'm going to get murdered here, and even if I was, Victoria probably wouldn't be able to stop it.

If I think of the money, I'll be fine. Wolfe might be odd, but he's also loaded.

Victoria follows Rustem but doesn't look happy about it.

When the door shuts, I arrange myself in the chair, back straight, shoulders back, staring at a far-off point. I want to be ready when he comes in.

"Welcome," a pleasant, soft voice says from the ceiling. "Please remain seated."

There's something canned about the voice that gives it away as computer generated. Like I'm about to go on a ride at a theme park.

"Okay," I say, mostly to amuse myself.

"Thank you," the voice replies so sweetly I almost believe it's human. I also almost jump out of my chair.

"Whoa!"

"I didn't mean to scare you." Its imitation of being contrite isn't quite right. "I'm Gulizar. I'm the smart home system."

She sounds almost proud, which makes me shiver. I'm reminded of the killer computer in *2001* for some reason, although this one sounds much more human than that one did. "What does Gulizar mean?"

"The woman with roses in her cheeks. It's Turkish—Rustem named me."

"It's lovely," I say automatically.

"Thank you."

It's deeply weird to be talking to a computer like this, but I can't help my curiosity. "What happened to the panels? Where exactly are you running in the house?"

There's a pause. "There was a breach. I had to be… confined."

Confined? "What happened with the breach?"

"He's coming." Gulizar's voice drops to a whisper.

"What—"

The lights go dark.

My heart slams into my ribs, compressing my lungs. A spike of adrenaline drives through me, locking all my muscles rigid.

"What the—"

"Hello, Ms. Robards." It's *him*. Gideon Wolfe, in the flesh, somewhere in the blackness. His voice, deep and dark as velvet, echoes through the room. "I'm so glad you came."

CHAPTER 2

I pop up out of the chair, my hands reaching out. There's nothing but blackness surrounding me.

Except for him. He's here, somewhere.

"Please, sit down." The please doesn't make that any less commanding. In fact, the please is almost mocking, given how much steel was in it.

A warm shiver runs through me, tingly and sharp.

"What's going on?" I demand.

"Sit down before you hurt yourself." This time he really means business.

I hit the chair with an audible thunk. My heart is pounding so fast he must hear that too. I force myself to slow my breath, assess the situation calmly, rationally. It's strange, but he hasn't hurt me. Not yet.

"Her heart rate is elevated." Gulizar says that with dead neutrality.

"Quiet," Wolfe growls to it. "Not another word."

Although the computer goes silent, I get the impression she's sulking.

"Is this a sick joke?" I ask coldly. "I don't appreciate having my time wasted."

"No joke," he says. "I want to hire you to completely over-haul my security. At the price you were quoted."

"I don't negotiate with someone I can't see."

"No visuals." That cracks out quick as a whip. "You can leave now if that's what you're here for."

Oh shit. He must be… I swallow hard. The rumors about his face melting in a fire might actually be true. Wolfe wasn't a publicity hound before—he was no Axel Beck—but photos of him exist. He's been taped in interviews, which is why I recognize his voice. Unless someone's pretending to be him.

"How do I know you're really Gideon Wolfe?"

"What," he barks with disbelief, "you think I murdered him, took over this house, and I'm doing an amazing impression of him?"

Okay, maybe that was a bit much. "Why can't I see you then? Usually job interviews happen face-to-face."

"Or on the phone." His voice is like… like a buzzer against the base of my spine, low and electric even though his tone is harsh. Something about not being able to see him is making my reactions to that deep, bittersweet tone so much more potent.

"Yes. Why not call then?"

"You needed to see the house. And I needed to see you."

My mind snags on the word *need*. He says it in such a particular, memorable way. It makes me shiver again.

"Okay, I saw the house. And the electronics panels. If I'm going to fix your system, I need to know what happened."

I sense the air around me gather, shift. Is he moving? I peer into the blackness, which isn't quite as bleak as I first thought. There's a little bit of light here.

There's a shadow, there by the TV screen. Distinct from the rest of the shadows in the room. It might be a man. Tall, well built. Broad shoulders, muscled arms, narrow waist.

When it moves, I realize I'm right. It's *him*.

I swallow and stare right at him, trying to make out more details, leaning forward as I do.

"You can see me." There's something like shock in his voice.

"Not very well." I relax my face. No point squinting at something that won't become more visible. "So what happened?"

Smoke, ambulances, the police—I've got the gist. I want the nitty-gritty though. And I really, really want to see him. Not out of any kind of gross, rubbernecking desire; I don't care if his face is melted. I just want *something* to match to that voice.

"The security failed," he says simply. "And that can't happen again."

"How did it fail?"

"Someone got in."

I press my lips tightly together. "How? Where? Were they after something? Did they take anything?"

"Do you need to know the details to build the system?" he asks coolly.

I suppose I don't need to know what they were after or if they got it—I mean, it was probably cash or valuables, considering the place they broke into. "I do need to know more about the specific failure if I'm going to build a system to prevent it."

"Mmm." That noise doesn't say yes, but it doesn't say no.

Jesus, this is like pulling teeth. I'm earning that obscene paycheck and then some. I ought to charge him a nuisance fee for this. "How did it fail?"

"An intruder."

We're getting somewhere. "Armed?"

The shadow shakes its head. There's more light now, I could swear. I can see the outline of his hair, thick and straight. The curve of his ear. He's still got both of those, so they didn't melt off at least.

"Did they take anything?"

"They tried to."

A shiver snakes down my spine. I'm not sure I want to know what happened to this intruder. "I didn't see a safe," I say. "Is there one?"

"In my bedroom."

We didn't get to see that on the tour. I wonder if the intruder was trying for the safe or somewhere else. But it doesn't matter because no one will be getting inside this house when I'm done.

I take a deep inhale. "All right. You want me to install a new security system. We can do that. And you won't be disappointed."

"Not just a new system." His tone is chillingly soft. "One that will never fail. Never be hacked. Never be penetrated."

"That's impossible," I say without thinking.

"Then we're done here." The shadow gathers, moves away.

"Wait!" I can't do what he wants, but I can't let him walk away. "I can build you a fully self-contained system. A walled garden. The only person who could touch it would have to be in the control room."

He stops moving.

I take that as permission to keep going. "You couldn't control it remotely. But it's the most secure system I can build. Motion sensors, facial recognition, machine vision: all the latest in threat-assessment technology. I can get you that."

He can probably get all that on his own—look at the stuff Rustem had—but he called me in. And that's what I can offer him.

"I won't need to operate it remotely," he says. "I'm not going anywhere."

"Wait." I frown. "Not going anywhere, like ever?" Like this is going to be his prison mansion or something?

"That's why I need the new security system. No one comes in. No one tries to steal from me."

Ooooh, that sounded nasty. And personal. Like whatever the intruder tried to take from him had deep meaning.

I lick my lips, steady my voice. "I can't make it completely secure. No one can. But I *can* build you the best security system money can buy."

It's a bold claim, but my company's never going to jump to the next level if I don't seize this chance with both hands. I don't know how he heard of us, but I've got him face-to-face —kind of—and I'm not letting go until I have the job, which I *know* we can do.

"I have *a lot* of money." It's a lick of amused velvet from the darkness. God, I wish I could see him.

"Then you'll be really secure."

There's a moment of considering silence. The shadow of him shifts, and I catch the outline of a hand running through his hair. When he lowers it, he stiffens and gasps like he's opened an old wound.

"Let's come to terms then," he grits out through his teeth.

I let myself exhale. I don't usually negotiate with clients— the prices are the prices and I know what I'm worth—but this man upends everything. Not only because of the kind of money he has but also himself. Even though I can't see him, his potency thrums through the air, supercharging everything.

"Well, the starting point is the offer you sent me," I say. The very generous offer he sent. If I'm going to take him on, I won't go lower than that.

"I'm finding that I require… more from you."

My pulse zigzags through me. My mouth is so dry it's hard to talk. "What would that be?"

"For these extras, I'm willing to pay double my initial offer."

I can't help my squeak even though it's super unprofessional. But *goddamn.* Not only could I clear my debts and my parents', they could retire. Like normal people are supposed to when they're too sick and tired to work.

"Do you need some time to think about it?"

"No." I say that too fast, but it's so much money I can't stop myself. "I can do it."

Now it's his turn to go quiet. I sense—and I have no idea how I do it—but I sense that he's weighing something. My response? His next response? I can't say.

"You don't even know what extras I'm going to ask for." His voice is dangerously soft. The hair on my arms rises but not solely from apprehension.

"I'm sure I can get whatever you need."

"Mmm." It's like the rumble of a jaguar. "Rustem will actually have to get it for you."

My head snaps up and back. "I'm sorry. What do you mean?" That makes zero sense.

"My condition for the... *bonus money,* we'll call it, is that you stay here. In this house. Until the job is done."

My mouth drops open in slow motion. "I can't... That's impossible."

"Then the deal is off." There's no room for argument there. "I made this offer to two security firms before you. They said no. Do you see them here?"

"But... why?" My throat is closing at the thought of being stuck in this place for... Oh Jesus. "This job could take up to three months. You can't keep me here that long!"

If the panic in me touches him at all, he doesn't show it. "I need someone I can trust. There can't be any leaks. Or pictures. Or rumors."

Well, if he didn't want rumors, he's a little late on that. I'm reminded of how the pharaohs used to entomb the architects of their pyramids with them so no one would know the plans. Oh God, I don't want to be entombed here.

"I'll sign an NDA," I say quickly. "You can sue me into oblivion if I break it." It won't take much to wipe out my finances, but he doesn't need to know that.

Except he's shaking his head, shadows moving against shadows. "No. No lawyers, no legal bullshit. You're under my personal watch while you do this."

I suddenly understand why he picked my firm for this. We're small, hungry, desperate to grow. Desperate enough to agree to this crazy scheme.

Except there are a lot of flaws in his request. "I have nothing here to do anything. No parts, no tools, no help. There's no way I could stay here and do the job."

"Ms. Shepard is your only other employee. You'll do the job on your own"—a small growl there, like I'm trying his patience—"it will just take a little longer than it would have with her. I'm willing to be patient—with the timetable."

My anxiety shoots into overdrive. "Is this some kind of sex thing?" I blurt out. I'm imagining all his billionaire buddies coming, using me in some kind of freaky hostage scene. When a man can have anything, what could be more alluring than the forbidden?

"Just breathe," he barks. "You're not breathing," he says when I continue to gasp.

"Should I call an ambulance?" Gulizar asks from the ceiling.

"I didn't say you could talk."

Although Gulizar has no feelings, I still flinch for her. And keep fighting for breath. This is too much. I can't do this no matter how much money he's offering.

"Hold up your phone." That's said to me, as cold and rigid as iron.

I do with surprisingly steady hands. Something about his command to breathe and hold up my phone short-circuits my panic. If he wanted to grab me, he could have done it many times before now. Hell, we're together in dark room and he hasn't done a damn thing.

And then there's the mystery of the broken panels. He went to a lot of trouble to smash those. I don't think this is a sex-slavery situation.

It's still weird though.

"You're really that paranoid?" I keep holding the phone up.

"If you'd been through what I have, you'd be just as para-noid." He's dead serious.

"I did a tour in Afghanistan—you'd be surprised at what I've seen," I mutter.

"Then staying here for a few weeks should be easy." His shadowed hand lifts, gestures to the phone. "Check your signal bars."

"They're full." Meaning I can call whoever I want now. Like, I can call for help. "Does this mean I'm keeping my phone?"

"Yes. And your associate can give anything you need to Rustem. He'll scan the items, then give them to you. If they clear."

"Where did he get those handheld devices?"

"From a friend of mine."

I'm guessing he means Gage, who founded an electronics firm that does a lot of business with the military. He's also a member of Wolfe's billionaire boys' club.

"Why not have your friend do the security then?" I don't let on that I know who he's probably talking about.

"Like I said, I can't trust anyone."

Shit. He can't even trust his friends, the ones who've been closest to him. At least if you believe the press about who he hangs out with.

"Call your friend," he orders. "Tell her where you are."

I dial Victoria quickly, waiting for him to do... something. But he doesn't.

"What is going on?" she yells into the phone the moment she picks up.

I wet my lips, watching the shadow of him. "I'm still here. Talking to Mr. Wolfe."

"That dude who works for him drove me all the way back to town." Victoria's very worked up. Wolfe can probably hear her through the tiny speaker. "I'm here with the van. It's going to take me half an hour to get back to you. This is mental!" There's a sharp intake of breath. "Are you okay? I've got the van started—"

"Don't." The shadow hasn't moved, but I can feel him listening to me. "I'm… I'm not leaving."

You could drop a hammer into that pause and not ever hear it hit bottom. "What?"

"If I take the job, I have to stay here. Everything has to be passed through Rustem. For security."

My pulse slows, steadies as I realize what that will mean. I'll be cut off completely except for my phone. If anything happens and I can't reach it…

"Why haven't you told him no yet?" Victoria is incredulous.

"Because… because he's offered to double our fee."

The shadow shifts, crosses his arms. He grunts softly as if something's hurting.

I can hear Victoria catch her breath. "Holy shit," she whispers.

"Exactly. And I can keep my phone. So I'll call you and my parents and my brother every. Single. Day." That last is aimed at Wolfe.

"You can't. It's not worth it. I'm ordering—" She catches herself before she goes full officer. "Tess, come on. You don't have to play along with this."

But I do. It's too much money to say no to. So I'm going to pretend that keeping my phone, my last link to the outside world, makes it all okay.

"It'll be fine," I say. "It's only a month or so. Sooner if I can swing it."

His shadow relaxes, his shoulders coming down and his arms uncrossing. So he wasn't quite as certain of my agreement as I thought.

"Tess." Victoria's tone is pleading, but she doesn't protest again. She takes a deep breath. "Okay. But if you're even a minute late calling, I'm breaking the door down. And I'm bringing my Ranger friends with me."

I have to smile because Victoria is dead serious. "If I'm designing the system, you guys won't be able to get in."

Wolfe laughs once, sharply, as if he's forgotten how and is surprised he still can. He cuts it off fast though.

"Just tell me this," Victoria asks, her voice dropping, "did you see him? Did he tell you what happened?"

"No and no." I stare at him, picking out what details I can. Some hair; an ear; a broad, long-fingered hand. Wide shoulders. "But I'm resourceful. I'll send you a supply list tonight."

"Mmm." Victoria's anything but convinced. "Stay safe."

"I will." I hang up and lower the phone.

"So that's a yes?" He said before he could be patient about the install, but he sounds anything but.

"It is. But I want a lock on my room." It's the smallest security measure, but it's better than nothing.

"You'll have the entire in-law unit," he says. "And you'll be the only one with the keys."

"I meant it about calling them every single day."

"I know." He clears his throat. "Lock down her phone."

Before I can even register that he's not talking to me, Gulizar says, "Done. Only outgoing and incoming calls now allowed."

My phone vibrates in my hand, a notification I've never seen before popping up. "Custom security mode activated," it tells me.

"What the hell?" I demand. "This was all a trick—

He cuts me off with a curt chop of his hand. "Access to the camera and voice recorder has been disabled. Along with internet access. You can still call and make calls. But that's it."

For a moment I'm tempted to turn the screen fully on him, bathing him in the light. It would be the fastest, most satisfying way to push him off his guard. Instead, I scroll through my app screen. Every square is grayed out except for the phone icon. I punch at a few, but nothing happens.

When I call up the phone app, it responds though. I immediately call Victoria again since it's the last call in the list.

"What happened?" she asks. "I can come get you."

I never look away from the shadow watching me. "It's okay. I accidentally dialed you. I might not have email access while I'm here—call if you need anything."

"Okay." There's a too-long pause. "Tess, seriously—"

"Bye. Talk to you soon." I hang up before Victoria can start again.

The shadow with me remains silent. He proved his power and skill, so why would he need to speak? In less than ten minutes, he's gotten me entirely under his thumb.

"If you can do all this," I say slowly, "you don't need me."

"But I do." His voice is so quiet it ghosts over my skin. He gestures to something, and then Rustem is opening the door. I have no idea how he knew to come in. And not enough light is coming through the door to see Wolfe's face, damn it. "One last thing."

"What, you want my firstborn now?" I might have agreed to the job, but I'm not going to cower when he speaks.

"No." There's a smile in his voice, but then it's gone. "The second floor is off-limits."

Okay, now that's completely unreasonable. "I can't install security if I can't go into that part of the house. It's impossible."

"Figure it out." He's so arrogant and unconcerned I want to scream. "Seriously, I catch you upstairs and…"

The emptiness he puts into that silence scares me more than anything else that's happened today.

CHAPTER 3

"Her staying here wasn't part of the plan."

I don't look up at Rustem's words, keeping my focus on the laptop open on my desk. "I had to change the plan."

Rustem doesn't know it, but the plan is more of a… set of guidelines. Fluid. Evolving.

"You don't have a plan," he says.

Okay, maybe Rustem suspects more than I thought. I spread my hands. "I don't know if you noticed, but shit's been fucked up around here."

He gives a pointed stare to the smashed security panel. "Everything looks normal to me."

His argument isn't lost on me. Okay, so I have a temper. I've never taken it out on anyone, but sometimes when I'm alone and things… malfunction, I start yelling. And sometimes punching things. But never people.

Mostly I growl. I'll admit to being a growler, which is perfectly acceptable to do to people who are fucking up. I didn't get to where I am by letting fuckups slide. Which gave me a reputation as a beastly boss.

When I realized that my top-of-the-line, insanely expensive security system wasn't worth shit—when I saw what I almost lost—I let my temper run wild. All the panels got caught up in it, but they were worthless anyway.

Having two broken fingers and I don't know how many broken ribs isn't helping my mood either.

"Where is she now?" I ask.

Gulizar answers before Rustem can. "I don't know. The panels in all rooms except this office and your bedroom are offline."

I sigh and pinch my nose. "I swear to God, I'm going to deactivate you." When I programmed the home control system, I'd thought to give it just a touch of personality. Something to make it sound human. And then the AI took off on its own and gave me Gulizar, who never misses an opportunity to remind me that I smashed her precious panels. She's more trouble than she's worth, and I don't know why I didn't deactivate her everywhere. It's not like hearing her voice from the ceiling is a comfort or anything.

"She's in the cottage," Rustem says. "Making a list of everything *I* have to pick up for her."

Great, now Rustem is joining in. "She'll get everything back to normal," I say. "Or better than normal."

"If you're sure."

I am. It's a small company, but she knows her shit. She came highly recommended, and when I looked over her plans, I couldn't find any flaws.

I couldn't find any flaws in her either. She was wearing a polo shirt and work pants, her hair up in a simple ponytail. Nothing about her should have been compelling, but goddamn if she wasn't. Those clothes did nothing to hide her curves and the way she looked at me—open, honest, like she wasn't a bit afraid. But her eyes were too wide, her mouth too soft to be anywhere near tough.

I can't get her out of my head. Which, yeah, might be part of why I forced her to stay here.

I also need her security system. I could have gone to Gage, had him put something in since he's the expert, but I wasn't exaggerating when I said I couldn't trust anyone. Even my oldest and closest friends. After what happened… It could've been any of them. And whoever it was is going to try again.

If the intruder was looking for what I think they were, one of my best friends *has* to be behind it. No one else knows the thing exists. My chest throbs with the ache that hasn't left me since the break-in. I'd suspect my sternum got cracked or bruised too, but the twinge only happens when I ponder who must have betrayed me.

"She has to stay here because I don't trust her," I say. "I need a new system put in, and someone has to do it. Once she's done, she's out."

"Are you going to kill her and entomb her with you just to be certain?"

I stare at Rustem. Sometimes it's hard to tell when he's making a joke. The man could teach deadpan to a cast-iron skillet. "No. She'll get her money, sign an airtight NDA, and we'll keep watching her."

Rustem raises his eyebrows at my tone. "Until when?"

"Until this is over."

"Which it might never be. You're assuming whoever broke in is going to reveal themselves."

"No, I know it." If it was one of the guys, they're for sure coming again. We don't give up until we get what we want. That attitude didn't serve us well when we were all a bunch of teenage punks, but once we channeled that force into making money, we were unstoppable. We directed it together, helping each other even though we had our own companies and interests. It was all for one and one for all. And we never breathed a word about what really bound us together, deep down.

Rustem doesn't know I suspect them though. He thinks

I'm just paranoid. He doesn't know what the intruder was really after.

"She isn't happy." Rustem crosses his arms. He's not pleased about the change in plans. He's also secretly soft-hearted under that dark suit and wrestler's build. He feeds kittens and rescues puppies. Not that he'd ever let anyone know about it.

I don't feed or rescue anything. Kitties and puppies and kids run away from me.

"She doesn't have to be happy." I shift in my chair, groan when my ribs catch. The intruder got in a couple of good punches when I grabbed them, but what really fucked me up was falling down the stairs. I couldn't go to the doctor—no one could know how serious the break-in had been—so I had to grit my way through the police visit, wave off the ambulance, and then have Rustem splint my fingers and wrap my ribs.

Everything in me fucking throbs, even a week later. Seeing Tess Robards made other places throb too, in a good way. Or at least it would have been good if everything wasn't a shit storm.

She was way too attractive. I wasn't expecting that. She was dressed in awful clothes—work clothes—but put her in something decent, something that would hug those curves harder than a Formula One car in a turn, and she'd be a killer. And that mouth, the way it wrapped around all that defiance she spit at me...

She wasn't scared of the dark either. When I told her she had to stay, then she panicked. But she recovered quickly. So quickly it made me want to test her in other ways. Sexier ways.

"You can make it easier for her," Rustem says. "Maybe be just a touch nicer?"

"She seems very nice," Gulizar puts in.

I ignore Gulizar, because what would a computer know

about nice? She only knows what I've programmed into her, and I'm definitely not nice.

I look back at the laptop. "I won't though." If she leaves here hating me, I don't care. The more she hates me, the farther away she'll keep herself. That suits me just fine. I don't need some curvaceous beauty entangling herself in my shit show. Even if I did force her to stay very, very close to me.

My phone rings then, loud and annoying. Rustem and I both stare at it.

"Cassian is calling," Gulizar announces since she's connected to the operating system on my phone. I swear she says it gleefully, which is impossible.

I groan. I can't ignore Cassian even if I want to. I've been hiding away from the world for almost a month now, but I can't hide away from the guys forever. Especially if one of them is behind all this.

My turning into a hermit hasn't lured the intruder back. So maybe it's time to pretend that everything is fine and I have no clue one of them is behind this.

Like I said, the plan is fluid.

I hit the Answer button and turn on the speakerphone.

"You asshole," I say. "I told you I'm on a deadline."

That isn't entirely a lie. In three weeks I have to attend the opening of a surgical department my company spon-sored. Our equipment is going inside state-of-the-art medical machinery guided by the most highly developed AI to help surgeons slice into brains. It's pretty much everything I've been working for since I dropped out of med school. The department looks like the crowning achievement of my impressive rise to fame and wealth, but only I know what it really is: a massive fuck-you to my parents.

"I love you too." Cassian makes kissy noises. "Where the fuck have you been?"

I look out the window at the sweep of lawn leading down

to the meditation pavilion. The landscaper thought it would be cute. I didn't give a shit, so I let her do whatever she wanted, which is why there're also several statues and a labyrinth.

I chased the intruder all the way to that pavilion. Then they disappeared into the darkness. I never found another hint of them out there. And then the cops and the whole circus came out and that was that.

"You know where I am." In my house, where I can guard the safe twenty-four seven. Where I'll stay until this intruder shows themselves and I can deal with them.

"Are you ready to talk about what happened?" Cassian asks. I can't tell if he's concerned or if there's something deeper. I fucking hate that I have to search his tone at all.

When I launched Wolfe Medical Industries, Cassian was the one who did all the branding. I didn't know shit about it, and it turned out that simply walking up to doctors at medical conferences and telling them how great my tech was didn't actually sell anything. They wanted slickness. They wanted to be sold to.

Cassian helped me with that. And when he needed help dealing with a rival who was determined to crush him before he could even get started, I reverse engineered the rival's ad software.

My chest throbs, hard.

"No." I force my voice to soften into something more casual. "Because nothing really happened. Some wacko tried to get into the house. I chased them off; nothing was taken. End of story."

"Which is why you haven't left the house since then. And why nobody's seen you in public."

"You've seen me. I promise I don't look that different."

"We don't count," Cassian says softly. "I don't give a fuck what you look like."

"That's very comforting," I say dryly.

Cassian doesn't laugh, which isn't usual for him. Not that he's lighthearted, except he usually runs more toward black humor. Like "look at how fucked up this world is, isn't it funny?"

He doesn't give a fuck about anything, and he comes at everything from a deep, deep well of cynicism. Which is why he founded a marketing company, one of the biggest in Silicon Valley. They say he could sell ice in the Arctic, and moreover, he'd also try just for fun. Only someone who believed deeply everyone else is as self-interested and misanthropic as he is would do that.

I used to think he cared about us though. Me, Gage, Archer, and Bishop. The messed-up kids who came up together and somehow achieved all their wildest dreams—and shared the same awful, secret nightmare.

After this break-in, I'm not so sure. Maybe Cassian's decided he actually doesn't give a shit about us. Maybe he's decided to just fucking blow it all up and snatch what he can.

"Something's changed," Cassian says. "You keep saying nothing happened, but you're shook."

I'm so glad he can't see my face. Cassian might also be a once-in-a-lifetime marketer because he reads people so well.

"I don't get shook," I say between my teeth.

There's a significant pause on his end. "You sure they weren't after anything in particular?"

He's getting at something. I go very still, very alert, but keep my voice expressionless. "I wouldn't know. They ran off before I could question them."

"Huh." I hear his teeth click. "They didn't try to go for the notebook, did they?"

Shit. He's just coming right out with it. If it was him, this is pretty fucking ballsy. He must be trying to feel me out.

Or maybe it wasn't him and he's genuinely curious. The full-frontal attack isn't really Cassian's style, but he could be pulling a misdirection here.

I rub my temples. Fuck, now even my head aches.

"The notebook is perfectly safe." I tell him to drop it with my cold tone. Let's see if he actually does.

He doesn't. "Did you ever think about opening it? Not yours, obviously, but the other one."

I'm horrified at the very suggestion. "It's Tynan's. Not mine."

"But he's dead." Cassian says it right out because he never does give a fuck. "It doesn't matter anymore."

I feel like someone's walking over my grave. "They never found a body."

"Come on, man, the car went off a cliff into the ocean. Anything could've happened to his body. Sharks. Currents."

"They found Ira."

We both go quiet with the heaviness that comes whenever his name is invoked. Our shared guilt, I suppose. We all still talk about him but always with that heaviness.

We almost never talk about Tynan.

"Yeah, well," Cassian finally says. "You should come to Archer's next Saturday. You can't hang out with just Rustem forever. You'll turn as surly as he is."

The joke is, I'm actually surlier. Rustem is the sunshine in our pair.

"I'll think about it." If he's trying to lure me out of the house, it won't work. But I can't keep avoiding them forever, not if I want to keep up the pretense that I don't suspect them.

Tess needs to get this security system in. And it needs to be everything she promised. I'm playing a dangerous game here, and everything is riding on her.

So no, I'm not letting her out of my reach any more than I'm letting that notebook out. The stakes are too high for me to release my grasp on either of them.

CHAPTER 4

The in-law unit is more than an in-law—it's an entire house, bigger than the one I grew up in. Definitely bigger than the house my parents live in now.

Big or not, it's still a prison, and whatever luxurious amenities are here—like the four-way showerhead, the deck with an entire outdoor kitchen, and even a mini movie theater—can't fully hide the fact. There's a TV and some books but nothing that looks too interesting. I'll have to see if Victoria can slip me my knitting needles and yarns through Rustem. Maybe we can pass them off as essential tools. Certainly knitting fuzzy scarves and shrugs and mittens keeps me sane.

I'll deal with that when I call Victoria. The fridge is fully stocked, so I grab a soda and sit on the sofa to call my parents.

"Hi, baby," Mom says when she answers. Her tone is gray, washed out, like it has been for months now.

"Mom." Even though I'm trapped here, I can't help but be excited. "I have the best news."

"Oh yeah?" She sounds tired. So damn tired.

"I've got this new contract. And Mom… It's enough to pay off the mortgage. And the legal fees. And my student loans."

She doesn't shout with excitement or gasp or do… anything. It's just quiet.

"Oh honey," she says finally. Just as gray as ever.

I don't understand. "This is really good, Mom. Seriously. It's everything we ever hoped for."

"You should keep the money, sweetie. Not give it to us."

There's something she's not telling me. I can hear it lurking in the fog of her tone. "What happened? And please don't tell me nothing."

Mom sighs. "We didn't want to have to tell you. You already worry so much."

My heart crashes into my stomach and gets tangled with it. "Oh no. Oh no."

"It's not that bad," Mom rushes to say. She always does this, always tries to make it sound okay—but it's not. And if I don't help, who will?

"It sounds pretty bad."

"Well…" She draws that out. "Nick took Elena back to court."

Nick is Elena's former business partner and her ex-husband. Both the marriage and the business split apart spectacularly, and whenever Nick gets a bug up his ass and wants to strike out at Elena, he files a bullshit lawsuit about custody arrangements or what's left of the business assets. And he usually gets a bug up his ass if he's heard Elena is dating again or just generally enjoying life.

He's put a hollow look in Elena's expression that she's never been able to shake. My sweet big sister is hollowed out because of him, and all I can do is help pay the lawyers to keep him away. It isn't enough though, and that haunts me.

"Okay." I force myself to breathe. "She's already got some legal bills. We'll just add to those. I should make enough here to cover whatever it is."

"It was a lot." Mom's voice is so quiet. "We took a second mortgage out on the house."

For a moment my mind goes blank. Total white noise.

"You did what?" My whisper is almost a scream. I shouldn't be talking to Mom like this, but I can't help it. Panic swamps me.

"We had to." Mom is defensive. "We didn't have a choice."

"Why didn't you tell me?"

"We didn't want you to worry." Mom sniffs like she's holding back tears. "You already take on so much—you deserve to be free of this."

"Elena's the one who deserves to be free." I feel tears burn my eyes. "I wish we could just… make him disappear." Which is a horrible thought, but I just want my sister to be happy. She's tried so hard to get rid of him, and we've done so much to help her.

It's never enough. The pressure in my chest is making it hard to breathe.

Mom doesn't even make a joke about hiring a hit man. She might have once, but years of dealing with Nick and his bullshit has rubbed the humor right out of her. "There's nothing else we can do. And then…"

"What else happened?" Dread settles in my stomach. "I know there's more. Just tell me."

There's no point in trying to protect me. Of course I have to know, because of course I have to help. We're all in this together.

Mom sucks in a shaky breath. "We're behind on the payments. I can stretch it out for another two months, but after that…"

After that, they could lose the house. I want to throw up. God, it just never ends. The debt piles up and up, and it's going to crush us. All of us. Unless I can stop the avalanche somehow.

And then the fog clears and I see my surroundings again. My gilded cage.

"I've got the solution," I say, making my tone steely. "This new job. It pays amazing, more than enough to cover a second mortgage." There goes any extra I wanted to save for myself though. Well, I guess having student loans for the rest of my life isn't that bad. It'll keep me normal.

"Honey, no." But her protest is weak. The relief in her voice is clear and strengthens my resolve. Mom needs me. They all need me. I can't let them down.

"It's fine. And I can finish in a month." I *have* to finish in a month, no matter what. I look around the house. It's a cage, but it's not too bad. I can do this.

I have to.

"I just don't know…" Mom's wavering. She's *this* close to giving in.

Something heavy settles on my heart. Love. Responsibility. Duty. We're a family and we all have to pull together if we're going to make it, but damn, I'd like to see some forward motion with all this pulling. Instead of feeling like we're doing our damnedest in order to stay in the same place. I hear the gray in my mom's voice, see it in Elena's expression, and I know it's creeping into me too. The money from this will push some of that back, bring more light into our lives. So I need to pull myself together and get through this.

"It's fine." I try to sound happy. I only manage super fake. "I'm working on-site, so I'll be in and out of touch. But I'll call you every night. If I miss a night, get ahold of Victoria right away."

"Is everything all right? Why wouldn't you be able to call?"

"Just call Victoria, okay? And don't worry. The money's coming. I've got it all taken care of."

"Well, of course I'm going to worry." Although Mom already sounds brighter. "You're a world-champion worrier and you learned from me."

After telling my mom I love her, I hang up and consider

what I'm going to do for dinner. There was some food in the fridge and probably in the pantry too, although I didn't check the shelves. But I don't really feel like cooking.

Actually, I almost never feel like cooking. I don't think ordering delivery is an option here though.

There's a knock at the door. When I open it, there's Rustem, looking happy as ever. It's oddly comforting. "I'm supposed to invite you up to dinner."

My eyes widen. "With Mr. Wolfe?"

Rustem's taken aback. "No. But there's food for you."

It sounds better than cooking for myself, so I follow him up to the main house.

Rustem serves me dinner in the main dining room, which is mildly uncomfortable because the expression on his face says he's clearly not into it. But when I start to protest, he shoots me a dark look and says, "I was told to get you dinner."

"You can eat with me." I gesture at all the empty spots at the massive table. "We're both employees, so it makes no sense for you to be serving me."

He considers it for a moment. "Maybe."

"Come on."

He rolls his shoulders and sighs heavily. "Okay." When he comes back from the kitchen, he's got a plate of his own, piled high with sliced meat, some kind of salad, a white, crumbly cheese, and flatbread. It looks amazing.

I push at my own chicken, which suddenly doesn't seem so appealing. "Where'd you get that?"

"My mother," he grunts as he settles into his chair.

"You live with your mom?"

He gives me a look that says he thinks I'm crazy. "Of course. A man should care for his parents once he's old enough."

That's incredibly sweet, especially coming from someone who looks like he snaps tree trunks over his thighs for fun.

"What did she make you?"

He points to each item. "Lamb kebab, shepherd's salad, and pita. Oh, and sheep's-milk cheese that she makes herself."

"Where does she get sheep's milk around here?" Can you even milk a sheep? I can't remember ever seeing udders on a sheep, not that I've ever stuck my head underneath one.

He's clearly suspicious, as if I'm going to cut in on his sheep's-milk source. "She knows a guy," he says cagily.

"Have you always been in security?" I ask. He's certainly distrustful enough to be born to the job.

He shakes his head. "I was a wrestler. A gold medalist actually. Captain of the Turkmenistan national team."

I recognize that this is not the time to ask him about Turkish oil wrestling, which ran like wildfire through my friends' text messages once we discovered it. Hot, muscled guys wearing leather pants and covering themselves in oil, grappling? Yeah, we were going to share those pictures over and over.

I don't think Rustem is talking about that kind of wrestling. And even if he was, it would offend his national pride to know we were drooling over it.

"That's impressive," I say. "Why aren't you coaching wrestling now or still doing something with it?"

"I insulted the leader of Turkmenistan. He brought his sons to me for training, and I told him they were spoiled, useless idiots." He shrugs one shoulder. "I had to escape across the border, but it was worth it. They were terrible."

I stare at him as he eats his lamb, completely uncon-cerned. It sounds like it could be true, but secretly fleeing a country because you insulted a man's kids seems like… a lot.

"Don't believe everything he tells you."

At Wolfe's voice behind me, I go completely still. Stone still.

The lights are on. I can turn around and finally see him.

Face-to-face. The urge to do so is so strong my stomach muscles ache. They're in knots. All of me is in knots.

I don't though. This feels like a test and he's already given me the answers: I'm not supposed to look back at him. So I tamp down the urge.

"I'll take it from here, Rustem."

I have no idea what Wolfe is taking over. Entertaining me?

Rustem gets up and takes his plate. As he leaves, the lights go down. I groan. Not this again.

"Don't worry." The bastard is actually amused, but this is his game we're playing, so why wouldn't he be? "You won't eat in the dark."

A light directly over my head comes on, catching me in a cone of brightness. I can see everything about two feet away from me but nothing beyond that.

"Has anyone ever told you you're a control freak?"

As he takes a seat at the far end of the table—I can see that much—I get the sense that he's smiling. "You have."

"Well, you keep proving it." I gesture toward the light. "This is arranged like stage lights. No one does this in their dining room."

"I do." If arrogance had mass, those two words would weigh hundreds of pounds.

I can't argue with that. It's his castle, I'm his captive, and these are his rules.

"Are you just going to watch me eat?"

"I thought we could talk." He says that like the thought pains him. "Rustem thinks I'm not hospitable enough. Turks are big on hospitality."

"Really? Because he was pretty surly when he called me up here to eat."

"It was *his* idea."

Interesting. Rustem seems to be hiding some softness

beneath that grumpy facade. I don't think I can say the same for Wolfe.

"You don't strike me as the kind of man who does things because his employees suggest them. Especially things you don't want to do."

"Maybe I was bored."

"A bored billionaire? Those don't exist."

"Really? Know many billionaires?"

Images of him with his billionaire friends flash through my mind. "No, but you do."

He laughs knowingly. "Go ahead. Ask me."

"Ask you what?"

"All those questions waiting on your lips."

I can't help but wet my suddenly dry lips. "You haven't exactly been forthcoming so far. Why would you answer my questions now?"

"I probably won't."

"So you're toying with me."

"No, I toy with attractive women in a very different way."

"Oh, I get the nonattractive toying then?"

He literally growls, like a jungle cat warning someone off. "I'm not toying with you. There is no nonattractive toying, and if you weren't hired for a job, I'd be doing the attractive kind of toying. The scorchingly attractive kind of toying."

My eyes widen and my breath sucks in. He thinks I'm *scorchingly attractive*. I have no idea what to say to that.

I have to admit that my dating experience is… sparse. Barren. After being harassed when I was in the Army, I was understandably wary of letting any man near me. So when I did date, I went for guys who were nice. Not intense. Which didn't mean they didn't have the potential to turn psycho, but it was easier to pretend they wouldn't.

Trouble was, they were all so nice and boring I didn't feel a thing when we eventually broke up.

Wolfe strikes me as the opposite of all those guys.

Strangely, I'm not afraid of him. Wary, yes. Super, super aware of him? For sure. But the high alert my body goes on when I see him has nothing to do with fear.

"No, we don't have orgies," he says harshly. "No, we don't share partners. No, we don't have threesomes or foursomes or whateversomes. Any other salacious rumors you want me to clear up?"

"I never asked you any of that," I say hotly. "So don't get mad at me."

"But you wanted to. Don't pretend you haven't heard all that shit. That you weren't curious. That you didn't come all the way out here to see for yourself what happened to me." He ends on a low, furious note. As if the thought of everyone staring at him makes him as crazed as a caged tiger.

He doesn't need my sympathy, but it surges through me all the same. I can't imagine having the entire world gossiping about you, dying to know in painful detail the awful thing that happened to you.

It wasn't the entire world, not for me. No, for me it was only a select few who were spreading lies about me, wanting to know exactly what he did and when and if he'd touched me. It was horrifying.

"I won't try to look at you," I say softly. I might be intensely curious and this whole constant darkness thing is strange, but I'll respect your wishes.

"Yes, but you won't stop wanting to see."

CHAPTER 5

He was right. I didn't stop wanting to see, although he never gave me a chance at all during dinner. A few minutes after telling me that, he left and all the lights came back up. By that point I was done eating and went back to the cottage to lie in the supersoft bed and stare at the ceiling. Sleep wasn't something I got a lot of last night.

But here I am, hard at work on one of the busted servers, trying to reconstruct the security software he was running. Rustem brought me my first supply run bright and early this morning, so I was able to put on clean clothes and get down to business. After Wolfe's mysterious appearance last night, I was more than ready to get into his system and see what the hell was going on.

I also kind of hoped I might see him or even just talk to him. But it's midafternoon already and I haven't heard a thing here in the spare office Rustem put me in. This place is soundproofed better than a recording studio... or I'm completely alone.

Since Rustem didn't say he was leaving and Wolfe doesn't leave anyway, I'm going with soundproofed. It's less creepy.

"Come on," I mutter to the busted hard drive I've plugged

into the laptop Rustem's given me—preloaded with all the software I requested. "Give me something."

The hard drive continues to spin uselessly, the folder on my screen totally empty.

I glance at the busted console on the wall. It might be nice if it was working and I could talk to Gulizar, even if she is only a computer program. Rustem told me that she only ran on the consoles, so if the wall panel was broken, she wouldn't be in that room.

I'm also tempted to ask her some pointed questions about what happened the night of the break-in. She might just answer me, and wouldn't that be something?

Too bad she's not here. I wonder if I could find my way back to the room that Wolfe interrogated me in. The console there definitely worked. And why did that one get saved when the rest were destroyed?

"Too many questions," I say to the laptop screen. "And you're still not working."

Time for something stronger. I call up the command window and set a different retrieval program to work on the hard drive. I suppose I could send it out to be rebuilt, but I don't think Wolfe would go for that. Which means I might have to rebuild it here, which is going to take more time and equipment. My heart sinks at the thought.

As I watch the program run, I go through the list of things I'll need to do next and the equipment Victoria will have to bring, jotting them all down. I miss the Notes app on my phone right now. "Jerk," I mutter to myself, but I mentally aim it at Wolfe.

A message notification chimes on the laptop. For a moment I stare at it, my heart thumping. This isn't my machine, so who could be sending me messages? Maybe Victoria? But I can't imagine her hacking into a computer that isn't hers. Not that she couldn't do it, just that she'd think it was too dishonorable.

I click on the message. *Wolfe* is listed as the sender. No first name, just... *Wolfe.* I suppose I should have guessed.

You have knitting needles and yarn on your list.

It's not what I'd ever expect him to say. Looks like Rustem is giving him my supply list to approve—I wonder what Gideon thought of the order I put in for cozy knitting mysteries.

Was that a question? Maybe I'm being too snarky, but if he's going to lock me in here, I'm going to keep myself entertained. With knitting, mysteries, and smart remarks launched from behind the safety of a computer screen.

I don't see what knitting has to do with security systems. He types that back so fast I can feel the growl in it.

It doesn't. Since I can't leave, I need something to do in my off hours.

The faster you work, the sooner you'll be done.

I can't argue with that, but I also have to occasionally sleep. *You ever hear of burnout?*

Burnout is for the weak.

I can hear his voice, rough and cold as I read it. Burnout is for lesser humans, not a billionaire CEO machine like him. But... what he's doing now—holing up in this house—could be a form of burnout. Or trauma. Things he would call weak.

I don't dare point that out to him.

I'm not a machine, I type back. *I have to have down time. And that means I knit. So if you want to think of me as a tool, think of that as maintenance.*

There's a long pause where I only see the bubble of him typing. Whatever he wants to say, it takes him several tries to get it out.

Are you knitting right now?

I bite my lip as I look up at the ceiling. Looks like Mr. Beast doesn't have any cameras in here to spy on me. If only he hadn't destroyed all those wall panels...

A little shimmy of relief moves through me. I didn't think

he was watching me, but it's good to have confirmation. It makes the whole being his prisoner a touch easier to bear.

No. I write back. *I'm trying to recover the data from this drive. And I'm talking to myself.*

Thank God I can't hear you, he types.

My mouth falls. Well, that's just rude. I know I'm only here for a job and he's a jerk, but it still stings. Probably because he's the only other person in the house. The only person I'm likely to see today—not that I'll actually see him. My chest gets heavy, my heart sinking. It's only been a day, but already I'm lonely and homesick.

I usually have Victoria to talk to. I hope he senses the tartness there. *So I have to talk to myself.*

Ever try silence?

Okay, now I'm really pissed. He can't control everything that I do. *You can't hear me, so why do you care?*

For a long time there's no response. Did I go too far? Am I about to lose this job that I so desperately need?

My hands hover over the keyboard, ready to type out an apology. A groveling, abject apology that I absolutely won't mean. My heart is thrumming in my throat.

Finally the typing bubble comes up. I hold my breath, waiting for him to tell me I'm fired.

Silence helps with focus. And if you're focused, you'll be out of here sooner. Which is what we both want.

I can't deny that. But I'm also tempted to tell him not to dictate how I work, which would probably be pushing it too far.

Okay, is what I reply, having zero intention of actually doing it. If he can't hear me, he can't catch me. *Is the knitting an approved item then?*

What do you knit?

I lean back from the laptop in surprise. "Do you really want to know? And why aren't *you* working, Mr. Billionaire?"

No reply comes, so I repeat it louder, taking childish glee in shouting at the top of my lungs. Not a peep comes back to me.

"I will not keep quiet," I say to myself as I start to type. *Whatever my friends want. Sweaters, scarves, shrugs.*

What the fuck is a shrug?

Wow, I could get really snarky here and respond that it's a motion of the shoulders to indicate ambivalence. I have to bite my tongue to stop myself. *It's a sweater that only covers the shoulders. I can make you one—what colors do you like? Teal? Magenta?*

He hates those colors—I can tell by the very dark, neutral color palette in the house. All browns and grays and deepest navy blues.

Do not make me a shrug. Or anything else. The letters practically vibrate with his irritation.

I have a sudden urge to make him something anyway—maybe some knitted animal. A beast just like him. But I'm guessing that's a no on the knitting stuff.

I blink hard. I really didn't think through this whole imprisonment thing when I said yes. But I should be thinking about the second mortgage and the legal bills and my student debt, not how hard this will be. So I won't have my knitting or my books or anything except my work? Big deal.

I can do this.

Fine, I write. *You're right. I don't need the knitting. I should only be working.*

To prove it, I go back to the laptop, which has finally pulled something off the hard drive. The files look like gibberish though. Which means I've got a long day—and night—ahead of me.

The knitting is approved. As long as it doesn't interfere with the job. Now get back to work.

I read over the message several times, the words making

my emotions jerk back and forth. He said I could have my knitting—but he also threatened to take it away from me. Reminding me that I've put myself entirely in his power here.

But he also had an entire conversation with me, about knitting of all things. He must be...

He must be lonely. The thought makes my chest squeeze. I tell myself to stop being stupid.

Of course he isn't lonely. He's got more money than God, and if he was scarred in the attack, he's rich enough to have everyone overlook it. In a moment he could be anywhere in the world. But he's locked himself up here.

Before my heart can squeeze again, I brutally remind myself that he's locked me up in here too.

CHAPTER 6

I know I shouldn't do what I'm about to, but I do it anyway.

I was good yesterday, only messaging Tess through the computer and then only for a brief time. The thought of her moving through the downstairs, only feet away from me, was an itch I couldn't get rid of. But I ignored it and focused on all the work I've let pile up. And my search for whoever was behind the break-in.

I didn't even wish her good night when she messaged me to tell me she was done for the day. Although I could have been a dick and told her sleep was for the weak. I certainly don't get more than four hours a night.

But I didn't. She better have appreciated that.

Rustem reported that she ate dinner by herself last night. And that she looked sad this morning, all the while eyeing me as if I were a monster.

I ignored him.

"Perhaps she's lonely?" Gulizar said.

"Of course she is," I snapped. "She's not here to make friends. She's here to do a job."

But their nagging stayed with me all day until finally in the afternoon I pick up my phone.

And I dial Tess's number.

"Hello?" she says on the second ring, all brisk business. It makes sensation dance along my spine, the way she says it.

For a moment my mind goes blank. I'm immediately furious because my mind never goes blank. "How's your progress?"

That comes out sharp and short, but it's also how I usually talk to my employees. Even the ones I've made my captive.

"Um…" She takes a breath like she's going to launch into a long explanation. "Okay."

"That's it? Okay? I'm paying you for more than okay."

I was also hoping to hear… more from her. At least something beyond a simple okay.

"I thought I was supposed to try silence."

Against my will, one corner of my mouth crooks up. "Somehow I don't think you're obeying."

"But you can't tell, can you?" The curl of her voice suggests that fact drives me crazy—and she likes it.

"Did you get your knitting?"

She's caught up by the change in subject. "Yes." She swallows. "Thank you."

Oh, she didn't care for that, having to thank me for giving her access to anything. But she did it. "You're welcome. Now give me a report that's better than okay."

She does, launching into the explanation that I was expecting before. Without explicitly saying so, she makes it clear she doesn't like the circumstances she's working under.

Too damn bad.

"All right," I say, stopping her midsentence. "You could be going faster, but it's fine."

She huffs, then bites it back quickly.

"We're having dinner tonight," I say.

The silence on the other end of the line runs over my skin. I shouldn't care about her reaction—or lack of one—but it bugs me anyway.

The only other person in this massive house doesn't want to be around me. It's exactly what I wanted. Which brings up *be careful what you wish for.*

"That wasn't an invitation." Her tone is flat.

"No." I don't see the point in a polite lie. "I want to have dinner with you. So I'm telling you to come."

"Does anyone ever tell you no?"

I have to think for a moment. Does breaking into my house and trying to steal from me count? Or is that more of a vicious middle finger?

"Are you about to tell me no?" I ask with deceptive softness. I know she won't—she wants this job. Look at what she agreed to do to get it.

Still, I hold my breath until she says, "Of course not. And I'll see you tonight."

She hangs up without another word, which impresses the hell out of me. I spend the rest of the afternoon with only half my focus on my work, waiting for dinner to come. Which irritates the hell out of me because I only asked her in response to Rustem and Gulizar's guilt trip.

When I enter the dining room, she's already there, sitting in the spotlight in the middle of the dark. I take my seat at the head of the table quietly, but she still goes on high alert at my presence. She fairly crackles with it, and my fingers itch to reach over and touch her.

Instead, I remain cloaked in the dark where she can't see me. But I can see her. And she's gorgeous. The light is harsh, but when it hits her skin, it softens, curving around her form, caressing her. She stares at where she thinks I am, her chin defiant.

"This is the oddest way I've ever had dinner in my life," she says.

"I'm glad I'm not boring." I have no food in front of me. I just want to study her.

"You're too rich to be boring." She stabs a piece of steak

and twirls her fork without taking a bite. "And you eat like a king."

"Better than a king," I say. "Have you ever eaten English food? No, all the nations with great cuisine—Italian, Turkish, Vietnamese—have no royalty."

"There's a Vietnamese place around the corner from my place." Her face falls. "I used to get takeout from there every Wednesday with Victoria. We called it our friend date."

For half a moment I'm tempted to offer to get some Vietnamese food for her, to fly in the best chef in the world to whip something up for her here. Partly to wipe that sad look off her face and partly just to show her exactly what I can do with all my wealth.

But it's not like she's never going to do that again. I'm only keeping her here for a month or so, not forever. I'm not a total monster.

"Sounds nice," I say shortly. "Very cozy."

"You're not a fan of cozy, are you?" Finally she takes a bite of the steak, rolling her lips around it in a way that makes sweat break out on my forehead. Thank God she can't see me.

I definitely don't like cozy. "Did the house give it away?"

She swallows, her throat bobbing gracefully. "That and the whole keeping me captive. And shutting off my phone. Those were all hints. And then there's the stories about you."

The way she says *stories*—like she hates that she loves hearing about me—is like a finger trailing down my spine. "Stories?"

"Oh, there's all kinds of rumors going around about you."

I lean forward, eager to hear. That's exactly what I wanted—the information to be confused, muddled, and nowhere near the truth. A swamp of stories for my intruder to wade into.

"Like what?" I make my voice bored although I very much care.

"Um…" She chews on her lip, suddenly uncertain. "Like…"

"Like I'm disfigured?" I supply.

She nods slowly. "Also, that you've lost your mind."

I snort. "They wish."

"Some people say that you started the fire. Because you went crazy."

I roll my eyes. "What else?"

"That it was a false flag." She tilts her head. "That you made it all up."

Huh. That wasn't one that I was expecting. What earthly purpose would a false flag serve? People spend too much time on conspiracy forums. "Is that it?"

Her lush mouth flattens. "Some people say that the attack was real but that you're totally fine. And that you're hiding away here for some reason known only to you."

So it looks like the truth *is* out there. "What do you think is true?"

Her eyes go wide. She wasn't expecting that at all. "Well." She sets down her fork, narrows her eyes. Whoa, when she gets hard-core thoughtful, it's amazingly attractive. "The panels are all broken." She starts to tick off on her fingers. "You have me isolated here and there's no one except Rustem. You… sometimes make a noise like you're hurt when you move."

I go very still. She noticed *that*?

"You hired me instead of whoever gave you those security scanners." She goes on, unaware she's stunned me. "And…" She bites her lip, her gaze so focused on me I swear she can see me. "And you won't let me see you," she finishes quietly.

The atmosphere pulses between us. "You want to, don't you? So bad."

She nods once, jerkily, inhaling hard.

"I warned you about always wanting to look," I rumble. "And I was right."

CHAPTER 7

He's right. I won't stop wanting to see. But probably not for the reasons he thinks.

"Even if I want to, I can control my urges."

I sense him shifting, like a big cat considering whether or not to pounce.

"I wonder," he says. "If I told you to close your eyes and keep them closed while I turned up the lights, would you do it? Or would the temptation to take a peek be too great?"

My eyelids flutter as if they want to open, but they already are. "I could do it."

"What if I came close? Close enough that you could peek through your eyelashes without me seeing?"

That would have to be pretty close. Close enough that I could smell his skin. Feel his heat. If he came that close, I wouldn't need to look. I'd have the rest of him to run my senses over.

"I wouldn't," I say confidently.

He drums his fingers on the table. There's a strange sound, like he's holding a metal pen in his fingers as he does it. The noise stops as he hisses like someone's pressed on a bruise.

"Are you okay?" I ask.

"Fine." His growl is back.

The lights go out.

I grab the table and gasp. Immediately my instincts go into overdrive. Was this deliberate? Is it a security breach?

"The power went out because of the wind."

I jump at his voice right next to me. He must have flown to get to me so quickly. "Are you sure?"

"It happens," he says. "Besides, if they're trying again, they're going to find out turning off the power was the worst thing they could do."

My brain sorts through possibilities. "The safe locks down without power."

He makes a little noise like he's surprised and pleased by me.

Acting on instinct, I reach out toward that noise, leaning into the darkness. My hand connects with heated firmness. A shoulder. He must be crouching next to me. My fingers turn upward, find the softer, hotter skin of his neck. His pulse is wild under the pad of my thumb.

I release a shaky exhale that he must feel. My hand slides up the powerful line of his throat, my fingers finding the blade of his jaw, rough with stubble. In the pictures I'd seen, he had a take-no-prisoners kind of jaw, and it feels like he still does.

I get the grit of his stubble under my fingers as I trace his cheek. His skin feels so good on mine, I don't even care if he might have scars. I just want to keep touching him.

As I leave the hollow of his cheek and reach the ridge of his cheekbone, he catches my wrist. I'm tugged forward until his mouth meets my palm.

As stony as his jaw is, his lips are amazingly soft. And hot. But not as hot and soft as his breath as it ghosts over my palm. He's not really kissing me—it's more like he's breathing in time with my pulse.

It's the sexiest fucking thing I've ever experienced. Up to and including orgasms.

I was right. There's nothing that is safe or nice about Gideon Wolfe. If I'm foolish enough to start something with him, I won't walk away unscarred.

Right now I don't care about scars. I just want to taste him. I lean forward, ready to find him with my mouth. The rhythm of his breath in the darkness is like a homing beacon.

Something in the background clicks, like door locks releasing. There's the short blare of an alarm, but then silence.

It's enough to break the spell between us.

He releases my hand. Air stirs near my face, and when he speaks again, he's moved away. "I'll have to start the generator."

I cradle my hand in my lap, my palm still tingling. "Do you need help?"

"No. And you should go home before I go to the generator."

Rats. I figured he wasn't going to let me get a look at him, but I'm not keen on stumbling home in the dark. "Sure," I say. "Just one small problem. I can't see shit."

He laughs. "Here. I'll walk you back." He pulls me out of the chair, his hand hot and firm on mine.

"How can you see?"

"Maybe I can see in the dark." There's a flash that might be the baring of his teeth. Or maybe I'm just desperate to see something, anything, of him.

He walks through the house confidently, navigating corners and walls as if the lights were on. He's either got the night vision of a freaking panther or...

"How many hours did you have to spend walking through the house in the dark to do this?"

"You think you're pretty clever, don't you?"

I don't know about that, but I think he's been preparing

for something like this, navigating through the dark in his own house. Which means he might have been expecting that break-in.

Every wealthy person expects a break-in—that's just natural. But they usually install security and hire guards and leave it at that. Not practice navigating through their house in pitch blackness.

"How long have you been doing MMA?" I ask.

He stops so fast I almost walk into him. But he starts moving again just in time.

He mutters something under his breath I don't catch, but I think it might be about my smart mouth and what he'd like to do to it. A shimmy of heat dances through me.

When we reach the in-law cottage, the lights are still off. The moon is a bare sliver in the sky, providing just enough light for Wolfe to find the doorknob. His back is to me, so I can't see anything of his face. I know by now it's deliberate. Which makes me desperate to see him. His touch, his voice, his presence are hooked into me, and I need all of him.

"I'll start the generator," he says, urging me into the house. "Sit tight here."

As I pass him, angling sideways to get inside, my breasts brush his arm. Immediately he clamps down on my shoulders, pulling me into him.

This time his lips are on my mouth and not my palm. They're soft but firm, and this kiss... it's hard. Engulfing. Like he needs something from me and he's going to get it.

It's such a contrast from how sweet his kiss into my palm was, my knees go weak. I'm not frightened of the shadows, and his mouth on mine is shadow and flame. Like he's going to take me into the darkness with him, he needs this so much.

I need it too. I part my lips, trace the seam of his with my tongue. He tastes like smoky tea and musk. He opens for me with a growly groan, half warning, half surrender.

I thought I knew what I was getting into when I kissed him back, but the thrust of his tongue against mine is something else entirely. I run my fingers through his hair, which is thick and silky. I can't remember the exact color from the pictures I've seen, but I'll remember the feel of it forever. I'll remember all this—a wild, feral kiss in the shadows of the moon—forever.

Finally he lets me go. I stumble backward, over the threshold, breathing hard.

"Are you really here just to get a look at me?" he asks in a rough whisper.

"No. I'm here for the money," I answer honestly. "I need it."

I hear his sharp inhale. The clouds shift and moonlight catches the outline of his shoulder, broad and muscular.

"But I kissed you because I wanted to," I say before closing the door.

CHAPTER 8

She touched me.

Of course I've been touched before, by any number of women. Women that other people would claim are more classically beautiful than Tess. They'd be wrong.

Illuminated in that cage of light at the dinner table, she owned the space. Her topaz eyes fucking pierced me, and she couldn't even see me.

I sink against the basement wall, staring at the rumbling generator. The lights have come back on, which means I should be upstairs and back at work. My business empire can't run itself, and since I can't leave the house for the immediate future, everything has to be done by email, which takes twice as long. I don't understand why people can't answer emails at midnight, but I've accepted that they won't.

I run my hand over my face, taking the same path Tess's hand did. She wasn't at all afraid, at least not of me. She just reached out and found me.

I didn't realize how much I needed that until she did it.

The concrete of the wall is cold and hard, the chill seeping into my spine. I welcome the discomfort, the ache in my ribs, the throb in my broken fingers. It reminds me of everything at stake, everything I'll put at risk if I draw Tess deeper into my world.

But as hard as I try, I can't make myself regret that kiss. My balls are tight just remembering the feel of her mouth on mine.

I need to get out of my own head. I need to check the safe.

I surge up out of my office chair and head upstairs, taking the steps three at a time. Behind me, my bedroom door locks with a heavy clunk, the bolts snapping into place. The alarm gives a warning beep, then quiets when it sees it's me.

"Open the safe."

There's a moment while Gulizar processes. "Your voice is different," she says.

I should have given that thing a more robotic voice. It's not quite human but close enough to be deeply unsettling.

"I'm pissed," I say. "Open the safe."

"Voice recognized," she says in a flat tone. Great, I've managed to trip the *pouty* subfunction in my AI.

The painting on the wall swings open, revealing the safe door. The panel on it lights up, the computer telling the two dozen bolts individually to open. They're all on separate circuits, the better to prevent any break-ins.

As the heavy safe door swings open, I hold my breath. I've done it since the break-in, waiting for the moment that the safe is revealed to be empty. Waiting to see that whoever's coming against me has won.

I exhale. The notebooks are still there. I grab one, leaving the other.

I walk over to the desk, kicking the chair out of the way. The notebook hits the desk with a thud. It's an ordinary lab notebook with a brown cover and stitched and glued binding, nothing special. I've filled hundreds of these with my notes, although this one wasn't written by me. I toss myself into the chair and open the book.

I can't read what's inside, of course. The writing is neat,

blocky, and covers each page from margin to margin. The sight of Ira's familiar handwriting makes my chest ache.

The letters themselves might be familiar, but I have no idea what the arrangement of them means. It's in a code I've never been able to break. One of Ira's little jokes. Or more likely an intellectual exercise. He was always setting up puzzles for us, things he said would keep us out of trouble. He said we weren't bad kids, we just needed our brains stretched.

I wasn't a kid when I met Ira, but he always referred to me as one. I was young though. I'd made it to med school before I hit twenty—my parents wouldn't expect anything less—and it wasn't for me. It so wasn't for me I was drinking my way through it. Passing all my classes, acing them actually, but I was a high-functioning drunk. I hated every second of it, I hated that I was so good at it, I hated that I was taking a spot from someone who'd actually give a damn, and I especially hated my parents.

An early death was looking good to me, and I was on my way there when I got called into the dean's office. I can't remember what for; maybe I'd puked in a trash can in class one too many times. I got read the riot act, told that if I didn't stop drinking I'd get kicked out no matter what my grades were and that this was so hurtful to the dean because he was such good friends with my parents.

I told him to fuck off and walked out. And right into Ira.

He was there to talk to somebody in the bioengineering department about direct neural interfaces. Ira wasn't a doctor, didn't know anything about biology, but he was fascinated by the idea that computers might one day think. Not exactly as humans did but in new, unique ways. He overheard me telling the dean he could take my grades and his school and shove them. Preferably up my parents' asses.

I have no idea what Ira saw in me, but he sorted things out with the dean and got me interested in AI and neural networks. I was so into programming that shit that I stopped drinking. I held on to med school a little longer, but as graduation approached, I cared less and less. My grades were excellent up until the very end, and I could see why medicine would be a calling for some people, but it wasn't *my* calling.

Ira was the one who encouraged me to quit. He said I wasn't meant to be a doctor; I was meant to build AIs. And he was right.

The rest of them had similar stories. Cassian was in his third stint in juvie and about to graduate into the adult criminal justice system. He'd been running scams, really sophisticated ones, involving email phishing. Ira managed to redirect Cassian's talents into something more useful and profitable.

Gage was getting into fights daily, and his parents were kicking him out of the house monthly. He was living on the streets. Bishop had been in and out of group homes and labeled "emotionally unstable." No one in the world wanted him or cared for him. Archer had a family more like mine, perfect on the outside and busted on the inside. He was keeping it together but about to fall apart, spectacularly.

Six boys on the cusp of becoming men, all ready to implode into something useless or destructive. Until Ira gave us all a purpose.

As for Tynan and his story... I don't let myself think about Tynan.

My fingers run down the notebook, Ira's legacy to me. That and the money he left me, which I used to start my company. We were all left very well off by Ira's death. Which was ironic enough to choke a fucking horse.

Ira took us in, gave us direction, and when he died, gave us the freedom and power to chart our own destinies. And he still managed to leave us each a notebook filled with a coded puzzle, one last exercise to stretch our minds.

God, I still miss him. So much. And it was all my fault. All our faults. But mostly mine.

Oscar, Ira's best friend and business partner, tried to fill the hole that losing Ira had left in our lives, and he did his best, but it wasn't the same. Nothing was ever the same after that.

I shut the notebook. It's useless to keep going over it. I tried to break the code at first, and I never got anywhere. I didn't ask if anyone else had figured out theirs or if they'd even tried. Anything to do with Ira was too painful at first, and then as time went on, we got on with our lives.

But someone's decided that it's time to drag these things back out again.

I put the notebook back into the safe, next to the other one.

The safe door swings shut with a weighty thunk, the bolts immediately snapping back into place. The alarm beeps softly as it rearms. I push the picture frame back into place and double-check the panel on the wall. Everything's as it should be. Everything's secure.

But I can't shake the sense that the intruder stole something, something I haven't even noticed is missing yet. Once they try again, and I catch them, I'll figure it out. I might not be able to bring back Ira—or Tynan—but I can do at least this for them.

I'll keep it up even if it's the last thing I do.

CHAPTER 9

Victoria calls as I'm eating breakfast in the kitchen of my temporary prison.

"Hello?" I say between bites of strawberries and yogurt. The strawberries taste like they came from heaven's own garden and the yogurt from the happiest, fattest cows on earth. Of course a billionaire would stock the best-tasting strawberries and yogurt I've ever had.

"You're still alive," she says with obvious relief.

I swallow. "Yep, still kicking. Honestly, I don't think he's going to stuff me into a suitcase or anything."

"Mmm. I'm going to keep being skeptical. I talked to Rustem this morning and got the list of things you need for today."

"Wow, he works fast." I look at the clock on the stove. "It's not even eight. Um, did he approve the knitting supplies?" He said he would, but I still haven't gotten my yarn.

"You're trapped in a billionaire's castle and you're worried about your knitting stuff?"

I scoop up more strawberries. "I agreed to work on-site, so I'm not technically trapped. And we're going to make lots of lovely money from this."

Victoria snorts. "Yes, he approved your knitting, you

degenerate. Along with everything else. I'm handing all of it over to him in about thirty minutes, so you should have it... I don't know? Today at some point? I have no idea how long his check will take."

"Thank you so much," I say. "I know this is all strange and awkward, and yes, kind of creepy, but it will be so worth it once it's over."

"If you say so." Victoria's tone shifts. "So, how was your first night there? Did you finally see him? Did you find the chamber where he keeps all his former wives?"

I run my fingers over my mouth. "Not exactly."

"What?" Victoria has snapped to attention. "What happened?"

I really don't know if I should tell her. She's worried already, and if I tell her, she'll go nuclear. But she is one of my closest friends. And I don't know how long I can hold this secret inside me.

"I kissed him. Or he kissed me. Or... we kissed."

The silence that follows is deafening. "You did what?" Victoria whispers. "You saw him and then he kissed you?"

"Well, I didn't see him. It was dark. And then the power went out." The more I tell the story, the more unbelievable it sounds. But it really did happen. It wasn't a dream, although parts of it felt that way.

I hear Victoria exhale slowly. "Tess, I'm worried about you. First you take this job, then you kiss the client? And you haven't even seen his face? This isn't like you, and even if it was like you, it'd be concerning. To put it mildly."

She's got a point. I should probably tell Wolfe to take this job and shove it and get out of this place. What was I thinking last night?

Well, I wasn't, which might have been the problem.

And then I remember my parents' mortgage. And the second mortgage. And the deadline looming.

My heart thuds like it's hammering something into place so firmly it can never be budged. I can't say no to this.

"It's fine," I say. "I won't do it again. I have my own separate house here, and he doesn't want to be seen. I'm going to get this job done, get our money, and get out of here."

"Do we really need the money that bad?"

"We do," I say bluntly.

"Okay." That's reluctantly dragged out of her. "Just promise you'll be more careful? Forget about trying to see him or figure out what happened—stay clear of him."

It's great advice and definitely something I should do. I just don't know if I can. I don't know if I *want* to, which is scariest of all.

"Sure," I say. "I can do that." I'm lying, but Victoria's already worried enough.

"Look, with what happened to you before..." Her tone is heavy. "I worry about you. This *really* isn't like you, and I wonder... what's happening there?"

She's right, and she's got reason to worry—she was my rock before when everything happened. It turns out that when you attract a psycho who lies about sleeping with you to everyone he knows, you need a rock to help you through it.

I was just a young soldier, trying to get through my enlistment. Victoria was my commanding officer, doing her best in her first command. And he was a captain, son of a full-bird colonel, who I pissed off when I told him some order he'd given me couldn't be carried out. I was as diplomatic as possible since he was an officer, but he was also a complete idiot.

He decided to teach me a lesson, so he began sending me messages online, anonymous ones, but with just enough info that I knew it was him. And then he started spreading rumors about how we were carrying on a torrid affair but couldn't be public because of Army regs.

The entire time he was doing that, I hardly ever saw him. It was all online messages and in-person whispers from mutual acquaintances. It made the entire situation surreal but no less upsetting and terrifying.

The brass wouldn't help me at all. It would have been career suicide to do so, so they didn't. Victoria was the only one who helped me, fought for me, and when she got nowhere…

I wasn't planning on staying in the military forever, but she was. The Army was her life. After what happened to me, she left it all behind. I owe her more than I can ever repay.

Once I was out of the Army, I guess he decided he'd punished me enough because the messages and rumors suddenly stopped. I haven't heard from or seen him since. But it made an unbreakable bond between Victoria and me, so silver linings in awful, awful storm clouds and all that.

I won't—can't—let her down. Any more than I can let my family down.

"I know what you're worried about," I say. "But it's nothing like that. I promise. I'm completely fine. I'm totally focused on finishing this job and getting that paycheck. I would never lie to you."

"I know that." Her voice is thick with emotion. "I don't think you're lying… just that you're too close to whatever is going on that you can't see what's really happening."

I stare out the window at the massive house Wolfe is holed up in, the layers of glass and metal looking like they're rising up out of the earth. "The problem is that I'm not close to anything. And I still have no real idea what's going on. But I'm going to do what I came here to do."

"Ooh, that gave me the shivers the way you said that. So determined."

I laugh because I didn't mean to be so dramatic. "Anyway, everything is fine, I won't lose my head again, and you don't have anything to worry about."

"I'm going to expect updates every day anyway," Victoria says with a healthy dose of skepticism.

"Yes, sir." I drop my empty bowl in the sink. "Thanks for getting those parts to Rustem. And a huge thank-you for the knitting, which will keep me busy. I'll call you tonight."

I hang up and get on with my day. Before I've even finished breakfast, Rustem's knocking at my door, handing over the parts. And then I'm walking up to the house, my heart pounding.

Light floods the ground floor, and there's zero sign of Wolfe. Not that I expected there to be, but I still bite my lip with disappointment. Instead of lingering on that, I get to work repairing the security panels in the main room.

Hours later, I'm totally in the zone. I exhale deeply, as steady as a sniper as I sink into my pulse, drop into stillness. The soldering iron in my hand arcs through the air in slow motion as I bring it to the control panel. I've got the chip into place, the solder wire in my other hand, and now I've come to the trickiest part.

I've got to apply the smallest amount of solder, just the barest bit, or else I'll completely ruin the chip. And then I'll lose a day waiting for Victoria to bring Rustem a new one.

Squinting, I judge the angle of my soldering iron, adjust it a hair. Okay, it's good. I need to just do it—

The front door swings open. I drop my arms, open my mouth, ready to tell Rustem to give me some privacy, but it's not Rustem coming in.

It's a man, someone who's vaguely familiar. I tense, readying myself for whatever he might do. And then I recognize him.

Gage Cannon. One of Wolfe's billionaire buddies. He's the military contractor one and probably the source of the handheld scanners Rustem had. He's thinner than Wolfe, sharper in the face. In the pictures of them together, Wolfe usually has a smile while Gage always looks serious. He looks very serious now.

I don't think he's supposed to be here. And damn, I need to fix that gate alarm pronto. Along with installing some proximity alarms on the grounds.

Before I can yell for Rustem, he comes in behind Gage. "He's not going to see you," Rustem rumbles.

"The hell he's not," Gage mutters. His gaze swings toward me. "He's got a woman here?"

I pin him with a stare as sharp and hot as the tip of my soldering iron. "I'm working."

Gage raises an eyebrow. "What the hell happened to all the panels?"

"I'm fixing them." I wave the thread of solder in my hand. "Or I would be if I hadn't been interrupted."

I'm acting way feistier than I really feel, because Gage is… something. Not as much of a presence as Wolfe even though I can actually see his face, but he still commands attention. I need to push back against him in a way I don't with Wolfe. Or at least in a different way with Wolfe—when I'm talking with *him*, everything in me wants to pull him closer.

I don't have that reaction to Gage, which is curious.

Gage stares at me. Long enough that it becomes uncomfortable. I stare back, but I try for stoic instead of challenging. I really shouldn't be antagonizing a guy that powerful.

Finally Gage turns to Rustem. "I already know where to find him." He disappears down the hall.

I look to Rustem. "Should you be stopping him?"

Rustem shrugs. "He won't hurt him."

"How do you know?" I gesture with the soldering iron. "He said he couldn't trust anyone."

"He won't hurt him" is all Rustem says. "And we'll hear if he does."

Oh, that's super reassuring. I shake my head. "Shouldn't you at least listen by the door?"

If Wolfe ends up dead, I won't get paid. And I'm not going to admit that my unease runs deeper than that.

Rustem sighs. "Gage wouldn't sneak around. He'd come right at Gideon." There's admiration in his tone. "He'd have been a great wrestler."

"I'll take your word for it." Figuring I'm not going to get anywhere with him, I turn back to the panel. This at least I can do something about.

As I start soldering, a thought occurs to me: Is Gage allowed to see Wolfe's face? And does he know the complete story about what happened here?

CHAPTER 10

The commotion down the hall warns me that I have an unwanted guest. There's still time for me to duck into somewhere private and avoid them, but I don't.

Hiding my face and letting the rumors spread hasn't tempted my enemies into attacking again. Maybe if they get a good look at my face, confirm what happened for themselves, they'll strike. And I'll be ready when they do.

The plan is fluid after all. And if Rustem hasn't tossed them out on their ass yet, they must be someone close to me. Probably one of the guys. There wouldn't be that much noise for Raven or Morgan.

I hear Gage before I see him. Huh. That's not who I would have expected to come first. Archer maybe—he's the closest to me out of all of them. Or at least he was. I haven't heard anything from him since the incident.

My sternum starts to throb.

I look up as Gage comes into my office, letting him see my entire face. I tense for a moment, then make myself relax. Gage forcing his way into my house is unusual, but not so unusual that I should lose my temper over it.

I'm tempted though. "Didn't you see the No Trespassing signs?" I ask, putting bite into it.

Gage pauses by the door. He looks the same as always—a lean and hungry look, Ira would say about him. Ira meant it as a compliment, a joke.

If Ira could see Gage today, he might not say it in amusement. Gage looks like he hasn't been sleeping. Same as me.

"Gage Cannon here to see you," Gulizar chirps.

I roll my eyes. "Thank you so much," I say with dripping sarcasm. Being a computer, she doesn't get it.

"Shit," Gage mutters. "You look awful."

"Thanks." I nod toward the door. "Shut that."

He does without ever taking his eyes off my face. "What's that woman doing here?"

Gage doesn't bother with preambles. He's never been one to waste words. At least this intrusion will be brief—as long as I've known Gage, I've never had a conversation last longer than ten minutes with him. "Installing the new security."

He doesn't sit down. Instead, he plants his fists on my desk. "Raven's worried about you. And so's Morgan, although she won't admit it."

I sigh. Those two are a… complication in all my plans. I don't want to hurt them. But it might be inevitable since they're tangled up with all of us even though they're the innocent ones. "I'll call Raven soon." Morgan can wait since Raven will pass on any information to her sister anyway.

"Today." Gage puts one thick finger on my phone.

"Shouldn't Bishop be the one bringing me messages from Raven?" Bishop is the protector of our group, the one who takes the world on his shoulders. So naturally he hovers over Raven. He feels responsible for the worst tragedy of her life.

We're all guilty there, but Bishop takes it hardest. Really, he should have been the one saving lives with medical devices. Instead, he uses his skills to decode the stock market, swimming with some of the bloodthirstiest sharks I've ever met.

I move the phone away from Gage, although he's right. I should call Raven. And Morgan.

Morgan doesn't need any of us hovering over her though. She and Tynan were close, and when he died, she distanced herself from the rest of us. If she knew what really happened…

"He's busy." Gage catches sight of the device on my desk. "How's that working out?"

"Nobody's snuck explosives in yet, so I'd say it's fine." I push it toward him. "Rustem loves it."

Gage picks it up and examines it. "When's he going to quit and come work for me? Running errands for you is a waste of his talents."

"He's not a mercenary."

"No, but he speaks some languages we could use." Gage tosses the device, then catches it, his fist flexing over it.

"Speaking of language, you're talkative today." Gage is monosyllabic at the best of times. This is like a fucking soliloquy from him.

Gage shrugs, his massive shoulders straining his suit. "Oscar's been asking about you too."

Our gazes meet.

"I don't answer to Oscar." Oscar's taking over as our mentor for Ira never quite worked out, no matter how hard Oscar tried. He's a good guy, but he's no Ira.

"Not anymore." Gage tosses the device again. "So, you're going to cut him off too? After everything he did for us? And Raven and Morgan? What the fuck did they ever do?"

I lean back in my chair. "Did you ever think, after what we did, that maybe we should have cut off Oscar and Raven and Morgan? Given back our inheritances to the girls, told Oscar he shouldn't be helping us with his contacts?"

I do. I think all the time about how I insisted the system was ready to test, that everything would be perfectly fine. About how fucking stupidly, deadly wrong I was.

"Every day," Gage says simply. "But we didn't. And now they care about us."

I run my hand over my face. "They shouldn't."

"Look, I'm not saying we deserve it. But it's there. Whatever happened to make you close off like this, even more than usual… it's not their fault."

It's not. But it might be his. Or Archer's, or Cassian's, or Bishop's.

Maybe it's time to come out of the shadows, see if I can lure them close enough to expose themselves. I'll have to weigh the danger of leaving the notebook alone though.

"When's Raven's next party?" I ask casually.

"It's Morgan's half birthday next Friday. Everyone will be there."

Half birthdays are a thing in that family, and Ira celebrated harder than anyone. We still get together for the girls' half birthdays, but it was never quite the same after he died. Missing a half-birthday party won't be that big of a deal.

But if they'll all be there, it'll be the perfect opportunity to observe them all, maybe press on them some.

I used to just enjoy those things. And now I'm plotting about them.

"Will Beck be there?" I ask, remembering what I did to the Inspiron car in my garage. Morgan, for whatever reason, decided that dating Axel Beck would be an awesome idea. I wonder if they ever find time to actually talk what with Beck documenting his every breath for Instagram.

"Unfortunately, yes." Gage looks as if he'd like to be sick. "I wish she'd dump that asshole."

"He wants her AI algorithms for his cars," I say bluntly. "There's no way that empty-headed pretty boy came up with their self-driving system all on his own."

Oh, he crows about it to every news outlet he can, about how revolutionary Inspiron's tech is, how his cars are the wave of the future and he's the genius behind all of it. But

I've been in the guts of those systems and I don't buy it. That AI has Morgan's fingerprints all over it. She should have started her own company instead of working for that idiot. And then to date him…

I shake my head. "Asshole," I mutter.

"We all agree," Gage says, "but as long as she's happy, we have to tolerate him."

"If he puts my picture on his shitty Instagram…"

"He won't." Gage's smile isn't nice. "You don't fit his brand."

That's for damn sure. Morgan does though—beautiful, intelligent, exactly the kind of person Beck thinks he is.

"I'll see if I can make it," I say lazily, making it sound like I probably won't.

"Just… try to show up. For them. They're Ira's daughters and his best friend. Or they were. Do it for Ira." He sets the device on the desk, where it hits with a heavy clatter. "I'll leave that for you. I think you still need it."

I do, but I can't confess that to him. I need him to go back to the rest of them and spread some more rumors. About my face, my injuries, what my security situation might be.

Gage and I used to be close before Ira died. It's weird, because we had such different backgrounds but maybe not so weird since neither of us are the most social of dudes. Sitting together silently is our idea of a good friendship. When things were getting really bad with my parents right after I dropped out of med school, Gage would work quietly next to me for hours on end—his way of showing me support. He never mentioned what was going on. He was just there.

And I did the same for him when his dad got sick for the last time.

I can't do that with him now. And suddenly I really, really hope he isn't behind all this so I can do it again.

"Thanks," I say.

He waits as if he expects me to say more. Then he gestures to his face. "Do you want me to tell Raven about…?"

I shrug. "Tell them whatever you want."

He watches me for a long moment, like he wants to say more. But he doesn't. He turns and leaves without another word.

I stare at the device for a while. He's right, which I hate to admit—I have to leave sometime. If only to see Raven, Morgan, and Oscar.

My phone buzzes. "Hello?"

"Is everything okay?" Tess's worry vibrates through the line. I texted her earlier to make sure she got whatever she needed for today—I guess she was too anxious to settle for a text this time. "I mean, I know who that was, but you said no one could come in. You said you couldn't trust anyone."

"It's fine. And if Gage wants to get in, I don't think we can stop him."

I stare at the device he left as I ponder that. If Gage wanted into my safe, he would have already been in there, I'm pretty sure.

Does that mean he's not behind it? Maybe.

Or maybe I'm overestimating him. Maybe the person who pushed me down the stairs is one of his mercenaries and I'm lucky not to have a broken neck.

This is like trying to solve a Rubik's Cube blindfolded with one hand tied behind my back. Each turn could bring me closer to the truth. Or take me further from it.

"Isn't the whole point stopping everyone?" Tess says.

She's right. And I can't trust anyone, not even Gage. "Right. So you need to work faster."

She stifles an angry noise. "I'm working as fast as I can. I have no access to my tools or shop or my employee—"

"Excuses," I snap. "I don't want to hear them. I want results. Today wasn't a great look, was it?"

I'm not mad at her, I'm mad at Gage, but she's close at

hand at the moment. Which is fucked up, but she was warned.

There's a sharp inhale. "He's your friend."

"I have no friends. And you should be working."

I hang up. For long moments I simply stare into space, my hands rhythmically curling into fists. God, I'm such a dick. But it's better that she realize that and stay away from me.

And fuck, I'm sick of myself. I pick up my phone again, dial Rustem. "Meet me in the gym."

He's already down there by the time I arrive, lacing up his gloves. I get into my own gear and climb grimly into the ring, my ribs burning and my broken fingers throbbing.

"What did Gage want?" Rustem jabs at my head.

I duck, try for a right cross. "To remind me of how loved I am."

Rustem manages to snort as he dances out of reach. "Did he take his stuff back?"

"Nope." I duck under his fist, looking for an opening. My ribs are fucking burning with stabbing pains with each breath, but I push harder, pulling more pain in. Just fucking eating it up. "But he did offer to hire you away."

"Maybe I'll say yes this time." He jabs once, twice, catching me on my uninjured side. I twist away from the blows, but my breath still hisses out like steam from a busted boiler.

"The fuck you will," I pant. "You just like to tease him." I circle, searching for a way to repay Rustem for those jabs. My broken fingers throb, reminding me that this is a stupid-ass idea.

I don't care.

"She was worried about you," Rustem says. "Wanted me to toss Gage out to protect you."

"You should have." A surge of energy rushes through me, and I drive him back, back, until the only thing he can do is to protect his head. When he meets the corner post, I let up.

I fall back into the ropes, my ribs on fire and my hand feeling like it's about to fall off. But my mind is clear.

Rustem, even though I boxed him into a corner, hardly looks winded. Probably because his ribs are intact. "Feel better?"

I nod. "How's she coming along?"

"You should go see for yourself."

I send him a warning look. "I've got work to do."

"You have time to get it done. It's not like you're going anywhere." He starts stripping off his gloves. "She asked for more supplies and for her friend to come help her."

"Yes to the supplies," I say. "No to the friend. Isn't that her employee though?"

"She's her friend too." Rustem swings a leg over the ropes and climbs out. "I'll arrange for the supplies."

"Order in some lunch and dinner for her too." I start to pull off my own gloves, wincing as my broken fingers come free. "Have it sent to the cottage."

The look Rustem sends me is too knowing. "You don't want to have dinner with her again?"

I do, which is entirely the problem. I want to watch her sit in a pool of light, then kiss her until we're both panting and feral. And beyond.

"Just take care of it," I say, tossing my gloves aside. "I'm getting back to work. This time see that no one disturbs me."

CHAPTER 11

Almost a week here and I haven't seen Wolfe at all. And I don't mean his face—I mean any of him. Rustem brings me my supplies, food is delivered to my house, and I call my parents and Victoria every night. And that's the sum total of my human interaction.

Wolfe hasn't appeared at all. Not at dinner, not in the shadows, not even on the phone or intercom. If he's here, he's good at keeping away from me.

And he is here. There's something in the air, a charge that makes my hair crackle, that could only come from him. I may not be able to see him, but I can sense him.

I haven't sought him out though. I've got work to do. I've managed to reestablish the security perimeter outside, hooking up the gates, the cameras, and the buried proximity sensor to a system running an operating system of my own design. And completely cut off from any other network. If someone wants to hack into it, they'll have to break into the security nerve center I'm setting up in an extra room inside the house. Which means they'll have to break through the perimeter first, which should be damn near impossible now.

No one's tried to come visit Wolfe since Gage Cannon came, so I haven't had a chance to really test it. Rustem was pretty game about helping me do some initial tests—I think he liked the idea of pretending to be a secret agent or ninja warrior—but a more realistic test would be better.

It'll have to wait though. And I've got plenty to do inside the house. I'm trying to repair one of the panels downstairs, but I need to get into the wiring, which is in the wall. And this particular panel has wiring that leads upstairs to the forbidden zone.

When I reach the stairs, I keep following the wires. I know he said I couldn't go upstairs, but I also can't do my job if I don't. It's ridiculous to expect me to avoid an entire floor. Besides, I'll be in and out before he knows it. I just need to know where this bundle of wires ends.

As I come up the stairs, I get the sense of the house changing. It's less vast and echoing, more cozy. There're even some pictures on the wall, personal photos.

I stop by one that's a group of teenagers, maybe even college kids, with an older man. The boys are grinning like they know something you don't, and the man looks so proud of them. There's two girls with them too, about the same age as the boys. They look so much alike they must be sisters, with long, dark curls, oval faces straight out of a Renaissance painting, and soulful eyes. One is dead serious in all the pictures, her mouth never once cracking into a smile. The other one is smiling at least, but it's small, uncertain.

As I look more closely, I realize I recognize some of them. There's Wolfe, looking much younger than the photos I've seen. And more carefree. His pictures now have a hardness to them, like he's always one irritation away from a snarl.

This Wolfe looks almost kind. But also arrogant, like he knows he's going to take the world by storm.

I lift my finger to the photo, tracing the same spot on his face as I did in the darkened dining room. But the flat surface can't tell me if the face there is anywhere near the same as the one I touched.

With surprise, I realize I recognize some of the others too. There's Gage, his smile sharper than all the rest. Cassian is there too, the most arrogant of them all. I can see he was trouble even as a teenager.

And there's Archer and Bishop too, both part of the big, happy group.

Holy crap. Wolfe doesn't just hang out with these guys in some billionaire social club—he grew up with them. And he said he couldn't trust anyone…

Meaning he can't trust them either.

The only people I don't recognize are the man, the girls, and one other boy. I wonder who they are and where they are now. And if Wolfe can't trust them either.

I keep going down the hall. There're more pictures of him and his friends as kids, the man and the girl appearing occasionally in them, along with the mystery boy I don't recognize. There're no pictures of anyone who looks like his parents. Or any siblings. The stuff about his personal life is pretty sparse online, so I have no idea if his parents are still alive or if he even has siblings.

Judging by the lack of pictures, he definitely doesn't trust them even if they do exist.

Finally I come to the destination of my wires. It's another control panel, broken like all the others. I guess I'm supposed to magically fix this one without ever coming up here.

Shaking my head, I start to clean it out. There're some salvageable parts here, and once I pull it off the main network and put a new operating system on it, the entire system will be pretty damn secure. Repairing the panels will take the most time.

I wonder if he broke the panels. He never did say.

As I turn to sneak back downstairs, a light flickers from behind an open door. An electronic light. Like from a display.

Huh. I thought all those were broken.

I step into the room, intending to take just a quick look. I haven't heard or seen anyone up here. I'm safe enough.

And suddenly I realize I'm in Wolfe's bedroom. The bed is massive and rumpled like he just rolled out of it, there're clothes on the floor and cuff links on the dresser, lying as if they were tossed aside hastily.

That's a very big bed. I can't stop staring at it. I didn't think they made beds that big.

Did he have a bed custom made for him? And why? To fit more people in?

My cheeks heat as I imagine Wolfe in that bed with several partners. He'd be in the center, the focus of everything that was happening. And he'd beckon to me with one strong hand, telling me there's always room for one more…

The heat has spread to my core now, washing over my skin. I force my gaze away from the bed, back to the panel, but the flush lingers.

I take a deep breath, focus. And frown. This panel is different from all the others. It's not broken, for one. And it's running an entirely different operating system.

I don't think this panel is running on the other security system. This looks entirely separate.

But what is it protecting?

The display itself doesn't give me any clue. It merely says Arm? like it's waiting for instructions. I'm tempted to touch it, but it might be fingerprint coded. If it is and I touch it, the alarm could go off.

I want to know what this thing is protecting, but I also want to explore this place more. Setting off the alarm would end all that, so I leave the panel alone.

This room doesn't have any pictures except for a massive oil painting on the wall opposite the bed, a kind of generic piece showing abstract flowers.

There's a safe behind that painting. I'd bet my salary from this job on it. I shake my head because it's so predictable it's sad. Of course a thief is going to look behind that painting first. They've all seen just as many movies as we have.

I look back at the panel. It must be running the system on the safe. That at least is a good idea, keeping it separate from the rest. I run through possible ways to make it even more secure. Maybe hide that panel better. Definitely change out that painting. A fake bookshelf could work as long as the books are real and look like they've been read recently.

A panic room would be best. Yeah, a panic room in the basement, with the safe in there and maybe some escape tunnels even—

"What the hell are you doing in here?"

I spin to face the growl behind me, my heart pounding wildly. *He's caught me.* I wasn't supposed to be here and he's caught me.

"I'm so sorry," I start to babble. Wolfe is towering over me, his fists clenched at his sides.

"I said never to come up here." He's talking over me, his voice so deep and rough it could have come from within a mine.

I look up, ready to plead my case.

I look up and finally see his face. The thing I've been longing to see.

His face. His *perfect, unblemished* face.

CHAPTER 12

He's completely fine. Nothing whatsoever is wrong with his face except that it's downright gorgeous. All the skulking in the dark, hiding in the shadows, was to cover up this.

Gideon Wolfe is completely fine *and* a psychotic liar.

"What the hell?" I gesture to his face, his broad shoulders, his narrow waist.

He takes a step back, surprised. Then his expression hardens again. "I told you not to come up here. *Very* explicitly."

I should be frightened of him, of losing this job and the money. Instead, I'm just really, really pissed. Here I was feeling so sorry for him, thinking something terrible had happened to him, wishing he trusted me enough to show me his face, and he was perfectly fine the whole time.

I feel betrayed too, although I shouldn't. I should have walked right out the moment he refused to show himself.

"No, you don't get to be offended," I say. "You hid yourself like something was terribly wrong with you, like one look at you would turn someone into stone. But in reality you look like... like..." I motion futilely to his face. "Like that!"

"You weren't hired to come look at me," he snarls. "You

were hired to install a security system. Which doesn't include sneaking into my bedroom." His expression goes flat, stony. "Fuck. You snuck into my bedroom." He takes a heavy step toward me. "Are you in on it?"

From overhead comes Gulizar's voice. "Your tones are agitated." There's a pause before *agitated,* like she had to search for and insert the right word. "Shall I call the police?"

"No," Wolfe grits out.

"Yes," I counter. "Because this is one sick game you're playing."

"Contacting the authorities," she says in an eerily neutral voice.

"No." Command vibrates through Wolfe's tone, enough to make it seem like the ground is shaking. "Cancel that. And shut up." He glares at me. "Stop talking to it."

"*She* can hear me no matter what." I set my jaw, my muscles tensing. "And I'm serious. You're crazy. I had nothing to do with whatever happened here before. I needed to follow some wiring. That's all."

He sneers. "You'll have to do better than that."

I notice two things then. One, he's holding a notebook in his hand, a heavy, bound one, like the kind you'd use for journaling. And two, if he takes just two steps to the left, he'll be between me and the door, blocking my way out.

If he's convinced I came here to steal from him, he's definitely going to stop me from leaving.

I go for the door, keeping my head up and my shoulders back, the picture of confidence. My stomach is in knots though, and my heartbeat is loud in my ears.

"Don't worry about firing me." Only two more steps to the door. "I quit."

"You can't." He watches me but doesn't follow. "We're not done here."

"But we are." I slip through the open door.

I take the steps two at a time, listening behind me for the sound of him coming after me. But there's nothing but the rasp of my shaky breaths and my own pulse. Still, I go as fast I can through the house without breaking into a run. I have to get out of here. This whole thing was a mistake.

I don't let myself think about the second mortgage, or the first, or my student loans, or the looming foreclosure. That will have to wait until I'm out of here.

I can't stop thinking about how he looked. The planes of his face, the hollows in his cheeks, how strong his jaw was, how blue his eyes were, how dark his hair was. And how sinfully plush his mouth was.

It doesn't matter how hot he is or how badly I want to kiss that mouth again—what he did was messed up. And as badly as I need the money, I don't need that.

I pass Rustem on the way to the back door. He watches me with surprise.

"What's—" he starts to say.

"I saw his face," I call to him as I speed away.

His eyes go wide. "Shit."

"Exactly. I'm out. I quit."

Rustem doesn't try to stop me either. I make it to the cottage without a single person behind me. Still, I shut and lock the door.

I collapse against it, panting.

None of this makes sense. He said he can't trust anyone, to the point where I can't leave the grounds… but he lets in Gage. He hides in the shadows as if he's ashamed of his face… but he's perfectly beautiful. He's got that safe upstairs, completely walled off from the rest of the security system. He didn't destroy that.

Rustem knew this whole time that Wolfe was fine. Gage must have known too. It was only me he was lying to. Asshole.

I push off from the door and march to my bedroom. In five minutes I'm packed and ready. There are tools of mine still in the house, but Rustem can send them to me later. It's the least he can do after being in on this with Wolfe.

With my bag slung over my shoulder, I head for the door. I dial Victoria once I'm outside and on my way to the main gate.

She doesn't answer. Shit. I leave a message, asking her to meet me on the road somewhere. I don't care where. I'm walking out of here, as far and as fast as I can.

Evening is falling once I make it out to the road. Somehow the truck trail looks even narrower and more dangerous in the low light. There's nothing but trees and mountains as far as I can see and then that one lonely road, disappearing into the dark.

I take a steadying breath. I've been through worse. As far as I know, there're no wild animals out here, so I should be fine until Victoria picks me up. She hasn't called me back yet, but she will. She's never let me down yet.

The first few miles are easy. And then the road starts to climb. I'm huffing and puffing by the third mile, my thighs burning. Jeez, I really wish I'd kept up with my PT. But I wasn't expecting to have to flee in the night from one of my clients.

As I come to a curve in the road, I step close to the guardrail and check my phone. Still nothing from Victoria. But maybe she's already on her way.

Headlights flash over the road, flicking in and out of the trees. I peer around the curve, expecting to see Victoria's car any moment.

Nothing comes around.

Then there's another set of headlights, whipping through the trees as if the car is jerking from one side of the road to the other. There's a squeal of tires, then a motor revving.

From around the corner comes a low-slung sports car,

going so fast my heart stops. The headlights blind me for half a second, and I put my hand up to shield my eyes.

I see a young kid in the driver's seat, not more than seventeen, his eyes wide.

He's coming right for me. There's no time to stop, no time to swerve. I'm going to be pinned between the car and the guardrail.

Suddenly the air rushes out of me as I'm tackled at the waist. I go flying over the guardrail and land on whoever sacked me. We bounce together, once, twice, and then gravity pulls us down the steep hillside.

I'm rolling down the hill, bouncing and bumping, held in a pair of amazingly strong arms. We come to a stop near the bottom, my rescuer underneath me, cushioning me.

Before I even open my eyes, I already know who it is. My hair's on end, my nerves are popping and sparking, and my skin feels too small for me.

It has to be Wolfe.

His eyes are closed, his head back.

Oh shit. Did he get knocked out?

I scramble off him, my hip shouting with pain. I must have wrenched something. But I'm worried about him.

I kneel beside him, checking for injuries. There's a massive gash in his forearm, like it got caught on a branch on the way down. And his fingers are at a funny angle.

I look again. Wait, his fingers are splinted—meaning they were broken before this. He had three broken fingers and he still managed to hold on to me as we rolled. I swallow hard as I remember his arms around me.

That gash needs to be taken care of. He might even need stitches. But his eyes still aren't open, which worries me the most. Head wounds aren't something I can handle on my own out here.

I look around for my bag or my purse. They're nowhere

to be found, which means my cell phone is gone too. Son of a bitch.

I hear more tires squealing and look up toward the road, but I can't see anything. Since the car isn't at the bottom of the hill here with us, I assume they made it okay and are getting the hell out of there. Little shits.

Wolfe still has his eyes closed. A spike of adrenaline hits my heart. I reach up and pat his cheek. "Mr. Wolfe." I pat harder. "Mr. Wolfe, are you okay?" Now I'm gently smacking him. "You need to wake up."

His eyelids flutter open, his thick, sooty lashes brushing over his cheeks. "Are you okay?" he mumbles.

I blow out a relieved exhale. Thank God. "I'm fine. But you need help."

He pushes himself and shakes his head, then winces. He grabs his ribs and grits his teeth, exhaling with a hiss.

"Is it your ribs?" I ask. He could have broken them on the way down, easy.

He shakes his head again, then nods. "They're broken, but they were before."

Broken ribs, broken fingers… What the hell happened?

I offer him my hand.

He looks at it for a long moment. "I'm supposed to be helping you."

"You saved my life."

He takes my hand then, and I drape his arm over my shoulders as I help him up the hill. His breath hitches with every step.

"Should we call the police?" I ask. "And you need to get to an ER."

"No." That's flat and final. "Rustem can stitch me up." He lifts his arm, studies the gash. "Hell, that doesn't even need stitches."

I'm not sure that's true, but if he won't go to the doctor, we'll never know.

"Someone just tried to kill us," I say. "And clearly something serious happened to you before. The police are definitely a good idea here."

He hauls himself around a bush, his feet slipping. I hold tight, trying to steady him. He's warm and solid, almost too big for me to support.

"I know that kid," he says. "Drives like an asshole around here when his parents are out of town. Wasn't intentional."

Man, I'd love to find that kid and give him a piece of my mind. "He's going to kill someone someday." And it would have been me if Wolfe hadn't miraculously been here. "Did you come to bring me back?"

He closes his eyes and grimaces. His ribs must be on fire. "You wanted to leave. I was going to offer you a ride. Can't walk here at night."

I can't leave now. Someone has to get him back to the house. And I don't have my phone to call anyone to come get us.

We're kind of fucked.

Finally we reach the road again, both of us climbing over the guardrail. Wolfe gestures with his chin down the road toward something.

A car is parked on the side of the road, lights on and doors open. I peek inside and see some books in a foreign language. Maybe Turkish.

There's only one dude in a fifty-mile radius who'd have Turkish books in his car.

"You took Rustem's car?" I ask as I help Wolfe into the passenger seat.

"Had to get to you." His voice is thready, breathless, as if he's fighting for every molecule of oxygen.

God, I hope his ribs didn't puncture a lung. I've had very basic battlefield medic training, but I've never had to actually use it.

"Hold on," I say. "We'll get you home."

He doesn't say anything, just lets his head fall back on the seat. It puts him in profile, his full lips a contrast to the stark lines of his nose and throat, the jut of his chin.

"Thank you for rescuing me." I'm not sure if he heard me.

I drive as fast as I dare on the narrow, twisting road, racing to get us both to safety.

CHAPTER 13

It turns out that Wolfe's injuries weren't as bad as I feared. At least according to Wolfe and Rustem.

"He's fine," Rustem says as I peer at the gash on Wolfe's arm.

Wolfe's stripped off his shirt, and I'm doing my best not to stare at his chest.

"Strong as an ox." And then he actually smacks Wolfe on the side of the head as if Wolfe really were an ox. And Wolfe, that idiot, grins.

"His ribs are broken," I say coldly. "And his fingers. And if these wounds don't get properly cleaned out, he could get a nasty infection."

"All that was already broken," Rustem says. But he hands me some gauze and iodine anyway.

I look straight at Wolfe. "How did that happen?"

He and Rustem exchange a glance.

I grit my teeth. "I think I'm owed some answers. I came here to help and you've both been lying to me the entire time. So actually, I'm *definitely* owed some answers."

Wolfe shrugs. "Someone broke in about a week ago. Went for the safe."

"You think," Rustem cuts in.

"They were definitely going for the safe," Wolfe says. "I caught them, tried to fight them off, and I ended up going down the stairs. They got away."

"And the police and the ambulance that came?" I'm staring at him, holding the gauze and iodine still, hardly believing what I'm hearing.

"Alarm system automatically calls them," Wolfe says. "I told them I was fine and to take off."

"And the smoke?"

Wolfe rolls his eyes. "I don't know how that one got started, but there was never any smoke."

"Yeah, it's not like you were stoking any of those crazy rumors with your behavior," I say dryly. "So why did you smash all the panels?"

His eyes flash blue at me. "Why? The fucking system failed me. Among other reasons." He looks to Rustem. "Go home. I'll be fine."

Rustem doesn't move.

I nod to him. "I'll take care of him." I don't let myself look at Wolfe as I say that.

"Call if you need anything," Rustem says.

Once he's gone, I keep my gaze on Wolfe's many scrapes and cuts. It's going to take a while to clean everything.

I dab at the abrasions with the gauze, but none of the gravel comes out. I'm going to have to get rougher, which I don't want to do. He's already in pain, his breath coming short, sweat on his forehead, and his pupils dilated so much his eyes are indigo.

"You need to have a doctor irrigate this," I say. "I'm worse than useless."

"Harder," he grits out. "I can take it. And I am a doctor."

My gaze flies to his. How did I not know that?

"Well, close to a doctor." He shrugs. "I dropped out of med school in my last year."

I didn't think my eyes could get any wider. "*You* couldn't finish med school?"

"I said dropped out, not flunked," he growls.

Well, at least he's feeling well enough to do that. "But why? If you were so close, why not finish?"

He doesn't answer. Instead, he turns his head away from me.

Fine. He wants to be surly, I don't care. I scrub at the wound, watching with grim satisfaction as some of the dirt comes out.

His breath hisses in. "Goddamn it," he mutters. "Goddamn it, god*damn* it, god*damn* it."

I keep scrubbing. More and more dirt comes out. I try to ignore his sounds of pain, but it's getting harder. I'm not made of stone. I whimper when he makes a particularly bad sound.

"My parents were surgeons," he says out of nowhere.

My mind trips on the past tense, my hand going still. "I'm so sorry."

He grimaces. "They *are.* Shit. I don't know why I always put it like that. They're still alive." He doesn't sound happy about that.

"Oh." I angle my head to get a better look at the scrape. I think I might be making progress after all. Just a few more bits of gravel and it will be clean. "Did they want you to go to med school?"

"I don't think they ever wanted anything for me." He gasps as I go after a particularly stubborn piece. "*Want* would be too tender. They expected me to go to med school. Expected me to do a lot of things."

I swallow hard. "But they must be proud of you now. You've built a company that saves lives. Way more lives than you ever could have as a doctor, working on your own."

He snorts. "Don't think I'm some kind of hero. I'm not. I started the company to get back at my parents. All this?" He points to everything surrounding us. "It's a giant fuck-you to them. The biggest fuck-you I could build. I'm not doing this for the good of humanity."

That's the coldest thing I've ever heard. I can't imagine feeling so bitter toward my parents. Feeling such hatred. It's like black ink seeping out of him and onto the floor it's so powerful.

"You say all that," I say quietly, "but you still do a lot of good in this world. Your heart's not as black as you claim."

I let the gauze fall into the trash and start to wrap the scrapes, my hand trembling slightly. I'm suddenly achingly aware of his bare chest, naked skin so close, so warm.

"What makes you think I have a heart?" he demands.

"Well, you did all this for your parents. So you must still care some even if you think you don't."

"My parents." He practically spits that out. "Someone who cuts people open for a living thinks nothing about cutting their own son's heart out."

My own heart goes cold, quiet. He's saying that like he really believes it. But I can't somehow. Even after the trick he pulled, I can't believe his heart is hollow. Maybe because there's still pain in how he talks about his parents. Somebody without a heart wouldn't care anymore.

"Rustem." I grab onto his name. "You definitely care about him."

"He's my employee." He flicks that out like he could fire Rustem at any moment.

Again, I call bullshit. "And your friend," I say defiantly. "Along with Gage, Archer, Cassian, and Bishop. You've been friends since you were young; I saw the pictures. You all came up together; you still hang out. You definitely care about them."

"You think it was some kind of shared childhood that bonds us together?" He's sneering at me. "Oh yeah, we share some stuff. But it's not great memories of summers at the swimming hole."

I stare at him for a long moment. At the sensuous lips turned cruelly, his drooping, sooty lashes, the iron line of his jaw. He's beautiful, but he's trying so hard to look like a monster.

"You want me to hate you," I say slowly.

A single, quick blink. "You're finally getting it." Relief, just the faintest hint, lurks under his words.

I won't hate him. I can't. But he wants me to so badly, and I'm desperate to know why. What could he have possibly done to think that way about himself? And it can't just be his parents, although it's clear they fucked him royally. I hope I'm never in a room with them, or I'll let loose.

I straighten up. "Fine. You're a monster. You're awful, hideous. A nightmare in human form. Something straight from a horror—"

"Okay, okay," he grumbles. "You don't have to go that far." His gaze locks with mine. "Promise me you'll remember though. No matter what happens."

He's deadly serious. As serious as he was when he first told me he couldn't trust anyone.

"I won't forget," I say just as solemnly. I won't say I hate him or anything like that, but I can promise that.

"Good." He nods to his hand. "Could you finish? Please?" he adds hastily.

I finish wrapping up his arm. As I do, the air between us shifts and eases. It's like making me admit he's a monster has made something in him open to me. Like he can trust me now that I know how bad he is.

When I'm done, he holds up both hands, one in bandages, the other in splints. "Shit," he mutters.

"I guess I'm doing the cooking tonight."

"I was thinking more about work." Gideon lowers his hands with a sigh. "Can you take dictation?"

The look I send him has him throwing up his hands again. "Just a suggestion."

"Cooking is my limit." I pause by the door. "I won't go upstairs again. I only did it to check on some wiring."

He raises an eyebrow.

"Okay, I went to check on the wiring," I confess, "but then I started to look around. But I won't again. Although there is a security system up there."

I wait for him to explain what it is. I don't think he will, but I won't pretend I don't know it's up there.

"If you need to go up there to install stuff, it's fine," he says gruffly. "I'd prefer you not to, but if you need to…" His jaw twitches. "Don't worry about the other security system."

I take a breath and take a chance. "Why pretend that something awful happened to you? Never letting anyone see you, never going out, letting the rumors fly? What's that about?"

He shifts in the chair and leans back. "I want people to think I'm hurt worse than I am."

"But you are hurt bad!" Realization dawns. "You want the intruder to think you can't defend yourself. You want them to try again."

It's madness but also the only thing that makes sense. All of this is bait. And he's setting himself up as the trap.

"You're crazy," I whisper.

He scoffs. "Crazy like a fox. I need to know who's behind this. And when I catch the fucker, I'll know."

"What are they after?" I ask. "This can't be about… cash in the safe or jewelry or whatever."

He looks away and grabs his ribs.

"They attacked you."

"Well…" His jaw works. "I tried to grab him, and when he fought back, I ended up going down the stairs."

Oh, that totally makes it better. "It's still bad. And way beyond what a run-of-the-mill burglar would do." I plant myself in the doorway. Nobody's getting any dinner until he talks.

"I guess you're owed some answers," he says, still not looking at me.

I cross my arms. "After you lied to me like this? Yeah, it'd be nice."

He sighs and gets up. "Fine. But I'm hungry. Let's do this in the kitchen."

Ten minutes later, there's a spread of hummus, cheese, flatbread, olives, and stuffed grape leaves. He pours us each a large glass of red wine.

"Should you have this?" I ask. "Did you take any pain meds?"

The look he sends me is pure annoyance. "This *is* my pain meds." He takes a long swallow, and I can't help watching his throat move.

I take a quick sip of my own wine, trying to chase away the sudden dryness in my throat.

"So." I set down my glass. "What's the story?"

He seems to look inward, as if viewing a memory. "I had a... a guy. You could call him a mentor. He helped all of us— me, Archer, Bishop, Cassian, Gage, and—" He cuts himself off and doesn't finish that. "Anyway, he helped us all turn our lives around."

"Turn your life around?" I ask. If he was in med school, his life couldn't have been that screwed up.

"Remember my dropping out of med school?" A sad smile flickers over his mouth. "I wasn't going to flunk out, but I was about to be kicked out."

My eyebrows fly up. "I mean, you're kind of... surly, but kicked out?"

"Surly?" he growls. "I've been really nice to you. Or tried to be."

"You mean you can be worse?" When he continues to

glare, I lift my palms. "You pretended to be horrifically scarred."

"No, you assumed," he says smugly. "And I wasn't doing it to you personally. Like you said, it was bait."

"For what? What's at the middle of all this?" I'm not going to be sidetracked here.

He rubs his face with his good hand. Or rather, his decent one—neither one is *good* at the moment. "I hated med school. I never wanted to go, but I couldn't make myself give up. So I developed a drinking problem. That's why I was about to get kicked out."

Wow. He had a drinking problem in med school but still got good enough grades to stay in. I'm impressed in spite of myself.

"Then what happened?" I ask, because he doesn't have an MD or a drinking problem now, at least as far as I can tell.

"Ira found me. Encouraged me to do AI and programming on the side. I'd always been interested in it but never gave it my full attention. He pushed all of us to be better, to design smarter, more elegant things." His tone is rich with affection. A small smile plays at the corners of his mouth. Everything that should have been in his voice when he talked about his parents is there now.

"When did he die?" I ask softly.

"Eight years ago." Gideon's staring at a point far, far away. Or maybe it doesn't even exist. "It was a car accident. Our friend Tynan was with him."

"I'm so sorry." It feels so small against Gideon's grief, but it's all I have.

He squares his shoulders. "Don't say that."

I flinch at his tone. I might not know him well—at all, really—but saying *I'm sorry* is pretty accepted when someone tells the story of how their father figure died.

"Ira left us all money in his will," Gideon goes on. "I was the executor. We used it to start our companies. And he left us…" He chews on possible word choices. "Notebooks. One for each of us, including Tynan. But since Tynan wasn't around, I held on to his."

"That's what's in the safe?"

He nods.

He thinks this is all about a notebook? I want to ask what was inside them, but considering the lengths he's gone to protect it, he's not going to tell me shit.

Whatever it is, it must be explosive. And what the hell is in *his* notebook then? The secrets to his success?

"But why now?" I ask. "Why not steal it when you lived someplace less secure?"

"I don't think the others knew Tynan had a notebook. Things were really confused right after. I never explicitly told them I had Tynan's notebook. They might have realized or figured out recently that it exists and I must have it."

"But they have their own. Why would they…?" I'm missing something big here. It's like trying to find my way around a boulder in the dark, but instead I'm inching around the things he won't tell me.

"Each notebook is different. We compared them when we first got them."

My mind starts to spin out possibilities. "So you think it's one of the guys then? Or what if it's one of Tynan's relatives? Shouldn't it have gone to his next of kin?"

He tears off some flatbread. "Tynan didn't have any relatives. No next of kin to give it to." He dips up some hummus. "Raven and Morgan are also possibilities."

"Raven and Morgan?"

"Ira's daughters," Gideon explains. "They got some money in the will, as much as the rest of us."

I frown. "They didn't get notebooks? And did Ira have a wife?"

"His wife died when the girls were young. But no, no notebooks for them. They did get the house though."

He doesn't elaborate on why their father didn't make the same bequests to his own family that he had for Gideon and his friends. Maybe because his daughters were girls. Only Ira's big, bad foster sons got a notebook, containing whatever it was. "Weren't they mad their dad didn't prepare notebooks for them?"

He pauses with a stuffed grape leaf halfway to his mouth. "No. They're not like that."

I tuck my tongue in my cheek. "They're good girls, never cause a fuss?"

He nods, totally oblivious. "They wouldn't care about that."

I'm not so sure, but I'll take his word for it for now. "So your only suspects are your best friends?"

"You can see why I've barricaded myself here," he says dryly. "If it's one of them, I have to be here to catch them."

"You don't have to go it alone," I say. "You have Rustem. And… well, me too, I guess."

Something flares deep in his eyes. "You? You'll take down an intruder? For me?"

I duck my head, because whatever is going on in his expression is too much for me. "Not that. But I can give you the best security system humanly possible."

The intensity in him fades. "I suppose I do have to trust you on that. But no, you should never be taking any intruder down. Rustem isn't either. It's my problem to solve. Tynan's gone, Ira's gone, so there's only me. And I'm not going to let them down."

It sounds so incredibly lonely. Like it's him against their ghosts and the world. My heart squeezes, hard, and this time I let it, because this time it feels like he's earned it.

CHAPTER 14

I never meant to tell her all that, but something about Tess Robards's gaze cracks me right open.

At least she didn't ask what was in the notebooks. I might have actually told her.

She's watching me with wide, solemn eyes. Like she wants to take the weight off my shoulders and onto her own. "You're not alone. Don't think that." She puts her hand on my face, just like she did before.

I suck in a sharp breath. Her touch is like no one else's. Soft but electrifying. "Don't feel responsible for me. That's the opposite of what should happen."

It's the opposite of what *is* happening—I'm imagining her trying to stop this thief, and my chest hurts so bad it's hard to draw air. I feel so responsible for her I'm going a little mad thinking about her in the face of danger.

I should let her go. Tell her to move back out, never come back. But her hand's on my face and I can't do anything but lean into her touch.

"But that's my superpower." Her eyes are sad. "Feeling responsible for everyone."

Tess looking sad is fucking gutting. Like seeing the sun

blotted from the sky. I never should have let her see my face, because she can get close now.

Too late though. I lean in and capture her lips.

Immediately I ignite. The hunger, the need she whips up in me is almost uncontrollable. I frame her face with both my hands, her jaw so delicate between them, and devour her. I don't even need to breathe anymore because she's got everything I've ever needed.

"Jesus," I mutter. "You're so fucking sweet and hot and goddamn gorgeous."

"I'm not." She sounds all dreamy, like I've kissed her into another world.

I don't know which part she's protesting, and I don't care, because it's all true. "Don't deny it," I demand. "And you'd better not give a shit about me after this."

Her eyes open. "You're a monster. I haven't forgotten."

The tight knot in my chest eases. Good. She's safe then. "That's right." I bend my head and kiss her again. Kiss her until the entire world starts to spin and my skin is aching for her.

"Let me touch you," I rumble, thrusting my thigh between hers. "Just touch you, that's all. With clothes, without, but if I can't get my hands on you, I'm gonna implode."

She makes a sort of whimper that's close enough to a yes for me. I bend her backward over the counter, spreading her legs with mine. Her pussy lands on my thigh, and the heat's so scorching I can feel it even through the fabric.

She thrusts against my leg like she just can't help herself. It's so hot I have to grit my teeth, because otherwise I'd be grabbing my cock and getting myself off. Only a few strokes and I'd be there, she's got me so wound up. And I haven't even touched her, not really.

I grab the curves of her ass and knead as best I can, dragging her core hard into me. Her mouth opens on a wordless gasp. I love that it feels so good I stole the noise from her throat.

If I had two good hands, no broken ribs, she'd be on the floor underneath me already. Or no, I'd carry her up to my bed. Tess deserves better than the cold, hard floor, no matter how wild she makes me.

I reach for the button of her jeans with my bad hand, figuring it's better to keep hold of her with my good one. She's fully on my thigh now, only her toes touching the floor, and I can't let her fall. I've picked her up and I've got to bring her down safely.

But my hand is too useless to get the button free. Stupid tight jeans and stupid stubborn button and stupid broken hand keeping me from her sweet pussy.

She reaches between us, flicks open her fly just like that. Her panties peep out in the gap, purple with a tiny bow. I never knew plain cotton could be so damn enticing.

I switch hands then, my broken fingers throbbing when they curl around her butt. I tell them to shut up and not ruin this. My good hand slips down the front of her jeans, cupping her sex through that ridiculously sexy purple cotton.

When my fingertips find wet fabric, I groan. When I brush the stiff bud of her clit, she groans.

"You don't have to… The jeans… Oh fuck," she pants.

I'm guessing she means I could get her off like this, right through her panties. But if she thinks I'm passing up the chance to stroke her bare pussy, she's dead wrong. I tease her clit with the fabric, watching her expression to see how far I can take her without pushing her over the edge. My other hand is clenched around her ass so firmly I might be breaking my fingers all over again, and my cock is so hard I might pop my pants button, but I've never felt so good in my life. It's like everything I've ever done was building to this moment.

When her eyes roll back, I slide my hand inside her

panties. It's a tight fit with her jeans still on and her riding my thigh, but I like that. Makes me get inventive, and I've got cleverness to spare.

Her folds are soft and slick, better than the finest silk. Her arousal perfumes the air around us. My mouth waters as I imagine how she'll taste.

Her clit is swollen and needy, and the second I touch it, she jerks in my arms. A noise that's pure crazed need leaves her mouth.

A few delicate strokes and some twists have her coming completely undone, her panting treading the line between breath and sobs.

"Oh God, oh God, oh God," she chants.

I hold her tight, giving her an anchor to ride on. She's so transcendent when she climaxes. I want to capture this image of her in my mind forever.

And then my bad hand gives out. She slips down my thigh several inches before I catch her.

"Fuck," I huff out. Betrayed by my own body. Except my cock is still raring to go.

She jumps off my leg, her pants still unbuttoned. "Are you okay? What were you thinking?"

"I was thinking you were too goddamn sexy to resist." I grin past the pain thrumming through my hand. "And I was right."

She shakes her head, a slight smile on her mouth. "You need rest. And real pain relief." She bites her lip. "And I should get back."

I hold in my sigh of regret. She's right, but my cock insists that we can still pull this off. My hand tells me that my cock is crazy.

"I'll walk you back."

She cups my cheek, presses a quick kiss to my mouth. "Thank you. I…" Her expression tips into pleased shyness, and I can't fucking take it. She turns me inside out with those eyes of hers.

"Let's go," I say gruffly.

I don't reach for her hand as we walk, because I don't entirely trust myself to let go. And I have to concentrate on walking straight since I fucked up my leg somehow earlier and I've got the devil's own hard-on.

When we reach her door, she kisses me again. Long and slow, like she wishes we could finish what we started.

I'm game. But she pulls away before I can suggest it, putting a hand on my chest. That touch says *I really regret this, but I have to go.*

So I let her leave and shut the door without any further protest. I do wait until I hear her turn the dead bolt.

As I walk back to the house, alone, her words about feeling responsible for everyone come back to me. I wonder who exactly the everyone is that she's talking about. And if I can use all this money I've amassed to take some of that weight off her shoulders.

CHAPTER 15

I wake up the next day with every fucking inch of my body hurting. Not just hurting—*screaming.*

"Fuck," I huff as I pull myself out of bed. I think I might have rebroken my ribs. But I drag my ass up and into the bathroom, getting myself ready for the day. A shower's doable, but I decide not to shave, which leaves me smelling like Irish Spring and looking like a damn pirate.

Strangely, my mood is pretty damn good. Probably 'cause I got to see Tess's O-face last night. I had some amazing dreams after that.

When I limp downstairs, Tess is already at work. She's wearing yoga pants today for some reason, and they're hugging her ass in a way that makes me wish like hell my hands weren't fucked up. And that she wasn't my employee. And that it wasn't broad daylight. Fingering her at night is one thing, but sneaking up on her while she's working is too beastly even for me. I do find myself wishing I was less of a gentleman as I take in her ass in those yoga pants though.

She turns as I come up to her, part of an electronic panel in her hand. "You look..." Her gaze runs up and down me, and I swear she lingers on my beard.

I rub at the stubble. Maybe I should keep it if she likes it.

"Like hell?" I ask softly.

A flush creeps up her neck and into her soft cheeks. "No. You look…" She swallows hard. "Good. Really good, considering what you went through last night."

Heat flares in her eyes, a brighter gold than her usual topaz. I know exactly what she's remembering from last night.

I reach out and lightly brush a dark mark on her jaw with my good hand. "You fell too. Are you okay?"

Her breath comes in sharp and quick. "I'm fine. Just a little stiff."

"I'll bet. You sleep okay?"

Her cheeks go pink. "It took me a while to fall asleep."

I want to lick that blush off her cheeks. And then keep licking all the way down. "Me too," I say huskily. Reluctantly I let my hand drop. "You got an early start."

"I've got a lot to do." She gestures at the panel. "Someone smashed all these for shits and giggles, and I've got to repair them."

"What an asshole." I scrub my hand through my hair. "I can help you."

Her flush deepens. "It's my job. You're paying me—a lot—to do this."

I am, but what I'm paying her is a drop in the bucket for me. A very tiny raindrop into a fricking lake.

"I want to make up for the asshole who did this."

She raises an eyebrow. God, but her eyebrows are… elegant? Expressive? I don't know exactly, but I can't look away from them.

I couldn't look away last night when she was caring for me. She tried to be gentle at first, but it didn't work. And then when she came, I definitely couldn't look away. Not if my life depended on it.

"You don't have better things to do?"

"I do." I reach out and touch the mark on her jaw again. "But I owe you. And I made your job harder."

She nibbles on her lip. "I could use some help. If you have the time."

If she keeps doing that with her lip, my head is going to explode. "How much do you trust your employee? The blond one?"

"With my life," she says without hesitation.

Damn. That's some real sincerity. I would have answered like that about the guys if I'd been asked the question before the break-in.

My sternum hurts. Again.

"You should have her come help you," I say gruffly. "This needs to get done."

For a moment it looks like she's going to light into me and remind me that banning her employee was my dumb idea. But all she says is "Thank you. I'll call her today."

I wait for her to make the next logical leap—to ask or demand to be released from her promise to stay here. If I'm giving away so many of my earlier demands, she's got to take advantage of it. Anyone would.

I don't want her to though. I want last night to mean something to her.

She watches me for a long moment, like she's… weighing me or something. I never had a woman look at me like that, not ever. Her look is deep.

I don't know what to make of it. I'm not afraid of it, but I already told her she's not going to like what she sees. If she stays, she's only going to see more. We react too explosively together to prevent it from happening again.

"I should probably keep staying in the in-law." Her tone is too casual. "To get this done faster."

My heart does something strange. Something like a leap.

To cover it up, I say roughly, "Good, because that wasn't on the table. We were only talking about your friend."

"Employee," she says. "But also my friend. Like you and Rustem."

I know what she's doing: she's reminding me of my human connections. Since she's staying, I'll let her get away with it.

"Why do you trust her so much?" I ask. "I mean, your *life*? Really?"

Her expression shifts, gets a touch haunted. "She gave up a lot for me. Almost everything."

There's a story behind that, a massive one, and I want to know it. "What happened?"

She sets down the part she's holding and sighs deeply. Like she has to gather herself to tell it. "I was in the Army," she says. "I enlisted the day after I graduated high school. No, two days after, actually."

And there's another story there, I can tell. This woman's got layers, and every new one she reveals just pulls me in deeper.

"Okay." I gesture like I'm rolling something up. "Start with that. Why two days?"

Color sneaks up her cheeks and her gaze drops. "I thought I'd have some time after high school to figure things out. Get an entry-level job, take some classes at the community college, decide what I wanted to do with my life. But then I… my parents had some debts that I found out about. Big ones. No job I could get with only a high school degree would be enough to help out as much as they needed. The Army would feed, clothe, house, and pay me." She shrugged. "It was a no-brainer."

Maybe a no-brainer, but not easy. "So you joined the Army. And helped your parents get out of financial trouble." She doesn't have to say that part—what I already know about her tells me she must have done that.

"I helped pay off those debts, yes," she says carefully.

Those debts. Meaning there were more debts after. I wonder how many of those she's helped pay off too. Not all of them, I'm sure—that must be why she took this job and kept it. Those debts held her here.

My long-dormant conscience stirs. I took advantage of her and lied to her. It's not the first time I've used someone to my benefit, and it won't be the last… but I haven't felt bad about it since I can't remember when.

So there's at least some of the people she feels responsible for. Her parents. And this employee too.

"You joined the Army then," I say irritably, because I don't like feeling bad. "Got yelled at by a drill sergeant and scrubbed toilets."

She tries to hold back a smile. "It's not quite as bad as *Full Metal Jacket*. I got assigned to the Signal Corps, doing pretty much what I am now. Except an Army base is way less nicer than this place."

"This house better be nicer," I mutter. "Considering what I paid for it." Secretly, I'm pleased. She likes this house. She wants to keep staying here, at least until the job is done.

Apparently I'm not enough of a monster to scare her away completely. Which was my plan all along—keep her at arm's length so that she'd get the job done quickly and never look back—but having my plan blow up turns out to be pretty good. I'm going to have her within arm's reach instead. My blood heats at the thought.

Maybe I should take her around the grounds. Show her the pool and the sauna. She ought to use those if she feels like it. And not to be a dick about it, but I wouldn't mind seeing her in a swimsuit. I definitely wouldn't mind at all.

Shit. My mouth's dry and my pulse is jacking up. Probably should think about something else. I want her to finish this story.

"Victoria was my lieutenant," Tess says. "Her family's been

in the military for four generations, and she was the first to go to West Point. She was really… committed. To being the best leader she could be."

The guilt in Tess's voice is like lead; heavy, dark. It makes my jaw tighten, because there's nothing Tess could have done to deserve that kind of guilt.

She takes a shaky inhale. "Someone higher up than both of us decided to start harassing me."

Immediately I'm on edge, my body bristling. "What the fuck? Is he still doing it? Give me his name. I'll take care of it." I won't even give it to Gage to deal with, although it's his specialty. I'll deal with this fucker entirely on my own.

She eyes me up and down. "No." Warmth creeps into her tone. "He eventually gave up, so you can stand down."

I don't feel like standing down. I feel like working out some of this anger on that dude's face. But I also want to hear the rest of this, so I force myself to relax. "Okay, I'm calming down."

She raises an eyebrow. "I guess that's relaxed, for you. So I had this… *problem.* And there wasn't much I could do about it because I was enlisted and he was an officer. Oh, and his dad was even higher in rank. But Victoria… she fought and fought for me. And kept fighting even when it went nowhere. Even when it endangered her own career."

Tess swallows hard, then wipes her hand across her brow. She's pale, almost trembling. I roar at her in the dark and she takes it on the chin, but telling this story has her rattled. Because she thinks it's all her fault.

My heart can't take much more of this.

"Hey." I say it loud to grab her attention and hold it. "It wasn't your fault. Victoria did the right thing. That's why she kept fighting for you. If the higher-ups were shitty, that's not on either of you."

She doesn't look at all convinced.

"If Victoria knew going in," I say, "that she'd ruin her

career over this, do you think she'd have done anything differently? I don't really know her, but based on what you've told me, I'm going to guess no. What do you think?"

Her blinks are long and slow, like she's coming out of a daydream. "She'd... she'd probably do exactly the same. She really believes in honor and responsibility. And doing the right thing no matter what."

I'll bet. And I'd guess Tess believes in it too even if she doesn't seem to think so. It's clear she feels very responsible for Victoria, even beyond the guilt issue.

"There you go," I say. "It sucks that you both were punished for that, but you're doing something better now anyway."

I'd still like to find the guy who harassed her, but if she'd stayed in the Army, she wouldn't be here in my house. And that would be a terrible loss.

Tess shakes her head. "But I never wanted an Army career. It wasn't my calling, not like it was with Victoria. And she gave it all up because of me."

"Because of you?" I ask. "Or because when push came to shove, the command wouldn't allow her to do what she was supposed to? Like protect her soldiers?"

Tess looks away, her expression vulnerable. "I suppose. But I still feel like I owe her. Like I'll never be able to repay her, no matter what." Her mouth purses. "I mean, I'd help her anyway even if she hadn't helped me. But... but I wish she could have held on to her dream."

And what about your dreams? All I've heard so far from Tess is what she wants to do for others. Not what she wants to do for herself.

"If you feel that way, why don't you make her a partner?" I ask. "She'd make more money."

"But she'd also have more risk. This way, when—*if*—the company goes under, she won't be left holding the bag."

But Tess will be. Those are some very small shoulders for

everything she's carrying. She might be after me to trust more people, to admit that I care about others, but she's got to let go of some of this responsibility. The weight of it is going to crush her.

Admitting that would be admitting that I care about her, for her. But that can't be right—I only just met her. I'm only feeling protective because she's staying with me and this place isn't exactly safe right now. Plus she almost got hit by a car last night. That's it.

I mean, I might have been terrified out of my mind before I reached her, thinking I might not make it before the car did, but I did make it. So whatever I felt before doesn't mean anything now.

"Nobody's going to be holding any bag," I say gruffly. "Have her come out if you need the help. And I'm transferring the first installment to your bank account today."

Her eyes widen. "But the contracted schedule—"

"I'm changing it. Are you seriously complaining about getting your money?"

I hadn't intended on paying her earlier than planned, but she needs the money. Or rather, her parents probably do. And having her friend around will make her happier.

But it also means she'll be done sooner and will leave sooner.

I shake my head. That's good. I mean, I like having her around, and I'm planning on getting her into my bed sooner rather than later, but the security system needs to be in like yesterday.

"I wasn't complaining," she says softly. "And thanks for letting me bring in Victoria."

"It's nothing." I clear my throat, step away from her. The softness of her voice—and the rest of her—is scrambling my thoughts. "I've got to get to work."

I leave to go do what I should be doing, which is not sharing confidences with the woman living with me.

Although I'm going to look more into her parents and this fucking sociopath that harassed her. Tess should never have to deal with that kind of guilt, not ever again.

CHAPTER 16

"So I'm finally allowed into the holy of holies?" Victoria asks as she looks around the main room on the ground floor.

"You've been here before." I don't know why, but her snark about the place kind of irritates me.

Maybe because I still have to admit to her what I did with Gideon last night. She's going to be worried and upset, and I can't blame her.

But I also can't regret it. The man has magic fingers. I haven't come that hard since… ever. And he didn't even get my clothes off.

"Yeah, and I almost came again last night," Victoria says.

That had taken some quick talking when Victoria had called in a panic. I assured her that I was fine, that Gideon and I had talked things over and everything was fine. Perfectly fine.

Telling her that I'd finally seen his face and he was handsome as ever helped to distract her. And then I'd told her most of what Gideon had confessed to me, which had really distracted her.

I left out the orgasm. I've really got to tell her. Soon.

I clear my throat, focus my attention back on the job. "I've already done the panels in here, but there are some to finish in the library and kitchen. I set up a control room next to the library—all the outdoor stuff is running on the machines there."

"Sensors, cameras, lights?"

I nod. "And I put our facial-recognition software on the camera system. So if someone tries again, we can ID them."

"Unless they're wearing a mask." Victoria looks sideways at me. "Was there any video of the first break-in?"

"There is, and I just got access to it this morning. They were wearing a ski mask," I say resignedly. "Which they'll probably do again."

"But if they don't…"

"Fingers crossed." It's all I can do, because I'm not sure how else to catch this would-be thief. Unless… "What if they said something?" I ask myself.

"What?"

"He's got voice recognition up there," I explain. "If the intruder said something, we might be able to get him through voice recognition."

"Possibly, if they did speak. But those databases aren't as extensive as the facial ones."

She's right, but it's worth a shot. "Let's look over the footage in the control room."

When we walk in, Gulizar says, "Welcome. I'm Gulizar, the home control system. And you are?"

Victoria pauses in the doorway, looking up at the speakers in the ceiling. "Um, Victoria Shepherd. Hi."

"Rustem named her," I say quietly to Victoria. "She's so happy to have the panels up and running again so she can operate throughout the house."

Victoria nods as if none of that makes sense but she's not going to question it.

I've done some redesigning in the room Gideon's let me have for all the security systems—it's very high-tech James

Bond now, with low, blue lights, sleek furniture, and everything arranged around a large main screen.

Victoria starts to laugh when she sees it. "You've wanted to do something like this for a long time."

I grin. "I wasn't going to pass up this chance. I've dreamed of building a security system like this one."

Victoria's smile drops. "And being held captive? And running in the middle of the night and almost being killed?"

I sigh as I bring up the security footage. "The car thing was an accident."

"And the rest of it? You said his face was just fine. And you're not moving out."

"It's just easier," I say weakly. "He wants it done quickly. And he's paid part of the invoice already."

That was a huge relief to see in my bank account this morning. I immediately transferred some money to my mom. It's not enough to pay off that second mortgage, but it's enough to at least keep them from being foreclosed on. Once I get the rest of the money, things should be fine.

"I don't know if there's enough money in the world to deal with this," Victoria mutters. "It still stinks."

I ignore that because Victoria's parents aren't up to their eyeballs in debt, so she can hang on to her ideals. Besides, it's really not that bad. Once Gideon's wounds were taken care of, he was almost… soft. A touch vulnerable. The rough edges were still there, but I could see more beyond those. Something intriguing. Enticing. And then there was his body…

After what happened in the kitchen, I can't wait to see him completely naked. Which is probably why I'm not saying anything to Victoria. I'm not ready to stop making mistakes with Gideon.

"Why are you smiling like that?" Victoria's tone is sharp.

I wipe the half smile off my mouth and focus on the screen. "Here's the video."

The camera caught the hallway outside Gideon's bedroom, empty and dark. There's a slice of light coming from his bedroom door, but not much. It looks like it could be from a table lamp or something.

"The image quality is amazing," Victoria says, her gaze glued to the screen.

"I know. I didn't even have to replace the cameras, although I did scrub everything off their systems. But the new operating system I put on them seems to be working out."

"With this kind of resolution, if you can get a clear shot of their face, you can get them from some database for sure."

I nod and suddenly realize I'm hoping the intruder will try again. Which is absolutely not what I should be doing—my job is keep those people out at all costs. Gideon's mad bravado must be rubbing off on me.

"I could," I say. "But let's see if we can snare their voice right now."

In the video, a figure walks down the hallway. The person is slim, dressed all in black, and moving with purpose. Like they know exactly where they're going.

I've watched the video before. I already know what's about to happen in it, but this time when I watch, there's a weight in my chest. It's heaviest right over my heart.

The first time, I was looking for any clues about the attacker's identity, where the cameras were placed, what parts of the hallway were in blind spots. Things relating to my job.

This time I'm looking for Gideon. He's about to be hurt, badly. And he hurt himself again last night saving me. He might be surly and secretive, but he's not afraid to put himself in danger when it's necessary.

I glance over at Victoria. She's done the same for me, only it was her career she put in danger, not her physical safety.

She might dislike Gideon—with good reason—but they share some traits.

And I suppose I feel responsible for them both now. Which is why I'm reacting so strongly to the video this time.

"They have a plan," Victoria says half to herself. "They already know what they're looking for."

"They came in through a downstairs window. Bypassed all kinds of valuables down there to come straight upstairs."

Victoria looks sideways at me. "So, what were they looking for up there?"

"I can't say." I've already told her that, but I knew she wouldn't let it go.

"But you know?"

I pause the video. "He told me what he thinks they were after. If that was it… then yeah, they knew exactly what they were going for."

Victoria sighs and I sense another lecture coming. "This guy, Gideon… I looked up more about who he is and who he runs with. These are powerful guys. If this burglar thinks they can tangle with him, they're serious business themselves."

I start the video again. "I know. I'm committed though. I have to see this through."

In more ways than one now.

The thief opens the bedroom door, flooding the hallway with light. So far there's no noise at all, not even their footsteps.

Then, at the end of the hallway, a tall, broad-shouldered figure appears. Gideon's entire face is visible, devastating with those cheekbones and that jawline. He looks like he was expecting this. Like he's not even surprised.

I remember again how easily he moved through the house in the dark. He'd practiced that. A lot.

It doesn't make any sense why he'd expect one of his

friends to betray him though. And over a notebook. A simple notebook.

But it can't be that simple if they're both going to such lengths to possess it. What secrets is that notebook hiding?

"You'll never reach it."

When Gideon tells the intruder that in the video, Victoria flinches. "He knows him."

I shake my head. "He doesn't."

She pinches her mouth tight. "That's not what it sounds like."

A prickle runs down the back of my neck. He thinks it could be one of his best friends behind this, so in a way, he does know the burglar. If he's correct.

The intruder pauses when Gideon speaks. Their head cocks like they're considering their next move. It's amazing how cool and collected they are even when they've been caught.

It's no ordinary cat burglar, that's for sure.

Gideon waits, power humming through his frame. He's ready to charge.

The intruder seems to know what Gideon has planned. They step forward, light, graceful, and Gideon rushes for them. Quicker than my eye can follow, they do something to get Gideon turned around so that he's rushing for the stairs instead of them.

Gideon catches himself just in time. He teeters on the top step and I hear his sharp inhale. He thinks he's safe.

The burglar doesn't take even a moment to consider. Fluid as water, they snap an elbow into Gideon's back, shoving him off the top stair and down, down, down.

As his arms come out to catch himself, one hand shoots back, snags on the burglar's shirt. When Gideon falls, the intruder goes with him, the two of them disappearing into the darkness of the stairwell together.

There's a long, sustained series of clatters and thunks,

each more painful-sounding than the last. The grunts I can tell come from Gideon. And occasionally a sort of suppressed scream, higher in pitch, which might be the burglar.

My heart is pounding when the noises fade. I already know the damage waiting for Gideon at the end of those stairs. Broken ribs, fingers, and all kind of bruises. And only Rustem to patch him up.

"Holy hell," Victoria breathes. "They were ready for him."

"Almost. He caught them at the very end."

"Still." Victoria is pale and I bet her heart is pounding too. "Did they say anything at all? Anything that we can use?"

I pull out just the audio file, jump ahead to when they're smashing down the stairs. I find that faint, odd scream and play it at a higher volume. "That might be them. I'm pretty sure the grunts are only Gideon."

Victoria's mouth twitches. "Really?" she drawls. "You know his grunts that well?"

I roll my eyes and ignore her, but my ears and cheeks are hot. I feed that tiny snippet of sound into our voice-recognition algo. "It's a long shot," I say, "but without their face, it's all we have."

Victoria taps her chin. "We've got a little bit more than that. We know whoever it is has trained in some kind of hand-to-hand fighting. Those moves didn't happen by accident."

Professionals are usually hired by someone. Good professionals are hired by someone with money. Gideon's closest friends, the ones he suspects the most, have tons of money.

"I don't think finding this particular person will answer any questions," I say. "Unless they give up the person who hired them."

"Not likely."

As if to prove that point, the voice-recognition algo spits

back an error message: Not enough features in the audio file for an identification.

I fall back in the chair. I knew it was a long shot, but I still hoped. "Nuts."

"Downstairs cameras?" Victoria suggests.

I call up the videos from those cameras. There's one that's aimed right at the foot of the stairs that should give us the clearest view.

Five seconds into the saved video, both Gideon and the intruder come crashing out of the stairwell. Gideon immediately jumps up although it's clear he's been battered, his breathing harsh and sawing.

The intruder doesn't wait or try anything fancy this time. They aim right for the door and sprint for it. Trouble is, they've done something to their leg in the fall, and every other step is hitched.

Still, they're faster than Gideon, slipping out the door before he can grab them and disappearing into the night.

"They vanished into the grounds after that," I say. "No trace on the outside cameras."

"He smashed all the cameras and panels but saved these videos." Victoria's chewing on this from every aspect.

"The videos were backed up to a remote server. They weren't touched when the system went down."

"No noises from them on that one."

I nibble on my lip. There's not, which means we're at a dead end. Again. And then it hits me—they were limping. "The hospital."

Victoria raises an eyebrow in question.

"They're hurt." I gesture toward the screen. "So maybe they ended up going to the hospital. If we check intake records from that night…"

Her skepticism only increases. "First off, we can't access those. It's illegal. Secondly, it wasn't a life-threatening injury. Even high-level thieves don't have the kind of benefits that include health insurance. No way they're going to a hospital."

"What's this about a hospital?"

Victoria and I both spin around at Gideon's voice from the doorway. Victoria grabs her throat, her eyes wide. I'm less surprised, mostly because I'm used to his mysterious comings and goings. But my heart still picks up its pace.

"Maybe your attacker went to the hospital," I say.

Victoria is looking him up and down, wide-eyed. Gideon raises an eyebrow at her, the beast. He knows exactly why she's staring at him, so he doesn't need to do that.

"So," I say loudly, "we were thinking of checking the hospitals."

"It's a HIPAA violation if they share info," he says. "And I already did it."

Well, that tells us. "We also ran voice recognition on the video clips. We couldn't do any facial recognition though. But if they come back and we get better footage—"

He cuts me off with a sweep of his hand. "You guys aren't supposed to be tracking them." Gideon is back to beast mode. "That's my job. You just keep them out."

"He has a point," Victoria says. "We don't catch the burglars."

Gideon looks surprised, like he never expected Victoria to be on his side.

"I'm not about to tackle them," I say, and Gideon's mouth flattens. "But even an ID would help."

There's a beat of silence. Gideon looks like he wants to argue more even though he knows I'm right. I'm ready to argue more because I am right.

Victoria offers her hand to him. "Victoria Shepard. We need to talk about your conditions for Tess. Specifically your forcing her to stay here."

Gideon's mouth twitches. "She told me you were protective."

"I'm right here." I wave my hands in front of both of them.

"Are you here against your will?" Gideon asks me silkily.

"This is coercion," Victoria says.

I want to roll my eyes at both of them, but this is kind of touching. Victoria's going after him because she cares about me, and Gideon is pushing back because…

Well, there's definitely something between us.

"It's fine," I say. "There's no coercion." I feel my face flood with heat when Gideon catches my eye. "None," I finish weakly.

Victoria catches what passes between us. She doesn't look happy, but she doesn't say anything.

"Good," Gideon says softly. He's staring right at me. "I need this system."

"Yes, because the other one was destroyed," Victoria says dryly.

That dissolves the moment. We've got a serious job to do here, one that needs some answers from Gideon if we're going to do it right. He was in confessing mood before—maybe he still is.

"Why did you smash the panels?" I ask. He didn't really give a full answer last night.

"Because when I went into the system, they were riddled with spyware." He glances at the ceiling. "Sorry, Gulizar, but they were."

"I understand," she says almost glumly.

"I didn't bother to check them," Gideon says, "because I was an idiot and assumed they were secure. The fucker was watching me for who knows how long."

"And the upstairs?" I look to the ceiling, not willing to say more in front of Victoria.

"Clean."

Which is why he left it untouched. That brings up the other thing that won't stop bugging me. "And the cars?"

His expression closes off so hard I swear I hear a metal door slam shut. "The cars aren't your concern."

Whoa. The cars are personal. Deeply personal.

"Okay," I say coolly. "We'll keep working on this then."

Something like guilt or maybe an apology flickers over his face, but then his phone buzzes. "Fuck," he says when he looks at the screen. "Why does everything fall apart when I'm out of the office?"

He disappears into his office without a farewell.

Slowly Victoria's gaze swings over to me. "I really, really hope you know what you're doing here," she says in a low voice.

I really hope so too.

CHAPTER 17

Victoria has already left for the day while I'm still working on installing software. Outside, night has fallen, a soft, quiet blanket of dark pressing against the windows. It's so quiet out here in the country, I almost feel like I'm meditating as I wait for the install to finish.

Things were tense today between us. Not like oh, we're in a fight tense. More like Victoria was really, really worried for me but couldn't tell me to not do anything with Gideon. I mean, I am an adult.

An adult who's hopelessly ensnared by a billionaire who can't trust anyone and is barricaded in his compound. At least this job gives me a firm end date for getting out of this. Whatever this is.

I usually date nice guys, guys who aren't dark, over-bearing beasts, but there's no way I can spin any of this as anything close to dating. It's intense and crazy, but it's not a relationship.

Nope. I shake my head as I watch the screen. Not a rela-tionship. Nothing we've done so far would fit into any kind of relationship activities.

When Gideon appears in the security office, I do a double take. It's eight at night, but he's got on a suit of a gray so dark it flirts with black. His shirt is white as an angel's wing, with cuff links the color of pewter. Except he's not wearing a tie, his shirt's open to the second button, so the whole effect is undone elegance. Like I caught him on his way to seducing me and he discarded his tie somewhere in the halls.

"I have to go somewhere tonight." He shoots his cuffs, the gesture graceful yet also somehow hesitant. Like he's using the motion to hide from me.

I haven't seen him since he said that thing about the cars. Which isn't unusual, but… I kind of hoped I would.

Wait—he just said he was *leaving*. I keep my surprise inside since I don't want to scare him off this decision. Not that someone like me could ever scare someone like him.

He's going to go back out into the world. He's not going to wait here, brooding, trying to catch shadows.

"Okay," I say. "I'll be fine here."

"I'll be here too," Gulizar says.

I smile in spite of myself. "See, I won't be alone. And the system is pretty much done." I gesture at the screens. "Well, not completely done, but enough that I can monitor all parts of the estate from here. If someone does come, I'll see them." I pull my hand back, take a breath. "But I won't go after them. Pinky promise. So everything will be fine. You can go."

I'm babbling, but I want him to know how secure things will be. I don't want him to feel trapped here.

"Not that it's completely done." Jeez, my mouth will not stop. "There's so much testing still to do, and a bunch of subsystems to install and integrate. And then there's the cottage, which I've left for last. So… another two weeks with Victoria helping me?"

I don't know why I spit all that out. Maybe because his leaving tonight feels like he's leaving *me* instead of just the house. He shouldn't worry about things here, but… I still have a role to play. I'm not done yet.

Gideon's fingers go quiet on his cuffs. "I'm not worried

about that," he says. "Well, I am, but not about your work. I *have* to do this. Gulizar?"

"Yes?"

"Can you talk to the security system?"

"No," she says immediately. "It can only alert me to contact you. I can't contact it."

I purposefully set it up so that not even Gulizar can talk to the security system—all communication with it is only one way.

Gideon nods like he's impressed. "Have you tested that yet?" he asks me.

I blink at him. "Um, no. But it should work."

His gaze meets mine, the blue of his eyes dark. "I want you to come with me. Gulizar, call us if anything happens."

My heart does a little shimmy. I ignore it. "Where are you going?" I point to his suit, which probably costs the same as a year of college. At an Ivy League. "I don't have anything that will go with that."

Is he taking me because he wants me there? Or because he doesn't want me in danger in case the intruder comes back? Or maybe both?

Either way, it's pretty flattering.

"It doesn't matter what you wear," he says. "I'm putting this on because… because I like wearing suits. And I'm going to need it for this."

My ears prick up. "Kind of like armor? So what is it?"

"A party."

My ears sink back down. "You want me to come to a party? I really don't have anything to wear then."

"It's at Raven's." He shoots his cuffs again. He's danger-ously handsome in a suit, I must say. "Everyone will be there. And by everyone, I mean Archer, Cassian, Gage—"

"Okay, you don't have to twist my arm." I start double-checking the system and the link to Gulizar. Everything looks good. "Give me five minutes to change."

I take ten since I'm about to meet some of the richest, most powerful men in Silicon Valley. Who might also be trying to steal from and/or murder my current client. Who is also the guy I'm kind of sleeping with.

Does a fully clothed orgasm in his kitchen count as sleeping with? I'm going to say yes since I know we're not stopping there.

Just as I'm putting on my lipstick, a car engine rumbles from outside. Something powerful and purring.

I walk out to find Gideon waiting in a vintage Porsche race car, sleek and silver and gorgeous. I guess the Inspirons aren't going anywhere with their electronics smashed. This is a pretty good substitute.

"Nice car," I say as he opens the door for me.

"Thanks." He hands me in like we're in a movie. "I like the dress. Actually, I love it."

The heat in his eyes makes me shiver pleasantly. It's only a simple sundress with a kicky skirt and little flowers printed on it, but he makes me feel like I'm wearing silk and jewels.

We head back down the truck trail, toward the freeways and civilization. He drives with total concentration, pushing the car to its full potential but never once letting it get away from him. I lean back and enjoy the rumble of the engine, the snap of the car through the curves of the road, and the intense expression on Gideon's face.

I could ask where we're going, but I decide to let that be a surprise.

"I want you to look at the safe's security system," Gideon says as he merges onto the 280. "When you're done with the rest of it."

I've been dying to get into that system, so I can't help my grin. "Who installed that? It's completely different from the other one."

"I did. Bought the safe, installed the panel, connected everything up, wrote the operating system myself." He drums his fingers on the steering wheel. "I wanted it to be secret, and I figured that was the best way to make sure it was."

But someone figured it out anyway. "Do you have cameras in the bedroom?"

He shakes his head. "Whatever they were capturing from the spyware on the cameras wouldn't have caught the safe. But it doesn't take a genius to realize you're seeing every part of the house except one."

I rub my temples. This is all so twisted and complicated. No wonder Gideon holed himself up in his house right afterward. Thinking through all this could take a person weeks.

"Of course I'll look," I say. "But the best thing would be to keep them from getting near the safe in the first place. Which the main security system should do." A thought occurs to me. "Have you considered hiring a security team?"

"I figured Gage could buy them off. He's got contacts everywhere in the security world. But maybe I should."

"You can't do everything yourself," I point out. "And besides, if he tries anything, you can use your contacts to have him poisoned the next time he goes to the doctor."

There's a long moment of stunned silence, like he can't believe I just said that. And then he throws back his head and laughs.

"You're a bloodthirsty little thing, aren't you?" he asks between laughs.

"Not really. I'm only pointing out your options."

"Mmm, I'm pretty sure that's a violation of the Hippocratic oath."

"Did you ever take that? How does that work?"

"I didn't," he says. "I never got that far. But my parents had it hanging on the wall of our house, so I memorized it anyway."

"Wow, that's hard-core. It's kind of pagan, isn't it? Like you have to swear to Dionysius and stuff?"

"Apollo," he says. "And some other healing gods. But that's

the old oath. There's a modern version. No gods invoked in that one."

My mouth twists. "That's disappointing. I'm imagining some crazy Greek rituals with wine and snakes and togas. Does it still say *First, do no harm?* It'd probably be smart to keep that part."

"Not exactly, but the whole thing is a long way of saying do no harm." He glances over at me, his gaze lingering on my jaw.

I lift my hand to that spot, finding the bruise I'd forgotten about. Does he think he's responsible for that? That he's done me harm?

"What happens after this?" I ask softly. "Between you and me, once I'm done with the job?"

His jaw goes tight. "I don't know. You can't get any more tangled up in this than you already are. My life... It's not safe for you to go any deeper into this." His gaze runs over me, hot, possessive. "But I know I can't resist you. The way you look at me... No one's ever looked at me like that. Not ever."

The wonder and awe in his voice makes my heart crack. With all the nice guys I've dated, none have ever talked about me like that.

This can't last. I'm only here to do a job for him even though he can't resist me. He's a billionaire with some serious trouble coming after him, and I'm... me.

Utterly irresistible to him. Oh boy, I'm in deep here, and I don't think I want to find a way out.

I clear my throat, try to find something like coherent words. "Um, that's... I can't resist you either. I don't want to."

My honesty makes something flare between us so brightly I'd swear it was midday. And then it fades, leaving the two of us holding the afterimage.

"I should send you away," he says gruffly. "To keep you safe. Face this on my own."

I release a noise of protest.

"I won't though," he says. "I'm too damn selfish. But once the job is done... You have to go then. I can't let you get harmed any worse than you already have been."

He's right, and I can't find a toehold to get an argument in. Some perverse part of me—probably the part that finds him irresistible—wants to try. "And if we find out who's behind it and stop them before I finish? What then?"

"That would change everything," he says. "But I'm not counting on that. And I forbid you to go looking for the intruder. I'm not going to be another one of your responsibilities."

It's too late for that, but I don't tell him differently. "Wait—you said *another* one of my responsibilities? I'm pretty sure I only told you about Victoria."

He purses his lips. "I, uh, looked into your background more. And I found out about the mortgages. They're paid now."

The blood drains to my feet so fast I see stars. I open my mouth, but nothing comes out. The mortgages are gone? "You paid both of them?" My tone is as faint as I feel.

It's unbelievable. He waved his hand at some point today, and something that's dogged me for years, tied my guts in knots, is just... dealt with.

"The paperwork will take some time," he says casually. "But yeah. So now you don't have to worry about it."

"Except now I owe you..." I calculate quickly, but my head's spinning too hard to make the math come out right. "I don't even know."

"You don't owe me anything." He's growling again. "Consider it payment for injuries incurred on the job. I can afford it, and I owe you. So it's done."

I get the feeling that if I say thank you, he'll snap my head off. "Okay," I say slowly. I wonder if he's found out about the legal bills and Nick and Elena. Or worse, tracked down my harasser.

Maybe he's leaving those surprises for tomorrow. After all, he's only had one day to start on my problems, and he's got an entire company to run. And betrayals to root out, secrets to protect.

"Your parents will have the deeds in a few weeks." His gaze is hard on the road. "I don't want to hear any more about it."

He did something nice for me, so nice it's mind-blowing. And he's acting like a lion with a thorn in his paw. My heart melts like chocolate left on a dashboard, because he wants so much to be bad, but he's just not.

"Thank you." It's softly daring, my attempt to pull the thorn.

He grumbles to himself. "You're welcome. And I mean it about not saying anything."

"Don't worry." I can't look away from him. "I haven't forgotten you're a monster."

Our destination turned out to be a gorgeous house on a cliff in Pacifica, shrouded in fog and surrounded by pines. The house itself is simple, painted dark blue and done in simple lines. The ocean and the cliffs are the stars here, and the builder knew it.

Without Gideon saying anything, I know this was Ira's house. And it's confirmed when I walk in and meet an older version of one of the girls from the pictures in Gideon's room: Raven. She immediately makes me feel at home, pulling me into a corner to ask me everything about me, but in a natural, easy way. It's the kindest interrogation ever.

Gideon was shooed away to go talk to people. "They missed you," Raven said accusingly. "You disappear for weeks and then you show up with a gorgeous, charming woman. I want to know all about it, but I'm going to chat up Tess first."

She pointed out a few of the people but hasn't introduced me yet. "They all know each other from way back," she says. "Let's get you cozy, and then you can brave the gauntlet. Besides, Gideon needs to talk to everyone first, and Archer isn't even here yet."

Archer might not be here, but I recognize quite a few other people. Gage gives me a sharp nod when I catch his eye, and I see Cassian, who's smirking at something Bishop Lund is telling him. Axel Beck is even here, snapping pictures with Raven's sister, Morgan.

Raven catches me watching them. "Oh yeah, the romance heard round the internet." She sighs. "I told him not to take pictures here, but he said he wouldn't get anyone else in the frame. It's part of his brand, and Axel can never not be on brand."

Morgan is the sister who wasn't smiling in Gideon's pictures, but she is for these. "They look very happy together," I offer.

And they do.

"They are," Raven says wistfully. I could be imagining it, but her gaze lingers on Bishop. "They met at work."

She explains to me that Morgan helped design the AI for Inspiron's cars, the very thing that makes them self-driving.

"Wow." Suddenly her and Axel's closeness takes on a new dimension. I guess they're not just together for social media. "So… everyone here does something with AI?"

"Gage does defense and security with an emphasis on AI." Raven points each of them out in turn. "Bishop does something with stocks, I'm not sure exactly what, but it involves AI. Cassian's marketing firm trumpets about their AI all the time."

"I already know what Archer does," I say before she can mention him.

Archer, the one who isn't here, has a company that uses AI to do translations, things way beyond a simple Google translation. There was a big splash last year when his AI translated a famous Spanish poem I'd never heard of. Decoding figurative language isn't exactly a strong suit of computers, but Archer claims to have done it.

"Are you in AI too?" I ask her.

Raven laughs. "Oh God, not me. I'm the black sheep of the family."

An older man I haven't seen before comes up to us, smiling widely. "Don't listen to her. She was the apple of Ira's eye." He holds out his hand. "Oscar Miller."

"Tess Robards. I'm…" I gesture weakly toward Gideon. "I'm here with Gideon."

Oscar winks at me. "No need to explain. I see how he looks at you."

I'm not sure what he means until I glance over at Gideon. Sure enough, he's watching me with a hungry look. Like he can't wait to get me alone.

I take a long sip from my glass, trying to cool my thoughts. "It's complicated."

"Don't tease her," Raven says to Oscar. "We can't scare her away." She glances back at me. "You're the only person Gideon's ever brought to one of our parties."

That sets me back on my heels. "Really? He's so—" I clamp my mouth shut before I can say anything embarrassing like *He's so hot, why doesn't he have people hanging on him all the time?*

Raven pats my arm. "Exactly. If I didn't know him so well, I'd want to date him myself." But her eyes slide toward Bishop, who's watching her right back.

"Gideon likes his secrets." Oscar is still smiling. "So he must be smitten with you if he invited you to meet all of us."

I like Oscar. In a room filled with billionaires, he strikes me as the most normal person here. "So how do you know everyone?"

"Oh, Ira and I were old friends from way back. When he… passed, I did what I could to help the kids. I couldn't take his place, of course, but I did what I could."

Raven smiles sadly and fondly at him. "You did good. We couldn't have made it through without you."

"I couldn't have done anything less for Ira. He would've done the same for me."

My breath catches. The affection between them is so strong. And Gideon thinks one of these people betrayed him?

I don't know that I see it. I haven't talked to the rest of them, not yet, but to turn on this kind of closeness and all for a notebook? It's a terrible thing.

Raven misreads my expression. "Sorry, we'll stop being maudlin. Come on, let's go let everyone meet you."

She leads me to Axel and Morgan first. I'm only a little stunned by how beautiful Axel is in person. Those photos he puts on Instagram aren't photoshopped at all, and I feel like a spotty, huge-pored monster next to him. But he's all smiles and charm, inviting me to come tour the Inspiron factory and attend his next get-together at the estate he's always featuring on his social media. I'm not sure if he really means it—I suspect he doesn't—but he offers it pretty enthusiastically.

Morgan is more reserved, taking me in with a quiet greeting. I get the sense she's sizing me up, judging if I'm worthy of Gideon. I suppose I understand the impulse.

"I understand you're in security." Her voice is low and soothing, quite the contrast to Raven's more chipper tones.

I nod. "That's... that's how Gideon and I met." I'm not sure how I'm going to explain the rest of it without betraying Gideon's trust.

Morgan's smile is knowing. "Gage mentioned you were working out there. I'm glad Gideon came out." She looks to him, her smile dimming. "We were all worried. Gideon tends to pull away when he's hurt, and when he disappeared... We were scared."

He doesn't seem to pull away from me when he's hurt. In fact, he told me to scrub harder at his arm, then opened up to me. And the orgasm...

I draw in a breath. "I'm glad we could come out tonight then."

"So am I."

We share a smile that feels like maybe we're friends now.

"Okay." Raven tugs on my arm. "Let's meet the rest of them."

I'm less certain I'll get a warm welcome from the guys. And I can't stop obsessing over which one of them might be trying to steal from Gideon. As if sensing my unease, Gideon appears at my side.

"I'll help with the introductions," he says smoothly.

Raven beams at him. "Isn't he sweet?"

Gideon's expression is so bland and mild you could feed it to an infant. "I really am."

I bite the inside of my cheek to keep from laughing.

We head toward Gage and Bishop first. Gage says hi as briefly as he can while Bishop looks me up and down. He's not hostile about it, more like curiously concerned.

"I hear you and Gage are in the same field." Bishop is a big guy, and his voice sounds like it's been dragged out of his massive chest.

"Um." I glance at Gage, who hasn't cracked a smile. "Kind of. Mine is more small scale. Personal security rather than national security."

"If I let Gage do the new security system," Gideon says, "I'd end up with a self-aware tank or something. Imagine Gulizar running one of those."

"You joke," I say, "but that's exactly the kind of thing the Army would dump on us with no training or even an instruction manual." I take a sip of my drink. "Just bam, one day we've got five self-aware tanks we've got to keep track of and have zero use for."

"You were in the Army?" That got Gage's attention.

I nod. "Signal Corps. That's how I got into working with electronics."

"Hmm." Gage's eyes narrow. "Have you ever thought of working in defense contracting? We could use more veterans."

Gideon's arm slips around my waist. "You're not stealing her away." There's more than amusement in his tone.

Bishop nods toward Gideon's fingers. "You broke those. Want to tell us how?"

I feel the cold, hard metal of the splint tap against my hip.

"Accident," Gideon says. He lies so coolly and quickly it almost scares me.

Bishop raises an eyebrow. "Gage is already the talkative one. You can't take that title."

"What did happen?" Raven asks. "All you said was that someone tried to break in. But the news made it sound much more serious."

A muscle in Gideon's cheek twitches. He doesn't want to say, but he doesn't want to be rude to Raven. His gaze focuses on Gage and Bishop like a laser.

"Someone went for my safe." He's watching them like a hawk, looking for any betraying flinches.

I'm watching them too, linked to Gideon by his hold on me, the two of us feeling these guys out together.

"He got hurt stopping them." I make my tone admiring even as I look for any guilty tells in Gage or Bishop.

Nothing. Bishop kind of frowns while Gage doesn't react at all.

"At least you stopped them," Bishop says.

"They sent an ambulance just for that?" Gage asks.

Raven rolls her eyes. "He shouldn't have done it in the first place. Whatever's in that safe isn't worth hurting yourself."

Neither of them react to that or ask what's in the safe. Huh. Either they have nothing to do with the break-in or they're really good at hiding their reactions. Considering that they've both built multibillion-dollar companies, they're probably excellent at hiding their reactions. I can't imagine you get far in Silicon Valley if people can read you easily.

"What's in that safe is irreplaceable," Gideon says.

Both Gage and Bishop go wide-eyed as they realize exactly what Gideon means by that.

"They're after—"

"What—"

They start and stop speaking together, clamping down when they remember that Raven is listening.

Clever Gideon. He just got them to reveal they had no idea what was in his safe until just now. Which means they had nothing to do with it.

Which leaves Cassian and Archer. Cassian is teasing Morgan about something, but he's watching us while we do. There's an edge to his gaze that makes my hair stand on end. All his smiles and laughs seem very fake, like he's covering up something much darker beneath.

Archer… I can't say anything about Archer's motives until he arrives and I get a look at him.

"They didn't reach the safe," Gideon reminds them. "No harm, no foul. And Tess is making sure they'll never get that close again."

I'm sharply aware of Cassian listening to every word.

"That's right," I say brightly. "I can monitor everything from here." I hold up my phone. "And I am."

Gideon pulls me closer. "Told you she was good."

Gage and Bishop look like they're holding in so many questions they could explode. But they manage it, anger clamping their jaws shut. And I don't think they're keeping quiet solely for my benefit—they looked to Raven, not me, and then shut up.

So Raven doesn't know much of anything about the notebooks. Interesting. I wonder what Morgan and Oscar know. Probably no more than Raven—there seems to be a very deep secret binding all these men together, a secret the other three have no idea exists.

"I'm glad you have someone looking out for you," Bishop says slowly. "You know, you can ask for anything you need."

Gage nods. "I can have a team at your place in five minutes. It can only help."

I elbow Gideon, because if we can trust these two now, we could definitely use that offer.

And faintly, flickering in the back of my mind, I wonder when we became *we*.

"We can discuss it later." Gideon cranes his head to look back at the entry. "Archer's here."

There was zero sound of his arrival, so how did Gideon know that? When I turn to see Archer in the flesh, I'm confronted with Gideon's twin. Not so much in looks and build—Archer is dark blond, his eyes the color of strong coffee, and less muscled than Gideon. But the way he holds himself, the way he looks out over the room, taking it all in— exactly the same as Gideon.

"Excuse me." Gideon drops a kiss on my forehead and walks over to Archer. Without a word to each other, they disappear down the hallway.

Gage, Bishop, and Raven are all staring at me when I turn back. I guess the kiss was kind of telling.

"So," I ask them all brightly, "do any of you like to knit?"

Raven tucks her arm into mine, a conspiratorial smile on her face. "I love it."

CHAPTER 19

We head back to our favorite room in the house without a word between us. If we're in Ira's house, we're going straight to our study.

It's a small room, not used as Ira's main office because it was too small. So Ira offered it to us, but it sort of became mine and Archer's. We planned a lot of shit in this room, filling the desk with scrap paper and schemes. The desks are completely clear, all our papers gone somewhere. Along with our schemes.

There's a wet bar now, probably because no one's expected to do any real work in here anymore. I pour myself a glass of tequila and take a sip. "You don't have any questions for me? Everyone else did."

Archer sprawls in his favorite chair, his legs stretched out. "You were up to something. I didn't want to interrupt." His gaze meets mine. "Did it succeed?"

"Still working on it."

Archer looks like what people mean when they say *fallen angel*—dark blond hair, midnight eyes, and a serious, almost pious expression. Look closer and you'll see he's no innocent.

If it's Archer behind all this, I'm going to have a hell of time maneuvering him into admitting it. He knows me too well to give anything away like the other two did. That unconcealed surprise when I revealed it was the notebook the thief was after? Dead giveaway.

So it wasn't those two. Which leaves Cassian or Archer.

Out of all of them, I don't want it to be Archer. I don't know if the rest of us would have stayed in touch if not for what happened with Ira—but Archer and I would have. He's like the brother I never had. Gage sat quietly when I was going through all the shit with my parents right after I dropped out, but Archer commiserated. Archer understood all that pressure, the need to be perfect, to be better than everyone, but only via the narrow path your parents defined.

He understands how it fucks with you, how you can never really let it go even as you hate it with your whole being.

After the break-in, Archer didn't call and my parents didn't call. I tap my sternum once, sharply. There's probably a good lesson for me in that.

"Are you pissed at me for not calling?" Archer asks with a raised eyebrow. "I figured you didn't want to be bothered."

He's right—I wanted the intruder to try again. I didn't want to field everyone's expressions of sympathy. Expressions that didn't do much to hide their selfish interest in getting the gossip.

"Nope." I knock my splint against my glass. "Like I keep saying, I'm fine."

"Good." Archer watches me closely. "Glad to hear it. Now, do you want to tell me what you're up to so I can help, or are you going to keep suspecting me of I don't even know what?"

Fuck it. This is Archer, and if he is behind it, I'd rather lock horns right now than keep dancing around it. It's giving me a fucking headache. "Looked at your notebook recently? Maybe figured out what it says?"

That was the other thing that came to me as I realized Gage and Bishop were innocent, something that should have come to me from the very beginning—someone's finally cracked the code of their notebook. And that's why they want the others."

Archer snaps up. "No. I haven't looked at that notebook since…" He's gone pale. "That's what they were after."

"Went right for the safe," I say. "Didn't even try for anything else."

"And you thought it was one of us. That explains the crazy rumors and your turning into a hermit."

"Can you blame me?"

Archer's dark eyes are intense. "No. I'd come to the exact same conclusion. Probably do the same thing. But why go after your notebook? I just keep mine in my office. Anyone could grab it."

I put my finger to my lips. "There was an entire CIA's worth of spyware on my security cameras. I'd move that notebook pronto and not say anything near any kind of recording device." I flop into a chair, relief flowing through me. Archer might still be behind it, but it feels good to finally talk about it openly. "And I think they were after Tynan's notebook."

"You have that?"

"I was the executor of the will. And there was no one else to give it to."

"You ever look inside it?"

I shake my head. "I figure it's the same as the rest of them. And it would be… It's Tynan's."

Archer leans forward and steeples his fingers. "The notebooks were mentioned in the will. Anyone could have found out they existed."

"But there's no other identifying details. Why care about something so random? Why not go after his other papers or the algorithms he designed? Those would look way more valuable. It has to be someone who knows there's more to the notebooks."

"So, one of us." Archer taps his fingers together. "You narrow it down any?"

"Probably not Gage or Bishop. They were definitely shocked when I said the notebook was in the safe."

"Leaving me and Cassian." Archer's smile is sharp. "I can tell you it wasn't me, but I know that doesn't mean shit."

I shrug. "You're my top suspect, to be honest."

"I'd be my top suspect too in your place." He's dryly resigned.

My sternum throbs again. "I really wish you weren't."

But it makes sense—if anyone could decode the notebook first, it'd be Archer. He was supposed to become a lawyer—part of his parents' grand life plan for him. He got into Harvard Law and was all set to join a white-shoe firm the second he graduated. Except... Archer wanted to study linguistics. Not at all prestigious, not at all well paying, in no way a credit to his parents. But he loved it.

Archer knows words. It's why he was able to create that translation program. And isn't a code just a type of language?

He gets up, pours himself some tequila. "So, it's all about the notebooks. I wish I had figured mine out, but I haven't. It could also be about that first algorithm."

Ice crackles along my spine. "That algo is crap. The field's moved way beyond that in the past few years, and it..."

I don't finish that because we both know what that algo did. And I was the one who told them to go ahead and put it into the car.

"What if it is about that?" Archer's voice is quiet.

I take a deep inhale. "It's a weird way to do blackmail. And we're all targets then."

"We're all targets if it's really about the notebooks even though those are useless."

I run my hand over my face. I miss the days when I only had to run a billion-dollar company and listen to my parents berate me for being a failure. Those fucking notebooks.

"Maybe they aren't just some puzzle Ira left for us. Maybe they have to be together to make sense. Assembled like Voltron or something."

Ira was always on us about how we were stronger together. The lesson didn't really stick until he died though.

"You'd have to let us look at Tynan's then."

"I told you, you're suspect number one."

"But you confessed all this to me anyway." Archer sprawls back in the chair. "What's up with the woman? Gage says she's living with you."

"She's not living with me," I say. Although she's most definitely sleeping with me tonight. "She's staying in the cottage while she rebuilds my security system."

Archer nods. "Yeah, I usually have contractors stay in my home while they're redoing the tile."

I shift my shoulders. "I'm feeling a little paranoid lately. I want to keep her close at hand."

"I can understand that. So you're not sleeping with her?"

I take a long sip of my tequila. Raven always manages to find the best liquor, then teases me by never saying where it's from. "Not yet."

"Is that smart? Considering your security situation at the moment."

"That's none of your business."

Archer snorts. "We grew up together. Your business is my business."

"I met you when I was twenty-two. How is that growing up together?"

"You know what I mean." His tone is dark.

I suddenly realize I've hurt his feelings. Archer isn't one for any kind of emotional expression. In fact, you could call him robotic if you wanted to be a dick. But he's got feelings even if he doesn't show them. He understands logically why I suspect him… but logic isn't everything.

I find myself wishing Tess were here, strangely enough.

She hasn't even met Archer, but she'd know what to say. She'd smooth things over so that I can make it better.

But she's not here because I can't pull her any deeper into this. And words alone can't fix it.

"You should meet her," I say. "You'd really like her. She's…" I recall her face as she cleaned my wounds last night. "She's got a soft heart. A huge sense of responsibility. And she's not afraid of me."

Archer lifts his glass. "Congratulations. It sounds like you've found the perfect woman."

Is she? He might be right about that. "Too bad my life is too fucked up for anything like perfection." I put all the weight pressing on my heart into that.

CHAPTER 20

The dynamics of this group are... puzzling to say the least.

Archer and Gideon finally came out after about an hour together, rejoining the rest of us. I wasn't lonely though, because Raven and Cassian did their best to keep me entertained. Cassian is beyond charming, making me laugh with every word out of his mouth.

He's also... not quite manipulative, but I am definitely being managed by a master of human interaction. It's not off-putting, but I am on guard. Victoria would hate him—she thinks men who try too hard to make you laugh are trying to hide something.

Maybe Cassian is trying to hide the fact that he's behind the break-in. I've been watching my phone like a hawk, checking for a message from Gulizar. Nothing so far.

But things here are going along—Cassian making me laugh, Raven chiming in at spots and keeping my wineglass full. And then Gideon and Archer come back, and the atmosphere starts to snap.

I don't know if the rest of them can sense it, but I'm pretty sure if it was only the guys here, there'd be some very intense discussions about some notebooks.

"Hey." Gideon appears by my side, looking subdued. I

wonder if he'll tell me what he and Archer talked about. I'm dying to know. "Where's Morgan and what's his face?"

Ha. As if Axel Beck isn't the most famous person here. "They left a few minutes ago. Oscar's in the kitchen."

Gideon stares at nothing for a moment, a glass of something forgotten in his hand.

"Hey." I give him a nudge, my voice only for him. "Everything okay?"

He nods, but his expression doesn't ease. "Everything okay at home?"

I'm amazed that this is the first time he's asking about it. I figured he'd have my phone glued to his hand. "Yep. Rustem has everything under control," I lie. I don't know why, but I don't want anyone to know only my security system is guarding the notebooks.

"You've still got Rustem working for you?" Archer asks this with a dark undercurrent to his tone.

"Sure. Why would I fire him?"

The tension ratchets up another notch. There's an itchiness to the guys that is spilling over to Raven and me.

"Too bad Rustem couldn't come too," Raven says too brightly. "I miss him. He promised to show me some wrestling techniques the next time I saw him."

Bishop's nostrils flare, but he tamps down his reaction as soon as it hits him.

"I can show you some moves," Gage says.

"She wants real self-defense not bare-knuckle brawling," Cassian says.

"Bare-knuckle brawling?" I repeat slowly. "And MMA. And wrestling. Are you guys part of some fight-club thing?"

My cheeks heat as I remember all the rumors about them being members of a sex club. Maybe it's a combo fight/sex club. Dudes would be into that probably.

Raven laughs. "Oh, they used to be. These guys..." She

takes them all in. "Man, when Dad first brought them home, I don't know what he was thinking."

"Really? Tell me about it."

Raven's only too happy to, although the guys don't look very pleased.

"Well, this one"—she points to Cassian—"was using some kind of phishing scam through email to get control of people's computers. Really beautifully written emails though. If he wasn't lying through his teeth, it would have been pure poetry."

"I never knew you saw those emails," Cassian says. "They were pretty good. But you have to be when you're convincing someone to click a phishing link."

Eww. I'm suddenly less sure Cassian isn't a total sleaze. "Isn't that illegal?"

His blue eyes go cold. "It was. But it fed my family for a couple of years."

Gideon clears this throat. "What Cassian won't tell you is that he paid all those people back with interest when he made his first million. And now his marketing emails—while still being pure poetry—are completely legal."

"You're going to ruin my rep." The coldness in Cassian's eyes hasn't thawed.

"Email phishing." Gage shakes his head. "As if that gives you a *rep.*"

Oooh, here comes the bare-knuckle part.

"Better than getting my head bashed in everyday by the village idiot," Cassian says back.

"Women love scars. And some wounds." Gage points to Gideon's broken fingers. "Just ask him."

I open my mouth, then close it. "We… It's not like that."

Archer gives me a look. "It's not? Because Gideon's never brought someone to one of these."

That's the second or third time someone's mentioned that.

"Don't start planning the wedding," I say dryly, mostly to hide my confusion. This wasn't supposed to be that serious. It was only supposed to be a party.

Archer actually smiles. Not just amused but also knowing.

"Told you you'd like her," Gideon says.

Great. They were talking about me in their little private session. The heat in my cheeks jumps ten degrees, and I must be beet red.

"Stop teasing her," Raven says. "And don't distract me from telling all about your scandalous pasts."

The tension clamps down even harder, every one of their mouths flattening. And then, with an effort, as if they'd all practiced, they relax again.

Huh.

Bishop smiles, but it's forced. "No scandals in my past. No email scams or street fights or dropping out of med school."

There's a quiet sadness to his voice that catches at me. Whatever brought Bishop to Ira's attention, it wasn't anything that could be spun as good.

I turn to Archer. "Have you done anything as terrible as dropping out of med school?"

"Worse. I dropped out of law school."

I can't help the face I pull, but after having Nick sue Elena every chance he gets—and what we have to pay to make those lawsuits go away—I don't have the greatest opinion of lawyers.

Archer isn't offended though. "That was my reaction exactly. My parents..." His gaze cuts to Gideon. "They weren't too happy about it."

"That's an understatement," Gideon says.

"They weren't as bad as your parents." Archer looks at me and points to Gideon. "When this guy dropped out, his parents went nuclear. Cut off all his funds, blocked his access to his bank account, reported all his credit cards for fraud—he was dead broke."

I put my hand to my throat, bile rising up. "That's terrible."

Gideon shrugs as if it's no big deal to have your parents ruin you financially. "I had this plan to sleep in my car."

Archer starts to laugh. "Yeah, but then they had it repo'd."

I don't find it funny at all. "How could they do that?"

"I opened up most of those accounts when I was in high school, on my way to college. My parents had to cosign on most of them, so they had the power to fuck with the accounts."

I didn't mean how could they logistically do it—more how they could *justify* doing it. Gideon had said his parents didn't care about him, but I hadn't understood the depths of that until now. "And all because you dropped out of med school?"

"If I went back, all would be forgiven." Gideon's expression is bitter.

Raven puts a hand on his arm. "But things are better now. They're coming to your gala at the neurosurgery department, aren't they?"

"That's still on?" Gage asks. "Considering..." He gestures to Gideon's splint.

"Sure. Can't disappoint my adoring fans."

"You'd better not cancel," Cassian says. "My team has been working on the campaign for months. It's some of their best work."

"Wait." I hold up a hand because we've gotten sidetracked. "What happened with the car and the frozen credit cards and all that? You would have been homeless at that point."

Ira must have taken him in then, let him stay in this cozy house.

"Archer let me share his garage. At least until we made our first million."

I blink because I must have misunderstood. "His garage?"

"It wasn't mine," Archer clarifies. "I was renting it. And living in it."

"Bay Area real estate at its finest," Cassian says.

Gideon nods. "It was freezing at night and an oven during the day. Just miserable." His tone is fond with memories though.

"Gage brought us those beds, remember? Otherwise we would have been on air mattresses." Archer's tone is also fond.

Gage shakes his head. "Those beds were a trade. I was working on the software for that detector, do you remember?"

"God." Bishop groans. "I tried to forget that. That one chip kept burning out."

"Until Archer and Gideon figured out what was wrong and saved the whole thing." Gage's expression tightens, releases. "I never would've gotten my company off the ground if not for that. So a couple of beds is hardly a fair trade."

"You gave me my first big loan," Gideon says. "I'd never have convinced investors to give me enough to buy all the equipment I needed. Or the money to start all those FDA trials."

"We could spend all night going through what we owe each other," Bishop says.

Raven's mouth twists wistfully. "Dad always said you guys could do anything when you got together." She sounds like she's on the outside looking in. Like her own dad kept *her* on the outside.

She didn't get a notebook, which strikes me as terribly sad, and suddenly I don't know if I like Ira so much. He might have saved all these guys, brought them together… but I don't know that he was good, exactly.

"You guys are lucky to have found each other." I don't say

that they're lucky Ira found them—I'm not ready to give him all the credit.

Suddenly I understand how awful it must be for Gideon to suspect them. Abandoned and punished by his parents, taken in and supported by these guys—they would have been his chosen family. He'd expect his parents to turn on him. But not these guys.

I reach for his hand, the injured one. I cradle it in mine, careful of the splints. There are some scrapes across his knuckles, fresh-looking. He must have gotten these when he saved me, and I didn't see them last night. Didn't clean them. I shouldn't have missed them.

Gideon looks down at our joined hands with surprise. But he doesn't pull away. Instead, he leans closer, brushing our linked fingers with his leg. Almost as if he's drawing comfort from it.

I really, really hope he is.

CHAPTER 21

The ride home was a tense one. But a good kind of tension, the kind I know is going to be relieved the moment we get to my bed.

They all loved Tess, just like I thought they would. And we've got an appointment tomorrow to go over the notebooks and figure out what might be going on. I'm not convinced one of them isn't behind it, but sitting alone in my house, waiting, isn't getting me anywhere.

We all agreed that we wouldn't open Tynan's notebook. It might hobble our efforts from the very beginning, but even the mention of his name is radioactive to us. We'll only open that notebook when we're desperate.

Cassian argued that it didn't matter, that he was dead and nothing was bringing him back. And Gage pointed out that it wasn't about bringing him back; it was about our responsibility for his death.

Tess and Raven weren't there to hear that. They were off with Oscar, looking at old pictures while the rest of us had a furious conference. If it's not one of them, then I'm at a dead end for suspects. I'll need their help to track down whoever it is.

It's making me grind my teeth even now, but it's done. I

pull the car into the garage, next to the busted Inspirons, then glance over at Tess. She raises one impudent eyebrow at me.

Immediately my pulse picks up. She's planning something, and it looks like something I'm going to like. I lean back against the door, letting the keys fall onto the dash. "Got plans for tonight?" I ask in a gravelly voice.

She shrugs with one shoulder. "Some knitting. An early bedtime."

The hell she is. I lean forward. "Is that really what you think you'll be doing?"

Her shiver is fucking delicious, ripe with anticipation. "What do you think I'll be doing?" She wets her lips.

"I can think of a lot of things." I tip her chin up and her eyes darken. "Want to hear some of them?"

"Mmm. Sounds"—she trails her fingers down her chest and flirts with her cleavage—"interesting."

I watch her fingers like a hawk sighting a shadow. "Are you… teasing me? I don't know if you're ready for what that's going to unleash."

"I don't think you're half the beast you pretend to be." Her eyes gleam. "And even if you are, I can handle it."

Holy hell. I bet she can. I grab her and pull her up and over the center console, kissing her like the beast I am. It's lips and tongues and teeth, so wild I want to throw my head back and roar. Her arms wrap around my neck, her breasts brushing against my chest. They're so soft, so full, like sexual works of art.

The Porsche is too small for what I have in mind, but somehow the confined space makes my urges that much more expansive. I want to blow the roof off this thing with the passion between us, and I'm sure we can.

She's panting into my mouth, her stiff nipples rubbing against my chest. Her sweetly fevered responsiveness is the greatest thing I've ever experienced. I could kiss this woman, all her soft spots rubbing against me, for an eternity. And when we got to the end of that, I'd start all over again.

"Gideon." Her fists clench in my shirt. "Gideon."

"That's right." I'm riding the edge of cruel. "Beg me. I'll give it all to you, but beg me."

She drags my mouth down to hers, demanding as all hell. She's not going to beg—she's going to take it. She wants me that bad.

I reach under her skirt, finding the smooth curves of her thigh. She gasps when I brush her knee, panting when I caress the soft welcome of her inner thigh. My other hand, the bad one, curls around her waist, lifting her up so that her legs fall open, giving me access to what she's got hiding under that skirt. But I can only lift her so high, my last two fingers refusing to do any work no matter how I command them.

"Your hands." Her voice is light and fluttery as a butterfly.

I want to say fuck my hands, I only need her. Being inside her will repair all the busted parts of me. But she's right—my hand's caught between her and the seat and if she twists just so… Snap, crackle, pop.

"We're going to my bed. Do whatever you need to do with the security system," I tell her, "because you're not leaving my bed until the next morning. At the earliest."

Her lips part, soft, wet. "Um…" She squeezes her eyes shut and clamps her thighs together.

Poor thing, trying to remember how to think. Once the system's set for the night, she won't have to worry about thinking again for hours. I'll make certain of that.

"It's already set. If anything happens, my phone will go off."

I'm so far gone in her, I don't even consider that the phone will go off. I'll have Tess in my bed and that's all that will matter. The world wouldn't dare to intrude.

I get out of the car, and she scrambles out after me, right over the console. Greedy, eager woman. I love it.

With my good hand, I catch her, help her out of the car and into the shelter of me. Every few steps, quick, frantic, I kiss her. I can't help it—if I go without the taste of her mouth for too long, I feel like the air's been driven out of me.

Her hands skim over me, her body pressed hard against mine. She's so damn soft, but there's strength in her too. The contrast makes my head spin.

My own body is alight, alive. There's pain, yes, because my hand and ribs are still broken, but it's faint, drowned out by the desire humming through me, rising and rising with each step we take toward my bed. It'll be a roar by the time we hit the mattress.

As soon as I open my bedroom door, a voice chimes, "You're back. Would you like me—"

"Shut up," I tell Gulizar. "No talking."

"Certainly." She almost sounds petulant.

Tess is laughing behind her hand. "You're the one who programmed her."

"I'm going to take away her voice capability," I growl. I look up at the ceiling, although that isn't where the program actually is. "You hear that? One word, and you're getting done like Hal 9000."

Nothing comes from the speakers. Good.

"Aww." Tess's face falls. "That's too much."

I advance on her, pushing her back toward the bed. "Really? What would you do to save that computer?" I nip at the side of her neck. "Anything?"

"You beast," she whispers, heat flaring in her eyes.

"That's right. Your beast for tonight." I lean into her ear and whisper, "Where do you want my fangs?"

She shudders so sweetly I want to snarl. Instead, I lay her out on the bed, her honey-brown hair spread out around her, her green eyes bright with wanting.

"Beast." This time it's almost affectionate. Her hand runs through my hair like she's petting me. Like she's taming me for her own.

It almost scares me how badly I want to be tamed by her and only her.

His bed looked too big when I saw it before, but once Gideon pulls me down to the mattress, I realize that it might actually be too small. Gideon's presence is so large it fills every inch of the space to overflowing. Add in his overpowering desire for me and I'm amazed there's still air to breathe.

And that line about his fangs... I shivered so hard I thought I might come just from the aftershocks.

"You never answered," he says severely, going to work on the buttons of my dress.

His fingers are pressing into my breasts, the touch sending a wave of heat through my belly. "Hmm?" If he wants coherence, he'll have to stop touching me. Judging by his expression, fat chance of that.

"My fangs." He pops open a button, revealing the swell of my breasts. "My mouth." Another button, and cool air hits my belly. "My tongue." He swipes his tongue over the skin he's uncovered, hot and firm. "My cock."

Gah. I can't take much more of this teasing. "My pussy," I pant. "I need it there. All of it."

He gives me a feral smile, then tears open the rest of my buttons. I hear them ping and scatter when they hit the floor.

I lift up, shake off my dress. When I lie back, I catch him looking at my white cotton panties with an odd expression.

"Jesus, those panties of yours…," he mutters to himself. "So fucking simple, but they're blowing my mind."

He looks more than ready to rip off some more clothes, so I quickly unhook my bra and toss it aside. That one's broken in just right, and I don't want to lose it to Mr. Beast Mode here.

My panties though… "You could take them off with your teeth." I have no idea what's gotten into me when I say that, but it's the same impulse that has me lifting my knee, my toes trailing over the silken sheets.

He rumbles deep in his chest, and it vibrates through my aching pussy. "You want to be ravished." One thick finger hooks in the waistband of my panties. "Don't you? Come on, admit it."

"If you want a confession, you'll have to earn it."

Heat flares in his gaze, and then there's a massive ripping sound. Cool air ruffles the curls between my legs, licks over my damp, hot pussy lips.

Thank God I got my bra to safety.

"Never, ever dare me." The dark warning has me widening my eyes. And then he lowers his head between my legs and I realize he's deadly, fucking serious.

I've never had oral sex like this before. The nice guys were okay, enough to get me off, but they'd either be too hesitant, like they didn't really enjoy it, or too sloppy, like pretending they really, really liked it would help.

Gideon is a fucking master. Precise, controlled, but with a hungry edge that says he enjoys it. Loves it. It's his reason for being. He's a genius sculptor of orgasms, and he's chiseling a work of art out of me with each sweep of his tongue.

The buildup starts deep within, nestled at the base of my spine, then radiates out in a gush of release that shakes the roots of my hair. My climax is so beautiful it should hang in the Louvre.

Once my body comes back down to earth, I pop open my eyes. Things are still blurry. "Wow." I blink away the last of the fuzziness. "Wow."

"You're not finished yet."

I gasp as he climbs up my body, the fabric of his pants scraping my sensitized inner thighs. He kisses me deep and fierce, pulling me up off the bed and into him. My nipples are pressed hard into his chest, and my pulse starts to race. Again.

"The noises you made when you came…" He buries his face into my neck, nips at the soft skin. "I can't even…"

It sounds like he wants to punish me for being so hot. He rocks his erection into my belly, thick and hard as steel. I can guess exactly what he wants to punish me with. My pussy clenches at the thought of being filled by him.

"It was so good." I start to pull at his shirt, desperate to have it off. To have him inside me. "Better than anything before."

Triumph flares in his expression, and then he gets to work helping me tear off his clothes. When the last of them come off, I catch myself at the sight.

Ace bandages are wound around his ribs. The splints on his fingers gleam cruelly in the low light. And the new cuts on his arm, the ones I cleaned out only two days ago, are covered in stark white bandages.

He's battered, my beast. But no less fierce because of his wounds.

"I swear to God," he mutters, "if you ask if I feel up to this…"

I glance down at his cock, rising proud and demanding from the nest of hair. "No, I'd say you're very *up*." I look into his eyes. "I was going to ask if I should be on top."

"*Hell* yes," he grits out. With his good hand, he helps me

straddle him. I reach down to steady myself, avoiding the bandages. I don't want to break his ribs all over again.

He looks up at me. "Jesus, your breasts from this angle. God shouldn't have made such perfect breasts. It's a crime that I can't be touching them all the damn time." He thrusts his hips up, making my chest bounce. "Oh God. So fucking gorgeous. You've got all this hidden under those ugly-ass clothes."

"Hey." I push gently. "Those work clothes are functional. I need those."

He reaches up and tweaks one of my nipples. "No, it's good. You'll be in those shitty cargo pants and that erection-killing polo shirt, but I'll know that hiding beneath is all this. *I'll* know."

He would. His eyes would run over me and strip off all those clothes, revealing the nakedness beneath. And he'd do it every time he looked at me.

My clit pulses at the idea. I'm going to be trying to work from now on, and he'll be looking at me, and my clit will be going crazy.

"Condom." I look around wildly as if one will magically appear.

"Top drawer."

We reach together for it, but I get there first. I roll it on with quick motions, because I'm shaking inside I'm so ready. His cock is insistent, so hard I imagine he's shaking with need too.

With one thrust, he's in me. So deep. He doesn't hesitate, doesn't take his time, just pumps into me. All beast-like.

He reaches between us, circles my clit. He's panting, but his touch is gentle, like he remembers that things get sensitive and tingly after an orgasm. "What do you need? Because you're coming again, all over my cock this time. Tell me how to get you there."

"Like that." I shift, helping his fingers find just the right spot. "Quicker. Firmer. Unghhh…"

I get lost in the rising wave of pleasure. Gideon pumps into me, his fingers working magic.

"So beautiful," he chants. "So gorgeous. Like a fucking goddess."

My pussy starts to clamp around his cock. The climax is coming on harder, faster than the last. And it's going to be so much better than the first one, if that's possible.

"That's right." He's working at me now, with fingers and cock. "Come so good, baby. You come so sweet."

Jesus. I orgasm with my entire body. Like even my toenails are overwhelmed with a tide of pleasure.

Gideon grunts, and then he's coming too. At last we're collapsing together into a sweaty, limp tangle of limbs.

I feel like I'll never catch my breath again. I don't want to, not if it means letting go of this feeling.

He wraps his arms around me. I can feel the splint on his fingers pressing into my back. We breathe together for long moments.

"How are your fingers? And ribs?" I ask after a while.

"Fine. You're the best kind of painkiller."

I smile into his skin. "Good. I don't want to have to move."

"You're not." His arms tighten around me. "You're not going anywhere."

CHAPTER 23

I never knew the morning after could be so… nice.

I've had *nice* mornings after before, with all the nice guys I've dated. But a morning after with a total beast of a man who turned me inside out sexually is another kind of good. Like I was at level-five nice before, but this is level eleven.

My body is pleasantly overstretched, my limbs still limp with remembered release. My hair is snarled around my face, and I'm totally naked. I must look like the best kind of mess.

Gideon is yawning like a lion next to me, all soft and sleepy. Well, his face is. The cock pressing into my leg is half-hard. His cock is coming awake faster than he is.

But he doesn't grab me right away. Instead, he smiles. It's like a slug to my heart because it's so… happy.

"Hey." I can't help smiling back even though sleeping with him was not the best idea. It's too late to go back now though. "Morning."

"Morning," he mumbles back, still smiling, still sleepy. God, he should not be this adorable first thing in the morning. It should be illegal how he looks right now.

I have to get up, get moving, get back to work. I have to finish this job he's hired me for. And then… I'll leave.

My throat closes. I'll have to leave then, but I can stay now. So I do.

"What are you up to today?" I'm impressed with how casual I keep that.

"Going into the office. It'll be fine," he says when my eyes widen. "I'm leaving Rustem here, and he's not to leave your side. And Gage is sending out a team this morning."

Rustem's going to love that. I can already see him scowling down at me all day. "I was thinking about you, not myself."

"You should be thinking about yourself." His voice deepens. "But I'll do some of it for you. I have to go in though. The place is going to fall apart without me."

"You have to go crack the whip?"

He nods.

I shake my head. "You pretend to be cranky and crabby, but Raven told me last night how you helped that man in your R&D division when his wife got sick. A nurse on call twenty-four seven, a nanny for the kids, and a driver."

"I never said that was me." His mouth flattens.

"Who else would it have been? You try to hide your kindness, but it won't work. People see it."

He makes a scoffing noise in the back of his throat. "More rumors. You can't prove anything."

Maybe not, but Raven had other stories like that one. Employees and their families at Wolfe Medical Industries getting special perks from anonymous sources. One employee getting an all-expenses-paid trip back to Iran to see his dying grandmother. Another employee having his kid's traveling soccer team entirely funded until the kid turned eighteen.

And then there's Rustem, saved from a dictator's wrath.

"How did you meet Rustem?" I can't imagine Gideon just ran into him on the streets of Ashgabat one day.

"I'm really into MMA," he says. "Just like you guessed.

There're a lot of great MMA fighters who are Turkmen. Rustem was training some of them in grappling techniques based on his wrestling training. They raved about him, so one day I went to meet him."

"Was this before or after the infamous dictator incident?"

Gideon chuckles. "So he told you about that. It was before. We kept in touch, and when the dictator tossed him in jail—"

"Wait." I sit up suddenly. "He was in jail?"

"Yep. Gage and I had to get a team together to bust him out."

My mouth goes slack. "You broke Rustem out of a foreign jail?"

"It wasn't foreign to him," Gideon points out. "But yeah. We had to get his mom out of the country too." There's a sadness to his tone. Like he regrets it.

"They can never go back, can they?" I ask.

"No." His tone is stark. "But it's better than being locked up, I guess."

"Is that why you trust him when you couldn't trust anyone else?"

Gideon twists a lock of my hair around his finger. I've never been a girl with the kind of hair that's good for that. It's too straight and limp and brown. But Gideon makes me feel like that girl. All sexy and seductive and gorgeous even though I've got sleep creases on my arm and God knows what else I can't see.

He releases my hair, then twines it up again as if he just can't help himself. Or he's avoiding my question.

"You and Rustem?" I prompt.

He releases a long, almost regretful breath. "Rustem feels like he owes me a life debt. *I* don't feel that way, but he does. When a man like Rustem feels that way... he means it. So." Gideon shrugs like he doesn't deserve that kind of loyalty.

Maybe he doesn't. Maybe no one does, but he also helped

Rustem escape, which is something most people wouldn't have done. Maybe loyalty can't be measured like a ledger book—I owe you, you owe me—but it's more like a web, catching each of them deeper with every good deed.

"You don't think you have that kind of bond with the rest of them?" I ask. "It certainly sounded like you'd done a lot for each other."

I sense a dark mood come over him, stiffening his body under mine. "It's complicated." There's a wealth of emotion in his tone, not all of it bad.

"Hmm." I walk my fingers up his torso, avoiding his bandaged ribs. "If you want to talk about it, I'm here."

So I hadn't been imagining some undercurrent running through their interactions last night. Something's going on, beyond the attempted theft. I wonder if it has anything to do with losing Ira.

But I won't pry. When he's ready to come to me and tell me, he will. I can let him stay in the shadows on this a while longer.

"I know." He captures my hand, presses it flat against his heart. "But you don't have to worry about it. You don't have to worry about anything, not anymore."

I wrap myself around him, trying to give him some comfort with the force of myself. "Now who's trying to be responsible for everyone?"

His chest rises and falls under my cheek. His skin is almost hot, as if too much burns inside him. He runs his hands down my back. "Thanks for going with me last night."

I recognize that he's not trying to change the subject— he's appreciating that I feel responsible for him. And if I'm reading him correctly, he feels responsible for me too.

"It was great," I say. "I got to hear all about Young Gideon, before he became… you."

His expression goes a touch smug. "I was always this

impressive." He shifts, and I fall a little more into the crook of him. "What did you want to be growing up?"

The blush comes on me so hard my ears buzz. It's such a stupid, silly thing, not even an ambition really. "I wanted… All I wanted was to be happy. And for my family to feel safe. All the other kids would write down being president or a football star or a princess, and I felt so dumb when that was the only thing I could think of." I clear my throat so he doesn't think I'm about to cry. "Anyway, I'd usually say a superhero or something even though it wasn't true."

"You said you were doing this job for the money." His hand runs slow and calming down my back. "Why did your parents have the second mortgage? And all those legal bills?"

I lean into his touch. "We never had a ton of money. I don't know, my family just never seemed to be able to get ahead. There were always the debts to worry about, and any unexpected stuff could send my mom into a tailspin, but somehow we always made it through. I think—although I don't know for sure and never asked—that my aunt helped out a lot. Until Nick came along and even my aunt's patience and money ran out."

Nick. What a goddamn useless jerkwad. And still a huge problem for my sister and my family. Gideon's made the debts disappear, but sadly he can't do that for Nick. Nick's eventually going to cause more trouble and cost more money. But this time I'll have my bonus from this job.

"Who's Nick?"

I raise my head. "You didn't snoop into that? You found the mortgages and paid those but didn't find Nick?"

He looks exasperated. "Financial shit is easy. People take more time, and I did it all in a few hours." He runs his thumb over my lower lip. "So who is he?"

Am I imagining the jealousy in his voice? Possibly. But there's something lurking there.

"Nick's my sister's ex-husband, former business partner,

and the father of my niece and nephew. Whenever he gets pissed about anything, he likes to take my sister to court. For all kinds of things."

"You don't sound as angry as I'd expect."

"I'm more tired than anything. It's like… It's like the hurt he caused is more like a bruise now. It still aches, it still needs to heal, but it's not acute."

He shifts as if he's the one feeling angry suddenly. "So that's what the second mortgage was for: legal fees."

"Yep. Nick has the money and the time to set up frivolous lawsuits, and he knows we don't. So that's what he does to hurt her."

Gideon is silent for a long time. I wonder what he's thinking about, but his hand is tracing the line of my spine, lulling me into drowsiness.

"Anyway," I mumble, "the debt stuff is taken care of. Thanks to you."

"Yeah." His voice rumbles out of his chest. "Don't worry about it. And let's make you some breakfast."

CHAPTER 24

I'm feeling kind of dreamy, which isn't the best mental state to be in when assembling electronics. But I can't help it after last night. The real world is too mundane to stay in, especially when I've got fantasies of Gideon to get lost in.

Which means when my phone rings, I jump like I've been zapped. Hell, I completely forgot I even had a phone. It's probably Victoria, giving me an update on the parts I sent her out for.

Except the caller ID says it's my mom. Oh crap. I totally forgot about Gideon paying off both the mortgages yesterday. She must have gotten some paperwork and is freaking out.

"Mom, everything's okay," I say when I answer.

"What is going on? There's all this new stuff on the mortgages, and it says they're paid off. I have no idea what it means." She's almost in tears.

God, I'm a shitty daughter. I should have called last night. Except there's the problem of exactly how I'm going to explain this. Gideon paid off the mortgage before we slept together, but it isn't going to sound great no matter how I spin it. Especially not to someone as prone to worry as my mom.

I could try the truth. Somehow I don't want to lie about anything involving Gideon. I want it all out there, no matter what others might think of it.

"You remember that client I'm working for?"

"The tech billionaire?" Mom's tone crackles with suspicion. "He's involved with this? Oh God, you took a loan from *him*. He's going to charge terrible interest." There's a beat of chilled silence. "Wait, you're already staying there. Oh God, oh God, oh—"

"*Mom*." I don't wait for her to catch her breath. "I'm not doing anything in exchange for paying off the mortgage. I swear to God, I'm not selling my body."

She makes a small noise. "Can you just start from the beginning?"

"Sure." I rub my hand on my thigh and inhale. "Look, Gideon Wolfe is just a... a good guy to his employees. I mentioned I needed this job really badly, and he went and found out about the mortgages and took care of them all on his own. It'll come out of my bonus. He does stuff like that all the time for his employees."

Like saving Rustem and his mom from a dictator, retrofitting a family's home when their grandfather came to live with them so that it was wheelchair accessible, and a dozen other stories like those that Raven told me last night. She was determined to paint Gideon in the best light, and it turns out she had an awful lot of paint to work with.

"That doesn't make any sense." Mom's voice is hard. "He wants something. He's a billionaire. Men like him don't get rich by being nice."

"He's definitely not nice." That's one thing I'm certain of. "But you can be good and care about others without being nice."

Mom snorts. "We thought Nick was nice and decent and too good to be true at first too. You're not dating him, are you?"

Oh boy. "I thought hearing this would be good news? You don't have to worry anymore."

Mom sighs. "We haven't cleared the debt—it's only been transferred. And I'm worried you're the price we'll have to pay now. At least more than you already were."

I slump into one of the chairs in the main room. It's sleek and modern but uncomfortable, with zero give. I wonder if I'm the first person to ever sit on it. "Mom, please trust me. I can't explain all of it, not yet, but this guy... he's the real deal."

I need her to believe it, because I believe it myself. Gideon is isolated, drawn inward, but when his humanity flashes out...

"Oh, honey," Mom says. "If you're sure, then... then I have to believe." She sighs. "There's all this paperwork, and I'm so lost."

"I bet if I ask Gideon, he'll recommend a lawyer we can consult. For free."

"Unfortunately, we're going to need one."

"Mom." I grip the phone tighter. "I love you. And this is a good thing."

"I love you too, sweetie. I'm trying to look on the bright side."

That's pretty good for Mom. We chat a little longer about nothing in particular, but already she sounds less tired. More vibrant.

Afterward, I get back to work. I might be sleeping with the boss, but I still have a job to finish. Although I leave behind my half-finished camera setup with a quickness when said boss texts me to come into his office.

When I walk in, he's behind his desk, wearing a too-satisfied smile.

"You rang?" I ask dryly. His summons was pretty polite for him, but it was still a summons. Not that I'm complaining about coming to see him in the middle of the day. Quite the opposite.

My heart is fluttering, my skin is tingling, and my nipples are already tight. All just from the sight of him.

"Good, you came." He flattens his palms on his desk. "I have an idea. And I want you to see."

This sounds intriguing. I take a chair and cross my legs. The squeeze of my thighs and him so close make my core pulse. I clear my throat, tell my body to behave. "Really? What is it?"

He grins, looking like a wickedly naughty boy. No, actually a wicked man. There's too much raw sex coming off him to be boyish. "What's the name of your sister's ex-husband?"

"Um, Nick Salantino." I lick my lips. "Why?"

"That's what I thought it was." He picks up his phone, taps the screen. From the speaker, a ring sounds. "Turns out it's ridiculously easy to find him on the internet."

His smile goes sharklike, hungry and sharp. Like he smells blood.

Oh no. If Nick gets pissed—and he will—he'll go after my sister again. He's always found a way to hurt her when he's angry. And he's still doing it.

"Please don't do this," I say. "He'll get mad, and then he'll do something awful again. You don't know what he's like."

"I know exactly what he's like," Gideon says coldly. "He's a bully who takes his inadequacies out on your sister, your family, and you. And I'm going to show him there's an even bigger dog in the yard now."

My eyes are wide. Gideon is definitely way more powerful than Nick. "Why would you do that?" My voice is small.

The phone is still ringing.

"Because he's threatening you," Gideon says simply. "And I can't allow that to happen. I protect my own."

His own could mean employee... or it could mean a lot

more. I swallow hard.

"Hello?" Nick's confused and little aggro. Like we're interrupting something important.

"Hey." Gideon's greeting is a verbal back pat. "It's Gideon, Gideon Wolfe. Wolfe Medical Industries. Is this Nick?"

"Yes." Nick's tone is filled with awe and greed. "This is Nick. CEO of Salantino Enterprises." His voice shifts like he's trying to sound as though he and Gideon are equals. But he's already given himself away.

"I'm so glad I caught you." There's a dangerous purr in Gideon's tone I think only I can hear. "I wanted to discuss something with you."

I can't see Nick, but I can definitely imagine what he's doing right now. He's sitting up straighter, a gleam in his eyes and sweat beading on his brow. He wants whatever Gideon's about to offer him. He wants it so badly he'll do anything. Nick was always more ambitious than clever or hardworking. If it promised to be easy, he jumped.

He doesn't even stop to wonder why Gideon Freaking Wolfe would want to do business with him. All he can see is dollar signs.

"Great." Nick's tone is thick with flop sweat. He wants to play it cool, but he's desperate too. "That's great. So we're doing—"

"I'm not interested in your company." Gideon's tone is as smooth and cold as silk left in snow. "I'm not calling about that."

Nick's swallow is audible. "Um, then what is this about?"

"Your ex-wife."

My entire body tenses, waiting for Nick's explosion. He's going to say something awful now. Or worse, take it out on Elena when he calls her later. That's always been his MO.

"Okay," Nick says slowly. He's being surprisingly reserved here, but he probably doesn't want to lose it in front of Gideon.

"You're never to contact her again. Not about anything. No more lawsuits, no more abuse, none of it. Forget she even exists."

"What?" Nick is utterly baffled. "Are you fucking her?"

Ah, there's the old snarl, the nasty anger. When Gideon growls, it's cute. When Nick growls, it's stomach turning.

"You really lack imagination, don't you?" Gideon steeples his fingers. "Do you understand what I'm requiring of you?"

"You've got some fucking nerve. That bitch isn't going to get rid of me that easy."

I flinch at what he called my sister. I know he's said worse, right to her face, but it's still gross. Sometimes I wish he'd get hit by a semi just so we'd never have to deal with him again. Which is a terrible thing to wish on someone.

"Yes, she is," Gideon says, deadly calm. "Because I say so. It doesn't matter why I'm doing this. You only need to know that I am. You won't contact her or any member of her family ever again. If you do, I'll know about it. And I'll bury you, because I'm Gideon fucking Wolfe. I'll make you disappear, and no one will miss you."

The silence on the other end of the line is deafening. But I can still hear my heart in my ears, loud, insistent. Even hopeful.

Turns out I might not need a semi to deal with Nick. I might just need Gideon fucking Wolfe.

"I…" Nick's mouth hangs open on that pause, so open I can hear the wind whistling past it over the line. "Okay."

I clap my hand over my mouth. He sounds so small and wormy, scared shitless. Which is how he should always sound, the bastard.

"Good. I'm glad that's settled." Gideon spins around in his chair as if he's just made a fantastic business deal instead of threatening someone's life. When he comes back to face me, he winks. "Tess will let me know if you've fucked up." Steel creeps into his tone, like metal frost, and I shiver even though it's not directed at me.

"Understand?" he finishes.

"Perfectly," Nick croaks.

"Great. Talk to you later." Gideon chuckles evilly. "Actually, you'd better fucking hope we don't. Bye."

I stare at him for a long moment. He stares back, cool as you please.

"I can't believe you just did that." The mortgage was one thing. This— *Holy shit, he didn't.* I lift my finger, stab it at him. "You cannot call *him.* Not him. I won't let you. He can't…" I'm shaking now. "He's forgotten about me. Don't let him remember."

Immediately Gideon is next to me, folding me up in his arms. "Jesus, honey. I won't do anything, just… just don't do this. Don't cry." He sounds helpless, which snaps me out of it. Gideon never sounds helpless.

"I won't." I rub furiously at my eyes. "You didn't find his name, did you? The guy in the Army?"

Gideon watches me for a long moment. "No," he says finally. "I haven't found him yet."

"But you were looking for him."

He glances away. "He can't get away with that. Any more than that asshole who married your sister can. I dealt with him, didn't I?"

He did, and I doubt Nick will screw with my sister or my family again. But my harasser is a different matter. I haven't heard from him or even heard about him since I left the Army. He's not an active threat. And I don't want to remind him I exist.

It's in the past. I've moved on, made a good life here, built a company with my friend. I don't need to bring him back into it or get revenge on him. He's gone, and I want to leave him that way.

"This is different," I say. "He hasn't done anything to me

in years. Don't remind him I exist."

Gideon's mouth flattens. "He wouldn't dare. Not once I was done with him. Don't you want him punished?"

"Honestly, I don't. What I really want is for him to never have done it in the first place. I want Victoria to have back the career she always wanted. Punishing him isn't going to change what happened."

"I'll find him eventually." Gideon is unyielding. "You know I will."

I blow out a breath of frustration. "You can't just attack all my problems. I've got a leaky sink. Are you going to glower at that too?"

His expression cracks, and he starts to laugh. "Maybe. But I've also got some wrenches. I can frown and then tighten it."

"Well, if you could fix it, that would be great. It drips all night and drives me crazy when I'm trying to watch TV." I take a deep breath. "But please. Please. Please. This is very important to me. Stop. Looking. For. Him. I've put that behind me, and I want to keep it there."

I hold his gaze, trying to impress on him how intensely I mean this. The mortgage thing was great, scaring off Nick was even more great, but there has to be a limit.

Eventually his shoulders ease and he sits back down. "Fine." He's being very ungracious. "I won't contact him. But if he pops his head back up and contacts you or even speaks your name, I'm going after him."

"Good. Thank you. Wait— How would you know he's speaking my name?"

He shakes his head. "Don't worry about it. But I promised and I mean it."

I reach up and cup his jaw. So hard, so dangerous-looking. But underneath, he's got a soft heart.

I don't dare tell him that. He'd snarl at me and demand I call him a monster. But now that I've seen the softness, I can't look away.

CHAPTER 25

I can't tell if I'm relieved when the guys show up with their notebooks or not. I suppose I am on some level—I've always fought with these guys by my side before, so tackling this with them feels familiar. And good. And really, we should have put our heads together about these books a long time ago.

I know why we didn't, but we should have.

But I'm also hesitant. There's something wrong here, something I'm missing, and it definitely involves one of them. One of my friends in med school said we were getting trained to be highly competent diagnostic algorithms, and it was true. After seeing your hundredth case of disease X, you knew in your gut what it was even if all the symptoms didn't align.

My gut sees the patterns of our work in this. How we come together to go at and around a problem. I can't explicitly identify what those clues are, but something deep inside me sees them anyway.

Which means one of the people coming into this room is the villain I'm searching for.

I'm almost certain it's not Gage or Bishop. Which leaves

Cassian and Archer. But try as hard as I can, the pattern of either of them being behind it just won't assemble.

That leaves Morgan and Raven, which makes no damn sense. To them the notebooks would be like Ira's fountain pens or his antique hand-built computers—curiosities that they wouldn't care much about.

So why does this thief care so much about the notebook? Unless they know what secrets are in them. Which *we* don't even know.

I've got both Tynan's and my notebook out on the desk. I know I said last night we shouldn't open Tynan's, but after thinking it over, I was wrong. Cassian's right—he's dead. No one will care if we look at his stuff. And if it holds clues to whatever is going on, we have to know.

But I still waited for them to come before I opened it.

Gage immediately goes for the carafe on my desk, pouring himself a cup of coffee. The man's addicted, which is weird because he's not jittery at all. In fact, he's positively low-key. Would he just be comatose if he stopped caffeine altogether?

Archer takes a chair by the window, looking out over the grounds. I've got a view of the west side of the property, and if the angle is just right, you can see the ocean way out in the distance. He puts his chin on his fist, his notebook tapping against his thigh.

Bishop is the fidgety one. He passes his notebook from hand to hand, riffling through the pages but never actually opening it. Instead of taking a chair, he starts to pace. He looks like he's about to defend his life before an unsympathetic judge.

Cassian walks right up to my desk, peering at the notebooks. "This is Tynan's?" He points to it.

I nod. Immediately he opens it and starts flipping through it. His mouth is set in a grim line, and for some reason I imagine he's doing an autopsy, trying not to breathe in the smell of cold formaldehyde.

He gets to the end and pauses, releasing a harsh breath. We all watch and wait. Even Bishop has stopped pacing.

"Nothing." Cassian tosses it down to the desk. "The same fucking gibberish that's in mine."

My attention flicks over to Archer, gauging his reaction. He's got the same strained relief on his face that we all do though.

I take my place behind my desk, setting Tynan's notebook back where I had it. Ira appointed me executor of his will, and I'm going to take charge here. I was always the natural leader of the group, urging us on to new and more daring things. Like putting our AI into Ira's car and turning it on.

Which makes it real fucking ironic that Ira made me the executor.

"So no one's decoded their books?"

Bishop starts to pace again. "I couldn't even look at it. I put it on the shelf and tried to forget about it."

"I looked when I first got it." Cassian's flipping through his own notebook now. "But I never tried to decode it."

Gage simply shakes his head.

"I tried for about two years." Archer looks out the window as he says it. "I figured out that it's probably an asymmetric algorithm, but that was as far as I got."

I groan. An asymmetric algorithm means that there are two encryption keys—one to encode and one to decode. So figuring out the encode key doesn't do shit for getting at the decode key.

"But it's not a difficult computation," Archer says. "Which means we should be able to break it with pen and paper. No supercomputer required."

"How do you figure that?" Cassian asks.

"I can see some patterns. And there are formulas in there. Math is easier to crack than language."

"Ira never left us puzzles that were impossible to do," Bishop reminds us. "In the end, we were always able to crack them no matter how difficult they appeared."

"He also never left us anything important in those puzzles," Cassian says. "The real work was done out in the open, not hidden behind some kiddie decoder-ring bullshit. This—" He holds up the book, his jaw tight with frustration. "This is just some fucking game. So why steal it?"

They all look to me. "I don't fucking know. But they went for the safe, and that's all I have in there."

"So why not steal one of ours?" Gage asks. "Shit, Bishop had his sitting on the bookshelf."

I stab a finger into Tynan's book. "Because this one doesn't belong to us."

The atmosphere becomes oppressive, crackling with tension.

"Has anyone considered blackmail as a motive?" Bishop asks.

Gage flinches. "We burned those books. Trashed that equipment."

"Not all of it," Cassian points out. "Not the most important piece of all."

"It's a home for crabs now," Archer insists angrily. "No one's going to recover that car."

I hold up my hands for silence. "The notebook proves nothing. If we can't read it, neither can anyone else."

"The thief might not know that," Gage says. "If they suspect something, they might be looking for proof. Specifically, proof among Tynan's things."

They all look to me. "He died intestate," I explain. "There was no will, and I wasn't the executor. As far I know, he had nothing and no one to give it to."

"Are we sure he had no family?" Bishop asks. "He never talked about them, but…" Bishop's expression makes it clear that he doesn't buy that Tynan had no one. And Bishop would know since he really does have no one. Except for us.

"I looked. The other executor looked, the one for Tynan's probate. There wasn't any family we could find. His parents died when he was young. All his grandparents died before he was born. No aunts, no uncles, no siblings. Not even a third cousin to contact."

Archer taps his toe against the hardwood floor. "So the only person who would want this notebook would be Tynan?"

"Or you guys," I shoot back. "Since you're alive and he's not, that complicates things, doesn't it?"

Gage looks like he wants to punch something. I can sympathize. "It has to be blackmail. Which means we need to catch this fucker."

"And then do what?" Archer points out mildly. "Sail out past the Golden Gate and drop them into the Pacific?"

We all ignore that wrinkle. "I've been trying to catch them. But pretending to be wounded hasn't worked."

Gage snorts. "You're shit-ass bait."

"I think I'm excellent bait." I bare my teeth. "Very tasty."

Cassian's smirk turns wicked. "All you've caught so far is Ms. Robards."

I growl at him because what I have with Tess isn't open for discussion. Or jokes.

"Oh leave him alone," Archer says. "You know he's shy about his crushes."

I look to the ceiling and pray for patience.

"He's so embarrassed he can't talk," Bishop says.

Gage makes a grunt that could be a laugh.

"Awesome. Very funny," I say. "Do we all feel better now?"

Bishop's mouth kicks into a half smile. "Actually, I do."

"Great." My tone is gruff, but there's a weird warmth in my chest. "Can we get back to this?"

Cassian crosses his legs, swinging his foot. "I'd rather keep riling you up about Tess. You *like* her."

More than like her, I'm pretty sure, although I'm not quite ready to put a name to how I feel about her. Besides, keeping her close to me only puts her in more danger, thanks to the very thing we're discussing right now.

"Yeah, I like her, and I'd like to deal with this situation so I don't need to worry about her safety while she's here." I sit back, square my shoulders. "So what are we going to do?"

"Find whatever Tynan might have left behind," Gage says.

"Okay, so we're going with the blackmail angle."

Cassian shakes his head. "No, that makes no sense. Who knew we put the system into Ira's car? Just us. There're no records of that. And we don't even know if it was on when the car crashed."

"If it was on," Archer says, "Tynan must have switched it on."

Bishop turns to him. "So you're blaming Tynan for his own death?"

Archer lifts his hands. "I'm not blaming anyone." His gaze flicks to me because I probably am the most to blame. "I'm only saying."

With a faraway look in his eyes, Bishop lifts his head. "We should confess."

There's a long beat of stunned silence.

"Confess to who?" I say. "We have no proof of anything."

We've got nothing but a lingering sense of guilt that hasn't lessened in the past five years. And rank suspicions that we'll never be able to shake.

"To Raven." Bishop's gone pale. "And Morgan."

There's a heavy, considering moment. We're all running through the possibilities in our heads, scoring the potential outcomes.

All the outcomes I come up with add up to less than zero.

"We're not saying anything." I set my palms down on the

desk. "We're making copies of our notebooks—physical only —and giving them to Archer. He's come the farthest on actually figuring the things out. Put the originals somewhere safe. Like… a safe."

"And where's Tynan's notebook going?" Cassian asks.

"It stays here. As bait."

Gage nods. "I'll send over a team. A discreet one—we don't want to scare this person off."

"And when you catch them?" Bishop asks quietly.

Gage and I exchange a look.

"We'll deal with that if we actually catch them," I say.

Bishop doesn't look pleased, but he doesn't say anything else.

Archer gets up. "I guess I've got some long nights ahead of me."

"I'll help," Bishop says.

"Me too." Cassian rises and stretches. "It'll beat acting as bait. By the way, is Tess still living here?"

I point to the door. "Goodbye."

They all laugh as they leave while I scowl. But beneath the scowl, I might be laughing too.

"So…" I set my chin on my hand. "How did your meeting go?"

Gideon pauses with his fork halfway to his mouth. We're having pork chops for dinner, and he's somehow made them so perfectly juicy I want to die. "You were waiting all day to ask me about that."

"Maybe not all day…"

He snorts. "Since you saw them all walking in."

I shrug. "Rustem was gone, and I got bored. Mostly I was waiting for programs to install and tests to run, so my mind was free to wander. And I managed to run out of the conversations stored in Gulizar's memory. Where is Rustem?"

"She should be able to compose new ones," he says. "And Rustem is running errands for me. He won't be back until tonight." Gideon goes back to eating.

I clear my throat delicately. He still hasn't answered my original question.

He lowers his fork and gives me a look. "It went fine. We're working together to figure out what's going on."

I raise my eyebrows but press my mouth shut tight.

"I haven't ruled any of them out," he says. "But they all

have notebooks too. It made sense to go through them together. Oh, and Gage is sending out a team."

"Yeah, I know," I say dryly. "I saw them on the monitors. Thankfully, Gage stopped to tell me they were coming."

"Oops." His grin is disarming. "I should've said something. But I got caught up with work. There's all this shit to do for the gala and making sure that the equipment is installed correctly before the opening. They want to let all the VIPs troop through the OR with a simulation running on the machines." He shakes his head. "Just a big dog and pony show."

"People love dogs and ponies. But I'm pretty sure your surgery center is more than a circus. How exactly will it work?"

He sets down his fork, his eyes lighting up. "So, you have to be awake for brain surgery. There're no pain receptors within the brain itself—did you know that?—so no need for deep anesthesia. And they need you awake so you can talk and perform tasks while they're cutting so they don't cut out the wrong bit."

My eyes are so wide I can feel my lids drying out. "That sounds… really primitive. The patient is just like 'hey, dude, you went far enough, you can stop now'? How would a person even know?"

Gideon's smile is wide and excited and proud. "That's where our setup comes in. We've got electrodes recording all around the areas where the surgeon is cutting and even within the scalpel itself. The computer is analyzing the neuronal activity in real time and using our deep-learning algorithm to identify what's normal and what's not. The signaling of the neurons themselves guides where to cut, not the input of the patient. Although that's important too. Of course, we had to build a whole new neurosurgery clinic for the hospital to accommodate it, and while we were at it, we paid to upgrade the entire surgery ward. Not just the neuro department."

I blink. It's so genius; it's like… it's like brain surgery. Only even more complicated and amazing. "That's brilliant. No wonder they want a dog and pony show. And a circus and probably fireworks and maybe even to give you the key to the city."

He dips his head, but his smile stays on. "Well, it was the team in charge of the programming who did most of it. I had the idea, but that was it. They put in all the hard work. And they'll probably tell you I yelled too much at them during development. But clearly I yelled just enough." He lifts his head. "I'm considered a horrible boss."

"Did you make them all live in your house while they were doing the work?"

"Um, no."

"I'm glad to know I'm special." I roll my eyes. "But I have no doubt that you're an utter ass to them in person, except Raven told me all about the stuff you do behind the scenes to help them. And even though you only came up with the idea, it was pretty brilliant."

His eyes narrow. "My parents would say it's not actual medicine. They *will* say it—they're going to be there."

"And you care what they think because…?"

He leans back, rolls his shoulders out. "I guess I want them just once to admit they're wrong. That I did the right thing in leaving med school." A hint of a crack comes in at the end.

"Do you think they'll ever do that?"

"Hell no." His answer is immediate. "But that doesn't stop me from wanting to hear them say it."

I can imagine him and his parents butting heads over this forever until their skulls crack. But they still wouldn't stop, because they're all that stubborn.

"Ira thought dropping out was a good idea." I tilt my head,

take him in. "What would he think of what you've done with the surgery center?"

He goes very still. "I know what you're doing."

"You're a supergenius. Of course you do," I say. "Now answer my question."

"Ira would have loved it," he snaps out. "But he's not here to see it."

"That doesn't change the fact you're doing what you should be. So seriously, screw your parents."

He's got an odd expression, like he can't believe I said that, and he also wants desperately to believe that he can just do it. Just let go of those old, bad feelings. "You're one to talk."

"The difference is, my parents support me. After I got out of the Army…" I lick my suddenly dry lips. "I kind of fell apart a little bit. Not like I had a full-blown mental issue, it was just… It was really hard to get out of bed. Every morning. They helped me get through that, fought with the VA, found a doctor, watched my reactions to medications—it was a lot, even though I wasn't that sick. But it would have been much worse if they hadn't been there to help me."

Gideon has said nothing this whole time, merely watched me with a shuttered expression. It's unnerving, so I dip my head.

"Anyway," I go on, "I'm fine now. But we stick together, us Robards. That's the difference."

"If that had happened to me…" Gideon's voice dies. "It *did* happen to me. Med school was fucking killing me. And my parents told me to keep going or die."

The bleakness in his voice hits my heart like an ice storm. I reach for his hands, both of them, grateful that we're eating at the small table in the kitchen and not that dining room monstrosity. "Then just say fuck them. And mean it."

He doesn't say anything. I can see the struggle deep in his

blue eyes. He wants to let go… but he can't give up that twisted dream. Not after holding it for so long.

I lean forward and kiss him to make him feel better. He shoves aside the food with a sweep of his arm, dragging me into his lap. He deepens the kiss so fast I go dizzy.

"Are you trying to distract me?" I say once I can get some air.

"I'm trying to distract myself." He gathers me up. I don't mention his ribs because he'd get mad. And it's also insanely hot that he can straight up lift me like a caveman. "We're going to bed, because I can't hold back another second. It's not even how you look, although you're amazingly fucking hot." He gives me another deep kiss. "It's the shit you say to me, the way you make me feel. Raw in the best fucking way."

I pull in a shaky breath, the oxygen scorching my lungs. Or maybe it's the intensity of his words that does it. "I feel the same."

From the moment I first met him, in the dark, *sensing* his presence, he's overwhelmed me. And he keeps doing it.

He carries me up to his bedroom, kissing me the entire way. Thank God he learned how to navigate this place in the dark. He takes his time undressing me, kissing and touching each new inch of bare skin he uncovers. The time he takes with my breasts and nipples is so decadent I'm sobbing by the time he gets to my stomach. And when he finally reaches my panties, my brain is fried. I'm reduced to pure throbbing, begging need. The second he looks at my clit, I'm going to explode.

With infinite care, he eases my panties over my hips, down my thighs, then tugs them off. I'm swollen and aching, and just pressing my thighs together has me biting my lip.

Gideon kneels before me, setting a hand on my thigh. "You need me, don't you? Look at how wet you are, how flushed your pretty pussy is." He opens my legs for a better look. "And that clit… Achy, isn't it?"

I nod once, frantic.

"I can do it like this, make you scream as you come," he says, "but I don't think you'll be able to hold yourself up. And I don't want my Tess to get hurt."

I grab his shoulders, dig in with my nails. I'm so far gone that even the walk to the bed looks impossible. But I can't form the words to tell him that.

Brilliant man that he is, he knows what I need without my telling him. In a moment I'm picked up and placed on the bed, the sheets cool and slick under me. Even that is almost too much in my overheated state, and I thrash my head and spread my legs, desperate for relief. Desperate for him.

He grips my knees, his fingers digging deep, anchoring me. "I've got you, beautiful."

Oh, he does. He has me so securely I never want to be released. His fingers skim my folds, testing my response. I suck in a breath because even that light touch is a lot. And I want more.

I lift my hips. "Please."

He lowers his head. The first swipe of his tongue has me panting. The second has me moaning. The third…

I come with a scream, my entire body seizing. He shouldn't be so good at this. I'm going to die of pleasure.

But I'm so, so glad he is.

He's got the condom on and is entering me before the aftershocks have faded. To be still half lost in my orgasm while he fills me so completely is beyond everything.

"Gideon." My voice splits around his name.

"I've got you, beautiful." He begins to move. "I've got you. Got you." He chants in time with his thrusts, telling me and showing me how deeply we're entwined.

My head falls back and I rise to meet him, to pull him even more into me. When he comes, he goes still, buried so far inside me I don't see how we might ever come undone.

CHAPTER 27

I come dead awake when the alarm first sounds, sitting straight up in bed, my eyes wide open and my heart slamming into my ribs.

"They're back."

I'm up and out of bed before Tess even stirs. In a flash I've got my shirt and shorts on, ready to finally catch this fucker.

"What?" Tess sits up, blinks the sleep out of her eyes.

"Get to the security room," I tell her. "Now. And shut down the audible alarm and all the lights up here."

There're stairs hidden in my closet, leading straight to the security room she's set up. Eventually the plan is to have it lead all the way to a panic room, but she should be safe enough in the security room. I fucking pray she is.

Thank God she doesn't argue. She simply pulls one of my T-shirts on and disappears into the closet.

I step out into the hallway, the alarm still blaring overhead. I know it's supposed to alert me no matter where I am in the house, but right now I'm worried it's scaring off the thief. A light flashes in the hallway—green. The proximity alarm. Someone's come over the fence and triggered the outdoor sensors.

I look right, look left. They might already be in the house, but if the system detected him, the alarm light would be orange.

"Rustem," I call down the hallway. There's no answer. Damn it, he was supposed to be back by now.

I don't know how long I have before the intruder tries for the safe. Suddenly the alarm is cut off. Everything goes quiet, and in the next second, everything goes dark.

Tess has reached the security room. I slink back into my room, my muscles remembering the route. Hopefully the thief thinks the power has gone off. I want him to feel nice and safe in the dark. And then I'm going to catch his ass.

I wait in my bedroom, hardly breathing, my muscles relaxed but ready.

There's a soft snick and then the slide of a window opening. The dude is coming through my bedroom window.

How the fuck did he get up to the second floor? He would have had to parachute onto the roof. But something definitely set off the proximity alarm by the fence.

No, I'm not dealing with any kind of superman here. This guy can be brought down, same as anyone else.

I keep waiting. One leg comes over the sill, then a torso. He straightens up, looks around the room. The dude is entirely in black and wearing a balaclava, which is a nice touch. Definitely got the cat burglar look down pat.

Without hesitation, he goes for the wall with the hidden door. Like he already knows how to trigger the mechanism and knows the safe is behind there. Fucker.

I rush him, aiming for his waist. He's not expecting it, and I catch him full on, lifting him up and over my shoulder. I wrap an arm around his chest and find—

Breasts? Those are definitely breasts.

Holy shit, he's a woman. I drop him—*her*—out of complete instinct. I just full-body tackled a woman.

She raises her forearm and punches me hard in the side of the head.

I stagger back. *"Fuck."* She's got a mean right hook.

What the fuck do I do know? She might be trying to steal from me, but I can't punch her back. I grab her wrist, try to twist her arm up behind her back. I can at least hold her here until I figure out what's going on.

She does this whip-snap twist, somehow tossing her body out of position and breaking my hold on her wrist.

Okay, I might have to play rough here. No way is she getting away.

I crouch and spread my arms, ready to grab her in a bear hug. Let her try to do some acrobatics out of that.

I get one arm around her, holding her tight. She doesn't fight, just goes very still. So I reach up and pull the balaclava off her head. A long fall of dark hair is released, and I get the impression of brown eyes.

Got you. I'm finally going to bring an end to this.

One knee lifts, her foot trailing along my leg. And then that foot cuts up between my legs. Hard.

I fall to my knees, my lungs emptying. Everything goes bright, then dark, then bright again, as if my eyes are on the fritz.

I see her climb back through the window. She looks back once, her eyes burning with anger. With one hand I reach out, the other cupping the fiery pain in my balls. But I can't reach her.

I don't even think I can have kids anymore. I curl up on the floor and pray to die. And pray that the thief has broken her neck jumping out of the window.

Rustem comes rushing in what feels like hours later. "What happened?"

"Go." I gesture to the window. My voice is creaky. "She went that way."

"She?" He frowns but looks out the window. "I don't see anything."

"Motherfucker." I grit my teeth and curl up into a tighter

ball. "She fucking got away again."

Last time she shoved me down some stairs. This time she gelded me. I'm going to enjoy catching her so much.

"That was a woman?" Rustem crouches next to me, watching me with detachment.

"Yes." I bang my head against the floor. "It was a woman. And she was going right for the safe."

Rustem shakes his head. "Why weren't you wearing a cup?"

I blink at him, my mouth dropping open. "Why the fuck would I wear a jockstrap in my own house?"

He shrugs. "So things like this don't happen. You have to be prepared."

"Are you wearing a cup right now? Do you *always* wear a cup?"

"A man has to be prepared," he says mysteriously.

"Do you wear it to bed?"

He doesn't say anything, which I take to be a yes.

I shake my head. "Must be interesting for your sex life."

Feet come pounding through the downstairs. Then up the stairs.

"Shit." I pull myself to a sitting position as best I can.

"I saw the whole thing on the cameras. Are you okay?" Tess demands the moment she sticks her head in the room. Her hair is falling down around her shoulders, her eyes are bright, and her cheeks are flushed. Even with the worry on her face—and my poor bruised dick—she looks amazingly enticing. And thank God she was safe.

"I am," I grit out. God, this pain will never end.

She falls to her knees next to me, so much more concerned than Rustem. "I couldn't quite see what happened at the end. Did she break a bone?"

Only the most important bone in my body.

"Got kicked in the nuts," Rustem says. "It's his own fault."

"No, it isn't." I haul myself up, wincing with every move.

But I do manage to hold out a hand to Tess and help her up. "He thinks I should be wearing a jockstrap."

Rustem nods solemnly.

She looks between us. "I think I missed something here."

"You missed a lot." I gingerly make my way to the bar hidden in the globe in a corner and pour myself a glass of scotch. I need some major pain relief, and this is one of the best scotches money can buy. "Came through that window"—I gesture with my glass—"and went straight for the safe."

"Jesus." She stares wide-eyed at the window. "But only the outdoor alarms went off. Should we call the police?"

"No." My answer is curt. "Nobody gets called. She'll try again. And I'll catch her next time."

Tess's eyes narrow. "You grabbed her breasts this time."

"By accident." I smile slowly. "You look cute when you're jealous."

She crosses her arms. "I'm not jealous."

But she is. "Rustem," I tell him without looking away from her, "go home. There's nothing more to do tonight."

"Cups," he says before he leaves.

I just shake my head. "Why do I keep him around again?"

"Come on," she says to me. "Let's find you an ice pack."

I try to look especially wounded. "I think I need your help to walk."

She falls for it, coming under my arm to brace me. I tuck her next to my broken ribs, sighing as she wraps her arm around my back. I was pretending to need the support, but it feels damn good to have her here.

"God, I'm so sorry," she says. "The alarms went off, but she still got in. I don't understand."

"Let's go through the footage," I say. "As soon as I get an ice pack."

"Oh!" Tess is so excited she pauses halfway down the

stairs. "You pulled off her mask—and we have a perfect shot of her face. We can ID her now."

I take in a slow breath. It doesn't matter that she got away; now that we have a good picture, we'll know exactly who she is in a matter of hours.

And from there I'll be able to track her down and trace who paid her to do this. Shit, I might not even have to find her physically. With a name, I can get bank accounts, credit cards… I'll have her entire life.

I start us down the stairs, pulling Tess along. "Finally some good news."

"You're feeling better," she says, trying to keep up.

"That news was the best painkiller I could have had."

I never thought my facial-recognition software ran particularly slowly, but as I wait for it to ID the intruder, I feel like time has stopped. Or is going backward.

Come on, come on, come on, I chant to myself.

I look over my shoulder at Gideon, who's watching the screen with a neutral expression. He should be way more excited about this, but maybe he's still in pain. He went down like she struck him with a two-by-four. Seeing it happen on the screen scared the shit out of me.

Without thinking, I turn to reach for him. He doesn't like to be coddled, but this isn't coddling. This is me reassuring myself.

He turns into my touch, the stubble on his jaw rasping against my palm. "I'm okay," he rumbles. "But I'm beginning to see Rustem's point about always wearing a cup."

He wants me to smile, but I'm not really feeling it. Suddenly I understand why he's so paranoid about… everything. That was terrifying, what just happened.

"We have to find this person," I say. "This has to stop."

One corner of his mouth quirks up. "Believe me, I want that too."

"I'm sorry I didn't build the perfect security system." Guilt clenches around my heart. The system went off, but it was useless in the end. He got hurt, again. And we're no closer to actually figuring out what's going on.

I've failed him, and that hurts like hell.

He wraps his fingers around my wrist, his thumb over my pulse. "No. I don't want to hear that. It worked. She came in through a second-story window, never got caught on the five million cameras and sensors you put out there—she knew we'd beefed up security. So she flipped the script."

It doesn't help ease the guilt. "But she didn't have wings, so how did she do it? And one of the sensors definitely went off. I sent one of Gage's guys to check it."

His mouth flattens. "They have more to answer for than you do. Seriously, they didn't see anything?"

Motion on one of the video cameras catches my eye. A fluttering from a tree branch, like a bird or something. But it doesn't quite move like a bird.

I zoom in and enhance the image. Huh. It's a piece of fabric, flapping in the breeze, but it's really high up in the tree; I doubt it got blown up there.

Suddenly it hits me. "She came in through the trees."

"What?" Gideon sits up. "That's impossible."

"Crap," I mutter to myself, cycling through the cameras, looking for the right ones, calling up the older video files. "I was looking at the ground, not the trees. And she knew it."

Sure enough, when I pull up whatever footage I've got of the trees just before the break-in, there's a telltale rustling through the branches, the opposite of how the wind is moving. And I can trace the odd disturbances from the fence line to the house, but I don't get any glimpse of the woman herself.

"That's impossible," Gideon says. "The trees aren't that close together. Some of them are twenty feet apart. The jump from the nearest tree to the roof is at least ten feet."

A member of the security team comes in then, looking

sheepish and holding what looks like a remote-control car in his hands. "We've informed Mr. Cannon about the breach," he says. "And we found this near the sensor that was triggered."

He hands it over. It is an RC car, only it's weighted so that it would trip the sensor.

Gideon looks ready to throw it into a wall. "A distraction. She set up a distraction with a fucking toy. And then went in through the trees."

"Do not punch or destroy anything," I warn him. "I worked too hard on this system."

"I wouldn't break anything you made," he says gruffly.

The security guy—I think his name is Steve—clears his throat. "About the trees… Todd thought he saw something, but we figured it was an owl."

"It wasn't." Anger vibrates through Gideon's tone.

I hold up my hands. "None of us was expecting this." I hold up the toy car. "Or this. I'll get together a fleet of drones and start flying them tomorrow."

I can't imagine what this thief is going to try next. The fence and the grounds have sensors, but I'll put in more cameras and point them up, and then the drones will be pointing down—everything will be covered. But I get the sense she's going to probe for every weakness.

"You can go," Gideon says to Steve. "I'll leave disciplining you for this failure up to Gage."

The man swallows hard, then leaves.

"Wasn't that kind of mean?" I ask. "You didn't lay into me, and it's mostly my fault."

"I don't care what *he* thinks of me."

I hold in my silly, pleased smile, because this isn't the time or place. But it's touching all the same.

The computer emits a low chime. My facial-recognition program is done running.

I reach for the mouse so fast I almost fall out of my chair. Gideon grabs my upper arm to steady me.

"One injury tonight is more than enough," he murmurs.

Face flushed, I scroll through the findings. The picture was good enough that the computer could pull out all the features, but…

"Doesn't exist in any government database?" I ask myself. "That's not possible. Did it run *all* the state and local databases?"

I look over the parameters again. Yep, it went through every database I have access to—federal, state, and local. Which covers pretty much everyone in the US and even has some nongovernmental databases as well.

"What's it mean?" Gideon asks.

"It means we've got a good picture of her," I say, "but we're the only people who do. She's never had her picture taken for any kind of official ID. Not even a college student ID card."

Gideon rubs his jaw. "Yeah, you're only looking into domestic databases. We should try some foreign ones."

I give him a look. "That… that might be illegal. And some of those are massive." Like Britain's, which uses surveillance *everywhere.* Or China, which has made a flipping art form out of recording and tracking literally everyone.

"I know a guy." He pulls out his phone and makes a call. "Gage?" he says as soon as they're connected.

"I already heard," Gage says tightly. "My guys aren't amateurs, but it sounds like they screwed up. What the fuck is happening there?"

"Our thief visited again. And she came in through the bedroom window."

"*She?*" There's a long pause. "And *your* bedroom window? On the second story?"

"She attacked him again," I supply helpfully. "But we got her picture. Well, Gideon did."

Gideon's expression clearly says that if I mention his wounding in any more detail, I'm going to be in big trouble. "As near as we can tell, she went through the trees. Tess is launching drones tomorrow," he says when Gage starts to interrupt. "The important thing is, she didn't get the notebook. And we've got a big lead on an ID. Except she's not in any domestic database. Tess already tried."

"Send over the picture," Gage says. "It could take all night though."

"We've got time." Gideon takes the keyboard from me, starts typing away. "Want me to use the usual server?"

"Yeah. You got hurt again?"

"A minor injury," Gideon says blandly, "to an unimportant body part."

"She hit you right in the balls, huh?"

I choke back my laugh, because it really isn't funny. She broke into the house, hurt Gideon, and she's still out there, biding her time. If I let go of this laugh, it will have a hysterical, wild edge.

"Got it," Gage says. "I'll run it now."

"Thanks," Gideon says. "And don't be too hard on your guys. Nobody even thought about someone coming in through the damn trees."

"Don't worry about them. And tell Rustem that job offer is still open."

"I definitely won't do that. Bye."

Once he's hung up the call, I pull up the photo of the intruder again. I didn't study it too closely before because I was so eager to run it through the facial-recognition algo.

She's young, maybe early twenties. Her hair is a deep, rich brown, the kind of color I wish mine were. The kind of brown that wealthy women pay for. Her eyes are wide set, her cheekbones high, and her mouth is stretched just enough to be interesting.

"She looks familiar." I've seen her somewhere recently, I'm almost sure.

"Yeah, she was just in my bedroom." Gideon squints at the picture. "Actually, I feel like… It's more like déjà vu when I look at her."

"I also just spent almost an hour running her picture through a facial-recognition program. That could be it."

But I'm not entirely sure about that. Something about her features snags at my brain and tugs.

"Maybe we've spent too much time obsessing over this woman." I tilt my head. At this angle, the familiarity is even more striking. Like I was looking at her cockeyed before.

Gideon sighs, rubs his hand over his face. "That's probably it. Come on, you need to get some rest."

"I'm fine," I insist even as I yawn. "What about you? You need rest too."

He pulls me up out of the chair suddenly and embraces me hard. "You shouldn't have been here tonight," he mutters into my hair.

He's the one who originally made me stay here, but I don't bring that up. Because I don't want to leave now.

"I'm fine," I say. "I mean, this person hurt you, but I don't think she really wants to *hurt* you. If you hadn't been in the room, she would have tried for the safe and that's it."

"But next time she might try something worse. She might get desperate." His hold on me tightens.

My heart kicks, but not at the idea of my getting hurt—if she gets desperate, he'll be the one she'll lash out at. She's already done it twice. I swallow hard. "She's not coming after me. I don't have anything she wants. And… and I'm not leaving you."

"I could make you," he threatens. But he doesn't let go.

"You won't."

He doesn't contradict me. He just leads me back to his bed.

CHAPTER 29

Tess is still sleeping when Gage walks into my office the next morning. She had a rough night, and I couldn't bear to wake her. I told Rustem to bring her breakfast once she was up and to make sure she had the coffee she likes.

I'm guessing I'll be stuck in here for a while. We've got a lot to discuss.

Archer comes in behind Gage, looking grim. Right as I'm handing out coffee, Bishop and Cassian show up.

Perfect. The gang's all here.

I pull up the photo of the intruder on my laptop, spin it around to show them without any preamble.

Nothing. No shock of recognition, although Gage has already seen it.

Cassian narrows his eyes. "Isn't that your bedroom?"

"Yep. Does that face ring a bell?"

They all start to shake their heads.

"Son of a bitch," Archer breathes. "It was *her*?"

There's a mutual exhalation as they all come to the same realization.

"Who is she?" Bishop asks.

I look at Gage. "Well?"

His smile is tight, humorless. "I don't know."

Fuck. That is not what I want to hear. "She wasn't in any database? Not a single one?"

"She was in a database." He holds up his fingers. "Three. Dubai, Vienna, São Paulo. Nothing to do with government records or any kind of ID. Dubai was a bank security system, Vienna was some cameras near Saint Stephan's Cathedral, and São Paulo was outside a private residence."

"You hacked the security cameras of a private residence?" Bishop is frowning.

"We share information." Gage looks pissed. Super pissed. "So no name. Yet. We're working on cross-referencing the bank records, seeing if we can pull anything from there. This particular bank can be… reluctant to provide aid."

Meaning they want to protect their clients' privacy because their clients are up to some shit.

I sigh, roll my head around on my shoulders to work the kinks out. "Okay. I'll leave it to you."

"So you trust us. Now." That's from Archer, who's never looked away from the photo on the laptop.

Cassian frowns. That's the first time I've seen him make that particular expression in years. "What?"

Archer finally looks up at me. His gaze is direct, unblinking. "If you trust them, they have a right to know."

That is one thing I hate about Archer even though I'm closest to him—he likes to push people into corners. Corners they can't get out of. He'll say some shit about how I owe these guys after everything we've been through together, but it's also just plain old shit stirring. There's no need for them to know.

But there's no way to keep it secret now, thanks to Archer.

"He thinks we're trying to steal the notebook." Gage is the first to figure it out.

"I did at first."

Bishop pinches the bridge of his nose. "That explains so

much of what you did right after. Jesus, Raven thought you were having a nervous breakdown. Or that you were pissed at her. At *her*."

Cassian runs the tip of his tongue over the edge of his teeth. "No, it makes sense. No one else knows about the books; no one else would care. And what does Gideon have that the rest of us don't? Tynan's notebook. That's why you asked if any of us had decoded ours."

"Son of a bitch," Gage says.

Archer merely watches all of us.

"You really thought of us first. You immediately thought we'd turn on you." Bishop's stance is cold, hard.

"It's not like we've stuck together all these years out of brotherly love." I don't back down. "Remember why we *have* to stick together?"

"Didn't we?" Archer asks softly.

"It doesn't matter," Gage snaps. "We're all stuck in this shit together, thanks to what we did." His gaze swings toward me. "Fine, you trust us now. Do we really have all the information? Anything else you're holding back?"

"No." I hold his gaze, steady as he is.

Cassian inhales long and sharp, clearing the atmosphere. "So we're back to blackmail. But who?"

"Or something valuable hidden in the notebook," I point out.

Bishop lifts a hand. "So what does the book say?"

We look to Archer.

"I don't know."

We all groan.

"Look, it's much more complicated than any other puzzle Ira made for us. I've identified some repeating elements through the books, meaning that he probably used the same cipher for all six of them."

My expression sags. "He could have invented *six* different ciphers?" Fuck, we never would have cracked that.

"Potentially. But he doesn't. There's a key, I just… I have to think about what Ira would have done. How he thought." His tone is strained. "It's been a while."

The entire room is tense because we all miss him and we're all responsible for him being gone.

I want to snarl, to roar, to place all this… darkness somewhere else.

I want Tess. Somehow all this doesn't seem so fucking awful when she's around. It used to be that these guys also made it less awful.

I sigh and turn my head slightly. The picture on the laptop is still there. Still eerily familiar.

"We're all doing what we can," I say. "And maybe we're all freaking out over nothing. It's been only two break-ins; nothing got taken."

"You got your ass kicked." Gage is cheered by the thought. "Twice, it looks like."

"Is that a mark for or against freaking out?" I ask.

"It's a mark for celebrating," Cassian says. "Your getting taken down a peg always is."

"Ha, ha, ha," I say with supreme dryness. But the dark weight in my chest has lightened up.

"Speaking of getting taken down a peg," Bishop says, "is your gala still on? Raven was wondering."

After this recent break-in, I'm tempted to cancel the whole damn thing. Just hole up here with Tess and tell my parents to fuck off like she wants me to.

But my team would be devastated, my clinic would lose out on great publicity, and my gala promises to bring a thousand potential donors swarming through the hospital. These guys are supposed to be there too, along with Raven and Morgan. I'm sure Axel will come along, checking his angles for Instagram.

Tess would come if I ask her to. She'd know these guys, so it wouldn't be awkward. And she'd know me.

She'd be on my arm. My date, my partner, smiling next to me as everyone told me how fucking amazing I was. She'd believe it too.

"Of course it's still on," I say. "I can't cancel. Are you going with Raven?"

Bishop flushes. "We're not going *together*." The muscles in his shoulders bunch. "I offered her a ride. She doesn't like driving in the City."

"Does Tess like driving in the City?" Cassian asks me, so very neutrally.

"Fuck off," I say. "And be nice to her at the gala."

CHAPTER 30

I've hardly seen Tess today, and I'm grumpy as all hell about it. I was busy with all kinds of bullshit, and she was finishing up the install of the security system and getting the drones together. I can hear one overhead now, a steady, low buzz in the air. A low-flying robot spying on me from above is kind of creepy when I think about it too long, so I don't.

Once we get to the bottom of all this, I can stop with the drones. I can stop with a lot of this bullshit.

Tess texted me today to say she had less than a week until she was finished with the security system, which means she'll be done in a month.

It's only been three weeks since I met her, but I don't want her to go.

I look at her in the bed. My bed. Her hair streams around her, a silken cloud of browns and golds and auburns. I never knew a woman's hair could hold so many colors.

I never knew a woman could hold so much of my heart.

This is a serious problem, my falling so fast for her and right in the middle of a shit storm like this. But I don't think I can stop it. Even if I wanted to.

Tess stretches and blinks up at me. She smiles like she was just dreaming of me.

"Come with me to the gala," I say suddenly.

Her eyebrows jump. "You're going?" She sits up, pulling the sheet to her chest. "But this whole thing with the intruder… You're going to leave the house?"

"I'll go if you do."

Her mouth flattens. "That makes it sound like you don't want to go."

"I don't." I sit on the bed next to her. I can feel the warmth of her through the sheets. "It's just going to be a bunch of rich assholes patting themselves on the back about how amazing they are for donating some money."

"Aren't you one of those rich assholes?"

I swallow hard. "My parents are going to be there."

Her face softens. "Oh Gideon." She cups my jaw. Her touch is softly painful, cracking open that wound I'd thought was healed.

"I'm not asking because of them. It's not like I want you to meet them." I wince. "That came out wrong. I don't want you to have to deal with them."

I'm not to the point where I can tell them to fuck off, but I can handle them. Tess shouldn't have to.

"I don't mind," she says softly. "I can deal with anything. For you."

God, what those two simple words do to me… I have to close my eyes for a moment. It's too much. She makes me feel too much.

"Including a gala filled with rich assholes?" I ask, giving her one last chance to say no.

"As long as you'll be one of the assholes." Her expression clouds. "I don't really have a nice gown. And I don't think my business suits will cut it. Not that I'm asking you to buy anything," she says hurriedly.

Gowns. She's worried about gowns. "Buy as many dresses as you want. Get your hair done, your makeup—go balls to the wall."

"You've already given me too much."

I stroke her hair, which spills over her shoulders. So soft and thick, more luxurious than the finest silk. But not so fine as her skin. "I'm not giving you anything." Although I'd give her whatever she might ask for at this point. "You're buying it yourself. With my credit card."

Her mouth twitches. "You're splitting hairs."

"It's just money."

Her expression flickers. "That's not something I'd ever think."

Christ, I shouldn't have said that. Money's not a joke to her. "Okay, well, think of it this way. I want you there with me. You need a gown to be there with me, as I've so selfishly demanded. So I'm forcing you to buy a dress. I'm being monstrous here, not nice. Does that convince you?"

Her hand runs over my shoulders. "I like you better when you're beastly, so yes."

"You're the only person in the world who does."

Heat flares in her gaze. "Did Gage find a name?" She's trailing her fingers over my chest. Which makes it hard for me to think about anything but her.

"No. He's got her on a few security cameras in places overseas, including a bank. But nothing with a name on it. He's checking the bank records now."

She blinks, slow and steady. "What's in the notebook?"

"We don't know."

If she's surprised by my response, she doesn't show it.

"They're all written in a code," I explain. "Ira was always giving us puzzles to solve. And he left us the biggest one of all in his will. We… After he died, we didn't really want to do puzzles anymore. So we didn't bother to decipher them."

"And Raven and Morgan got nothing?"

"He didn't make puzzles for them." I frown. "It wouldn't be them."

"Why not?"

"Because Ira was always pushing us. He wanted us to live up to our potential, to do better, but we were also… projects to him. His girls weren't anything like that for him. They were just… his kids."

I don't have to elaborate—Tess immediately understands. "Then who? If it's not Raven or Morgan or Archer or Bishop or Cassian or Gage, then who?"

I stroke her hair and don't answer. I don't have any answers. Strangely, when I'm holding Tess, that doesn't matter so much. All the bits and fragments of this thing that won't assemble into something recognizable aren't so looming. Gage will find a name and Archer will decode the books—the intruder can't hide forever. And I'm willing to wait as long as it takes, as long as Tess is with me.

Tess makes the past and its echoes manageable. She makes me want to look to the future. Like this gala.

Suddenly I want this intruder problem gone and not simply because Tynan's notebook is my sacred trust and no one will touch it. I want it gone because it's standing between Tess and me and whatever we might have without that hanging over us.

You know what? Fuck this intruder and whatever game she's playing.

I'm going to that gala, and I'm going to enjoy it. I'm going to enjoy the fuck out of it. I'm going to show off everything I've accomplished since Ira died, to my parents, to the guys, to the entire world.

And I'm going to do it with Tess by my side.

CHAPTER 31

"I don't think this is the place we should be looking."

I take in the rotunda and stained glass soaring above me, everything about the store—Neiman Marcus at Union Square—screaming that it's not for someone like me.

Victoria grabs my arm and drags me along. "You've got a limitless credit line sitting in your purse," she says. "This place is definitely for you."

"Maybe I should get something I can wear again."

We pass a beauty counter that looks like the inside of a sci-fi lab. Like they're ready to reprogram you at the cellular level to make you more attractive.

"If it's something you can wear again, then it's not nice enough."

I can't argue with that. "I never even had a prom dress."

"We had formals at West Point." Victoria shudders but she never slows down. She's on a mission. "There was a flipping PowerPoint explaining the dress code. I'm going to enjoy this vicariously at least."

My phone buzzes. As I read the text message Gideon sent, I start to smile. "Awww."

Victoria sighs. "Do I want to know? Can you even share it?"

I hold the phone in front of her face. "Gideon wants you to come to the gala too. And he wants you to get a dress. His treat."

Victoria looks torn. "I really shouldn't. I mean, he's *your* boyfriend."

That catches me up short. Is he really? What we have feels more compressed and intense than simple dating, but there's not a good word for it. "He's my looover."

She snorts. "Please don't ever use that word again. I almost lost my lunch. At any rate, your…" She pretends to gag. "Whatever he is, it's improper for him to buy me clothes."

I stop in front of a shoe display that looks like it belongs in a movie about Marie Antoinette. "Did you get that from a Jane Austen movie?"

"No." She catches sight of the shoes and her eyes go wide. "I don't think I could even walk in those, but I want them."

I nudge her. "And maybe a dress to go with them?"

She pinches her lips together.

"Come on," I wheedle. "If you don't go, I'll be all by myself. Surrounded by the richest people in Silicon Valley with nothing to talk about. Like, someone's going to talk about their latest jade-egg vagina-steaming session and how amazing it was, and I'll have nothing."

Victoria is laughing so hard she's doubled over. Some of the other shoppers are staring, but I ignore them.

"Okay," she says as she tries to catch her breath. "I'll come, just to save you from vagina-steaming conversations."

I give her a half hug. "Thank you," I say sincerely. "I didn't want to go in there alone. And hey, we can do some networking. Wealthy people need security systems."

Victoria makes a noise that could mean anything. "You wouldn't be alone," she says carefully. "There's always Gideon."

My heart sinks, although I understand. "You still don't like him."

She starts to say something, rethinks it. "It's not that. You're so different with him than you ever were with any other guy. It's hard to get my head around it because it's not exactly a normal relationship."

That's very true, but the weirdness of how I met him and the crazy shit going on around him doesn't change how I feel about him. "I like him."

"I know. And I have to admit I really like who you are with him. You're… giddy." She pulls a face briefly.

"Giddy is bad?"

"Giddy is good. And honestly, I am coming around to the idea of you two together. I'm glad you're happy. Like, really glad."

That gives me a warm tingling all over. I squeeze her arm. "Thanks. It means a lot."

She bumps my hip, Victoria's version of a bear hug. "If you're happy, I'll be happy for you."

My phone buzzes again. This time Gideon's texted, *Where are you shopping?*

Neiman's, I text back. *Is that okay?*

Suddenly I feel like maybe a dress from here would be too much, that I've overstepped by coming. There are probably more expensive stores in San Francisco, but I don't know what those stores are. This was my idea of the most high-end place to go.

Perfect, he replies. *Get whatever you guys want.*

I release an exhale. "Okay, let's do this thing."

By the time we find the formal wear, we've done an extended tour of the store, stopping to look at some of the price tags. I feel faintly dizzy every time I see what some of these things cost.

"Ms. Robards." A salesperson comes up to me right away, sleek and sophisticated. She's wearing a blouse and skirt that fit her perfectly and are elegant without being flashy. I immediately feel very, very plain.

"Yes? Is there a problem?" They know already that this is not my credit card, that I don't belong in a place like this, and I'm about to suffer the utter humiliation of being asked to leave.

Victoria comes to my side, chin up, ready to do battle.

"No, not at all." The woman's smile never flickers. "I'm Gina Weatherby." She offers to shake. We both introduce ourselves as we do. "Mr. Wolfe called and said you would be coming. We have a private room for you to view the gowns in if you'd be more comfortable that way."

A private room? I bet it comes with free champagne. And I guess that's what Gideon was up to, asking me where we were.

"Sure. We'd love that." I try to be smooth but fail, because *private room.* All for me to look at fancy dresses.

Becoming Cinderella is a fantasy I thought I'd left behind as a kid, but it turns out that living it out as an adult is pretty neat.

Victoria and I exchange goggle-eyed expressions, hastily wiping them off our faces when Gina ushers us into our private room.

I can't help my gasp. It's a perfect jewel of a room with tasteful wallpaper, low velvet couches, and a three-way mirror discreetly tucked into a corner. It's a room to languidly lounge in, sipping champagne and eating chocolate-covered strawberries, and maybe, if you feel like it, trying on fifty-thousand-dollar dresses.

Speaking of the champagne and strawberries, there's an ice bucket with a bottle waiting and a tray of assorted tidbits.

"Will this do?"

It'll more than do. I try not to look so stunned as I take a seat. "This is perfect." I take a breath, wondering how I'm supposed to start this. Do I go out and point out the gowns I want?

"Mr. Wolfe suggested something that would bring out your hair," Gina says.

I finger a strand of my hair, my face twisting up. This hair? It's… brown. Not sable, not chocolate, not even dark blond. Plain old brown. Like a crayon straight from the box.

"Um, I can't—"

"That'd be great," Victoria says.

"She needs something too. Something to bring out her eyes."

Victoria's eyes, which are a lovely greenish gray, narrow at me. "Right."

I grin back at her.

"I'm sure we have something that will work."

Five minutes later, we're in the shopping montage from a movie. There're a ton of gorgeous dresses hanging on a rack —no throwing these gowns on the floor—the champagne is delicious, and Gina is determined to make us happy no matter what.

"I'm sorry that last one didn't work out," she says even though she has nothing to apologize for. The dress was beautiful on the hanger, and it was me that made it look like an overpriced sack.

"I've got too many curves." The champagne is making me giddy, because normally I'd never say anything like that.

"Shut up," Victoria says. "You know that's not true."

I do, but some of these dresses seemed specifically designed for a direct hit on my self-esteem.

"What about this one?" Gina has a steel-gray silk sheath on her arm. "For Miss Victoria?"

It looks kind of plain, but once Victoria has it on, she transforms it. The gray of the dress echoes the gray in her eyes and makes the green look otherworldly. Her skin picks up the sheen of the silk and glows with it, while the simple lines skim all her best features.

She's so beautiful. I'm so glad she could come with me, and I'm so glad she'll be at the gala with me wearing this.

"Wow." Victoria is looking in the mirror, her expression stunned. "This is… Wow."

"We'll take it," I say.

Victoria's mouth compresses. "Do I have to take it off?"

Gina clears her throat. "Well, we can hem it for you and press it. And you might want a garment bag to carry it in."

I raise my glass. "And you don't want to spill champagne on it."

Victoria takes off the dress, but she isn't happy about it. When she flops back down on the couch next to me, back in her old clothes, she says, "What about you?"

"We'll find something." But I'm not so sure it will be as perfect as that dress is for Victoria.

Gina comes back with a dress in a garment bag. Two garment bags, actually. "This one just came in. We haven't even put it out on the floor, but I think it will be exactly what you need."

When she unzips the bag, a fall of red velvet spills out. The kind of red velvet that's dark as sin, meant to be worn by a king's mistress. It's way too sensual for the queen.

"That doesn't look like my kind of color." I was thinking something cool, like navy blue. Or a nice green. Not something that flipping… sexy.

"Just wait." Gina pulls it free and shakes it out. The dress is a simple column of red velvet, nothing to distract from my curves. The back is gathered at the neckline, creating a sort of short train.

But the neckline and shoulders are what take my breath away. It's a golden jeweled capelet, like a necklace except for the shoulders. The capelet is almost like the shrugs I knit, if I could use pure gold and jewels instead of yarn. The dress is gorgeous and unique, and I'm terrified that I'll look awful in it.

I want this dress. I want to look like a goddess in this dress.

"Yes?" Gina asks.

I can only nod.

Once it's on, I hold my breath as I make my way to the mirrors. *Please, please, please.*

When I see myself, I exhale so fast my lungs burn. My mouth opens, but nothing comes out.

My hair is… it's glowing. The red in the dress has picked up and highlighted red notes in my hair that I never knew were there. My skin looks as soft and alluring as the velvet, and the golden jewelry on my shoulders makes my eyes look like a lioness's.

I can't believe it's me in the mirror. And I don't even have my hair and makeup done.

"I don't even know what to say." I spread my arms wide. "How is this dress that amazing? Did a wizard sew it?"

Victoria shakes her head. "It's you, not the dress. It wouldn't look that way on anyone else."

Gina nods, looking smug. "I knew this would be perfect." Suddenly her expression clears. "I mean, do you like it?"

I hug myself, feeling the heavy nap of the velvet under my palms. "I want to live in this dress. Eat, sleep, and work in it —I want to be buried in this."

"I think that's a yes," Victoria says dryly. "Should I snap a pic for Gideon?"

"No." I turn to stop her. I don't know why, but I'm suddenly feeling very superstitious. "He can't see it until the night of."

Victoria lowers the phone. "Okay. I guess we're done then."

I look back at myself in the mirror. "I should probably take this off."

Both Gina and Victoria laugh at my glum tone.

"We're not done," Gina says with a gleam in her eye. "There're still shoes to pick out. And we have a full-service hair and makeup salon here—perhaps you'd like to try out some styles and looks with your dresses?"

She wants us to play Cinderella all day? Victoria and I exchange a glance like we can't believe our luck.

"Sure," Victoria says.

"We'd love to," I say. And then we clink our champagne glasses as we wait for the shoes to be brought in.

CHAPTER 32

"You're seriously not going to tell me about your dress?"

I realize I'm whining—a touch—but Tess is refusing to even drop a hint about what her dress looks like. I never cared much before what my dates wore, but I'm finding that I'm desperately curious about what Tess picked out today.

"You'll have to wait." She tilts her head and smiles like she doesn't even care about my pain. She's just walked into my office after being gone all day, and I have to admit I was concerned. Gage had a team following her, just in case, which she didn't know about, but I still worried.

I narrow my eyes. "You don't have any shopping bags. Did you not buy anything else?"

She wrinkles her nose. "The rest of the clothes there wouldn't have worked in my job. I can't be wearing five-thousand-dollar pants when I'm in some attic crawl space."

I was thinking more that she could wear them if we went out somewhere, but I don't bring it up. We'll start with the gala and go from there. Besides, if the thief tries again while I'm gone…

"Next time buy more stuff," I growl.

She kisses me as if she finds me too funny. "Right. Next

time." It's casual, but underneath there's an odd hitch to her voice.

"Yes," I say firmly. "Next time. Once this is done…" I reach up, stroke her hair.

"Did Gage find anything else?"

I shake my head. "No. But something will come up. It has to."

She bites her lip and steps away. "But what if it doesn't? What if you never find this person? What if you never decode the notebooks? What if all this is never resolved?"

Something cold and dreadful creeps into my chest. "It will be."

Her expression hardens. "But if it isn't? Are you going to stay here forever, guarding this thing?"

I sense she's not angry exactly, but she's working some things out. Like our future together maybe. It's a fair question.

"I'm going to the gala," I say carefully. "I'm not a hermit."

"And if I wasn't going?"

"I didn't want to go *before* I met you," I point out. "It was only something I was going to endure. Having you there will make it… good."

She bites her lip. "And after the gala? What happens after that?"

"What happens is we come home and keep on with what we have. If you want." If she doesn't want to, I don't know what I'll do, so I don't let myself think of it. "I'm not going to let this person, whoever they are, determine how I live my life. Or yours."

That's what she needs to hear, I think. That's what she's been angling for—reassurance that no matter what, we have a future.

Her chin starts to tremble. "I had so much fun this afternoon, and I couldn't stop thinking about you. Then I got to thinking about what's going to happen next, and there were no good answers." She sucks in a shaky breath. "It's just that I'll be done soon, and this entire situation may never be solved, and I…"

I pull her into my arms, kiss her hair. "What's going to happen is," I say forcefully, "once you're done installing the security, you're not going to worry about it ever again. It won't touch you, I swear." I'll keep it separate, isolated, walled off. The same way I kept our role in Ira's death walled off from Raven and Morgan. I held that secret for years. I can hold this off forever, for Tess. "The only thing you'll have to worry about it is how I'm going to make you happy. Which is going to be my main focus going forward."

She presses her face into my chest. It feels so good to be able to be her comfort. "It sounds too good to be true."

"It's not." I run my hand down her back, savoring the warmth of her skin through her shirt. "I'll make it true."

"I'll have to move out of the cottage," she says. "I can't keep staying there."

"Of course." I'm planning for her to spend most nights in my bed, so that's fine with me. If she wants to keep her apartment, I can pay the rent, but I'll work up to suggesting that.

"And I won't be at your beck and call anymore."

"Nope," I say mildly. I don't like the idea of that, but I'll adjust. Besides, I've been neglecting my own work since she arrived. I can't give her everything she's ever wanted if I'm suddenly broke.

"And I'll need time to spend with Victoria and my other friends and my family. My mom is already worried about your paying for the house, and Victoria thinks I've abandoned her."

"I would never monopolize your time." I totally would. But I won't, because she asked me not to.

"I feel like you're not really listening and just agreeing to everything."

I look straight into her eyes. "I won't lie. I'm greedy. I want all of you, all the time."

She shivers and licks her lips. She likes that fantasy.

"But your loyalty to your family, your love for your friends, how damn good you are at your job are what make you who you are. And I don't want you to lose any of that."

She swallows hard and blinks rapidly. "I… I could say the same about you."

She couldn't, actually. I have no loyalty to my parents, I suspected my friends immediately after the break-in, and while I'm good at what I do, I don't do it out of any kind of higher ideals. She's still got me all wrong, but I'll take it.

"Well then," I say, "we're perfect for each other."

She doesn't say anything, just tucks herself closer to me. Right as I'm thinking I could stay like this forever and to hell with the rest of the world, Rustem comes in.

I get ready to tell him to buzz off, but then I catch his expression. He looks like something awful just happened. Tess lifts her head as I go tense.

"What's going on?" I immediately think of the safe. But there's been no alarm.

"Cassian's here," Rustem says. "Along with the rest of them. Says he needs to see you right away, looks like he's… It looks bad."

I hear raised voices coming from the main room. It sounds bad too.

When I come in, Tess and Rustem on my heels, they're all there. Everyone is wearing a taut, strained expression. Cassian's is stretched to the breaking point.

In his hands is a metal box with wires trailing out of it. Something about it—

Holy shit. My pulse hammers through me as I realize why they're all looking like they've just seen a ghost.

It's because what Cassian's holding in his hand should be at the bottom of the Pacific, along with Ira's car. And Tynan.

CHAPTER 33

"What the fuck is that?" I stab a finger at it, although I already know what it is. It's my past, coming back for retribution. "Is it a replica? How the fuck could she build that?"

It has to be the work of the thief, making this… *thing* to fuck with us. It has to be blackmail, and this is her sick way of telling us she knows what we did.

Cassian doesn't say a word, just opens the back panel. There, scratched into the metal, are all six of our names in our own handwriting.

We'd been so proud of what we'd built we put our names on it. There's no way anyone could have replicated that.

"That's impossible." I run my hand over my face. "There's no way anyone could have that."

Tess comes up behind me, puts a comforting hand in the small of my back. I don't shake her off.

"It's really it," Cassian says. "I found it in my office this afternoon. No one saw anything, and the security-camera footage was erased."

"This is bigger than the notebooks," Archer says.

Oh, it is so much bigger.

"I don't understand." Tess's voice is clear and sweet, even with the confusion. "What is that?"

"We called it Drive-Less," I say, my voice toneless. "A stupid name, but Cassian wasn't a branding genius yet. It was our very first AI system, at least the first that worked like it was supposed to."

Gage snorts. "Supposed to?"

"But Morgan does driverless cars," Tess says. "You guys never developed anything like that. Did you?"

"I do what?" Morgan's in the doorway, Raven waiting behind her. We were all so preoccupied we didn't even hear them come in.

Bishop is furious as he turns on Cassian. "They don't need to see this."

"They do." Cassian shoves the box into his face. "It's past time that we told them what really happened. They deserve the truth."

"What truth?" Raven's eyes are wide, her cheeks pale. "What is that?"

There's a long beat of silence as the old instinct to hide, to never confess, takes hold of our tongues. There's no bringing back Ira or Tynan. No point in telling them what will only hurt them.

Bishop is the first to speak. He stares straight at Raven, his hold on her gaze never breaking.

"I'm sorry," he says, almost as if he's saying goodbye.

"For what?" Raven asks.

"Fuck," Archer mutters, looking up at the ceiling. "Just say it."

Bishop steels himself like he's facing a firing squad. "We killed Ira and Tynan."

At first denial flashes across both the sisters' faces. "That's stupid," Morgan says bluntly.

Raven gives a high, wild laugh, as if she's just heard a joke she can't believe someone would actually say. "No. No, it's…" Slowly her face crumples as she looks at each of us in turn.

I take a deep inhale, preparing to tell the rest. Bishop did the hard part—I can take over. And with Tess listening, I have to be the one to finish this confession.

"A driverless car was our first big project together," I say. "Our only big project together. Ira thought it was a great idea, that after all our experience working on smaller AI projects, we were ready to make something groundbreaking."

I can still see his face in my mind, so patient, encouraging. It wasn't even that he gave us full access to his labs and equipment—we had full access to his time and attention, which were even more valuable.

"We tested it on golf carts," Gage says, lost in memories.

"I thought they were radio controlled," Morgan says quietly. "That's what Dad told me when I asked, that you'd built a remote-controlled golf cart."

I feel Tess flinch next to me. I can't make myself look at her though, can't see the expression on her face.

"No, it was entirely controlled by the computer," Archer says. "We thought it was great. That we'd solved this huge problem that people had been talking about for years. Decades even."

We hadn't though. We'd only been arrogant and stupid, thinking that we'd created this perfect thing. And I was the most arrogant and stupid of all.

I clear my throat. "Once the golf cart worked, we were eager to test it on road conditions. So we put it into Ira's Mercedes and took it out on the road." I take a shaky breath. "*I* convinced the rest of them it was ready for real-world testing."

"You tested it on the road with other people? People who didn't know the car had no driver?" The horror in Tess's voice pierces my chest.

"We did," Bishop says heavily. "We were in the car and

could take control if needed, so we convinced ourselves that made it right."

"There was an on/off switch too," Cassian says. "Unless you were convinced it was safe enough, you were supposed to leave it off."

"Oh my God." Raven puts her hands over her mouth. "Oh my God," she says through her fingers.

"You think they had it on that night." Morgan's face is stony, her words hard. "That the car went off the road because your AI failed. And killed them both."

There's no room for doubt there—she's convinced we did it. That it's entirely our fault.

"We don't know exactly what happened," Archer says gently. "But we suspect."

Morgan looks like she wants to spit fire at him. Raven just keeps moaning behind her hands.

"Why didn't you tell them?" Tess demands.

Finally, finally I make myself look at her. Her expression is both angry and stricken, like she's feeling Morgan's *and* Raven's emotions for them.

"Because we weren't sure," Gage says.

"Because we didn't want to be blamed," I say. Both those things are true.

"Because we love you both," Bishop says. "Like sisters."

Morgan closes her eyes tight and shakes her head. In that moment, I feel the bond holding her to us snap. "No. My sister would never do this to me." She points to the box. "What is that?"

"It's the computer we put in the car," Cassian says. "This is what the AI was loaded on; it's what controlled the car." He flicks the switch on the side, bright orange rust flaking off as the switch reluctantly moves. "It was set to On when I saw it on my desk. It's rusted in place, so… it must have been in that position when it went down with the car."

"If it was in the car," Raven says slowly, "how did it get here?"

"We think it might have something to do with the notebooks," I say. "And whoever's trying to steal them."

"Notebooks? What notebooks?" Morgan demands.

"Ira left each of us a notebook in his will," Archer says. "They're encrypted so we can't read them. We thought they were a puzzle he left us, like he used to—"

"He never made puzzles for us," Morgan says.

Raven shakes her head at her sister. "Not now."

"We think they might be more than that though," I say. "That's what the intruder was after at my place. My notebook and Tynan's."

Morgan goes stiff. "You have Tynan's notebook?" There's a strange note of hope in her voice.

"I was the executor of Ira's estate," I explain. "There was no one to give Tynan's things to. So I kept it."

Morgan looks from me to the box, then back again. "Tynan might be alive then."

Archer gives her a sympathetic look. "I don't think that's possible. They never found the car—"

She jabs her hand at the box. "Well, clearly someone did!"

For a moment silence falls and we all wrestle with the slim possibility of that. Tynan, alive, out there somewhere. It's too fantastical to be real.

"We all wish he were still here with us," Bishop says. "Along with Ira."

"But this has to be blackmail, not Tynan." Gage's expression is almost gentle.

Morgan runs her hand over her face. "I need to talk to Axel." She grabs Raven's hand. "Come on. We'll finish this later." She glares at the rest of us. "This is…" She blinks hard and sniffs. "I don't even know what to say."

Raven puts her arm around her sister, giving us a hard

look. "It's okay," she tells Morgan as they walk out. "It'll be okay."

But it won't. We might have been responsible for the death of their father. We certainly kept it from them for years.

We knew saying anything would shatter everything. And we were right.

A heavy silence falls as we stare at the box, risen from a watery grave. Dimly I'm aware of Tess and Rustem watching us.

"You don't know if it was your fault," Tess says quietly. "You said yourself it was supposed to be off if it wasn't safe."

She's still trying to find the best in me. After I tell this awful, terrible thing, and the even worse sin of covering it up for so long, she still wants me to be *good*.

I look them both full in the face. "You're fired. Yes, both of you. You have twenty minutes to pack your things and leave. And don't come back."

Rustem doesn't even argue. He simply lifts his chin, all betrayed and dignified, and walks out.

I already know I'll never see him again.

Tess though… Tess is still fighting for me. "I know why you're doing this." Her eyes are bright with tears. "You want me to say you're a monster? Okay, you're a monster. The worst of the worst. Is that what you want to hear?"

I know she doesn't mean it, which kills me. "Remember what this place looked like when you first came? Remember the cars? Well, now you know why. Yes, I am a monster. And no one is safe with me."

"Gideon," Archer says softly.

"Stay out of it," I snarl. "She has to go. How many more people we care about have to be hurt because of our mistakes?"

That shuts them all up. Except for Tess.

"Okay, what you did was wrong. A terrible mistake. But

you've done so much good since then. Think about the clinic, a whole new way to do *brain surgery*—"

I cut her off with a swipe of my hand. I can't look at her, and I can't take this anymore. "I did that solely to piss off my parents. I told you from the very beginning what I was and you wouldn't believe." My chest hurts so much I think it might crack open and my heart might spill out. "So here it is again, right in your face: I'm a monster. And I'm kicking you out. This is over. Believe me now?"

Finally something gets through to her. Maybe it's my twisted expression, maybe it's the ice in my tone, or maybe it's the way the rest of them watch the entire thing without trying to stop me.

"Fine." She lifts her chin, looking as proud and fierce and unbent as that first time I saw her. "I'm leaving. I won't be back." She walks to the security panel in the wall and arms the system. "Your new security system is complete—no one will ever get in again. You'll be completely, utterly alone. No one will ever touch your safe or your notebook. And I'll be sending you a bill."

Then she's gone, leaving me alone with the mistakes of my past.

CHAPTER 34

It's the night of the gala, and I'm sitting at home, in my pajamas, eating cinnamon twists and lukewarm delivery pizza while watching a series about living in Alaska. Cinderella I am not.

"They really are beautiful dresses," Victoria says. She's sitting next to me on the couch, wearing an old West Point T-shirt and yoga pants.

The dresses are hanging in the doorway to my bedroom. We figured we should at least look at the pretty since we wouldn't get to wear it. But maybe that was a mistake. Maybe it's making us more depressed.

The real mistake was saying yes to Gideon's job offer in the first place. I haven't heard from him since I walked out. I did send him an invoice, which was promptly paid along with a very, very generous bonus. Like generous enough for me to never work again. I recognized it for what it was— payment for me to forget him.

It's not working. The paperwork on my parents' house came through, and they now own it, free and clear. Elena's legal debt is wiped out, and for the first time ever, she hasn't heard from Nick in weeks. She commented on how strange and lovely it is and wondered why it was happening. I only said I was so happy for her and that I hoped Nick kept keeping silent.

I haven't tried to contact Gideon. I already know he won't respond. I called Rustem, who did answer, and I ended up having dinner at his house with him and his mom. After meeting her, I can see why he became a wrestler—she's the most take-no-shit woman I've ever met while also being incredibly hospitable. I'm going again for dinner next week. We didn't talk about Gideon.

I did text Morgan, telling her how sorry I was about her dad and what she'd learned. No response from her, but I expected that. Raven did respond though, and we had a short chat. She wasn't ready to talk about most of it, but she did tell me she appreciated hearing from me. And that while her feelings about Gideon were very conflicted at the moment, he never looked so happy as when he was with me.

I was glad when she ended the call shortly after.

Victoria was more than eager to talk about *everything* though. I couldn't keep holding in all those secrets, not after that last explosive confrontation between all of them, so I poured everything out after swearing her to secrecy.

I can't tell if she's glad or sad that Gideon is out of my life. She's been so supportive it's hard to say what her real feelings are. And since she keeps bringing me comfort food and binge-watching TV shows with me, I won't ask.

"We should move to Alaska," I say. "Look, that shipping container they're living in is way nicer than some of the FOBs we were stationed at."

"That's the worst compliment ever. *Better than a FOB in Afghanistan.*" She gives me a sideways look. "And moving to Alaska isn't going to help you get over him."

I take a defiant bite of cinnamon twist. It's really only pizza dough rolled in cinnamon sugar and covered with cheap frosting, and somehow it tastes as despairing as I feel. "I'm doing fine," I say. "We've got that new job, my parents are debt-free for the first time in their lives, and I'm finally free to hang out with you again."

"While I'm very glad you're not holed up in his castle anymore," Victoria says, "all the good things come from *him*. And that makes it very hard for you to get over him."

She says *him* like Gideon is this boulder between us she has to talk around to get to me.

"I feel like I'm doing really well," I say. "And yeah, the new job is totally because he talked us up to that firm. Would you like me to tell them no, actually, we can't install a new system for you and make a ton of money for us?"

"Of course not." Victoria looks toward the dresses. "I'm just thinking maybe we should put them away."

The red velvet seems to look back at me, like it's so sad I'm not wearing it and wants to know what it's done wrong.

"Maybe we should put them on."

Victoria chokes on her wine. "I thought the plan was getting over him. Not wallowing!"

"It's not wallowing." I stand up and grab the dress off the doorjamb. "It's defiance. I bought this thing to wear to one single event. I can never wear it again. So I'm going to enjoy it and to hell with Gideon Wolfe."

Victoria's eyes are wide. "Oh my God, let's do our hair and makeup too."

Thirty minutes later, we've finished the bottle of wine and we look like a million dollars. No, a billion dollars. I'm not drunk, but my mood definitely feels fizzy. And very, very take-no-prisoners.

"I can't believe he's never going to see me in this." I take in the effect in the mirror from all sides. Here I am, looking like this with nowhere to go.

I wonder where Gideon is now. I'm certain he's not going to the gala. He's probably at his house, in the security control room, watching the feed from the drones. Or taking apart the car computer box. Or trying to decode his precious note-book. Or doing all three at once.

He'll be alone, without even Rustem to talk to. The other guys will probably be coming and going, but they'll be just as obsessed with the car thing and the notebooks as he is.

"Look what we're missing." Victoria holds her phone out to me. She's pulled up the gala's hashtag on Instagram. Morgan and Axel are there and so is Archer.

"Wait." I take the phone from her. "They're at it?"

She nods. "And I saw a picture of Gage too."

They're all there. At least most of them. Gideon's parents will be there too. God, he was so upset about having to deal with them even if he didn't show it. All those people gathered to celebrate his remarkable achievement… and he won't be there. He thinks he doesn't deserve to be there.

"We're going to this thing."

Victoria takes her phone back. "What? I know you didn't drink that much."

"We have two tickets, we're all dressed up… We're going."

She looks skeptical, but she reaches for her purse anyway. "Is this more defiance?" she asks hopefully. "One last screw-you?"

I smile sadly. "It's much, much worse. I think it's love."

CHAPTER 35

I've done everything I can to make Tess happy, to make sure her life is secure. Except for this one last thing.

I tap the folded paper with the name on it on my desk, my notebook open to a random page. We've been working around the clock to decode the notebooks and gotten nowhere. We've even gone through Tynan's notebook along with everything of his left behind that we could find. Nothing.

We're also taking apart the control box from the car, although that's more difficult because we used discarded electronics to build it five years ago. It was almost obsolete then, and it's super obsolete now. Finding even the cables to connect to it is proving difficult. Cassian had to get in touch with a lab in Russia to get one of them that we needed.

Cassian's taken the lead on the car computer. He says since it was given to him, it's his responsibility.

If I had it here, I'd destroy it. Just smash it to bits, then burn both the notebooks. I'd leave the ashes and broken parts for the thief to find. It'd be my greatest fuck-you yet.

They want to blackmail me, fuck with my mind? Fine. The people who'd be hurt the worst by our secrets—Morgan and Raven—already know. We pulled the pin on that grenade. Anyone else? I don't care about them.

I do care about Tess. Deeply. But if she stays, if whoever's behind this sees what she means to me… Without the box and the notebooks to threaten us with, they might go after Tess next.

So I'll stay here, luring them back. Holding on to these fucking notebooks and playing Clue with the box they somehow fished out of the ocean. And I'll never let them know how badly I want to be with Tess. How much I miss her.

All this time I thought it might be one of the guys who started this, and they're the only ones left around me. Morgan won't answer my texts, Raven says she isn't ready to talk, and Rustem and Tess are gone. I drove them away to save them, but their absence echoes through the house. Especially Tess's.

I open the scrap of paper and study the name there. A few calls and his life is over. And one last call when it's done and he'll know exactly why I did it. It'll be exactly like when I called that piece of shit who married Tess's sister, only so much more satisfying.

Because this is the man who hurt Tess. I found her harasser. And I'm going to absolutely destroy him.

I can't touch the car control box or the notebooks, and I definitely can't smash any more security panels—not when Tess put them in with her own two hands—but I can smash the shit out of him. At least figuratively.

I pick up my phone. Time to make the first call in a long series, a series that will end in his ruin. He's about to get all his debts called in—every single one. He's sure as shit going to lose his cushy defense contracting job.

My eye falls on the knitted stuffed animal on my desk. It's a horned bear-lion thing—a beast that Tess knitted just for me. She left it as a surprise the morning after we first made love, giggling at my horrified reaction.

It's knobby and cuddly and so not me. I love it.

"Gulizar," I say.

"Yes?" She sounds infinitely patient. But of course she is—I programmed her to be that way.

"Remember how I said I was going to deactivate you?"

I did it in the heat of the aftermath of the car computer showing up. She wouldn't stop suggesting things, saying that my heart rate was too elevated, my movements too agitated, that I needed to calm down.

I told her I was going to shut her down and to shut up.

There's a pause. "Did I do something wrong?"

Fuck. How can a goddamn computer make me feel like such an utter monster? I pick up the stuffed toy, rubbing my thumb over its horns. I kept warning her I was a monster. But she fell for me anyway.

"Mr. Wolfe?" Gulizar says tentatively.

I give the toy one last stroke. "I'm not going to deactivate you. I'm sorry I said that."

I'm also not going to call anyone. Instead, Tess's plea that I not do anything about it comes back to me. What had she said —that he didn't remember her? That she'd put it all behind her?

It made no sense. The whole situation was unresolved. Her asshole was never punished. How could she put it behind her?

But she had. She built a company, helped her friend, was helping her parents and would be still helping them if I hadn't stepped in.

Tess is *brave.* Life sets her back again and again, and she keeps going forward. Keeps insisting on taking her loved ones with her as she goes forward. She doesn't want to bring up her harasser again not because she's afraid—although she is—it's because she's past him now.

The idiot brother-in-law was still an active threat, so she let me handle him. But if he stays gone, she'll leave him behind too.

I wonder what she'll do now, without the debts and the brother-in-law and her pick of clients. She'll still feel responsible for her family, for Victoria, and she'll be able to do whatever makes them happy. Because making them happy, keeping them safe, makes her happy.

But who's going to do that for her? See what's troubling her, what's a threat to her, and deal with it so she doesn't have to?

It could have been me if I hadn't run her off. We would have done that for each other. And more.

I was waiting for my past to be perfectly tied up in a neat bow before I fully committed to Tess, but she saw the truth: that will never happen. If I wait for everything to be resolved, I'll never be with her. And I need her.

She thinks I'm still worthy, even after she heard in painful detail what I'd done. The secrets that I'd kept. Maybe the only way to tie up my past, even with only a messy, incomplete knot, is with her by my side.

My phone buzzes with a text message. It's from Archer, who only says, *She's here.*

It takes me a moment and then I realize. He's at the gala.

And Tess is there too.

She went in spite of it all. Probably because she believes in some nonsense about celebrating the good I've done. And she's going to run into my parents. She'll meet them alone, without me by her side.

I never did get to see her dress.

Be there in twenty, I text back.

Carefully I put the little beast back in his spot on my desk. I get up, grab the notebooks, ready to put them both back in the safe. I'll have to arm the security system, make sure the drones are flying, and let Gage's team know I'm leaving.

But as I'm going through my mental checklist and walking out of the office, I pause. I stare at Tynan's notebook in my left hand, identical to mine except for the name on the cover. I've been holding on to this thing for five years. I spent the past few weeks guarding it with my life.

I should leave it out on the desk when I go.

It doesn't belong to whoever's trying to take it, but it doesn't belong to me either. We all assumed whoever tried to steal the notebook and sent the car computer system was trying to fuck with us or blackmail us... but what if they were trying to warn us?

I can't read the notebook. It's useless to me even if I were tempted to take what was Tynan's for my own gain. Maybe... maybe I shouldn't lock it up. See what happens.

Tess would probably tell me to let go of my past. To leave the notebook and this house and celebrate the good I've done. I won't be papering over my mistakes if I do it—we still have the car computer. We're not abandoning that.

I walk back to the desk and carefully set Tynan's notebook there. It's right out in the open for whoever wants to find it. Mine, I'm keeping. I think that's fair.

With an easy mind, I walk out of the office to get ready for the gala.

CHAPTER 36

The moment we step out of the car at the gala, I'm hit with a wave of indecision. We have tickets and we're dressed appropriately, but I'm worried we'll be turned away. Or even worse, kicked out once we get inside.

"Was this such a good idea?" I ask Victoria.

She raises her palms. "You're having second thoughts now?"

"I hope not."

We both turn at the sound of Cassian's voice to find him watching us from a side entrance. The new clinic is in the Dogpatch neighborhood, and we ended up parking next to a self-storage place. We definitely look out of place next to the industrial units.

"Gideon's not here, is he?" I ask.

"Of course not." Cassian's mouth quirks up. "But that's all the more reason for you to come." He offers an arm to Victoria.

She looks as if she'd like to refuse but doesn't want to be rude. And of course Cassian picks up on it.

"I don't bite."

Victoria raises an eyebrow. "Isn't this the point where you add *Unless you want me to.*"

"You want me to bite you?" Cassian wags a finger at her. "We've only just met."

Victoria's cheeks go red. "No. I don't. And I don't need someone to lean on."

"That's too bad," Cassian murmurs. "Because I was looking forward to being your escort."

I can't tell if Cassian is teasing her on purpose or if this is just how he is. The end result is the same: a very flustered Victoria. She hates charming men.

"Okay." I take a deep breath and throw my shoulders back. "We came all this way. We're going in."

There's an approving glint in Cassian's eye as he offers me his arm. After I take it, Victoria reluctantly takes his other arm.

The moment we walk in, we immediately attract attention. Since Gideon isn't here, everyone seems to want to talk with anyone who's connected with him.

"Is he coming?" one woman comes up to ask Cassian.

"Gideon does what he wants." Cassian smiles blandly at her. "If you'll excuse me, my dates need a drink."

"Dates?" Victoria hisses at him as we walk away.

"A turn of phrase. No one in this crowd will even bat an eye."

They don't, but many eyes are on us as we move through the main atrium. The entrance of the clinic is a large, airy space with an abundance of plants and trees and tiled paths snaking through them. I half expect a butterfly to land on my shoulders, attracted by the glitter of my golden capelet.

"The architects really outdid themselves with this," I say, reaching out to touch a flower drooping into the pathway.

"It was Gideon's idea," Cassian says. "But he'd want you to see the surgery rooms."

The rooms are cordoned off so we can peer inside but not tramp through. Gideon would have been happy to see that.

There are screens inside, playing a demo video, and someone from the development team is explaining how the surgery system works.

A family is watching as the developer talks, the woman pointing out something to the little girl. "See? That's what they had to do to Auntie to make her better." The woman waves to the developer, and she waves back like they're old friends. They must have gotten to know each other during the clinical trials or something.

Gideon helped save someone these people love. I bet these aren't the only people here who had loved ones go through the clinical trials.

I swallow hard and look away from the family because it's just too touching. Gideon should be here to see this. As I do, I catch sight of an older couple watching the demo video, their eyes narrowed as they take it all in. They look more like professionals at a conference than people enjoying a party.

It hits me then: they're Gideon's parents. There's nothing about them that particularly stands out, they don't even really look like him, but somehow I know.

When the woman catches my eye, recognition flashes over her face.

She knows me. How does she know me?

"You're Tess." She comes over with no hesitation.

"Yes," I say slowly. I notice that Cassian and Victoria have disappeared; I must have wandered away from them. "Have we met?"

I know we haven't, but I can't just blurt out that she's Gideon's mother. And I can't yell at her about messing him up so badly.

"I'm Dr. Talisa Wolfe, Gideon's mother. And this is his father, Jason." She gestures to the man next to her, who nods his head. I still don't see anything of Gideon in these people. "Gideon told us about you." She doesn't shake my hand, but she isn't exactly combative either. Curious is what I'd say. "He said that you'd be here with him."

Gideon told his parents about me? I'm so shocked—and touched—that I'm speechless.

Talisa looks around. "Where is he?"

I make myself smile. "Something came up. Are you enjoying the party?"

She sniffs. "When is he coming? I wanted to point out some things he needs to change."

"I couldn't say." I keep my smile plastered on. "Like I said, something came up. I'm so impressed that some of the patients and families are here—it's lovely to see the people this has already helped."

"They really shouldn't have people wandering through here," Jason says. "It's a clinic, not a ballroom."

Gideon said that exact same thing, but somehow it makes me grind my teeth coming from his dad. Maybe it's because they're his fricking parents and they should be over-the-moon proud, no matter what they think of the location.

"But it is nice that everyone can see it before it officially opens." I don't know why I'm trying to shove sunshine up their rears, but I suppose it beats getting angry with them.

Talisa gives me a look that says she suspects what I'm up to but isn't quite sure what to do about it. "You're not what I was expecting."

"Thanks," I say brightly. "So I'll tell Gideon that you really liked it then."

Her mouth flattens. Oh, she's definitely on to me now. "Never mind. You're exactly what I was expecting."

"Brilliant and beautiful and the perfect woman?" Gideon's arm slides around my waist at the same moment he speaks those words.

Words that leave me stunned and speechless. He came and he's... saying *that* to his parents? I must be dreaming.

But he's so large, so solid, and I can smell his soap, which has never happened in my dreams before.

He presses a kiss to my temple. "Hey. Sorry I'm late."

"Hey," I say weakly. I'm glad he's got his arm around me because my knees are wobbly with shock.

"Mom. Dad." His smile is so sharp I'm amazed his mouth isn't bleeding. "So glad you could make it."

I lean into him to remind him that he doesn't have to do this. He can be polite, distant, and not let them get to him.

He glances down at me and his expression softens. "I'm so glad you already met Tess," he says to his parents without looking away from me.

"They were telling me how much they like the clinic."

Gideon looks like he wants to laugh at that obvious lie, but he appreciates it anyway. "Good. I'm glad it has the approval of two highly regarded surgeons."

As opposed to all the neurosurgeons his team worked with to develop the system and the ones who'll be working in here day to day.

"About that—" His dad holds up a finger, finally contributing to the conversation. "There're things you need to change—"

I clutch at Gideon's arm. "Oh no, there's Raven and she looks upset. I'm so sorry," I say to his parents, "but we have to go deal with this. I hope we can chat later!"

I then hustle Gideon away as fast as I can. He should see some of the good things happening here tonight before his parents go in on him. Or maybe we can avoid his parents altogether.

"*Is* Raven here?" he asks, a faint note of hope in his tone.

"I'm sorry," I say. "She was the first person who came to mind."

He looks around, then ducks us both past a No Admittance sign into a deserted hallway. From there, he pulls us into an empty office.

"I don't think we're supposed to be here," I say.

His expression is amused. "My name's on the building. Also, how much did that dress cost? Because whatever you paid for it wasn't enough—you look fucking fantastic. Like a goddamn queen."

My face flushes as I look up at him. He slides a hand along my jaw, cupping my warm cheeks.

"You came," I say wonderingly.

"I did. And I'm sorry I'm late. Without you around to tell me to pull my head out of my ass, it takes me a while to actually pull my head out of my ass."

He hasn't said anything about the notebooks or the intruder or the car control system or Raven or Morgan. Which means none of that has been resolved.

But he still came.

"Why did you decide to come?" I ask.

"It was you and your bravery."

"My bravery?" I frown. "But I didn't do anything."

"About the past," he says. "You didn't let yourself obsess like I did. You went forward, built something that could help your family, help your friend. You didn't hole yourself up in some compound."

"I didn't have a compound to hole up in," I point out. "And I did wallow a bit when I got back. And my parents helped me."

He shakes his head. "But you still did it. And when I tried to drag the past back into your life, you wouldn't let me. You tried your damnedest to drag *me* out of *my* past."

"You've done great things." I gesture to the clinic. "And awful ones too. I don't want the awful ones to be all that defines you because…"

I can't finish. It's too raw, always so raw with him. Maybe that's why I love him—because he strips me down to my essence so easily. I mean, we're in the middle of a massive black-tie event and having this intense, intimate confession. And it feels raw and right.

"I don't want them to be either." His tone is quiet, serious. "Because I love you and want to be worthy of you."

Aww, jeez. I bite my lip. "I'm not…" I shake my head. "You are."

He kisses me then, soft and slow. "Don't argue," he says, his words full to the brim of affection. "Just kiss me."

I'm very tempted to. "Wait." I put my hand in the middle of his chest. "Didn't you just say that you love me?"

He nods.

"Don't you need me to say it too?"

"No. It's enough that you're here with me." But something pained flickers deep in his eyes.

Ah, my beautiful beast. He wants the words, but he loves me enough to be with me without them. He doesn't have to choose though.

"Too bad. Because I'm going to say it. I love you."

The expression that comes over his face… It's like he can't even believe emotions like he's experiencing exist, but he's so, so grateful they do.

He kisses me again, deep and slow, and we breathe together. Live in this exquisite moment together.

"Let's get out of here," he growls after a while.

Reluctantly I shake my head. "Everyone is here to see you. And it would mean a lot to your team if you went and saw the demos."

"I gave them a bonus," he grumbles. "A very generous one."

If the bonus he gave me is any measure, they got a super generous bonus. "You still need to say hi and show your face."

His scowl doesn't let up.

"The champagne is pretty good," I say. "And I did get all dressed up."

That finally makes him give in. "Okay. Twenty minutes. And then we go home."

"Thirty. Literally every person here is here to see you."

He sighs as he takes my arm. "I love that you make me a better person, yet I also hate it."

I nestle close to him, savoring his nearness. "You'll have the rest of your life to get used to it."

"God," he says fervently, "that's the best thing I've heard in forever."

CHAPTER 37

When we arrive at the house, I go immediately to my office. Yeah, I know I'm turning over a new leaf and leaving the past behind—and Tess was so happy when I told her what I'd done—but I still need to see what's happened.

The notebook is still there, right where I left it.

The tension leaves me in a rush. I'm not exactly happy to see the notebook still there, although I suppose I am relieved.

Tess comes in behind me, in her gorgeous dress. I've been dreaming of tearing it off her the entire car ride. I'd leave the shoulder-jewelry thing though.

Her mouth compresses when she sees the notebook. "I was hoping it would be gone."

"Me too," I confess. I shake my head. "I thought… I guess I was wrong though."

"Maybe you should put it back. Just in case."

She's right. It feels heavier than usual when I pick it up, but that's just an illusion. It's the psychic weight of it that's gotten to me, not the physical weight.

"I can just take it from you now."

I spin at the strange voice, putting Tess behind me.

The thief is there. Her mask is off, her hair loose over her shoulders. She's all in black again and looking very, very relaxed.

"The cameras are on," I warn her.

She shrugs. "The mask is a precaution, but I have others. I doubt you found anything from the last picture you got." Her expression turns smug. "Actually, I know you didn't."

"Who's paying you?" Tess asks. "We could negotiate something."

Smart Tess, offering to pay more. I don't think this person will take it, but it's worth a shot.

"It's not about the money." A touch of anger threads through the thief's tone. "I only want the notebook."

"Why? Can you read it?"

Surprise flickers through her before she can catch it. "It's not for me. And who's paying me isn't your business. You can hand it to me now, or we can keep playing this game. Your system is good, but you have to be lucky all the time. I only have to be lucky once."

My stance hardens. That sounds suspiciously like a threat. "And what happens to me once you have the notebook? You keep coming for… I don't even know what."

"Once I have the notebook and deliver it safely, we're done."

I narrow my eyes. "And the computer?"

Again, she can't quite catch her confusion in time. "I'm only here for the notebook."

She doesn't know about the computer sent to Cassian, and she doesn't know the notebook's in code. We could try harder to get the name of her client out of her, but I'm beginning to suspect she might not know that either.

But she did get mad when Tess made the offer of more money…

I hand over the notebook, keeping my expression hard and still. "It's useless to me."

Tess's hands reach for me, her fingers curling into the fabric of my shirt. "Are you sure?" she whispers.

I keep holding out the notebook. I'm not sure actually, but it's time to move forward. The past—and this fucking notebook—aren't going to chain me down anymore.

The intruder comes forward slowly, cautiously. She's not quite as certain about this as she pretends to be. But she takes hold of the notebook as soon as she's close enough.

I don't let go right away. "Gage is going to find you."

That brings back some of her bravado. "Good luck to him then." She pulls the notebook out of my grip. "Thanks."

"Tell him…" My voice falters. I hadn't really prepared what I wanted to say and my thoughts are scrambled. "Tell him we're waiting for him."

"I don't know who you're talking about." This time the intruder's not surprised.

And then she's gone.

I reach behind me for Tess's arm, wrap it around my waist. I sure as shit hope I did the right thing. But having Tess here helps with the guilt and second-guessing. And everything, really.

"Why did you do that?" Tess asks. "After everything, you just… let it go." She sounded horrified and impressed in equal measures.

I take her hand and lead her toward the door. We have to get to the security room, run the new pictures we've got just in case. "One, Archer has a copy now. Two, I put a nanotracker inside it, in the binding."

"When did you do that?"

"When I first got the thing. I didn't want to lose it."

She blinks up at me as we move through the hallway. "I have a feeling there's a three."

"Oh yeah. There's a three." I stop dead when I see Rustem in the hallway, going toward the kitchen. He lifts his chin and grunts in greeting, which is the most effusive welcome he's ever given me.

I'm happy to see him too.

Tess waves to him and gets a smile.

"I texted him while we were at the gala," she says. "You know you wanted him to come back."

I did, and it would have taken me forever to figure out how to approach him without losing face. And Tess just up and texted him and here he is.

I kiss her forehead because I'm so goddamn lucky she's here. "I'm going to enjoy you turning my life inside out, aren't I?"

"I'm definitely going to enjoy doing it." Her smile fades. "Wait, what was number three?"

Oh yeah, number three. Can't forget that one.

"I think Tynan's alive," I say. "And he's the one who hired her to take the book."

CHAPTER 38

"He can't be alive."

Bishop looks as stunned as the rest of them, but only he says out loud what they all must be thinking.

Except for maybe Archer. I don't know him that well, but he seems not as surprised.

"It's the simplest explanation," Gideon says. He's called them all to his office, Raven and Morgan included, to tell them about what happened last night.

"Yes, someone coming back from the dead is very simple," Gage says.

Morgan goes pale. "I can hardly believe it," she says. "All this time I thought…"

Raven reaches over and squeezes her hand. She looks hopefully at Gideon. "If Tynan's alive, does that mean Dad might have gotten out too?"

Bishop closes his eyes briefly, tightly. "We saw him though. When we…"

"When we closed the coffin," Archer finishes.

"Right." Raven nods her head sharply. "Right."

Morgan lifts her hand. "But Tynan might have gotten out, right? And he's… he's sending you things from the car? And trying to steal his notebook that Dad left him?"

"I realize it sounds like… a lot," Gideon says gently. "But it makes the most sense."

Morgan inhales sharply. "But why disappear? Why hide from us?"

"And why come back now?" Cassian asks. He holds up the car computer, which he's brought with him. "Why send us this?"

Gage rubs at his forehead. "Because something happened when the car crashed. Something that made him think it wasn't an accident."

"So he suspects it was one of us trying to kill him?" Bishop rumbles.

Gideon nods. "It's what I did. Maybe…" He gestures to the computer Cassian is still holding. "Maybe there's something in there we need to find. Or maybe he's warning us he's back for his revenge."

"I can help." That comes from Victoria, who's been sitting quietly and taking it all in this entire time. She came home with us last night and stayed in the cottage. "It looks like some of the equipment we had to use in the Army."

It does, but I'm surprised Victoria offered. This isn't her fight, although she is here in the room. And she doesn't like Cassian.

Cassian looks solemn, like he knows that offer from Victoria shouldn't have happened. "Thank you."

Victoria goes pink. "I just want to get inside that thing." Then she goes red as she realizes how that sounds.

Cassian opens his mouth, thinks better of it, closes it again.

Gideon clears his throat. "Like I said, maybe there's something to find there. And maybe there's something in the notebooks Tynan needs to find."

"The thief did say that she only wanted the notebook," I say. "And she didn't seem to know anything about the computer. So if Tynan did suspect you at first, he seems to have changed his mind."

Gideon shakes his head. "Don't assume that. He's been gone so long we can't even begin to guess at what he's thinking. We have to allow for the possibility he's not on our side. Or that he's actively against us."

"Even assuming that, why not show himself?" Morgan is pleading now.

"I don't know," Gideon says. "He must suspect we'll guess he's still alive. So he doesn't want the rest of the world to know he's alive."

Archer nods. "We have to keep quiet about this. All of us."

"So we're back exactly where we started," Gage says curtly. "Holding jack shit."

"That's not true." Morgan's tone is quiet. "We know that Tynan's probably still alive. That's… that's huge."

"And you guys finally told us the truth about the accident," Raven says. She and her sister exchange a look. "Which you should have done from the very beginning."

"We know," Bishop says, not looking at her.

"I want to see the notebooks too," Morgan says. "You guys owe me at least that much."

"You can't show Beck," Gage says.

"He's my partner." Morgan's stance is tight with defiance. "In every sense of the word. Of course I'll show him."

"Let her see them," Archer says. "She'll probably catch something that I've missed."

Gage doesn't look happy, but he doesn't protest.

"So," Gideon says, "we have notebooks to decode." He looks to Archer. "A computer to resurrect and search through." Cassian nods. "And a thief to track." Gage raises his eyebrows in acknowledgment.

"What about Tynan?" Bishop asks. "Assuming he really is alive."

"We'll look for him," Raven says. "Starting by going

through everything he left behind, everything we can remember of him."

Morgan swallows hard. "I can help."

"I didn't want to presume," Raven says.

Morgan smiles faintly. "As if you ever could."

Gideon spreads his hands. "Looks like we're holding quite a bit more than jack shit." He closes his hands, his expression going solemn. "And we're all together again. Like we really haven't been since Ira died. That has to count for something."

There's a long moment where they soak that in. A moment filled with affection, solidarity, and a tinge of sadness too. Grief binds them together as much as a shared history does.

"It does." Morgan says that, which surprises me. I thought she'd hold out the longest. "But without Tynan, we're not all together."

"And that's why we're going to find him," Bishop says.

"Damn straight," Gideon says.

I reach for his arm because I have to touch him right now. He's bringing them all back together.

Archer sees and a faint smile crosses his mouth. "Well, we should get to it then. And let you two get back to whatever you were doing."

Raven's eyes go wide. "Oh my God, that's right. We interrupted you guys."

"No," I say, right as Gideon says very seriously, "Yes, you did."

"Interrupted you doing what?" Archer asks with a knowing look.

"Work," I insist, my cheeks heating. "Seriously, we've been running the new pictures we have—and the voice files— through the recognition software. And I have a new client, one who's got a ton of work for me."

"Oh yes, definitely work." Gideon says that so deadpan I have to give him a very hard look.

Raven rushes over to hug me. I'm so shocked I simply stand there in her arms.

"Stop teasing her," Raven commands them all. "Do you want to scare her away?"

"It'll take more than that." Gideon is smiling at me with love, affection, and all the warmth in the world.

"I'm not scared," I say as Raven squeezes me again.

"We'll get out of your hair." She winks, then turns to the rest of them. "Come on, we have work to do."

They head to the door, all of them looking happier than when they came in. Or at least resolved and determined—it's a stretch to call Gage's expression happy.

"Could someone give me a ride to the Caltrain station?" Victoria asks.

Before I can tell her we'll call for a car, Cassian says, "I'll take you. All the way home." He shrugs as if he doesn't really care if she accepts his offer. "We can talk about the computer on the way."

"Sure." Victoria's expression is strained, but she follows him out. *Call me*, I mouth to her as she goes by.

When they're gone, I turn to Gideon. He's watching me with a solemn, almost puzzled expression.

"You brought everyone back together," I say. "You should be proud."

"I tore us apart to begin with." But his protest is routine.

"Then you put it back together, which is good."

He pulls me close, kisses me quick and sweet. "You just won't give up on this, will you?"

"I won't give up on you. Not ever."

"And thank God for it." He seals that with a deep, romantic kiss. The kind that will last.

CHAPTER 39

When it's all over and the guys have finally left, I feel like I've been through several rounds in the boxing ring with Rustem —exhausted, wrung out, but satisfied.

Speaking of Rustem, I need to find him tomorrow and let him beat the piss out of me in the gym. I owe him for tossing him out like that. Luckily Tess was here to save me from myself.

"We really should get back to work," she says regretfully, still nestled in my arms.

She's right, and now's not the time to drag her upstairs and have my wicked way with her. Tonight will be though.

With a sigh to let her know I'm doing this against my will, I lead her out of the office. "My parents found me again last night," I say as we walk back to the security room.

"I hope they told you how proud they were of you."

I snort. "They told me everything I should have changed before we even started building the place. They never, ever stop."

She looks so damn mad my heart lightens. Tess is ready to take on my parents, and I love it.

"They shouldn't have done that," she says angrily. "I hope you told them to fuck off."

I shake my head. "It would have caused a scene, and it wasn't worth it. I did that thing that you did and talked around everything she said. It drove her nuts. I don't think I've ever seen her that seethingly angry. At least not since I dropped out of med school."

"I'm so sorry."

Although I don't need it, I let Tess's sympathy wash over me. This is what it means to be loved—to take this comfort and goodness even though you don't technically *need* it. But it makes you feel so complete you'll always take it.

"It doesn't matter," I say. "I've got you, Tynan might still be alive, and my closest friends haven't turned on me like I thought. My parents' approval would be nothing compared to those."

She leans her head into my chest. It comforts and strengthens me all at once.

"Honestly," I say, "as they were walking away, I realized I really didn't care. At all. I just wanted to find you again and get home. And to say thank you to my team. They did something really amazing."

"You helped."

"A little," I admit. "I want to build more of those clinics. All over the country."

"You will. Even if we never find where Tynan is or what secrets are hiding in the notebooks, you'll continue to do good things."

I pause in the doorway of the security room and take her in. Precious, beautiful, wondrous Tess. Who thinks I do good in this world even though I've definitely done bad.

But she still appreciates—and loves—the beast inside of me.

"I still don't count this as a real vacation," Gideon growls as he helps me into the hired car.

I can see his point. It's ninety degrees and about to rain, the air is too thick to breathe, and we are technically working. But we're just now leaving the Phillips Collection, and we're supposed to spend all day tomorrow at Glenstone, and we spent yesterday afternoon on the National Mall, so yeah, it's a vacation for me. I've never been to DC before, and Gideon is determined to show me *everything*.

And the work part isn't anything boring—Gideon is here to talk to the head of the VA medical system about putting his neurosurgery systems in their clinics. I'm between big jobs at the moment, and I've hired on an entire crew since things are so busy, so I get to simply sit in the background and listen as he sells them on his amazingness.

"Trust me, this is definitely a vacation," I say.

Gideon slides in next to me and shuts the door. He nods to the driver, who puts up the privacy partition and then pulls into traffic.

"Wait until the yacht," Gideon says. "Then you'll see this is nothing."

He might have a point. Gideon hired a private yacht with

a complete crew to take us, my parents, and my sister on a trip to Hawaii and other islands in the Pacific. When he told me about it, he said, "Your parents and sister deserve it," which was a pretty sneaky way to get me to agree. But he was right—they do.

"Yes, but you won't be impressing high-level members of the government on the yacht."

He rolls his eyes. "It doesn't take much to turn your head, does it?"

I snuggle up next to him. "*You* turn my head." I trail my fingers down his thigh. "Along with other parts of me."

His laugh is low and wicked. "I didn't know that part of you could turn."

"Maybe you just haven't explored it thoroughly enough."

He narrows his eyes. "Is that a dare? Because I'm pretty damn thorough with you every night. But we could go deeper..."

I shiver at the idea. He'll make that threat real and turn me inside out in the process. I swallow hard. "Let's forget dinner and go back to the hotel."

"This is why I love you," he says with a knowing smile. "Because you have the best plans. Of course, we could start right here."

"And that's why I love you," I say as he dips his head, his fingers finding my buttons. "Because you make my plans even better."

ABOUT THE AUTHOR

Raleigh fell in love with billionaire romance as a teenager thanks to Harlequin Presents. She fell in love with San Francisco in her twenties thanks to how charming the city was. And she fell for a coding genius thanks to how charming *he* was.

Naturally, she had to put all of the things she loved into her romances.

You can find her online at www.raleighdavis.com.

Alois Essigmann

Sagen und Märchen Altindiens

Teil 1. Vom Weltalter der Götter bis zum Herrschergeschlecht Kaurava. Mit Begriffsregister.

Meine liebe, stille Mutter!

Als Du vor drei Jahrzehnten Deinen Kindern Märchen vorlasest, waren sie alle erstaunt: Du konntest Deine sanfte Stimme zur Härte zwingen, wenn Du als Harun al Raschid den bösen Kalum-Bel verurteiltest. – Nie hatten sie solches von Dir erwartet.

Wie recht tatest Du, keinerlei Pathos an diese flache Tatsachenwelt zu verschwenden, Maß zu halten in allem was sich messen lässt, und dafür in der Unendlichkeit der Phantasie zu schwelgen! Wenn ich diese Arbeit Deinem Andenken weihe, so dankt der Mann seiner Kindheit. Das gärende Werden, das zwischen Anfang und Reife liegt, lag auch zwischen Mutter und Sohn, wie die Jugend zwischen Kind und Mann.

Es ist vorbei! Alle Irrwege haben sich zum sicheren Pfad vereinigt.

Nimm hier die erste Frucht, die ich an diesem Wege zum Glück gepflückt habe. Du bist ja noch unter uns, als wärest Du am Leben!

Dein dankschuldiger Sohn
Alois Essigmann.

Inhaltsverzeichnis

Diese Sagen und Märchen sind nicht nur Tausende von Jahren alt, sie sind auch im Laufe vieler Jahrhunderte, vielleicht Jahrtausende, entstanden, lange Zeit nur mündlich überliefert, und auch nach der Niederschrift noch durch Jahrhunderte hindurch geändert, erweitert, den Sitten und Gebräuchen der Zeit, sowie dem Geschmack der jeweiligen Dichter angepasst worden.

So erklärt sich mancher Widerspruch in der Auffassung und Verehrung von Göttern und Helden, in Landesbräuchen usw.

Zu merken wäre, dass die ältesten Inder ein sehr kriegerisches Volk waren und leibhaftige Naturkräfte als Gottheiten verehrten (Indra, Varuna, Agni usw.). Später aber riss der Priesterstand die Herrschaft an sich, die Naturgötter mussten sich den erdachten Repräsentanten der sittlichen Ordnung (Brahma, Wischnu, Dharma usw.), und Könige, Krieger und Volk, ihren Priestern, den Brahmanen, beugen.

Mit dem der Allgemeinheit geläufigen Buchstabenmaterial ist es nicht möglich, ein vollkommen klangtreues Lautbild der altindischen Namen und Worte zu geben. Ich habe mich deshalb mit einer Annäherung begnügt und möchte nur noch bemerken, dass bei der von mir gewählten Schreibweise das Sch, sch, im Anlaut *weich* gesprochen wird. Die letzte Silbe der Frauennamen ist lang.

Im Anhang habe ich ein alphabetisches Namensverzeichnis angefügt, welches manchen durch die vielen Namen vielleicht verwirrten Leser rasch über die Beziehung einzelner Personen zur Erzählung orientieren mag.

Im Weltalter der Götter

Schöpfung und Flut

Eine Ewigkeit hatte Brahma als Nichts auf dem Rücken der Urschlange Sescha geruht und sich zum All gesammelt.

Dann schuf sein Denken die zehn Schöpfer!

Sie wurden die Väter der Götter und Dämonen, die Ahnherren der Menschen, und bauten mit ihnen Welten aus dem All.

Kaschjapa, einer der Schöpfer, nahm die Töchter des Schöpfers Dakscha zu Gattinnen:

Aditi schenkte ihm die Adita oder Götter, Diti die Daitia und Danu die Danawa, zwei den Göttern feindliche Dämonengeschlechter.

Der Sohn der Sonne aber war Manu, der erste Mensch.

Im Auf und Ab der Zeiten vermehrten sich die Geschöpfe schier ins Unendliche, da dem Leben noch kein Ende gesetzt war.

Brahma versank in tiefes Denken:

Er wollte dem wuchernden Leben Einhalt gebieten, doch er konnte kein Mittel finden, den Strom der Fruchtbarkeit einzudämmen: Sein schöpferischer Wille hatte ihn hervorgebracht, und der war für ewige Zeiten unabänderlich.

Da schlugen, im Zorn über seine Hilflosigkeit lohende Flammen aus den Augen des ohnmächtigen Allmächtigen und drohten die Welt zu verzehren!

Der Gott Schiwa aber fühlte inniges Mitleid mit allem Leben und bat den Erhabenen seinen Zorn zu mäßigen, dass dessen Feuer das herrliche All nicht fräße.

Die Flammen erloschen vor diesem Hauch des Alleinempfindens!

Ein Tropfen fiel von der Stirne Brahmas und ward zu einem ernsten, schwarzäugigen Weib in purpurnem Kleide.

Nach Süden wandte es sich um von dannen zu schreiten, als der Herr es anrief: „Du Furcht meines Denkens über Vernichtung des Lebens sollst Tod heißen: Du geh und schlage Weise wie Tore, Gute wie Böse und alles was lebt, auf dass es nicht mehr erstehe, denn die Welt sinkt schier ins Wasser von seiner Last!"

Laut weinend warf sich die Lotusgeschmückte vor dem Allmächtigen auf die Knie und barg ihr Antlitz in seinen Händen.

„Gnade! Du Herr der Welt!", schluchzte sie. „Soll ich Kindern und Greisen, Starken und Schwachen, Sündern und Büßern mit gleichem Maß messen? – Wie wird man mich hassen, wenn Vater und Mutter, Gattin, Freund und das Kind in der Wiege dahinschwinden! Durch alle Ewigkeiten werden die Tränen der Unglücklichen mich brennen! – Gnade! Du gütiger Vater der Wesen!"

„Mein Wort ist unabänderlich und ewig!", sprach der Herr: „Tod soll das Leben enden! Doch Du wirst vor den Geschöpfen ohne Schuld sein: Du liebst sie, Du sollst sie befreien! Zorn, Hass und Neid werden ihren Untergang zeitigen, ehe sie in Deinen Armen Ruhe finden; die Tränen, die Du in meine Hand geweint, will ich als Siechtum über die Erde streuen, sodass die Vergehenden Dich als Erlösung ehren: Mögen die Sünder durch ihre Sünden vergehen – Du bist die sühnende Gerechtigkeit, die sie, ohne Hass, ohne Liebe, aufnimmt! Und Yama, der Herr über das Recht ist, soll auch Herr sein über Dich, Tod!"

So war Tod in die Welt gekommen, auf dass sie sich ewig erneuere!

Noch einmal drohte allem Atmenden der Untergang, als ein Danawa dem ruhenden Brahma die heilige Lehre Weda stahl, die dem schlafenden Gott über die Lippen quoll.

Der Erwachte beschloss eine Flut über die Erde fegen zu lassen und sich eines edlen Menschen zu bedienen, um die entsühnte Welt mit neuen Geschöpfen zu bevölkern:

An den Ufern der Wirni stand Manu, in strenger Bußübung die Arme zum Himmel erhoben, den Blick in die eilenden Wellen des Flusses versenkt.

Da schwamm ein kleines Fischlein auf ihn zu und sprach mit menschlicher Stimme:

„Sieh! Du büßender Gerechter: Die großen Fische fressen die kleinen, die Starken verdrängen die Schwachen! Ich bin in steter Sorge um mein Leben. Rette mich, edelmütiger Büß0er, vor dieser verzehrenden Furcht!"

Voll Mitleid schöpfte Manu das Fischlein mit der hohlen Hand aus dem Fluss und trug es rasch nach Hause. Dort setzte er es in eine silberne Schüssel, pflegte seinen Schützling voll frommen Eifers und liebte ihn wie einen Sohn.

Aber das Fischlein wuchs unter der Sorgfalt des Guten rasch und hatte bald nicht genug Raum in der Schüssel.

Auf seine Bitte setzte Manu es in einen großen Weiher: der maß drei Meilen in der Länge und eine in der Breite.

Doch der Fisch wuchs weiter und nach einiger Zeit ward ihm auch dieses Wasser zu eng.

Wieder bat er seinen gütigen Pfleger, ihn in ein größeres Gewässer zu setzen:

„Zur Ganga bringe mich, zu des Meeres Gattin! Dort möchte ich mich tummeln, Du Lieber! Doch tu wie Du willst – Du bist der Herr, denn Deiner Güte verdank' ich das Wachstum, Du Sündenloser!"

So brachte Manu den Fisch nach der Ganga, und als ihn auch die Ufer dieses Stromes beengten, trug er ihn nach dem weiten Meer. Dort setzte er den Riesenfisch, der einen himmlischen Wohlgeruch ausströmte, in die lockende Flut.

Der Fisch aber sprach mit freundlichem Lächeln:

„Du, Glückseliger, hast mich in treuer Sorge erhalten, so höre meinen Rat und handle darnach:

Bald wird die große Reinigungsflut über die Erde fegen, denn Lebendem und Totem ist die Zeit des Schreckens nahe!

Baue ein Schiff und besteig es mit den sieben Heiligen! Und Samen aller Ort nimm auf und bewahre ihn wohl! Harre meiner, wenn die Flut Dich trägt! An einem Horne sollst Du mich erkennen!" „Ich will tun, wie Du geraten hast!", sprach Manu, und als der Fisch untertauchte, schritt er in den Wald und begann den Schiffbau.

Als das Schiff fertig und genau nach des Fisches Rat beladen war, hob sich die Flut über die Erde und Manu glitt auf den Wogen dahin.

Und als er des wunderbaren Fisches gedachte, kam dieser geschwommen, und Manu sah an seiner Stirne ein großes Horn.

Daran musste nun der Büßer sein Schiff binden, und in schneller Fahrt zog es der Fisch über die weite Meeresflut.

Stürme tobten über das Wasser, dass sie schier Sonne, Mond und Sterne verlöschten! Nur die sieben Heiligen, die mit Manu über das Wasser glitten, erglänzten im reinen Licht ihres sündenlosen Seins. Das Schiff tanzte über die Wellen, wie ein liebetrunkenes Weib. Alles Land war versunken, und schier endlos schienen die Wasser.

Viele Jahre zog der Fisch schweigend das Schiff durch die Nacht!

Endlich stieß es an den höchsten Gipfel des Himawat und Manu musste es auf Geheiß des Fisches dort
anbinden; heute noch nennt das indische Volk den Berg
„Schiffsbindung".

Der geheimnisvolle Fisch aber sprach zu Manu:

„Ich bin Brahma, das höchste und ewige Wesen!

Dich habe ich aus der Flut gerettet, auf dass Du meine
Welt mit neuen Geschöpfen bevölkerst: Bete und schaffe,
so wird es Dir gelingen!"

Damit verschwand der Gott vor den Augen Manus.

Als die Wasser sich verliefen, reinigte der Gerettete
seine Seele in frommer Sammlung, dann breitete er neues
Leben über die weite Erde.

Die Götter und ihre Feinde

Mitten im Weltall ragt der Berg Meru in den Himmel
und durch die Erde in die Unterwelt.

Er ist der geheiligte Sitz der Götter, den Sonne, Mond
und Sterne voll Ehrfurcht rechtshin umwandeln und von
allen Seiten mit ihrer Lichtflut umspülen.

Wie Strahlen um einen Stern, liegen die Erdteile um ihn.

Auf seinen Höhen wohnen die Götter unter der Herrschaft des kriegerischen *Indras.*

Schakra, der Mächtige, heißt er allen, denn er hat die
schwankende Erde befestigt und das Blau des Himmels
darüber gespannt. Er verteidigt sie gegen Daitia und
Danawa in ruhmreichen Kämpfen und segnet sie mit
fruchtbringendem Regen in schenkendem Frieden.

Die *Wasu* oder Erdengötter, die Rudra und Maruta,
Wind- und Wettergötter, die lieblichen Apsaras, himmli-
sche Wasserjungfrauen, und des Himmels Spielleute: die
Gandharva, sie alle ziehen in Indras Gefolge einher und

beglücken Mensch und Tier, Baum und Gras, ja den dürstenden Sand in der Wüste, mit ihren freundlichen Gaben.

Schatschi, die Macht, ist des Götterkönigs Gattin, ein ragendes Beispiel weiblicher Treue. Sie kost mit dem geliebten Gatten, wenn er aus der Schlacht kommt, sie schmückt ihm den Herdsitz, wenn er ruht nach friedlicher Reise, auf der er Flüsse, Seen und Teiche gefüllt und nach der Ordnung in den Reichen der Erde gesehen hat.

Der große, blonde Sohn der Aditi ist der Vorkämpfer der Götter, wenn die Dämonenscharen der Diti- und Danusöhne sich gegen den Himmel wälzen. Er ist Meister aller Waffen, und siebenfarbig ist sein großer Bogen, der nach dem Kampf am Himmel hängt.

Varuna steht neben Indra, der mächtige Herr der Gewässer. Sein Reich ist das unendliche Meer mit all seinen Schätzen und die gewaltigen Ströme, die flinken Wasser der Erde. Geheimnisvoll wirkt er noch in dem kleinsten Grashalm, denn seinem Gesetze gehorcht alles Leben. Er ist ein mächtiger Hüter der Menschheit und wacht über ihre Sitte: Der Unklarheit, der Unwahrheit ist er Feind und straft sie mit Krankheit und heillosem Siechtum.

Agni, der milde Gott des Feuers, ist des Götterkönigs getreuer Freund und Kampfgenosse. Sein Wagen ist mit roten Stuten bespannt, und so stürmt er die hölzernen Burgen der Feinde.

Er ist der ewig Junge, der sich stets erneuert!

Gerne wohnt er bei den Menschen und trägt ihre Opfer zu den Göttern.

Auch Agni ist ein Freund der Wahrheit, und die Liebe zu ihr hat einst den Fluch eines Heiligen auf ihn geladen:

Der Seher Bhrigu warb um Puloma, die Braut eines Riesen, und führte sie als Gattin in seine Einsiedelei.

Verzweifelt irrte der verlassene Riese durch die Wälder, und als er zufällig die leere Klause des Heiligen betrat, warf er sich betend vor dem flackernden Hausfeuer nieder und flehte Agni um Wahrheit an: „Wo ist Puloma? – Du schwarzpfadiger Gott! wo weilt sie, deren liebliches Lachen mir eine glückliche Zukunft verhieß? Sprich, Du Siebenzüngiger, vor dessen Sitz die Ehen geschlossen werden: War sie die Meine, da sie sich mir versprochen? – Ward sie mir nicht *geraubt*? – Oh Du, der Du die ganze Welt durchziehst, der Du in Sonne, Mond und Sternen bist, wie in dem kleinsten Spanlicht; im opferfressenden Feuer, wie im winzigsten Tröpflein Blut – Du Allesseher! gib mir Wahrheit: wo weilt Puloma, und ist sie die Meine?“

Um der Wahrheit willen sagte Agni, dass Puloma des Riesen Weib sein müsste, dass sie aber nun als Gattin Bhrigus in der Einsiedelei hause.

Da verbarg sich der Riese in der Nähe und raubte die Heimkehrende ihrem Gatten.

Als Bhrigu sah, dass er sein Weib verloren hatte, verfluchte er den schwatzhaften Agni;

„Werde zum verachteten Allesesser! verzehre was Du berührst, – sei es rein oder unrein, erlaubt oder verpönt vom religiösen Gesetz – Dich soll darnach hungern, mundschneller Gott! – selbst Leichen sollen Dir noch als köstliche Speise munden!“

Entsetzt floh Agni vor dem Fluch des zürnenden Heiligen und verbarg seine Schmach im Meer, da der Hohn seine Feinde ihn ‚Allesfresser‘ nannte.

Mit einem Schlag hörten alle Opferfeuer zu brennen auf, die Götter hungerten, und die Menschen verkamen in Sittenlosigkeit.

In dieser Not baten die sieben Heiligen Brahma um Hilfe, denn ein feierlicher Fluch nimmt unaufhaltsam wie das Schicksal seinen Lauf: Das schnelle Wort kann nicht zurückgenommen, nur in seiner Wirkung gemildert werden.

Und der Allmächtige rief Agni vor sein Angesicht und sprach zu dem Betrübten: „Du wirst bis ans Ende der Zeiten dem Fluche folgen und verzehren was Du berührst! doch ich schenke Dir auch die Gabe, zu reinigen, was Du berührst. So bist Du zwar ein Allesesser, aber nichts Unreines wirst Du essen, denn Deine Berührung reinigt alles!"

Pavaka, der Reiniger, heißt Agni seither den Andächtigen.

Yama, der ernste Völkerversammler, der über den Tod und das Recht herrscht, ist ein nimmermüder Freund der Menschen und getreuer Hüter der Ordnung. Im Gefolge des schweigsamen Herrschers schreiten die Ahnen und Väter der Lebenden. Seine Boten schweifen über die Erde und führen die Gezeichneten in sein gastliches Haus.

Surya und *Soma*, der Gott der Sonne und des Mondes, teilen die Ewigkeit, auf dass sie als Zeit geregelt erscheine. *Surya* ruft täglich zu neuem Leben, und *Soma* lässt sein balsamisches Licht in die Nächte fließen, auf dass die Menschen darin Heilung und neue Kraft finden.

Uschas, die liebliche Morgenröte, erfreut Götter und Menschen, wenn sie das Himmelstor öffnet. Sie sendet alltäglich ihre beiden Reiter aus, um Verzweifelnde aus den Schrecken der Nacht zu erlösen.

Aswinas heißen die schönen Jünglinge, die auch die Ärzte des Himmels sind.

Kama, der Liebesgott, reitet als ewiger Jüngling auf einem bunten Papageien und schwingt seinen goldenen Bogen, an welchem eine Schnur wilder Bienen die Sehne ist. Duftende Blüten sind die Spitzen seiner sehnsuchtbefiederten Pfeile, und ihre Wunden heilt allein Kamas Gattin: *Rati*, die Lust.

Wischnu und *Schiwa*, Erhalter und Zerstörer, sind Teile des Schöpfers, sind er selbst, der urewig geheimnisvolle, dreieinige Gott *Brahma*.

Brihaspati, der weise Sohn des Angiras, versieht als Priester den Opferdienst im Himmel. Er ist der gütige Mittler zwischen den Aditisöhnen und Brahma, dem ehernen Schicksal, dem sich auch die Götter beugen müssen.

Nicht sorglos fließt ihr Leben dahin; sie kämpfen um ihr Dasein, wie die Erdenkinder, und ihre schrecklichsten Feinde sind die starken Söhne der Diti und Danu, die wilden Dämonen der Finsternis, der Dürre, der sengenden Glut.

Auf kühner Streife war es einst Bala, dem Danawafürsten, gelungen, die Kühe der Götter zu rauben und sie in der weiten Höhle eines Berges einzuschließen.

Indra zog an der Spitze des Götterheeres aus, die milchspendenden Freunde aller Geschöpfe zu befreien und die Frevler zu strafen.

Auf seinem edelsteingeschmückten Streitwagen, mit den goldenen Radbüchsen und Schienen, brauste der starkarmige Götterkönig durch die Luft, gefolgt von den flechtentragenden Windgenien in gefleckten Fellen, deren goldene Helme und Lanzen weithin über den Himmel glänzten.

In heißem Pfeil- und Speerkampf wurden die Danawa zurückgedrängt und der dreiköpfige Wischwarupa von Indra im Keulenkampf erschlagen. Ein Wurf mit der niefehlenden Indralanze spaltete den Berg und befreite die Kühe, so dass sie ihr Labsal über die ganze Erde ergießen konnten.

Doch bald darauf führte Bala seine Dämonenscharen aufs Neue gegen den Meru.

In heißer Schlacht entriss er dem Indra die Herrschaft über die Erde und flehte in brünstigem Opferdienst, dass Brahma ihn in dem neuen Besitz erhalte.

Da erschien Wischnu in Zwergengestalt, mit der weißen Schnur des Brahmanenstandes um die Brust, vor dem Opfernden, gewann in weiser Rede die Gunst des mächtigen Dämonenfürsten, und als dieser dem Lobredner eine Weihgabe bot, bat Wischnu, ihm drei Schritte Landes zu schenken.

Gerne bewilligte der Fromme dem priesterlichen Zwerg diese Bitte.

Vor den Augen des Dämonenfürsten wuchs nun der Gott ins Unendliche *und nahm mit drei Schritten die ganze Welt!*

Indra, dem Götterkönig, hat er sie wiedergegeben!

Mit Agni, dem kühnen Freund, zog nun Schakra abermals gegen Bala und schlug das Heer der Dämonen aufs Haupt, dass seine Herrschaft aufs Neue befestigt war.

Indessen wuchs dem gewaltigen Herrn des Himmels in Writra, dem Fürsten der Kalakeya, einem Riesengeschlecht der Danawa, ein schier unbezwinglicher Gegner heran.

Writra wälzte mit seinen Riesen Berge gegen den Meru, dass die Erde erzitterte. Darauf stürmten die Kalakeya vor und warfen sich gegen die Götter. Der Meru schien in lohenden Flammen zu stehen, so funkelten die goldenen Panzer, die eisernen Keulen, der Danawa. Tapfer wehrten sich die Götter, und zu Hunderten und Tausenden fielen die abgehauenen Köpfe der Riesen aus der Luft. Aber Writras Kühnheit hatte unzählige Scharen der Dämonen angelockt, und die Götter wurden zurückgedrängt. Als stürzten Berge ein, so tobte es in den Lüften, beim Zusammenstoß der feindlichen Helden.

Vergebens stritt Indra mit all seiner Tapferkeit und Stärke, mit allen seinen göttlichen Waffen gegen Writra. Der Danawa in seiner goldenen Wehr schien unverwundbar, und sein gellender Schlachtschrei trieb die Seinen zu tollster Kampfeswut und entmutigte die göttlichen Heerscharen.

Da trat Indra vor Brahma, um von dem Allmächtigen Rat zu erbitten. Brahma wusste, warum der Götterkönig vor ihm stand, und sprach:

„Lass aus den Knochen eines Sündenlosen eine sechszackige Keule machen: damit wirst Du Writra töten!"

Die Götter baten darauf den Heiligen Dadhitscha ihnen zu helfen, und willig opferte der Edle sein Leben zum Heile der Welt.

Twaschter, der Götterschmied, verfertigte aus den Knochen des Sündenlosen den Sechszack, und, wieder voll Mut, warfen sich die Götter den Dämonen aufs Neue entgegen.

Furchtbar war der Anprall Leib an Leib! wieder schienen die Danawa die Stärkeren zu sein, die Götter weichen zu wollen. Schon klang Writras Kriegsschrei wie ein Siegesjauchzen – da warf Indra den Sechszack:

Schauerlich rollte der erste Donner durch die Lüfte, die Danawascharen mit Entsetzen erfüllend. Writra sank mit gespaltenem Schädel zu Boden und war tot!

Jetzt drangen die göttlichen Heerscharen auf die entsetzten Dämonen ein und schlugen ihrer viele Tausende nieder. Heulend flohen die letzten vom Schlachtfeld und verbargen sich voll Angst im Meer.

Seither ist der Donnerkeil Indras Lieblingswaffe. Freundlich spricht er mit dem Zackigen vor der Schlacht, und dieser glüht vor Kampflust in Schakras Hand, wenn der Feind sich naht.

Ein mächtiger Helfer gegen die Dämonen erstand bald darauf dem Götterkönig in dem Kriegsgotte *Skanda*:

Agni hatte beim Opfer die Gattinnen der sieben heiligen Seher erschaut, und sein Herz entbrannte in heißer Liebe zu den holden Frauen. Seufzend und sinnend zog er sich in den Wald zurück und fand keinen anderen Gedanken, als den an die tugendhaften Schönen, die er ewig meiden musste.

Svaha, des Feuergottes Gattin, erkannte in ihrem liebenden Herzen den Kummer des Gemahls und, um den Treulosen nicht zu verlieren, nahm sie die Gestalt der Gattin des ersten Sehers an und ging am Morgen zu Agni in den Wald. Voll Freude umarmte der Verliebte seine Gattin und verlebte den ganzen Tag in Lust und Freude mit ihr, ohne sie zu erkennen.

In der Dämmerung aber schlich Svaha ins Dickicht, verwandelte sich in einen Geier und flog nach dem Berge Sveta. Dort ruhte sie die ganze Nacht in einem goldenen Bett, von Schlangen und Geistern bewacht.

Am nächsten Morgen flog sie nach dem Wald zurück und nahte sich ihrem Gatten als Frau des zweiten Sehers. Wieder verlebte sie unerkannt einen glücklichen Tag mit Agni. Und wieder ruhte sie des Nachts in ihrem goldenen Bett auf dem Berge Sveta. Und noch viermal gelang es ihr, den geliebten Gatten zu täuschen. Nur die Gestalt der Arundhati, der Gattin des siebenten Sehers, konnte sie nicht annehmen: Ihre Zauberkraft versagte vor der unendlichen Liebe der beiden Gatten zueinander!

Die ersten sechs Seher aber hörten von den schwatzhaften Tieren des Waldes, dass ihre Frauen sich mit Agni erlustigt hatten, und jagten die Ungetreuen aus dem Hause.

Unschuldig verdammt, irrten die Unglücklichen durch die Welt, bis Brahma sie als Sternbild an den Himmel setzte.

Svaha aber gebar auf dem Berg Sveta den sechsköpfigen Skanda. Dann flog sie als Geier davon, und niemand kannte die Mutter des starken Gottes, der in vier Tagen zum Manne erwachsen war.

Um diese Zeit raubte der Dämon Keschin Dewasena und Daitiasena, die Töchter des Schöpfers Pratschapati.

Indra besiegte Keschin und löste die Fesseln Dewasenas, während der starke Daitiafürst mit der Schwester der Befreiten entfloh.

Weinend beklagte die herrliche Dewasena das Los der Unglücklichen und schwor nur den zum Gatten zu nehmen, der stärker als Götter und Dämonen sei.

Da trat der sechsköpfige Skanda auf den Plan.

Voll Kühnheit verfolgte er den Entführer und besiegte ihn nach heißem Kampf. Dann drang er weit in das Reich der Daitia ein und schlug Bana, den Sohn Balas, in schwerer Schlacht. Als der Dämonenfürst sich voll Angst in den Berg Krauntscha verkroch, spaltete der Gewaltige das Gebirge und tötete den Feigen durch einen Lanzenwurf. Indra, Schiwa und viele andere Götter hatten sich dem kühnen Skanda angeschlossen und lieferten den Dämonen blutige Schlachten.

Nun trat der Riese Mahisa an die Spitze der Dämonen und führte eine Schar ihrer Besten zum Angriff. Mit unwiderstehlicher Kraft fraßen sich die kühnen Recken in das Götterheer und drohten es zu vernichten. Bis dicht vor den Streitwagen des gewaltigen Schiwa rollte die feindliche Woge. Da tötete Skandas Lanze den Mahisa, der seine Keule schon gegen Schiwa erhoben hatte. Dann sprang der Starke unter die führerlose Schar und warf sie mit dem Schwert, wie der Schnitter die Halme. Der Riese Taraka stellte sich dem Sechsköpfigen entgegen: ein furchtbares Ringen hob an, und die Erde erdröhnte von dem Gestampf der beiden gewaltigen Kämpfer. Doch der sechsfachen Kraft des Gottes war keiner gewachsen: Skanda erwürgte den Riesen wie einen tollen Hund.

Indra neigte sich vor dem gewaltigen Kämpfer und bot ihm seine Herrschaft an, doch Skanda wies sie aus Ehrfurcht vor dem mächtigen Writratöter zurück und bat nur, ihm die Führung des Götterheeres anzuvertrauen.

Seither ist Skanda Indras starker und kluger Feldherr und der glückliche Gatte der Dewasena, die ihn stärker als alle Götter und Dämonen gesehen hat. Der rote Hahn, das Banner, welches Skanda von Agni erhalten hat, zieht dem Heere der Götter voran.

Katscha und Dewajani

Wirschaparwan, der König der Danawa, hatte dem bußereichen Brahmanen Uschanas das Seelenheil der Seinen anvertraut. Als Hauspriester des Königs war der Fromme oberster Priester im Danawareich.

Uschanas hatte in strengster Askese und tiefinnerster Sammlung der Natur das Geheimnis des Sterbens abgelauscht. Wen immer er mit seinen Zauberworten rufen mochte, der brach jede Fessel des Todes und trat lebend vor den gewaltigen Büßer. Da war die Weltherrschaft der Götter in Gefahr! Mochten ihre Waffen auch tausend und aber tausend Dämonen in der Schlacht töten, das Zauberwort des Danawapriesters rief alle wieder ins Leben zurück. Und die Leichen aus dem Heerbann der Götter blieben tot, denn der edle Brihaspati kannte das Zauberwort nicht. Jede Schlacht, und mochte sie auch für die Götter siegreich sein, zehrte an der Macht der Himmlischen.

Mit Mrauen gedachten die Götter des Lichtes der Zeit, da die Dämonen der Finsternis, der verzehrenden Dürre, die Herrschaft der Welt an sich reisten, die alte Ordnung zertrümmern und Elend über die Erde breiten würden.

Sie gingen zu Katscha, dem Sohn ihres Priesters Brihaspati, und baten ihn, Schüler und Jünger des mächtigen Dämonenpriesters zu werden.

Vielleicht lernte er die Kunst des Wiederbelebens von seinem Meister, vielleicht fand der schöne Jüngling Gnade vor den Augen Dewajanis, der holden Tochter Uschanas: Auch die Götter mussten den Tod überwinden lernen, wenn die Welt fürder unter ihrer Herrschaft blühen sollte!

Katscha neigte sich ehrfürchtig vor den hehren Hütern der Welt und kam ihrem Wunsche freudig nach:

Im Schülerkleid, mit einer Tracht Brennholz auf dem Arm, so trat er, wie es die Sitte erheischte, vor Uschanas, nannte seinen Namen und seine Herkunft, und bat den würdigen Asketen, ihm tausend Jahre als Jünger dienen und von ihm die heilige Lehre des Weda und alle Bräuche der Priesterkaste hören zu dürfen.

„Gerne nehme ich dich als Schüler auf, edler Jüngling!", sprach Uschanas, „denn Dein Vater, der ehrwürdige Götterpriester, ist mir wert! – Sei willkommen!". So lebte nun Kotscha im Hause des Danawapriesters, und seine Dienstwilligkeit, seine bescheidene Freundlichkeit, sein kindliches Lachen, machte ihn dem Alten und seinem jungfräulichen Töchterlein Dewajani immer lieber.

Fünfhundert Jahre hatte er schon gelernt und gedient, da hörten die Danawa erst, dass Uschanas Jünger der Sohn des Götterpriesters sei. Voll Sorge um das Geheimnis, dem allein sie ihre Macht verdankten, lauerten sie Katscha auf.

Als er eines Morgens die Kühe seines Lehrers auf die Weide trieb, erschlugen sie den edlen Jüngling und gaben seinen Leichnam den Wölfen zum Fraß.

Dewajani ahnte nichts Gutes, als die Kühe ohne den Hirten heimkehrten. Und als vollends die Stunde der Abendandacht schlug, ohne dass der eifrige Brahmanenschüler nach Hause gekommen wäre, litt es sie nicht länger in ihrer Sorge um den lieben Freund.

Sie wandte sich mit Tränen im Auge zum Vater und sprach: „Oh, Vater! Katscha fehlt zur Abendandacht – er, der jeder Pflicht des Priesterstandes so pünktlich nachkommt – oh – er ist gestorben – sie haben ihn ermordet – oh – ich will nicht leben ohne ihn!"

Tröstend strich Uschanas über die Flechten seines lieblichen Kindes und rief den Vermissten mit seiner geheimnisvollen Zauberformel.

Da zerriss Katscha die Leiber der Wölfe, die ihn gefressen hatten, lief nach Hause und erzählte der treubesorgten Dewajanh was ihm geschehen war.

Bald darauf lauerten die Danawa dem Wiedererstandenen vom neuen auf und töteten ihn, als er beim Blumensuchen zu weit in den Wald geraten war.

Sie warfen den Leichnam ins Meer, doch Uschanas Zauberwort reichte auch in dessen Tiefen, und Dewajani konnte den schmerzlich vermissten Gespielen bald wieder begrüße.

Zum dritten Mal erschlugen nun die Danawa den Jüngling, verbrannten seinen Leichnam, und gaben die Asche seinem Meister in Sura, einem berauschenden Getränk, zu trinken.

Wieder klagte Dewajani dem Vater ihr Leid, doch dieser weigerte sich das Zauberwort zu sprechen: „Wie oft ich auch Katscha erwecken wollte, die Danawa würden ihn stets wieder erschlagen!", sprach er. „Lass ihn ruhen! weine nicht um den armseligen Schüler, da Götter und Danawa um deine Liebe werben."

„Oh–oh!", schluchzte Dewajani. „Wie kann ich meinem Schmerz um den edlen Jüngling, den lieben Gespielen, gebieten? – nein, Vater, nein! – hungern will ich und dürsten, bis Du mich mit ihm vereinst – oder der Tod!"

„So will ich ihn noch einmal rufen!", sprach Uschanas, „und die Brahmanenmörder mit schweren Strafen bedrohen –."

„Halt ein!", rief da Katscha aus Uschanas Leib. „Rufe mich nicht, ehrwürdiger Lehrer, denn Du müsstest sterben.

Die Danawa haben Dir meine Asche im Abendtrunk gegeben! Du stirbst, wenn ich die Fesseln des Todes breche!"

„Nun, Dewajani, hast Du die Wahl: gilt Dir des Gespielen Leben mehr als das des Vaters?", sprach Uschanas ernst.

„Weh mir!", schluchzte Dewajani. „Wie soll ich einen missen, von zweien, die ich liebe? – Oh lass mich – Vater – lass mich sterben!" „Wie schön, wie edel bist Du, Katscha! dass meine Tochter so Dich liebt!", rief Uschanas. „Ersteh aus meinem Blut aufs Neue als mein Sohn – doch nimm zuerst den Zauber, der ins Leben ruft, dass Du mich, Deinen Vater, aus des Todes Banden lösest!"

Darauf murmelte er die Zauberformel, und als der wiedererstehende Katscha des Greises Adern sprengte, fiel dieser um und war tot.

Doch rasch belebte das Zauberwort des kundigen Schülers den Toten. Freudig schlossen die Drei einander in die Arme.

Der Asketenfürst aber, welcher durch sein Suratrinken so viel Glück gefährdet hatte, verfluchte für alle Zeiten jeden Brahmanen, der der Lockung des berauschenden Trankes nicht widerstehen könnte: An Leib und Seele sollte der suratrinkende Priester gestraft werden, wie der Mörder eines Gerechten!

Katscha blieb bis ans Ende seiner tausendjährigen Lehrzeit bei Uschanas. Als er Abschied nahm, um nach der Götterstadt zurückzukehren, bat Dewajani ihn hold verschämt, sie als Gattin in sein Haus zu führen.

„Oh Schwesterlein!", sprach Katscha dawider, „wie könnte ich Dich freien, da wir doch beide eines Blutes sind? Uschanas, der mich aus seinem Blut zu neuem Leben gerufen hat, ist mein Vater, wie der Deine! – Der heilige Weda und aller Völker Gebrauch verbietet solchen Bund. – Sonniges Glück wünsche ich Dir, holde Schwester, doch unsere Wege müssen sich scheiden!"

Damit grüßte er die Betrübte und eilte nach dem Himmel. Dort feierten ihn die Götter als Befreier aus schwerer Not mit vielen Ehren und jubelnder Freude.

Dewajani aber drohte sich schier zu verzehren vor Sehnsucht nach dem Geliebten. Als Uschanas sein geliebtes Kind von Tag zu Tag bleicher werden sah, da verfluchte er die Zauberformel, die an allem Schuld trug, auf dass sie für ewige Zeiten im Gedächtnis aller Geschöpfe erlösche.

Seither bleiben Tote tot und kein Götter-, kein Dämonenwort kann sie ins Leben rufen.

Mada, der Riese Leidenschaft

Der Bhrigusohn Tschiawana hatte seine Klause an dem Ufer des Flusses Narmada gebaut und lebte dort in strengster Askese. Schier unerschöpfliche Gnadenschätze häufte er durch fromme Buße auf: Während des glühenden indischen Sommers saß er nackend zwischen vier hochlodernden Feuern und ließ sich die Sonne auf den Scheitel brennen. Viele Jahre hindurch hielt er das strenge Gelübde des Schweigens und seine Nahrung bestand in Wasser und wenigen Wurzeln. Zuletzt stand er regungslos, wie eine Säule, im Wald, und Ameisen bauten an ihm ihr Bauwerk empor. Sein Scheitel ward noch überdeckt, nur die blitzenden Augen lugten aus dem Gewirr von Halmen, Nadeln und Sandkörnern.

Scharjati, der Herrscher des Reiches, kam um diese Zeit mit seinem Töchterlein Sukanja in Tschiawanas Waldeinsamkeit. Ihm folgten sein riesiges Heer und ein Tross von Sklaven und Frauen der Prinzessin.

Sukanja tollte mit ihren Gespielinnen durch den stillen Einsiedlerwald, und in fröhlichem Haschen und Suchen verlor ihr Gefolge sie aus den Augen. Bald stand sie allein vor Tschiawanas Klause und musterte neugierig das Niegesehene.

Der büßende Bhrigusohn in seinem Ameisenhaufen sah das holde Mädchen, und in sein altes Herz fiel heiße Liebe und glühende Sehnsucht nach dieser blühenden Jugend.

Leise rief er Sukanja an, doch die Neugierige hörte oder beachtete den Ruf nicht. Sie sah etwas Funkelndes in dem Ameisenhügel, und während sie spielend darin mit einem langen Dorn herumstocherte, fragte sie harmlos: „Was mag das sein?“. Da ihr keine Antwort ward, lief sie wieder in den Wald und suchte ihre Gespielinnen. Sie hatte dem büßenden Heiligen die Augen ausgestochen!

In seinem Zorn sandte der Blinde eine schwere Seuche über Scharjatis Heer.

Vergebens forschte der König in seinem Gefolge und bei den Kriegern nach des Übels Ursache; wiederholt fragte er, ob keiner von ihnen den heiligen Bhrigusohn, der hier in der Nähe hause, gekränkt habe. Endlich erzählte Sukanja, wie sie, im Walde spielend, zwei funkelnde Sterne in einem Ameisenbau zerstört habe.

Böses ahnend, ließ sich Scharjati dorthin führen und fand mitten im Ameisenhaufen den geblendeter Büßer.

„Verzeih! Du mächtiger Heiliger!“, rief er mit flehend erhobenen Händen. „Verzeih, was Dir meines Kindes Unverstand getan hat! Sei gnädig, frommer Einsiedler, und nimm die Strafe von meinem Heer, von meinem Land!“

„Hochmut und Verachtung für den schmutzigen Greis haben Dein Kind verleitet mich zu blenden. So soll es als Gattin des Verachteten seine Armut teilen, den Geblendeten führen! Dann will ich Dir und den Deinen wieder gnädig sein!“, sprach der Heilige.

Schweren Herzens gab Scharjati dem Asketenfürsten die liebe Tochter, doch willig nahm Sukanja die Buße für ihren jugendlichen Übermut auf sich. Freundlich, wie eine liebevolle Tochter, pflegte sie ihren greisen Gatten und ward nicht müde in seiner Wartung.

Einst zogen die schönen Morgenrotreiter, die Aswinas, die Götterärzte, durch den Wald und sahen die Liebliche, wie sie am Ufer der Narmada das Kochgerät wusch.

„Wer bist du, schönste Blume des Waldes?", fragten die beiden Jünglinge.

Da erzählte Sukanja von ihrer Herkunft, von dem schrecklichen Unheil, das sie in kindischem Unverstand verschuldet hatte, und dass sie jetzt das Weib des geblendeten Büßers sei und ihn voll Reue und kindlicher Liebe pflege.

„Mir dünkt, Du bist zu jung zu diesem traurigen Amt und für die Waldeinsamkeit zu schön!", sprach einer der Jünglinge.

„Ja, komm mit uns," sprach der andere. „Komm mit nach der Götterstadt und wähle einen Jungen zum Hatten. Lass Dich mit köstlichem Geschmeide schmücken und Dir den Weg zu Götterfreuden zeigen!" „Ich liebe Tschiawana, denn er ist weise und gut!", erwiderte Sukanja mit leisem Seufzen.

„Wir sind die Götterärzte! wir wollen den Heiligen gesund und jung machen, dann magst Du zwischen ihm und uns beiden wählen!"

Alle drei traten vor Tschiawana, und die Aswinas wiederholten ihren Vorschlag.

Der blinde Heilige war zufrieden, und die Heilkundigen führten ihn in den Fluss, bis allen dreien die Wellen über dem Kopf zusammenschlugen.

Als sie wieder auftauchten, war Tschiawana ein helläugiger Jüngling geworden: schön wie die Morgenrotreiter und lachend wie der Gatte des leibhaftigen Glückes!

„Nun wähle!", riefen die Aswinas der staunenden Sukanja zu.

Da wählte sie mit holdem Erröten ihren Gatten!

Neidlos beglückwünschten die Götterärzte das herrliche Paar.

Tschiawana aber sprach: „Ihr habt meinen Augen die Schönheit der Welt, meinem Leib die Lust der Jugend geschenkt! ich will es euch danken: Künftig sollen die Menschen auch euch den köstlichen Somatrank opfern, wie jetzt nur Indra und den höchsten der Götter!"

Frohen Mutes stiegen die Morgenrotreiter zum Himmel hinan, und das junge Paar trug sein stilles Glück in die Klause.

Als bald darauf Scharjati mit großem Gefolge die Einsiedelei besuchte, um sich an der jungen Freude seiner Tochter zu weiden, rüstete Tschiawana ein feierliches Opfer.

In seliger Dankbarkeit hob er die geweihte Schale mit dem berauschenden Soma und rief die Ashwinas an, um die Spende für sie zu vergießen.

Da erschien Indra vor dem Altar und rief dem Heiligen ein drohendes Halt zu: „Du sollst nicht rütteln an Althergebrachtem!", schrie er zornig. „Die Aswinas sind Halbgötter, sind Ärzte und Diener der Götter! Sie sollen nicht an meiner Tafel schwelgen!"

„Oh König der Götter!", sprach Tschiawana ernst, „wie magst Du die Edlen schmähen, die die Schrecken der Nacht verscheuchen, wenn sie vor Urschas Wagen reiten, die Götter und Menschen heilen mit ihrer Kunst, die mir das Licht und die Jugend wiedergegeben haben! – Sie sollt' ich nicht ehren dürfen als Götter? – Nein, Schakra, fröhlicher Somatrinker! ich spende den Aswinas Opfer, wie den anderen Göttern!"

Und wieder hob er die Schale, um das Opfer zu vollenden.

„Halt!", rief Indra, „und hörst Du nicht auf mein Wort, so wird mein Donnerkeil Dich treffen, Unseliger!"

Zornig funkelten des Writratöters Augen, und in seiner Rechten schwang er dräuend den Sechszack.

Tschiawana aber erschuf aus dem Gnadenschatz seiner Buße Mada, den Riesen Leidenschaft! Unermesslich war dessen Leib und sein Rachen gähnte von der Erde bis zum Himmel. Zähne wie Bäume und Hauer wie Türme standen darin. Die Augen glänzten wie Sonnen und die Arme glichen Bergketten. Glühend heiß loderte es aus seinem Rachen und ein Meer von Schlamm geiferte über die zuckende Zunge.

Mit furchtbarem Brüllen stürzte Mada gegen Indra und drohte den Gott zu verschlingen.

Dem tapferen Götterkönig erlahmte vor Schrecken der Arm, der den Donnerkeil schwang.

„Wahrlich!", sprach er, „würdig sind die Aswinas des Somaopfers, wenn Du, mächtiger Bhrigusohn, ihnen den Schatz Deiner Gnade leihst!"

Schnell rief Tschiawana den Riesen Leidenschaft zurück und verteilte sein Wesen auf Trinken und Spielen, auf Hassen und Lieben! Furchtbar sind auch noch die Teile des Riesen, vor welchem einst Indra gebebt hatte!

Tschiawana vollendete das Opfer, und die segenspendenden Aswinas sitzen seither an der Somatafel.

Der dankbare Heilige aber lebte mit seiner holden Sukanja noch viele Jahre im stillen Waldesglück, als Freund der Götter und Menschen.

Nahuscha

In Naumutschi, dem Daitiakönig, war den Dämonen ein neuer Writra erstanden. Als ein gewaltiger Kriegsheld führte er seine Scharen gegen die Götter und entriss der Herrschaft Indras weite Gebiete.

Wieder und wieder stellte der Donnerer seine Heere von Rudras, Marutas und Gandharvas diesen Schrecken der Welt entgegen, wieder und wieder maß er sich im Einzelkampf mit dem furchtbaren Dämonenherrscher: der Sieg blieb aus!

Naumutschi behauptete, was er erstritten hatte, und stürzte die Welt in Sorge, durch neue Raubzüge in glückliches Land.

Die Götter fragten die Rischi, die sieben heiligen Seher der Urzeit, um Rat, und die Heiligen rieten zu einem ehrlichen Frieden.

Da auch die Götter nicht bessere Hilfe wussten, und Indra gestand, dass ihm der Daitiakönig an Kraft und Geschicklichkeit gewachsen sei, so gingen alle zur Grenze des Daitiareiches und die sieben Rischi suchten Naumutschi auf.

Der Dämonenfürst empfing die Heiligen voll Ehrerbietung und hörte ihre Friedensvorschläge willigen Herzens.

„Ich bin bereit einen ewigen Frieden zu schließen!“, sprach er ernst, „doch trau’ ich dem mächtigen Donnerer nicht. Er ist vernarrt in sein Spielzeug: die Menschen und Tiere, Felder und Wälder. Das Herz möchte ihm schier brechen, wenn ich mich in Frieden über die Erde lege und mit den Meinen Flüsse und Weiher austrinke, so dass die Geschöpfe ein wenig dürften müssen. Ich traue dem Jähzornigen nicht! – Heilige Eide müssten ihn binden, sonst schlägt er mich tot, sobald ich die Waffen abgelegt habe! – Er schwöre, mich nicht zu töten: bei Tage nicht und nicht bei Nacht, mit Wasser nicht und nicht mit Feuer, noch mit Waffen aus Stein, Erz, Holz oder allem was fest ist!

Spricht er den Eid, so will ich Frieden halten und das Jahr mit ihm teilen!“

Und Indra sprach den Eid: „Bei Tage nicht und nicht bei Nacht, mit Wasser nicht und nicht mit Feuer, noch mit Waffen aus Stein, Erz, Holz oder allem was fest ist, will ich den starken Naumutschi töten!". So ward der Friede geschlossen, und im Sommer streckte sich der Dämonenfürst über die Erde, um sie ein halbes Jahr lang zu drücken.

Furchtbar litten alle Geschöpfe unter der verzehrenden Dürre. Weiher und Flüsse waren von den Dämonen ausgetrunken, versengt die einst blühenden Matten, die duftenden Wälder; und flehend stiegen die Gebete aus vertrockneten Kehlen zum Himmel empor. Nie noch hatte der Gabenspender Indra so lange gezögert. Das Ende aller Wesen schien nahe!

Traurig saß der Weltenherr auf seinem funkelnden Thron und sann, wie er die Erde von der Schreckensherrschaft Naumutschis befreie.

Oh, sein geliebter Donnerkeil! – doch der war eine Waffe – war aus Festem geschmiedet – das Feuer barg er in sich – oh! des schrecklichen Eides!

Zornig sprang Indra auf und eilte zu seiner gequälten Erde.

Da lag sein Feind im Dämmerlicht des Abends, lang hingestreckt, durch den Frieden geschützt, und schlief!

Sein Haupt reichte bis ans Ufer des Meeres, und dem schnarchendem Rachen entstieg eine verzehrende Glut, die das Wasser des Meeres kochen machte, dass seine Oberfläche eitel Schaum war.

Wie der Blitz fuhr's in Indras Gedanken:

Nicht Wasser ist der Schaum des Meeres und nicht Feuer! Waffe ist er nicht und nicht aus Stein, noch Erz, noch sonst aus Festem! und die Dämmerung ist nicht Tag noch Nacht!

Jauchzend schlug er den Donnerkeil in die kochende Meerflut, dass eine Schaumwoge hochauf zum Himmel stieg und im Niederfallen den neuen Writra erschlug.

Hei! wie jubelten Götter und Genien, wie trieben Waju, der Sturm, und die singenden Maruta strotzende Regenwolken herbei und ergossen deren Labsal auf die lobpreisende Erde!

Indra aber sank zu Boden und vergrub sein Antlitz vor Scham im Sande:

Er hatte seinen Eid gebrochen!

Lange lag der Heißblütige so, dann schlich er im Dunkel der Nacht von dannen.

Winzig klein geworden, verbarg er sich vor aller Welt im Wasser, im Stängel einer frisch erblühten Lotusblume.

Kaum war der Götterkönig verschwunden, versiegte der Regen, die Erde vertrocknete aufs Neue, Bäche, Weiher, Flüsse und Seen versickerten, denn Götter und Genien fühlten nicht mehr die Zügel der Herrschaft. Die Welt war ohne König. Zucht und Gesetzmäßigkeit im Schwinden.

Wieder traten die Götter vor die sieben Seher und baten sie um Rat, baten, ihnen einen neuen Herrscher zu geben.

Die Heiligen sahen die Not der Welt und schlugen den König Nahuscha, der in Weisheit und Milde über die Menschen herrschte, zum Himmelsherrn vor. Sie versprachen, ihn mit den Schätzen ihrer Gnade zu überhäufen, auf dass er stark genug werde, um über die Dreiwelt des Himmels, der Erde und der Unterwelt zu herrschen.

Des waren die Götter zufrieden, und im feierlichem Zuge holten sie den Erwählten aus seinem irdischen Reich:

Nahuscha trat auf das Tigerfell vor dem Weltenthron, Weihwasser rieselte auf den Beglückten nieder, und so ward er der Beherrscher der Dreiwelt.

Doch Nahuscha war ein Mensch!

Als er sich über Götter, Genien, Heilige und die ganze Erde gesetzt sah, vergaß er die schweren Pflichten seiner Erhöhung und langte gierig nach ihren leichten Freuden.

Mit den schönen und heiteren Apsaras durchstreifte er die heiligen Haine in tollem Taumel, schwelgte mit den

Welthütern an der Somatafel, und lieh sein Ohr nur den lustigen Weisen der Gandharva, den preisenden Heldenliedern der brahmanischen Dichter, und nicht den klagenden Gebeten der leidenden Menschheit.

Einst feierte er ein stolzes Fest in Indras Garten Naudana:

Narada, der Götterbote, pries die kriegerischen Ahnen des Weltenherrn in begeisterten Hymnen; Apsaras tanzten über die blumigen Wiesen, und die Schellen an ihren zarten Knöcheln klirrten leise in die fröhlichen Weisen der Gandharva. Wohlgerüche erfüllten die Luft und ein kühler Wind erfrischte die tafelnden Götter.

Um Nahuscha waren die sechs Jahreszeiten versammelt, die dem Herrn der Welt ihre köstlichsten Gaben gebracht hatten.

Nach dem Somagelage streifte der Fröhliche durch den weiten Götterhain und erblickte die trauernde Schatschi.

„Ist das nicht Schatschi, die Macht?", rief er „des verschollenen Indra Eheweib? – Warum dient sie mir nicht? – Ich bin nun Indra – ich der Götterkönig– der Herr der Welt! – Und wahrlich! so schön ist Schatschi, dass sie stets nur das Weib des Erhabensten sein soll! – Bringt sie in mein Haus!", sprach er zu seinem Gefolge. „Ich will sie zu meiner Gattin erheben!"

Als Schatschi die Worte Nahuschas hörte, entfloh sie und verbarg sich bei Brihaspati, dem guten Götterpriester.

Dieser gewährte der Treuen gastlichen Schutz und prophezeite, dass Indra wieder erscheinen und über die Dreiwelt herrschen werde.

Nahuscha tobte, dass die Welt erzitterte, als er hörte, dass Schatschi sich unter des Brahmanen Schutz begeben hatte.

Die Götter baten ihn, seinen Grimm zu beherrschen, auf dass dieser nicht die Welt vernichte. Doch eigensinnig bestand der Götterkönig darauf, dass Indras Weib in sein Haus geführt werde.

Da gingen die Götter, denen vor dem Zorne des Starken bangte, zu Brihaspati und baten ihn, um der Welt willen Schatschi auszuliefern, auf dass sie die Gattin des furchtbaren Götterkönigs Nahuscha werde.

„Gib sie heraus! oh Ehrwürdiger!“, sprachen sie.

„Nahuschas Grimm verzehrt sonst die Welt, denn weit stärker als Indra ist der neue Herrscher, da die sieben Heiligen ihm den Schatz ihrer Buße geliehen haben!“

Doch Brihaspati sprach:

„Wie kann ich die Schutzsuchende dem Verfolger ausliefern? – glaubt ihr, so wenig gälten einem Brahmanen die Lehren des Weda?

Muss ich die heiligen Sprüche erst nennen? – Euch sagen, dass kein Regen fällt auf die Saat dessen, der einen Schützling ausliefert, dass Speise und Trank ihn verzehren, statt zu nähren, dass seine Kinder früh ins Grab sinken und seine Ahnen keine Ruhe finden, dass die Götter seine Gaben verschmähen und ihre Gaben ihm Not und Tod bringen!

Habt ihr vergessen, wie Indra einst den König Usinara prüfte und belohnte? – So will ich es euch wiedererzählen:

Der vielgepriesene Länderherr saß vor dem lodernden Opferfeuer, als eine Taube sich in seinen Schoß flüchtete.

Ein schneller Habicht verfolgte die Zitternde, flog bis vor Usinaras Thron und forderte seine Beute von dem König.

„Gerecht wirst Du gepriesen, oh Herr!“, so sprach der Habicht. „Gib mir was ich erjagt habe, mich plagt der Hunger!“

„Wie könnt’ ich gegen die heilige Lehre verstoßen?“, sprach der König. „Wie dem Verfolger geben, was sich vertrauend zu mir geflüchtet hat? – Die Schuld würde lasten auf mir, als hätt' ich eine Kuh, eine Weltmutter, erschlagen oder einen Brahmanen erwürgt! – Nie geb' ich den Schützling heraus!"

„So willst Du mich dem Hungertode preisgeben? – mich? und, bin ich tot, mein Weib und meine Kleinen? oh – vergiss nicht, weiser König: Pflicht steht gegen Pflicht! Lasst doch die kleinere um die große zu erfüllen: gib mir die Taube! Es ist den Habichten gesetzt, die Tauben zu fressen!"

„Nimm einen Büffel, kluger Vogel – einen Eber oder Hirschen – alles lasse ich Dir geben, doch der Schützling ist mir heilig!", rief Usinara.

„Nicht Büffel, Hirsch und Eber will ich von Dir erbetteln, König!", sprach der Habicht. „Die Taube gib mir, meine müdgehetzte Beute und jene Nahrung, die des Schöpfers Willen mir zugesprochen hat!"

„Nimm mein Reich und alles was ich habe, der Schützling bleibt in meiner Hut!", erwiderte Usinara ernst.

„Gib mir von Deinem Fleisch so viel als diese Taube wiegt, wenn Du um alles an die Pflicht Dich bindest!", rief der Habicht.

„Gerecht ist Deine Forderung, weiser Vogel!", sprach der König und ließ eine Waage bringen.

Dann schnitt er sich ein Stück Fleisch vom Leibe und wog es gegen die Taube.

Doch der kleine Vogel wog schwerer als das blutige Fleisch des Edlen. Noch einmal schnitt das Messer in des Dulders Leib, und wieder ward das Opfer zu leicht befunden.

Da trat Usinara auf die Waage und bot sich dem Habicht zur Speise.

„Indra bin ich!", rief der Vogel jetzt, „und die Taube ist Agui! Wir kamen Dich zu prüfen, viel besungener Herr der

Gerechtigkeit, und Du hast bestanden wie Gold im Feuer, glücklicher Weiser! Steig auf zu meinem Himmel und leuchte der Menschheit als Beispiel!"

„So schützt ein Weiser, was sich seinem Schutze anvertraut! – Nie liefere ich Schatschi dem Drohenden aus!", schloss Brihaspati seine Rede.

„So rate uns, wie wir die Welt beschützen, vor dem Grimmigen, der die Gnade der Rischi besitzt!", sprachen die Götter ergeben.

Da dachte der edle Priester nach und sagte:

„Schatschi mag Nahuscha sagen lassen, dass sie dem Gewaltigen in sein Haus folgen werde, wenn er die sieben Heiligen vor seinen Wagen spannt. In einem Gefährte, so kostbar, wie noch keiner eins lenkte, fährt die Macht mit dem Allbezwinger zum Altar! – Hochmut ist Nahuschas Fehler, Hochmut wird ihn stürzen!"

„Die Götter brachten ihrem König die Botschaft der Entflohenen, und der Herr der Welt freute sich über Schatschis Willigkeit und das seinem Stolze schmeichelnde Verlangen. Er suchte die heiligen Seher auf und spannte sie an seinen Streitwagen: Zwei an jede Seite und drei an die Stange.

Indessen hatte Brihaspati ein stilles Opfer zur Auffindung Indras gerüstet. Der Agni der Opferflamme durchstreifte im Fluge die ganze Welt, doch fand er seinen Herrn und Freund nicht auf der festen Erde, noch in der blauen Luft. Unter Brihaspatis kräftigen Zaubersprüchen fuhr er in das gefürchtete Wasser und sah hier Indra in der Lotusblüte verborgen.

Rasch rief er alle Götter herbei.

Und als die Herrlichen reinen Herzens des gewaltigen Writratöters Kriegstaten und seine weise Friedensherrschaft priesen, da wuchs der in Sünde und Reue klein gewordene Indra und stand plötzlich in seiner alten Stärke unter ihnen.

Nun erzählten die Frohen ihm von Nahuschas schlechter Herrschaft und baten den mächtigen Donnerer, den Unwürdigen vom Thron der Welt zu stürzen und sie wieder, wie einst, zu beherrschen. Doch Indra schüttelte das Haupt: „Woher nähm' ich die Kraft, den Nahuscha zu stürzen? – Ich, der unter der Sünde des Eidbruches seufzt, ihn, den die Gnade der Heiligen trägt!"

Und schweigend schritten die Götter alle zum Himmel.

Dort hatte Nahuscha indessen sein seltsames Gespann gegen Brihaspatis Haus gelenkt, um die heißbegehrte Braut im Triumphe abzuholen.

Dem ungeduldigen Verliebten zogen die Ehrwürdigen zu langsam des Weges.

„Schleicht nicht so!", schrie er zornig und spornte den heiligen Agastha mit der Ferse.

Da war das Maß des Frevels voll, und die Macht des zum Weltherrscher erhobenen Menschen gebrochen!

Die Heiligen hielten an, und auf Agasthas Fluch: „So schleiche Du durch die Ewigkeit!", stürzte Nahuscha als Schlange vom Wagen. Heute noch steht am Himmel das Sternbild: die sieben leuchtenden Heiligen an den Wagen gespannt, und daneben die stürzende Schlange!

Indra aber ward im Himmel mit lautem Jubel empfangen.

In einem sühnenden Rossopfer wälzten die Heiligen die schreckliche Schuld von seinem Herzen und verteilten ihr Wesen in der ganzen Schöpfung: Die Berge nahmen ein Drittel auf sich und bekamen davon die Schrunden und Risse; die Bäume tragen das zweite Drittel und schwitzen Harz unter der schweren Last; die Frauen büßen das letzte, in stets wiederkehrender Schwäche.

Indra aber ward rein und thront wieder mächtig über der Dreiwelt, an der Seite seiner getreuen Schatschi.

Der Fluch der Schlangenmutter

Die Schwestern Kadru und Winata waren Gattinnen des Schöpfers Kaschjapa. Kadru brachte tausend und aber tausend Kinder zur Welt. Sie war die Mutter aller Schlangen und liebte ihre klugen und zierlichen Sprösslinge voll Stolz und Freude.

Winata sah voll Neid auf die Scharen blühender Kinder und erflehte vom Schöpfer einen Nachwuchs, weit mächtiger als das Schlangengeschlecht der Schwester.

Sie gebar den Aruna und den Garuda.

Aruna, ein schöner Knabe, war ohne Beine zur Welt gekommen. Der Sonnengott nahm ihn als Wagenlenker, und morgens und abends sieht man den Herrlichen das rote Siebengespann leiten, das im goldenen Joch den perlengeschmückten Wagen Suryas durch den Äther zieht.

Garuda war der Fürst der Geier, ein furchtbarer Feind seiner schleichenden Vettern. Stark war er und weitflügelig, der größte Vogel der Welt! Dem erhabenen Gott Wischnu diente Garuda als Reittier, oder er saß in der Dämonenschlacht auf dem Bannerschaft seines Streitwagens. Voll Stolz strich er durch den Weltenraum und deuchte sich selbst dem Götterkönig an Kraft gewachsen. Als Indra einst den Schlangenprinzen Sumucha, den Schwiegersohn seines Wagenlenkers Matali, vor Garuda beschützte, stritt der stolze Vogel mit dem Herrn der Welt und prahlte mit seiner grimmigen Stärke. Lächelnd legte Indra dem Zornigen seine Linke auf die Schulter, dass diesem schier der Flügel brach unter der Last der Faust, die einst die Erde befestigt hatte.

Kleinlaut bat der Wischnuvogel ihn zu schonen, und spottend warf Indra ihm Sumuchas abgestreifte Haut um den nackten Hals.

Durch alle Zeiten trägt Garudas Volk diese Krause, als Zeichen der schmählichen Prahlsucht seines Ahnherrn.

Kadru und Winata waren voll Eifersucht gegeneinander, denn jede war stolz auf ihre Kinder und sah in ihnen die Krone der Schöpfung.

Einst gerieten die beiden in Streit über die Farbe des Götterrosses Utschaisrawa: schwarz! Sagte Kadru; weiß! Winata.

„Wir wollen um die Freiheit wetten!“, schlug Kadru vor, denn sie hatte einen Plan, der die verhasste Schwester in ihre Gewalt bringen sollte. „Wir wollen wetten, und wer verliert, dient der anderen als Sklavin!“

Winata war damit einverstanden, denn sie wusste bestimmt, dass Utschaisrawa weiß sei.

„So wollen wir morgen an das Ufer des Meeres gehen und das herrliche, hochohrige Ross betrachten, wenn es bäumend aus den Fluten steigt!“, sprach Kadru.

„Dann sandte sie einige ihrer Söhne bei dem Schlangenvolk umher und befahl, dass alle ihre Kinder sich am anderen Morgen als schwarze Haare an das Götterross heften sollten, auf dass ihre Mutter nicht der Sklaverei verfiele.

Doch die Schlangen sind gar leichtsinnige Geschöpfe: Im strömenden Regen der Nacht badeten sie voll Wonne und sonnten sich träge am nächsten Morgen.

Nur wenige hatten der Mutter Befehl befolgt. Und als Utschaisrawa aus den Fluten stieg, war der Hengst silberweiß und trug nur einen schwarzen Schweif aus den wenigen getreuen Kindern Kadrus.

Da verfluchte die der Sklaverei verfallene Mutter ihre ungehorsamen Kinder:

„Sterben sollt ihr alle bis zum Letzten! Wenn Dschanamedschaja das Schlangenopfer feiert, soll das Feuer euch verzehren! Alle mögen enden auf dem Opferherd, den der Sohn Parikschits aus dem Kuruhause baut!"

Und der Schöpfer der Welt hörte den Fluch und verhängte seine Erfüllung als Strafgericht über das Schlangenvolk, denn bösen Schaden hatten die Giftzähne der Kadrusöhne seinen Menschen und Tieren schon zugefügt.

Die listigen Schlangen aber versammelten sich in einer Steinwüste und hielten Rat, wie sie dem schrecklichen Fluch der Mutter entgingen.

Einer riet, das Kurugeschlecht unter den Bissen der Nattern sterben zu lassen, auf dass nie ein Parikschit, noch ein Dschanamedschaja geboren werde.

Ein zweiter wollte ruhig die Zeit abwarten bis Dschanamedschaja das Opfer rüste und ihn dann in Brahmanengestalt so eindringlich bitten und warnen, dass er sicher von der Ausführung seines Vorhabens abstünde.

Ein dritter riet, den Priester, der das Schlangenopfer leiten wolle, zu töten. Andere wollten im Regen die Opferfeuer löschen oder die heiligen Geräte verunreinigen, so dass die Zeremonie unwirksam bleibe, Dschanamedschaja töten und noch manches andere.

Doch Wasuki, der Schlangenkönig, sprach mit ernster Miene: „Was schwätzt ihr da von Königs- und Brahmanenmord, ihr Überklugen! – Glaubt ihr Sünde löscht Sünde aus? – Mag dem und jenem Fluch die List entkommen, doch unabwendbar ist ein Mutterfluch! – So unabwendbar wie das Schicksal! – Bei ihm will ich Hilfe suchen, in einer Stunde, da die Götter uns gnädig sind. Vielleicht mildert Brahma den Fluch auf ihre freundliche Fürsprache. Harret und hoffet!"

Traurig, furchtsam und doch voll Hoffnung auf die Weisheit ihres Königs, schlichen die Schlangen hinweg, und Wasuki sann, wie er den Göttern dienen könnte, um sein geliebtes Volk zu erretten.

Amrita, der Göttertrank

Nun war in jener Zeit der Götter Sehnsucht nach ewiger Jugend und Unsterblichkeit erwacht. Die Zauberformel, welche Katscha von den Danawa geholt hatte, war durch Uschanas' Fluch der Welt verloren gegangen und hatte bei allen die Liebe zu ewigem Leben erweckt.

Da traten die Aditisöhne vor Brahma und baten ihn um Rat. Und der Ewige sprach:

„Sehet! im Wasser ist alles, was das Leben erhält! Das winzigste Kräutlein zieht seine Kraft daraus, wie der mächtige Elefant der Berge. Und das Wasser des Himmels fließt in Bächen und Strömen über alles Verwesende, nimmt die letzten Lebenssäfte Lebenskräfte mit und trägt sie in das weite Meer.

Im Ozean ruht das ewige Leben!

Auf! Sondert das Amrita, den köstlichen Unsterblichkeitstrank, von der salzigen Flut, wie der Hirte die goldgelbe Butter von dem bläulichen Nass der Milch!"

Die Götter riefen die Dämonen herbei, denn sie wären allein für das Riesenwerk zu schwach gewesen. Die Söhne der Diti und der Aditi schlossen Frieden und machten sich an die segenverheißende Arbeit.

Der Berg Mandara wurde zum Rührstock ausersehen.

In gewaltiger Anstrengung rissen Götter und Dämonen ihn aus seinen Grundfesten und schleppten ihn zum Meer. Der Schildkrötenkönig Akupara bot seinen starken Rücken als Lager für den Riesenquirl, und Indra hob den Mandara auf den hochgewölbten Panzer des geduldigen Tieres.

Nun fehlte es an einem Strick, um den mächtigen Rührstock zu drehen.

Da hielt der Schlangenkönig Wasuki die Stunde für gekommen, in der er für sich und die Seinen der Götter

Freundschaft und Dankbarkeit erwerben konnte: Er bot sich den Suchenden als Quirlstrick an.

Der tausend Meilen lange Schlangenkönig schlang sich um den Mandara.

Die Götter fassten seinen Kopf, die Dämonen den Schwanz, und in gleichmäßigem Hin und Her wirbelten sie das Meer durcheinander, dass der Gischt in die Wolken spritzte.

Huii! sauste und rauschte das, als die Wellen hier Abgründe aufrissen, dort Berge auftürmten! – Wie im Donner erzitterte die Erde unter dem mächtigen Wogenprall.

In jähem Wirbel wurden zuerst alle Fische in den brodelnden Abgrund gerissen. Immer schneller drehten Götter und Dämonen! Die Drehstürme rissen Vögel aus der Luft und warfen sie in den schäumenden Kessel. Und der Riesenquirl tanzte immer schneller! Die Tiere der Uferwälder wurden von Luftwirbeln in die Tiefe geschleudert, und alles Leben da unten zerstoßen, zermalmt, zerrieben! Baum und Gras wurden hineingerissen, und der Mandara glühte mitten im Meer und ergoss Ströme geschmolzenen Goldes und Silbers ins Wasser!

Da gerannen plötzlich die tobenden Fluten. – Ein wunderschönes Weib in goldgelbem Kleide hob sich aus dem Schaum, in der Rechten eine Schale aus einem einzigen Edelstein tragend: darin war Amrita, der Trank der Unsterblichkeit.

Das herrliche Weib war Lakschmi, die Göttin des Glückes, die leibhaftige Schönheit!

Sie schlang den Arm um Wischnus Hals und wählte ihn zu ihrem Gatten.

Die Götter tranken von dem köstlichen Amrita und gedachten nicht der Dämonen, die jenseits des Berges standen. Die leuchtende Schale ging von Hand zu Hand und ward nicht leer.

Plötzlich bemerkten Sonne und Mond, dass sich Rahu, ein Dämon der Finsternis, unter die trinkenden Götter gemischt hatte und eben an der kostbaren Schale nippte. Erschreckt, riefen sie Wischnu an, und dieser schleuderte seine nie fehlende Wurfscheibe und schnitt damit Rahus Haupt vom Rumpfe.

Tot sank der Leib des Dämonen zu Boden, denn der Unsterblichkeitstrank war noch nicht durch die Kehle gelaufen. Das abgeschnittene Haupt aber fliegt ewig durch den Weltenraum, denn unsterblich ist es durch das Amrita geworden:

Brüllend verfolgt es Sonne und Mond, kommt bald diesem, bald jener nahe und droht die Leuchtenden zu verschlingen – denn sie haben Rahu an Wischnu verraten.

Als die Dämonen sich von den Göttern um das Amrita betrogen sahen, stürzten sie hinter dem Berg hervor, und es kam zu fürchterlichem Kampf.

Aber die Unsterblichen erschlugen der Dämonen so viele als sie umdrängten. Nur wenige konnten sich vor den streitbaren Lichtgöttern in die Tiefe des Meeres retten.

Nachdem die Götter den Berg Mandara wieder auf seinen Platz gestellt hatten, traten sie mit dem Schlangenkönig Wasuki vor Brahmas Angesicht.

Sie priesen dem Ewigen die guten Dienste, die der Herr der Schlangen ihnen geleistet hatte, und baten den Weltenschöpfer, den Fluch der Kadru zu mildern, denn die Sorge um die Zukunft der Seinen verzehre den wackren Wasuki.

Da sprach der milde Herr der Geschöpfe:

„Unauslöschlich steht der Mutter Fluch in meinem Sinne! und zu viele der Giftwürmer schleichen unter meinen geliebten Geschöpfen umher. Sie sollen untergehen, auf dass die Welt gedeihe und der Mutter Wort geachtet werde wie meines. Nur eine kleine Schar von ihnen will meine Gnade erretten:

Wenn Wasukis Schwester Dscharatkaru die Gattin eines frommen Einsiedlers wird, der, trotz seiner Gelübde, um ein Weib bettelt, so wird sie einen edlen Sohn gebären, welcher die letzten Schlangen vor den unwiderstehlich lockenden Zaubersprüchen des Opferpriesters bewahrt!"

Traurig ob des unabwendbaren Verhängnisses schlich Wasuki von dem Lotusthron des Ewigen hinweg.

Er sandte die Klügsten seines Volkes durch alle Lande, dass sie den Büßer suchten, welchen das Schicksal seiner schönen Schwester zum Gatten bestimmt hatte: Das Geschlecht der Zickzackläufer sollte nicht aus der Welt verschwinden.

Patala, die Unterwelt

Die letzten Dämonen hatten sich im Meer verborgen und brüteten Rache.

„Lasst uns Glauben und Sitte vernichten!", sprachen sie. „Ist die Zucht der Frommen dahin, so bleiben die Götter ohne Opfer, und ihre Kraft schwindet, wie Schnee vor der Sonne. Schweigt die Lehre, so stirbt Sitte und Brauch; keiner wird dann ein Opferfeuer entzünden und den Himmlischen Speise und Trank bieten!"

Des Nachts schlichen sie aus den Gewässern, erwürgten die frommen Brahmanen, die Einsiedler und Büßer, und fraßen ihr Fleisch, dass die Knochen und Schädel in der Wildnis bleichten.

Von Tag zu Tag wurden weniger der Frommen, die allein die heiligen Opferbräuche und das alles ordnende Wissen des Weda kannten. Die Feuer erloschen auf den Altären, die Menschen wüteten gegeneinander in Hass und Mord, denn kein Gesetz, keine Vätersitte zügelte ihr wildes Wesen, seit die Überlieferung mit den Lehrern der

Menschheit dahinschwand. Einer scheute den andern, wie das Lamm den Tiger, und sie flohen einander und bargen sich in den Höhlen und Klüften der wildesten Berge.

Nur wenige, in denen die alte Tugendlehre durch einzelne, den Dämonen entgangene Brahmanen lebendig erhalten worden war, zogen als Helden gegen die Schrecken der Finsternis. Doch sie blieben im Kampf mit den Unholden.

Die Lichtgötter verloren an Kraft und Macht, als die Opfer ausblieben, denn der Glaube stärkt Menschheit und Gottheit.

In dieser Not kamen die Himmlischen zu dem allewig Unveränderlichen und baten ihn um Hilfe für seine Welt.

„Ihr sollt die Brahmanenmörder vernichten!", sprach Brahma, „und müsstet ihr dazu den Meeresgrund trocken legen! – Bittet den Heiligen Agastya! Die Bußkraft dieses Frommen ist mächtig genug um euch zu helfen!"

Da gingen sie nach der Klause des Heiligen und sprachen zu ihm: „Du frommer Seher der Urzeit, der Du dem Windhiaberge das Wachsen verboten, als er voll Neid auf den Meru die Sonne verdunkeln wollte! Du Starker, der den Frevler Nahuscha vom Weltenthron gestürzt! Du Edler, der stets der Welt aus aller Not geholfen! Hilf ihr aus diesem verderbenbringenden Elend! Leere den Ozean, dass wir die tückischen Brahmanenmörder fassen und vernichten können!"

Da neigte sich der Gewaltige zum Gestade hinab und trank das Meer aus, bis auf den letzten Tropfen!

Die Götter aber stürmten über den Meeresgrund und töteten die aufgeschreckten Dämonen zu Tausenden und aber Tausenden. Nur eine kleine Schar der Verfolgten grub sich durch die Erde und floh in die Unterwelt, wo Kapila, der Beherrscher des grausigen Patala, thront.

Die sieghaften Götter umwandelten den Heiligen Agastya rechtshin und priesen seine weltbefreiende Tat. Dann baten sie ihn, den Ozean wieder zu füllen, dass in der Welt die alte Ordnung herrsche.

Doch Agastya vertröstete sie auf kommende Zeiten, da Bhagiratha, ein König aus dem Geschlecht der Ikschwakuiden, dem Himmelsstrom Ganga den Weg ins leere Becken des Ozeans weisen würde.

Damals herrschte zu Ajodhia Sagara, ein Urenkel Ikschwakus.

Seine erste Gattin hatte ihm den Stammhalter Asamandscha geschenkt, die zweite einen Kürbis, aus dessen Kernen ihm sechzigtausend starke Söhne erwuchsen. Denn der Segen des heiligen Bhrigu ruhte auf Sagaras Haus.

Die sechzigtausend Sagariden waren gefürchtet auf der weiten Erde. Als gewaltige Kämpfer zogen sie durch die Lande, und ihr hochgemuter Stolz kannte keine Grenzen.

Als der König ein Pferdeopfer feiern wollte, vertraute er das Opferross der Hut seiner tapferen Söhne an.

Dem strengen Opferbrauch gemäß, schweifte der todgeweihte Hengst, jeder Fessel ledig, durch das Land. Als er auf den trockenen Grund des Meeres geriet, verlor er sich durch die Dämonenschlucht in die Unterwelt.

Lange suchten die Sagariden ihn auf der ganzen Erde, denn ein unvollendetes Opfer musste ihrem Haus, ja dem ganzen Lande, schweres Unheil bringen.

Endlich kehrten sie, ohne das ihrer Sorge anvertraute Tier, nach Ajodhia zurück und berichteten dem Vater von ihrem Unglück.

Da fuhr Sagara zornig empor und schrie: „Bringt mir das Ross zum Opfer! und wenn ihr es aus der Unterwelt holen müsstet! – Sonst will mein Auge euch nicht mehr sehen!"

Die Sagariden suchten aufs Neue die Erde und den Meeresgrund ab und fanden endlich die Schlucht, durch welche die letzten Dämonen zum Patala gefahren waren.

Diese betraten sie mutig und, Schritt für Schritt gegen Schlangen und Drachen, Geister und Riesen kämpfend, kamen sie endlich bis zum höllischen Feuer, dem funkelnden Throne des mächtigen Kapila.

Das lange gesuchte Opferross sprang mutwillig neben dem Throne umher.

Und, statt sich ehrfürchtig vor dem Herrn der Unterwelt zu neigen, umstellten die stolzen Recken den flüchtigen Renner und wollten ihn nach der Oberwelt treiben.

Darob ergrimmte der Herr des Feuers, und ein Zornesblick aus seinen Augen verbrannte sie alle zu Asche. Sechzigtausend weiße Häuflein lagen rings um das Pferd.

Zu Ajodhia aber harrte Sagara lange Jahre seiner Söhne und des Hengstes, denn er mochte nicht sterben, ohne das Opfer vollendet zu haben. Asamandscha, der für den Greis die Herrschaft geführt hatte, war ihm schon in den Tod vorausgegangen. Nun sandte er dessen Sohn Ansuman, einen gewinnenden Heldenjüngling, aus, die Sagariden samt dem Opferross zu suchen.

Ansuman fragte sich durch die Welt und fand so die Schlucht, durch welche seine Oheime kämpfend geschritten waren.

Als er vor Kapilas Thron kam umwandelte er den Ehrwürdigen rechtshin und bat ihn, das Opferross, welches friedlich neben dem Höllenfürsten stand, dem Großvater zur Vollendung des Opfers bringen zu dürfen.

Freundlich gab der Mächtige dem schönen Jüngling seine Einwilligung.

Die Asche der Sagariden und Kapilas Erzählung, wie die Stolzen geendet hatten, erinnerten ihn an seine Pflicht als Enkel: Er müsste für ihre Ruhe im Tode sorgen, ihnen den Weg zu Indras Himmel bahnen!

Wieder wandte er sich voll Ehrfurcht an den Herrn der Unterwelt.

„Wenn Ganga, die Tochter des Bergriesen Himawat, ihre Asche benetzt, so werden die Sagariden Ruhe finden!", sprach der Ehrwürdige.

Und Ansuman kehrte mit dem Opferross nach Adjodhia zurück, entschlossen, durch fromme Opfer die Gnade de ergtochter zu gewinnen und die Seelen seiner Ahnherrn von den Schrecken der Unterwelt zu befreien.

Ganga, die Dreipfadige

Zu Ajodhia war das Opfer gefeiert worden, Sagara war gestorben und auch sein Enkel Ansuman.

Auch dem Gebet seines Sohnes Dilipa war es nicht gelungen, die hehre Göttin Ganga von, ihrem funkelnden Lauf am nächtlichen Himmel herabzurufen.

Erst Bhagiratha, dem Enkel Ansumans, erschien die stolze Tochter des Gebirges, als er in schier übermenschlicher Buße seine Jahre am Fuße des Eisstarrenden hinbrachte.

Gnädig fragte die Herrliche nach dem Ziel seiner Buße.

Bhagiratha schilderte den Tod seiner Ahnen und seine Pflicht, als Enkel für die Ruhe der Vorfahren zu sorgen, wenn er einst im Tode den Frieden finden wolle. Er sprach von der Hoffnung, die Kapila seinem Großvater erweckt habe, und bat die Erhabene, sich doch zur Erde herabzulassen und die Ahnen aus der Unterwelt zu erlösen.

Ganga versprach dem Frommen Erfüllung seines brünstigen Flehens, doch müsse Schiwa sie auffangen, sonst würde die Gewalt ihres Sturzes die Erde zerschmettern.

Nun legte Bhagiratha seine Andacht dem starken Gotte Schiwa zu Füßen, und der Erhabene erhörte seine Bitte:

Er trat mit Bhagiratha an den Fuß des Himawat, und als der König rief, stürzten in brausendem Fall die Fluten auf das Haupt des Gottes.

Vom höchsten Gipfel des ehrwürdigen Berges, der in den Himmel ragt, schäumten die Wogen in blitzendem Spiel herab, und alle Götter sahen dem herrlichen Schauspiel zu. Der starke Gott aber empfing den Strom mit der Stirne, wie der Sieger den Kranz. Durch die schwarzglänzenden Locken des Dreizackschwingers brach sich die Herrliche Bahn und rieselte in sieben Strömen über die Brust des Gewaltigen hernieder.

„Nun weise mir den Weg, Bhagiratha!", rief die stolze Tochter des Bergriesen.

In feierlichem Zuge ging es durch Indiens Lande:

Voran Bhagiratha im Büßerkleid. Ihm folgten die Fische, Schildkröten, Schlangen und alles Getier des Meeres. Dann kam die herrliche Tochter des Berges und segnete das Land in weitem Umkreis. Götter und Genien schritten an ihrer Seite und jubelten ob des Glückes der Erde.

Singend und tanzend kam der Zug bis ans Gestade des Meeres und brausend ergoss sich die Flut in das leere Becken.

Noch schritt Bhagiratha voran! und er führte die Hehre über den Boden des Ozeans nach der Dämonenschlucht: Abwärts stürzten die Wasser in gurgelndem Lauf und wanden sich rechtshin um Kapilas Thron.

Die heiligen Fluten netzten die Asche der Sagariden, und sogleich erstanden die stolzen Helden in Göttergestalt und schritten fröhlich nach Indras Himmel.

Bhagiratha eilte zur Erde zurück und zog das Büßerkleid aus, nachdem er der Pflicht gegen die Ahnen genügt hatte.

Als weiser und starker König herrschte er noch lange über Ajodhia.

Ganga aber, deren Weg vom Sternenhimmel über die Erde nach der Unterwelt führt, heißt bei allen Gläubigen die Dreipfadige und ist der Segen der Menschheit.

Das Schlangenopfer

Tausend und aber tausend Jahre waren durch die Welt geeilt.

Dem Weltalter der Götter und ihrer Verehrung war das des Zweifels und großen Kampfes gefolgt.

Parikschit, der Enkel Ardschunas, herrschte zu Hastinapura über das Reich seiner Väter.

Er war edel und kühn und ein großer Freund der Jagd.

Einst hetzte er hinter einem Hirschen her, den sein Bogen weidwund geschossen hatte. Voll Eifer folgte der Jäger der blutigen Spur, bis sie sich auf einer Lichtung verlor. Im eifrigsten Suchen stieß er auf einen Brahmanen, der still seine Kühe hütete.

„Ehrwürdiger!", rief er hastig, „sahst Du nicht einen weidwunden Hirschen vorüberspringen? – Sprich! Ich bin der König!"

Der fromme Büßer erwiderte nichts auf die schnelle Frage, denn er hatte am Morgen gelobt, den Göttern zu Ehren einen Tag lang zu schweigen.

„He! Sprich!", rief Parikschit ungeduldig. „Ich bin Herrscher in diesem Lande!"

Vor dem gleichmütigen Schweigen des Priesters überfiel den eifrigen Jäger der Zorn. Verächtlich schnellte er mit dem Ende des Bogens eine tote Schlange gegen den Büßer und lief davon, aufs Neue den Hirschen zu suchen.

Der Schlangenleib aber hatte sich wie eine Kette um des geduldigen Hals gelegt. Freundlichen Auges sah der Büßer dem enteilenden König nach und freute sich dieser Prüfung.

Demütig trug er das Aas am Halse: in würdiger Beherrschung seines Zornes die Schmach zum Schmucke verwandelnd!

Schamika hieß der gute Heilige, und er hatte ein Söhnlein namens Schringin. Der war ein lebhafter Knabe, welcher über seine Gespielen zu herrschen gewohnt war.

Als die Knabenschar den Heftigen am nächsten Tag verspottete, weil sein Vater den sonderbaren Schmuck auch ferner trug, da wallte Schringinis heißes Blut über.

Weihwasser sprengend rief er aus:

„Stirb, Parikschit! Du Eitler, der einen Weisen zu schmähen wagte, stirb am siebenten Tag von heute: Das Gift des Natternkönigs Takschaka soll Dich töten!"

Und das Schicksal hörte den Fluch des Heiligensohnes und verhängte seine Erfüllung über Parikschit.

Schringin aber lief zu seinem Vater und erzählte, schluchzend vor Zorn und Freude, wie er die schändliche Tat des Königs gerächt habe.

„Wehe"! mein Sohn!", rief Schamika erschreckt. „Was hast Du getan? – Nie soll ein Frommer den Zorn für sich sprechen lassen: Geduld und Weisheit sind die Zauberwaffen des Brahmanen!

Du hast den edlen König Parikschit dem Tode geweiht! – Weh uns! Im Lande ohne König herrscht Not und Elend – Recht und Pflicht vergehen, wo keine starke Hand sie schützt – Indra versagt dem königlosen Land den Regen, und die Dämonen der Dürre heben froh ihr Haupt! – Wer soll die Frommen schützen, wo keine Macht die Bösen bändigt? –

Und Parikschit ist gut – der Jagdeifer nur hatte ihn hingerissen – er kannte mein Schweigegelübde nicht und hielt sich für verhöhnt! – Oh schneller Zorn der Jugend!"

„Mein Vater, was ich sprach wird sich erfüllen!", rief Schringin, „sei's lieb Dir oder leid! – Ich sprach noch nie ein Wort, und wär's im Scherz gewesen, das nicht der Wahrheit folgte, sie verkündete: Heut über sieben Tage stirbt der König vom Gifte Takschakas!"

„Weh uns! – Ich lass den Guten warnen! – Und Du – lern' Selbstbeherrschung! zügle Deinen Zorn, wenn er Dich nicht ins Elend reißen soll! – Der Weise trägt die Welt in sich – nichts außer ihm kann ihn zu Wort und Tat entflammen! – Wie fern bist Du davon, mein Sohn!“

Darauf sandte Schamika einen seiner Jünger nach Hastinapura und ließ dem König sagen, dass Schringin ihn in schnellem Zorn verflucht habe.

Voll Schrecken über die Gefahr, versammelte Parikschit seinen Rat, und dieser traf alle Vorsichtsmaßregeln, um den geliebten Herrscher vor der Natter zu schützen:

Der König wurde ins innerste Gelass des Palastes gebracht. Jeder Eingang, jede Spalte und Ritze wurde aufs Sorgfältigste bewacht. Die besten Ärzte rief man aus dem ganzen Land herbei und stellte Heilkräuter und Gegengifte bereit. Und doch ward der siebente Tag voll Sorge erwartet!

In der Schlangenwelt aber herrschte eitel Freude: Voll Angst hatten die von Mutter Kadru verfluchten Geschöpfe der Erfüllung des Fluches entgegengesehen.

Parikschits künftiger Sohn sollte das vernichtende Opfer feiern, und noch hatte Wasukis Schwester den ihr bestimmten Gatten nicht finden können. Nun befahl der Fluch Schringins, dass Takschaka Parikschit töte! und – Parikschit hatte noch keinen Sohn. – Konnte ein Fluch den anderen aufheben?

Frohen Herzens zog Takschaka gegen Hastinapura. Vor dem Stadttor traf er Kasiap, den berühmtesten der Ärzte. Flugs nahm er die Gestalt eines Brahmanen an und näherte sich dem Weisen.

„Wohin so eilig? würdiger Arzt!“, rief er ihn an.

„Zum König! Takschaka will ihn heute beißen, und ich werde ihn heilen!“

„Oh, Weiser! Ich bin Takschaka, und meinem Gift ist Deine Kunst wohl nicht gewachsen! – Sieh hier den

Baum! – ich beiße ihn in die Wurzel – und schon verdorren seine Blätter – Zweig' und Äste fallen –"

„Halt!", rief Kasiap. Rasch machte er sich an dem sterbenden Baum zu schaffen, und wenige Augenblicke später trieb der Geheilte neue Knospen und grünendes Laub.

Takschaka stand betroffen da.

„Ich staune über Deine Kunst, weiser Arzt!", sprach er dann. „Und doch wird es Dir nicht gelingen, den König zu retten: Eines Brahmanen Fluch wirkt stärker als alles Gift!"

Und da er den Arzt nachdenklich werden sah, fuhr der Schlaue fort:

„Kehre um, Weiser, und lasse Deine Kunst nicht vor dem Schicksal zu schanden werden! Soviel als Dir der König geboten hat, soviel und noch mehr will ich Dir geben."

Damit war Kasiap zufrieden, und, nachdem er des Schlangenkönigs Geld genommen hatte, wandte er Hastinapura den Rücken und ging nach Hause.

Takschaka schritt durch das Tor und kam bis zum Palaste des Königs. Als er sich hier von Wachen angehalten sah, ging er hinweg und rief einige seiner Schlangen. Diese verwandelte er in Brahmanen und ließ sie am Tor des Palastes köstliche Früchte, als Huldigungsgabe für den bedrohten König, abgeben.

Parikschit freute sich über die ehrerbietige Spende, doch als er einen der Apfel öffnete, sah er darin ein kleines Würmchen. Erschrak er auch zuerst vor dem winzigen Schlänglein, so fasste er sich doch bald und sprach:

„Der kleine Heilige soll wahr gesprochen haben: Ich will dies kleine Abbild der Schlange ‚Takschaka' nennen und mich von ihm beißen lassen!"

Lachend hielt er den zappelnden Wurm an seinen Hals.

Doch der schwoll zwischen seinen Fingern zum wahren König der Nattern an, umstrickte den Leib des Entsetzten, und schlug seine Zähne in dessen nackten Hals.

Tod fiel Parikschit zu Boden, und im selben Augenblick
brachte seine Gattin ein Knäblein zur Welt und nannte es
Dschanamedschaja.

Zu jener Zeit zog ein büßender Brahmane namens Dscharatkaru als Bettler durch die Lande. Als ihn die Lust der
Jugend zum ersten Mal geschüttelt hatte, war sein feierliches Gelübde zum Himmel gestiegen:

„Ohne Freude will ich durch die Welt wandern, ohne
Haus und Eigentum leben; wo mich die Nacht findet, will
ich mich schlafen legen! Herr will ich bleiben über Leib
und Geist, Lust und Schmerz, Hass und Liebe! Dscharatkaru soll Dscharatkaru genügen!“

In stiller Versunkenheit war er seither durch die Lande
gezogen und hatte viel fromme Weisheit in sich gefunden.

Einst kam er auf seiner Wanderschaft an einen Abgrund.
Ein schwankendes Rohr sah er über die gähnende Tiefe
ragen, und daran hingen, kopfabwärts, viele Seelen von
Verstorbenen. Das Rohr hing nur noch an einer einzigen Wurzelfaser, und daran nagten, abwechselnd, eine
schwarze und eine weiße Maus.

Entsetzt schrie er auf:

„Oh ihr Unglücklichen! gleich wird die letzte Wurzelfaser reißen, und ihr stürzt in den schrecklichen Abgrund.
Oh könnt’ ich euch helfen! Ein Viertel – die Hälfte – ja
meine ganze Buße will ich hingeben – wenn das euch retten kann, denn mein Herz ist von Mitleid erfüllt!“

„Nicht an Buße mangelt es uns, Du Guter!“, sprachen
die Seelen. „Wir sind das fromme Geschlecht der Iajawara
und haben die schönsten Plätze im Himmel! doch werden
wir sie bald verlieren.

Du weißt, die Seelen der Abgeschiedenen vergehen,
wenn kein Enkel ihrer im Opfer gedenkt. Und Dscharatkaru, der letzte unsres Stammes, will unvermählt sterben.

Siehe das Rohr, das uns trägt, ist unser starkes Geschlecht. Die letzte Wurzelfaser ist der letzte unseres Stammes.

Schwarz und weiß nagen Nacht und Tag an seinem Leben. Ist es zu Ende, so stürzen wir in den Abgrund der Hölle!

Oh edler Fremdling, der Du das Leid mit uns fühlst, suche Dscharatkaru und sage ihm, er soll ein Weib nehmen, auf dass sein Sohn den Stamm fortsetze, wie Brahma es den Menschen gesetzt hat!"

Da warf sich Dscharatkaru an dem Abgrund nieder und schrie:

„Ich Unglücklicher bin Dscharatkaru, euer Sohn und Enkel! Durch Weltflucht wollt' ich euch und mir den Himmel verdienen, und mein strenges Gelübde droht euch nun mit dem Höllenpfuhl. Oh – oh – wie bedrückt mein Schwur die Seele, seit ich euch über dem Abgrund sehe! – Ich will ein Weib suchen – ich kann mein Gelübde nicht brechen –!

Find' ich ein Mädchen namens Dscharatkaru – denn: Dscharatkaru soll Dscharatkaru genügen! – und ist es bereit mein Bettlerdasein zu teilen, so rette ich euch und mich!"

Und wie ein Wahnwitziger eilte er hinweg und schrie durch den Wald: „Wer schenkt seine Tochter einem Bettler? – Aus Barmherzigkeit!"

Die Mädchen aber flohen vor dem schmutzigen, vom Fasten halb verhungerten, Frommen, und er irrte weiter durch die Welt, überall seinen Bettelspruch um ein Weib wiederholend.

Als die Schlangen den Einsiedler um ein Weib betteln hörten, gedachten sie der milden Worte Brahmas und brachten die Nachricht ihrem König Wasuki.

Rasch eilte der um die Rettungseines Volkes Besorgte zu dem frommen Dscharatkaru und bot ihm seine schöne Schwester zur Gattin an.

„Wie heißt Deine Schwester?", fragte der Büßer.

„Dscharatkaru, wie Du!"

„Und weißt Du, dass ich sie nicht ernähren kann? denn ich bin ein Bettler und habe gelobt es zu bleiben."

„Ich will sie beschenken und erhalten, als würde sie das Weib eines Königs!", sprach Wasuki.

Da ging Dscharatkaru in Wasukis Palast, und vor dem heiligen Hausfeuer nahm er die Schlangenprinzessin in feierlicher Hochzeit zum Weibe.

Als Dscharatkaru ihrem Gatten ein Knäblein schenkte, nannte sie es Astika, und der fromme Brahmane weihte es der Gattin Brahmas, Sarasvati, der Schirmherrin von Kunst und Wissen, der Göttin der Beredsamkeit. Aus dem reichen Gnadenschatz seiner Buße, schenkte Dscharatkaru dem Söhnlein die Gabe, dass niemand seinen Bitten widerstehen können sollte.

Im Königspalast zu Hastinapura war einstweilen Dschanamedschaja zum gewaltigen Helden herangewachsen, und er führte die Herrschaft als kluger und tapferer König.

Als er einst im Triumph von der Bestrafung eines raubsüchtigen Nachbarn heimkehrte, trat ihm Ruru, ein junger Brahmane, entgegen.

„Du glaubst von einer großen Tat zu kommen, König!", sprach er zu Dschanamedschaja. „Und doch hast Du nur Raub an Deinem Eigentum bestraft, und der Mord an Deinem Vater ist noch ungerochen!"

„Was sprichst Du da? Jüngling aus edlem Geschlecht!", rief der König. „Wer bist Du? und wie starb mein Vater?"

„Ruru heiße ich, und vor wenigen Monden hat eine Natter meine Braut zu Tode gebissen. Yama, der gute Gott des Todes, hat auf mein inniges Flehen gewährt, dass ich das mir zugemessene Stück Leben mit ihr teile. So lebt sie wieder und ist meine Gattin, bis Yamas Boten uns – ach!

lange vor der Zeit – holen werden. Doch den Nattern habe ich Rache geschworen und komme, Dich, König, mahnen! Auch Du hast die Pflicht die Argen zu vertilgen, denn Dein Vater Parikschit fiel unter dem Giftzahn des Natternkönigs!"

Da berief Dschanamedschaja den weisen Priester Utanka nach Hastinapura und ließ von ihm das große Schlangenopfer rüsten, denn der allein kannte die verborgensten Opferbräuche und die zwingenden Zaubersprüche.

In der Opferhalle saß der junge König. Erlauchte Gäste aus allen Ländern umgaben ihn: Herrscher aus den benachbarten Reichen, Freunde und Vasallen, viele edle Frauen und würdige Priester.

Wyasa war gekommen, der greise Heilige, der als Sänger die Heldentaten der Vorfahren pries und von der großen Schlacht am Kurufelde sang.

In weiser Rede und Gegenrede glänzten die ehrwürdigen Brahmanen vor dem ganzen Hof und empfingen reiche Geschenke von dem freigebigen Herrscher.

Und vor der Halle loderten die Opferfeuer! Priester in schwarzen Talaren schritten dazwischen umher und nährten sie mit Sandel und anderen kostbaren Hölzern, sprengten Weihwasser aus goldenen Becken nach allen Himmelsrichtungen und wiederholten Utankas halblaut gesungenen

SCHLANGENZAUBER

Kommt, ihr Sanften, Klugen, Schnellen!
Kommt, ihr Kinder Mutter Kadrus!
Grüne, gelbe, blaue, rote,
Schwarze Brut der braunen Erde!

Wärmt euch an der hellen Flamme,
Wie im Schein der goldnen Sonne,
Kühlt euch in geweihtem Wasser,
Wie in Indras Regenflut!

Kommt! und ruft die ganze Sippe:
Vater, Oheim, Bruder, Schwester
Und der Schwester flinken Gatten!
Kommt in Rudeln, Kommt in Scharen!
Komm, Du ganzes Volk der Schlangen!
Fünfundfünfzig,
Siebenundsiebzig,
Neunundneunzigtausend Völker
Kluger Schlangen, eilt herbei!
Beißzahn, Schnellzung', Zähneschärfer,
Tausendgift, Gazellenwerfer,
Würger, Viper, Otter, Natter,
Ewigfresser, ewig Satter:
Hört und eilt und kommt herbei!

Wohl! ihr naht:
Es glänzt das Feuer,
Sprüht das Wasser wie ein Regen
Aus den güldenen Gefäßen,
Die des Priesters Hand geweiht!
Schwarzer Rauch steigt gegen Himmel
Und die ersten Opfer brennen,
Sterben nach der Mutter Fluch!

Weiter, weiter!
Kommt in Scharen,
Kommt in Heeren!

Komm, Du gift'ges Volk der Schlangen!
Fünfundfünfzig,
Siebenundsiebzig,
Neunundneunzigtausend Völker
Gift'ger Schlangen, eilt herbei!

Seht ihr, wie die Flamme loht?
Und die Flamme loht zum Tod!
Stürzt ins lodernde Verderben –
Alles end' im großen Sterben!
Die ihr in den Wäldern lauert,
Die ihr unter Steinen kauert,
Die ihr kriechet durch den Kot:
Kommt! – Nun prasselt euch der Tod!

Kommt, ihr Bösen, Gift'gen, Falschen!
Kommt, ihr Kinder Mutter Kadrus!
Grüne, gelbe, blaue, rote,
Schwarze Brut, der braunen Erde!.
Brennt! ihr schnellen Zickzackläufer,
Dass ihr niemals wiederkehret!
Endet für und mit dem Mörder:
Takschaka! ich rufe Dich!

Lockend und drohend klang es in die Wälder hinaus, fand seinen Weg zum Ohr und Herzen der Schlangen, koste den schlanken Leib und schüttelte ihn vor Entsetzen.

Langsam folgten die gerufenen der unwiderstehlichen Lockung. Langsam, doch stetig!

Angstvoll hielten sie nach den ersten Windungen an, riefen Verwandte und Freunde, um in ihnen Kraft zum Widerstreben zu finden, und rissen die Herbeigeeilten nur mit auf den Weg zum Verderben.

Das Säuseln des Windes trug die Zauberformel durch alle Lande: süß schmeichelnd und lockend, trotzig drohend und fesselnd!

In allen Wäldern raschelte das Laub den seltsamen Spruch und lockte die Schwachen zum Tode; die Bäche murmelten ihn auf ihrem Lauf und die heißen Steine klirrten ihn in die Sonne!

Weit und breit bedeckten sich die Wege nach Hastinapura mit gleitenden Schlangenleibern, und alles wogte nach den lodernden Feuern vor der Opferhalle. Das glitt und sprang und warnte den Nachbar vor der Gefahr, die ihn selbst anzog. Wie ein Rausch war es über die klugen Geschöpfe gekommen, wie ein vernichtender Rausch und ein verzehrender Durst nach Tod und Todesfurcht!

Wochen, Monde und Jahre währte das Opfer.

Hundert- und aber hunderttausend Schlangen waren dem lockenden Rufe Utankas und seiner Priester schon gefolgt – waren ins lodernde Feuer geglitten und ihrer Mutter zu Ehren verbrannt.

Wenige bargen sich noch in den geheimsten Schlupfwinkeln, doch zwingend klang auch dorthin das geheimnisvolle Raunen vom Feuer auf der Opferstätte.

Takschaka war mit Wasuki zu dessen Schwester geflohen, die als Weib eines Brahmanen über den Zauber erhaben war. Doch blutenden Herzens beklagte die gute Dscharatkaru den Untergang ihres lieben Volkes.

Wasuki seufzte, dass Astika, das Söhnlein der Schwester, erst zwölf Jahre alt sei, denn von ihm sollte den letzten des Schlangenvolkes Rettung werden, nach Brahmas mildem Spruch. – Ach! es würde zu spät sein! denn wenige waren nur, die dem Zauber noch widerstanden hatten.

Als Astika die Klagen der Mutter und des Oheims hörte, tröstete er sie mit verheißenden Worten und eilte an den

Hof Dschanamedschajas, um die letzten vom Geschlecht seiner Mutter zu erretten.

Takschaka aber fühlte den Zauber in seinem Herzen bohren und locken, und floh vor Entsetzen zu Indra, dass dieser traute Freund des regenfrohen Schlangenvolkes ihn vor dem sengenden Tod beschütze.

Und zu Hastinapura ging das Opfer weiter:

> *Kommt, ihr Bösen, Gift'gen, Falschen!*
> *Kommt, ihr Kinder Mutter Kadrus!*
> *Grüne, gelbe, blaue, rote,*
> *Schwarze Brut der braunen Erde!*
> *Brennt! ihr schnellen Zickzackläufer,*
> *Dass ihr niemals wiederkehret!*
> *Endet für und mit dem Mörder:*
> *Takschaka, ich rufe Dich!*

So klang es in den Wald hinein, als der schöne Knabe Astika zur Opferstätte kam.

Doch wehe: Die Wachen, die Diener des Palastes, die Priester – alle wiesen das Kind von der Stätte ernster Andacht, denn sie fürchteten eine Störung des Opfers, und Takschaka, das Ziel des jahrelangen Mühens, war von den lockenden Zaubersprüchen noch nicht bezwungen worden.

Da stand Astika an der weiten Pforte, die zur Opferstätte führte, und sah die Priester mit rauchroten Augen die Feuer schüren, den König und seine Gäste mit Andacht der heiligen Handlung folgen und über alles eine ernste Schönheit gebreitet.

Begeistert hob er seine helle Knabenstimme, und jubelnd klang es zur Weihestätte:

„Oh seht das herrliche Opfer!

Die Feuer leuchten wie die Sterne am Himmel, und der Opferherr thront unter ihnen wie der lichte Mond.

Golden und schwarzrandig loht es zum Himmel, und rechtshin streicht der duftende Opferrauch, zur Freude der Götter.

Frommen Herzens wandeln die Priester zwischen den Feuern, und ihre Weisheit ist die Brücke zwischen Menschen und Göttern.

Reich wird der Opferdank des gastfreien Königs sein, denn er ist der Herrlichste unter den Gatten der Erde –den Vätern der Völker!

Segen ist in seinem Lande, soweit ein Auge nur reicht, denn er ist tapfer und gerecht und der Stolz seines Geschlechtes!

Strengstes Opfer, das jemals zum Himmel flammte! Beste Brahmanen, die je einen Herrscher gepriesen! Edelster König, der Indra gleicht, wie er in den Wolken thront: seid gesegnet!"

„Wer ist der Knabe mit der milden Weisheit eines Alten?", fragte Dschanamedschaja und ließ Astika vor seinen Thron führen.

„Heil Dir, Herr der Erde!", sprach das schöne Kind, als es vor dem König stand. „Ich frage nicht, wie es die Sitte erheischt, ob Segen herrscht in Deinem Reiche, ob Dein Schatz gefüllt und Dein Heer stark ist, ob Du den Sechsten nach Recht und Pflicht nimmst! denn Dein Auge verrät, dass Du ein guter, ein Edler, ein Weiser bist, und mit solchen ist das Glück und die Gnade der Götter!"

„Du bist ein Weiser, liebliches Brahmanenkind!", sprach der König voll Freude, „und ich will Dir jegliche Gnade erweisen, die Du erbittest. Fordere! Alles sei Dir gewährt!"

„Halt! edler König!", rief Utanka in diesem Augenblick. „Mein sündenloses Auge sieht Takschaka, den lange vergebens gerufenen, in Indras Palast. Nun will ich ihn mit der

Zange meiner Worte packen und herunterziehen ins verzehrende Feuer. Spare solang Deine Bitte, schöner Knabe,
und Du Deine Gabe, schenkender Herrscher, bis ich ihn
fallen seh' in den glühenden Tod!"

Und ins tiefste Schweigen der Andacht sang der Priester
sein lockendes Lied und schloss mit dem zwingenden:

Takschaka! Dich rufe ich!

Und da litt es den Natternkönig nicht länger an des Freundes Seite; lautlos schlich er aus der Halle des Götterkönigs
und glitt am Himmelsgewölbe abwärts, gegen die leuchtende Opferstätte von Hastinapura.

Indra wollte den treuen Freund retten, ihn zurückhalten
von sicherem Verderben. Er sprang ihm nach und umklam-
merte den Abwärtsfliehenden mit seinen starken Armen.

Aber Utankas Ruf zog den Natternkönig wie an einer
eisernen Kette, und Indra musste ihn lassen, wenn er den
Sturz in den Tod nicht mitmachen wollte.

Schneller nun fiel der Verlassene und war wie ein
leuchtender Blitz am Himmel zu sehen.

„Jetzt ist Takschaka mir sicher!", rief der Opferer Utanka.

„Nun sprich Deine Bitte, lieblicher Knabe, ehe er und
die letzten seines Geschlechtes in den Flammen prasseln!"

„So will ich, dass das Opfer zu Ende sei!", rief der Sohn
der Schlangenprinzessin, und ein Wink seiner Hand hielt
den fallenden Takschaka am Himmel auf.

Bestürzt rief der König:

„Was sinnst Du, Knabe? – Um Takschakas willen ward
dies furchtbare Opfer gefeiert, denn er hat meinen Vater
getötet!"

„Und willst Du darum das ganze Geschlecht meiner
Mutter ausrotten?", sprach flehenden Auges Astika.

Da schwieg der König, und auf seinen Wink wurden die
Opferfeuer verlöscht.

Astika hatte die letzten Schlangen vor dem Verderben
bewahrt, und ihm danken die munteren Zickzackläufer,
dass sie sich heute noch sonnen und in Indras Fluten küh-
len können.

Takschaka aber steht als Sternbild am Himmel, dort wo
Astikas Wink ihn festgehalten hat. Ein leuchtendes Beispiel für die zwingende Gewalt geheiligter Bräuche und die
alles besiegende Macht des reinen Geistes!

Nala und Damayanti

In uralter Zeit herrschte zu Nischada, einem der vielen Reiche Indiens, der junge König Nala. Stärke, Schönheit und Tugend zierten ihn vor allen anderen Männern. Die tapfersten Helden hatte er mit Schwert und Keule besiegt, führte den Streitwagen so sicher wie der Sonnengott, und traf auf hundert Schritte eine Nuss mit dem Pfeil. Vor der Schar seiner Helden glänzte er wie die Vorausreiter der Morgenröte und war erzogen in tiefster Ehrfurcht vor den Göttern und ihren Gesetzen in Liebe zur Wahrheit und Treue am Wort, so dass ihn Freund und Feind den Makellosen nannte. Seine Weisheit und der Adel seines Wesens wurden in allen Landen besungen, sein Glück ward sprichwörtlich.

Einst jagte er mit seinem Freund und Rosselenker Warschneja in den Wäldern Nischadas.

Der Rosselenker des Königs war in Altindien ein gar hoher Herr, denn er führte den Streitwagen seines Gebieters im Gefecht, und an seiner Umsicht und Geschicklichkeit hing oft das Leben des Königs. Er war der Marschall, dem die königlichen Ställe unterstellt sind, war der erste Rat des Königs in weltlichen Dingen, sein Herold und, als nächster Mitkämpfer, der berufene Sänger seiner Heldentaten.

Nala und Warschneja lagerten sich am Ufer eines romantischen Weihers und der liederkundige Rosselenker kürzte seinem königlichen Freund die Zeit durch die folgende Erzählung:

„In Widarbha, dem großen Reiche, herrscht heute noch der greise König Bhima, der der Schrecken seiner Feinde heißt. Vor vielen Sommern hat er Opfer um Opfer gebracht, dass der Himmel ihm Kinder schenke, denn, wie Du weißt, o Herr, öffnet nur das Gebet des eigenen Kindes den lichten Himmel Yamas. Lange flehte er vergeblich, doch ward er nicht müde im Opferdienst und hoffte auf die dreiunddreißig Götter. Einst kam ein Büßer aus dem heiligen Hain zu Bhima. König und Königin empfingen ihn an der Pforte, in demütigem Gruß die Hände faltend. Bhima führte ihn nach dem Ehrensitze und bot ihm Fußwasser; die Königin brachte die gastliche Spende: den gewürzten Reis und einen Trunk klaren Wassers. Dann saßen sie zu seinen Füßen und lauschten seinen weisen Reden.

Der heilige Mann war über die ehrerbietige Gastfreundschaft erfreut, und seiner Fürsprache beim Herrn der Welt dankten sie den heiß ersehnten Segen: Drei Knäblein schenkte die Königin ihrem Gatten und ein holdes Mägdlein. Zu Helden sind die Knaben herangewachsen, und Damayanti, König Bhimas Tochter, ist die schönste Jungfrau auf Erden: Glanzlockig und zartgliedrig steht sie inmitten ihrer hundert Gespielinnen, wie der Mond unter den Abendwolken, nur Lakschmi, der meerentstiegenen Göttin des Glückes, zu vergleichen, die noch keines Sterblichen Auge gesehen. Fröhlichen Sinnes ist sie, und ihr Lachen klingt wie die Stimme des Bergquells; wie Edelsteine blitzen ihre Mandelaugen unter den schönen Brauen, und ihre Wangen sind wie Blumenblätter ...“

„Sieh, König!“, unterbrach sich Warschneja, „der goldflügelige Schwan, der sich uns naht, wär' eine Beute, des königlichen Jägers würdig!“

„Lass nur den Schwan“, sprach sinnend der König, „und sprich mir von Damayanti, denn ich liebe das holde Kind, seit ich von ihm gehört!“

„Dank! König Nala, dass Dein todbringender Pfeil mich verschont!", rief der Schwan über das Wasser. „Ich will Dir's lohnen: zu Damayanti flieg' ich nun und will ihr von König Nala singen und sagen, bis sie Dich liebt, wie Du sie!". Und auf flog der Goldflügler vom Wasser und strich in langen Zügen gegen Widharba. Nala aber wurde nicht müde von Damayanti zu hören und zu sinnen wie er sie erwerbe.

Zu Kundina, der Hauptstadt Widharbas, ergötzte sich Damayanti mit ihren Gespielinnen im Garten des königlichen Palastes. Als eine Schar von Wasservögeln nach dem Teiche strich, liefen alle hin, um sie mit Brot und Früchten zu füttern, im Spiele zu haschen und sich an ihrer Schönheit zu erfreuen. Der Führer der Vögel aber, ein goldflügeliger Schwan, schwamm zu Damayanti und sprach mit menschlicher Stimme:

„Damayanti! In Nischada herrscht König Nala, den man den Makellosen nennt. Er ist der schönste der schwerttragenden Männer, ihr Klügster und Tapferster! Strahlend wie die Reiter des Morgenrotes, stark wie der Tiger, des Waldes König, und weise wie ein Heiliger. Dir gilt all sein Denken, denn er entbrannte in Liebe zu Dir, als er von Deiner Anmut gehört, und schreitet nun über die Erde wie die fleischgewordene Liebe. Niemand ist ihm zu vergleichen: kein Mensch und keiner der himmlischen Spielleute, kein Genius und kein verführerischer Teufel. Er ist der Diamant der Mannheit, wie Du die Perle der Frauen bist. Wir Luftdurchsegler wissen es, denn wir kennen alle Geschöpfe Gottes. Wenn er Dein Gatte würde: das Köstlichste zum Köstlichsten käme, dann erst wäre die Welt vollkommen!"

Als der Schwan wieder aufflog, winkte ihm die Blume von Widharba und rief errötend: „Grüß' König Nala!". Und sinnend ging sie vor ihren Frauen ins Haus; das sehnsuchtbefiederte Blütengeschoss Kamas, des Liebesgottes, hatte über weite Lande hin getroffen. Tag und Nacht trug die Lotusäugige ein heißes Sehnen im Herzen und lernte Lust und Qual der Liebe kennen. Wenn die Mädchen sich in fröhlichem Reigen auf dem Anger schwangen, sah sie nach den jagenden Wolken und seufzte; wenn alle lachten, so weinte sie; wenn alles schlief, sah sie in die Nacht hinaus und bat jede Sternschnuppe: Grüß' König Nala! Ihre Gespielinnen sahen sie immer bleicher werden und hörten nicht mehr ihr fröhliches Lachen.

Da lief die kluge Kesini, Damayantis Gürtelmagd, zu König Bhima und klagte ihm, dass ihre Gebieterin an einem unbekannten Leid sieche. Vater und Mutter aber ahnten, was Damayantis Herz bedrücke, und sandten Boten in alle Lande, die dort verkündigen mussten: Nach sieben Monden wird König Bhimas Tochter im Hause des Vaters den Gatten wählen!

Nun rüsteten die Könige und Prinzen aller Länder zur Reise und zogen in hellen Scharen nach Kundina, denn jeder hoffte auf das Glück, vor Damayantis Augen Gnade zu finden. Sie kamen mit Rossen und Wagen, auf Elefanten und Kamelen, geschmückt mit Blumenkränzen und allen Schätzen Indiens, in glänzenden Waffen, von stolzen Vasallen umgeben und erfüllten die gastfreien Hallen und Höfe in Bhimas Palast mit Waffenlärm, Lachen und Singen, und manchem Seufzer der Liebe.

Nun geschah es zu jener Zeit, dass zwei heilige Männer, bußereiche Einsiedler, ihr Erdenwallen vollendet hatten und in den strahlenden Himmel Yamas einzogen.

Dort fanden sie unter dem mächtigen Feigenbaum, im nieverlöschenden Licht, die Herrn des Himmels und der Erde beim berauschenden Somatrank sitzen. Indra saß da auf dem Ehrensitz, den des Götterschmieds kundige Hand aus Gold getrieben hatte, das Urbild des Kriegers: hoch und breitbrüstig, mit Armen wie Keulen, das Haupt von hellen Locken und mächtigem Barte umrahmt, die Augen voll Feuer; Varuna, der Herr der Gewässer und Schirmherr der Rosse, im goldschimmernden Panzer; Agni, der Feuergott, der ewig junge, ewig neue, der als Freund der Menschen seine roten Stuten über die Erde treibt, und Yama, der ernste Gott des Todes und des Rechtes, an dessen Füße sich zwei vieräugige Hunde schmiegten.

Die Heiligen grüßten die Götter und fragten, wie es die Sitte heischte, gar artig den obersten: „Gabenreicher Indra, mächtiger Dämonenbezwinger, bist Du und die Fürsten bei gutem Wohlsein?". Indra dankte und sprach die Hoffnung aus, dass die Heiligen während ihres Erdenwallens reiche Schätze an Buße aufgehäuft hätten. Dann fragte er, wie es wohl käme, dass ihn schon mondenlang keiner von den Helden der Erde besucht habe. „Diese, meine Welt der Seligkeiten, die jeden Wunsch erfüllt, steht allen offen, die ehrlichen Schlachtentod fanden!", so sprach er.

„O, Götterkönig!", rief einer der Büßer „so weißt Du nicht, dass alle Waffen ruhen, bis Damayanti den Gatten gewählt hat! Damayanti, des Widharberkönigs holdes Kind, das an Schönheit alle Frauen der Erde übertrifft, den Götterjungfrauen gleicht und der fußlos wandelnden Sonne! Zu Damayantis Gattenwahl ziehen alle Fürsten der Erde, denn für sie schlagen aller Helden Herzen!"

„Bei Writra, den mein Donnerkeil erschlagen hat! da wollen wir dabei sein!", rief Indra, und die Götter stimmten freudig ein.

Als die vier Welthüter zur Erde fuhren, sahen sie König Nala, der auf den Ruf von Bhimas Boten zur Gattenwahl Damayantis reiste. Und weil er so schön von Gestalt war und von makellosem Ruf, so wollten sie ihn zu ihrem Boten wählen. Sie stiegen aus den Wolken nieder, und Indra rief: „He, König der Nischader, Herr unter den Königen, Du bist worttreu und ein Freund der Wahrheit: Sei uns Beistand und Bote, edelster der Männer!"

„Ich will es sein!“, gelobte Nala den Strahlenden und neigte sich mit ehrfürchtigem Händefalten. „Wer seid ihr? und an wen wollt ihr mich senden?“

„Unsterbliche sind wir, die um Damayanti, die schönste der Sterblichen, werben wollen. Indra heiß’ ich, hier Agni und der Herr der Gewässer, dort Yama, der Menschheit Richter im Leben und im Tod. Melde der Lieblichen: Indra, Agni, Varuna oder Yama, einen der vier soll sie zum Gatten wählen.“

Demütig bat Nala: „Erlasset mir diesen Dienst, ihr Welthüter voller Gnade! Wie kann ich tun, was mir das Herz bricht? Ich wollt’ um Damayanti werben, wie kann ich eure Sache gut führen!“

„Du hast’s gelobt, nun halt’ Dein Wort!“

„Wie komme ich durch die Wachen vor dem Frauenhaus?“, fragte Nala traurig.

„Sie sollen Dich nicht sehen!“, sprach Indra, und schweren Herzens ging der Nischader, um sein Wort redlich zu halten.

Unbelästigt kam er in den Hof des Frauenhauses. Dort wusch Kesini den weißen Mantel ihrer Herrin im Abendtau und bleichte ihn im Mondenschein. Die Kluge sah den Herrlichen und führte ihn vor Damayanti und ihre Frauen. War das ein Staunen und Raunen unter den Mädchen, als der Held in den Saal trat. „Wer mag der Herrliche sein?“ „Sieh sein strahlendes Auge!“ „Ist’s ein Gott?“. So flüsterte es durcheinander, und aller Augen hafteten an Nala, die Wangen röteten sich verschämt, und die Herzen schlugen schneller. Damayanti mochte wohl ahnen, wer vor ihr stand, und fragte frohen Herzens: „Wer bist Du, Strahlender, der meine Pulse fliegen macht? Bist Du ein Gott, dass Du trotz aller Wachen ins Frauenhaus findest?“

„Ich bin König Nala und komme als Götterbote, so fand ich ungesehen Einlass: Indra, Agni, Varuna und Yama werben um Dich, holde Jungfrau, wähle einen der vier Welthüter zum Gatten! Ich habe gesprochen, nun tu nach Deinem Sinn, zu Deinem Heil!"

Als Damayanti von der Werbung der Götter hörte, neigte sie sich in Demut und traurig; als sie aber in Nalas Augen sah, ward sie wieder froh, schüttelte das Köpfchen und sprach:

„Die Götter bete ich an – Dich liebe ich, Nala! und wenn Du mich nicht erhörst, so muss ich sterben vor Scham und Herzeleid!". Ernst sprach König Nala: „Nicht eigne Sache führe ich heute, mein Herz muss schweigen, bis mein Amt erfüllt! Als Götterbote frag ich Dich: Wer kann versagen, wo Indra wirbt, der Held der Helden, der Wolkenspalter, Sieger, Gott der Götter! Wo Agni freit, der Opfernehmer, der milde Freund, der Schirmer des Heims, und Varuna, der Herr der Meere, der mit den Perlen spielt? Wer schlägt Yama aus, der vom Leid erlöst und den Himmel öffnet? Luftraumbezwinger, Feuerbeherrscher, Wassergebieter, des Irdischen Herr! – Wähle Du, Weib! – Ich muss gehorchen."

„Du kennst Deine Pflicht!", sprach Damayanti „und ich die meine: Der Zorn der Götter darf Dich nicht treffen! Sage den Unsterblichen: Wenn alle Fürsten zur Feier versammelt sind, wird Damayanti wählen! –und in der Götter Gegenwart will ich *Dich* wählen, Makelloser!", und errötend schlüpfte die Schöne aus dem Saal.

Da ging Nala zu den Göttern und sagte ihnen alles. Sie dankten dem worttreuen Wahrheitsfreund und entbanden ihn seiner Botenpflicht.

König Bhimas Hausbrahmane hatte einstweilen die Zeichen erforscht, Mond und Sterne befragt und die günstigste Stunde für die Gattenwahl bestimmt.

Da kamen alle die fürstlichen Gäste zur großen, säulengetragenen Halle im Königspalast von Widharba. Schöne und starke Männer, in reichen, bunten Gewändern, mit

Gold und Edelsteinen auf der Brust und in den Ohren und ihren guten Waffen in den Händen! Reichbekränzt zogen sie durch die Ehrenpforte ein und lagerten sich auf Pfühlen und Stühlen.

Als Damayanti, schüchtern und stolz, erschien, schlugen ihr alle Herzen entgegen, und jeder freute sich des holden Anblickes. Sie aber schaute nur flüchtig über die Helden hin: ihr Auge suchte König Nala.

Doch wie erschrak sie: Der Geliebte, den sie gesucht, stand hier und dort und wieder da – fünf Gestalten zählte sie, die König Nala glichen. Wie sollte sie den Rechten wählen? Ängstlich spähte sie nach den Götterzeichen – umsonst! es waren lauter Menschen, liebe Menschen, aber Menschen, die sich nicht im Kleinsten unterschieden. Und in der Not ihres Herzens beschloss sie bei den Göttern Hilfe zu suchen. Demütig faltete sie die Hände und betete zitternd:

„Ihr Himmlischen, zeiget mir König Nala! So wahr ich keines anderen Mannes gedachte, seit mir der Schwan von Nala gesprochen, so innig seid gebeten: zeigt mir König Nala! So wahr die Götter mir selbst Nala zum Gatten bestimmten, so heiß seid beschworen: zeigt mir König Nala! So wahr ich Nala ehren will als meinen Gatten und ihn ewig nie mit Willen kränken, so klar mögt ihr Himmlischen in eurem Glanz erscheinen, dass ich erkennen kann meinen Nala, den Gebieter und Herrn!"

Die einfältige Treue der lieblichen Jungfrau rührte die Götter, und sie erfüllten ihre Bitte:

Schattenlos standen sie über dem Boden, schweißlos und staublos, strahlenden Blickes, und ihre Kränze blühten wie am Strauch.

Nala dagegen stand fest am Boden, schattenwerfend, Schweiß und Staub auf der Stirn, im Sonnenlicht blinzelnd, und sein Kranz begann zu welken.

Da ergriff Damayanti den Saum seines Kleides und legte dem Helden ihr Blumengewinde ums Haupt: sie hatte den Gatten gewählt!

Tosender Jubel scholl durch die Halle, und alle priesen den Nischader glücklich.

König Nala aber gelobte sein Weib zu lieben, zu ehren, und es nie zu verlassen.

Als nun die Hochzeit gefeiert wurde, und das Brautpaar Hand in Hand das Hausfeuer feierlich rechtshin umwandelt hatte, da beschenkten die Götter es reichlich; Damayanti verhießen sie zwei schöne Kindlein, und dem Nischader verlieh Indra ein helles Auge, das die Gottheit beim Opfer leibhaftig sieht, und den stets aufrechten Gang, selbst wenn er durch Mauern schritte. Agni gab ihm Gewalt über das Feuer und Varuna über das Wasser, Yama aber die Kunst gar köstliche Speisen zu bereiten. Segen und Schutz verhießen die Götter Nalas Haus, solang er die Opferbräuche achte. Nachdem sie das Paar so beglückt hatten, nahmen sie Abschied, um nach dem Himmel zurückzukehren.

Vor dem Tor von Kundina begegneten sie Kali und Dwapara. Kali war der leibhaftige Böse, den man ‚Spielteufel‘ nennen kann, denn das Würfelspiel war damals das ärgste und meist verbreitete Laster im Lande. Dwapara, das heißt ‚Fehlwurf‘, war ein dienender Geist Kalis.

Die Welthüter hielten sie an und fragten: „Wohin des Weges?“

„Zu Damayantis Gattenwahl“, lachte Kali „ich will mich unter die Bewerber mischen. Hat doch schon manches schöne Weib den leibhaftigen Teufel gewählt. Vielleicht habe ich Glück, ich liebe sie schon lange.“

„Du kommst zu spät, dummer Teufel!“, lachte Indra dagegen „die Gattenwahl ist längst vorüber, und Damayanti hat, vor uns, den Nischaderkönig Nala gewählt.“

„Vor Euch? dass Dich –!“, brummte Kali „das soll sie
büßen, dass sie den Sterblichen einem Unsterblichen vor-
gezogen hat!“

„Wir hatten es ihr erlaubt, denn Nala glänzt vor den
Männern, wie Damayanti vor den Frauen. Er ist ein tapferer und weiser Fürst, hält strenge alle Vorschriften der
heiligen Bücher, spendet Opfer, dass alle Unsterblichen in
seinem Hause satt werden, und ist ein Vorbild der Treue,
Wahrhaftigkeit und Rechtschaffenheit. Und wer es sich,
trotz seiner Frömmigkeit, einfallen ließe ihn zu quälen,
Kali, der möcht’ es wohl am eignen Leibe büßen, Kali! und
müsst’ im tiefsten Höllenpfuhle enden!“

Also sprach Indra, mit gerunzelter Braue, und die vier
Welthüter setzten ihre Fahrt fort.

„Eine derbe Lektion!“, zischte Kali „aber euer Affe soll
es mir büßen! Dwapara, Du musst ihm in die Würfel fahren, wenn ich ihn je zum Spielen bringen kann!“

Und von der Stund’ an hefteten sich die beiden unsichtbar an des Nischaders Fersen.

Die Neuvermählten hatten die Festwochen im gastfreien Palaste König Bhimas verbracht und waren sodann
mit dem Segen der Eltern nach Nischada gezogen.

Dort empfing sie des Volkes Jubel ob der schönen
Königin.

Frieden und Glück herrschten im Reich, die Opferfeuer
brannten reichlich, und des Himmels Segen ruhte auf
allem durch manches Jahr.

Eines Abends begab es sich, dass der König vom
Weihwasser nippte, aber der vorgeschriebenen Fußwa-
schung vergaß.

Da gewann Kali Macht über ihn und fuhr in den
Vergesslichen!

Als Puschkara, des Königs Bruder, ihn am andern Tage
zum Würfeln aufforderte, da konnte der vom Spielteufel

Besessene nicht widerstehen. Und Dwapara, der Fehlwurf, beherrschte seine Würfel!

Als es Mittag ward, hatte Nala all sein Gold verspielt und würfelte weiter.

Der Hausbrahmane warnte ihn, doch er predigte tauben Ohren!

Und als es Abend ward, hatte Nala Haus und Hof, Rosse und Sklaven verspielt und würfelte weiter.

Warschneja kam, der Treue, an der Spitze des Volkes und bat den Unseligen vom Spiele zu lassen. Der König hörte ihn nicht!

Und als es Mitternacht ward, da hatte er das Reich verspielt an seinen Bruder Puschkara.

Damayanti kam und flehte ihn an, doch jetzt vom Spiele zu lassen und mit ihr und den Kindern zu Bhima zu fliehen. Doch des Königs Ohr blieb verschlossen!

Da nahm sie Warschneja beiseite und sandte ihn mit ihren Kindern nach Kundina. Dann setzte sie sich zu ihrem Gatten.

Und als der Morgen dämmerte, da hatte Nala seine Waffen verspielt, bis auf ein schlechtes Messer, und alle Kleider, bis auf einen alten Mantel.

„Jetzt!", rief Puschkara „soll es Damayanti gelten!"

Da erwachte der Unglückliche, legte Stück um Stück die Waffen, Schmuck und Kleider von sich, und ging mit Damayanti und den Resten seiner Habe ins Elend.

Warschneja brachte die Kinder zu den Großeltern und zog dann nach Ajodhia, wo er beim Kosalerkönig Rituparna Wagenlenker wurde.

Nala und Damayanti wanderten im Wald und aßen Wurzeln und Beeren. Als sich ein Schwarm Vögel vor ihnen niederließ, warf Nala seinen Mantel wie ein Netz darüber, um einige zu fangen. Da flogen sie mit dem Mantel davon und krächzten:

Würfel sind wir! unser Neid
Raubt Dir auch das letzte Kleid.
Würfel nehmen alles!

Wär' ein König noch so groß,
Würfelaugen sehn ihn bloß.
Würfel nehmen alles!

Reich und Schwert und was einst Dein,
Bettelsuppenknöchelein,
Würfel, nahmen alles!

Da stand der Unglückliche vor seinem Weib und sprach: „Sieh, soweit ist es mit mir gekommen!“

Damayanti aber schlug das Ende ihres Mantels um den Nackten und beide in ein Kleid gehüllt zogen die Gatten weiter.

Wo sie auf einen Weg stießen, da sagte Nala: „Hier geht's nach Kosala!“ oder „Der führt zu den Vindhyabergen, wo die heiligen Büßer hausen!“. Da bangte Damayanti, dass der Gram- und Schamverzehrte sie verlassen könnte, und sie bat: „Lass uns nach Widarbha gehen: der Vater nimmt uns gerne auf!“

„Ich kann nicht betteln!“, sprach Nala, und im Weiter-schreiten beschrieb er den Weg nach Widarbha.

Damayanti weinte und sprach: „Wie könnt', ich Dich verlassen, Du armer, nackter König! Wer soll Dich trös-ten, wenn Du leidest, wer Dir Nahrung reichen, wenn Du hungerst, und Wasser, wenn Du dürstest? Wo willst Du, Müder, Dein Haupt betten, als in meinem Schoß? Bin ich schuld an Deinem Elend? – Du? – Nein! der *Böse* ist's, der an Deinem Herzen frisst! Und wo fände ein Arzt bessere Heilmittel für einen Kranken, als in dessen treuen Weibes Sinn!“

So klagte die Edle, bis sie an eine leere Hütte kamen, die wohl vor langer Zeit ein Einsiedler verlassen haben mochte.

Darin legten sie sich auf die bloße Erde, bedeckten sich mit ihrem einzigen Gewand und schliefen bekümmert ein.

Als der Mond durch das löchrige Dach in die Hütte schien, erwachte Nala und sah sein Weib im tiefen Schlaf der Erschöpfung liegen. Und so sehr hatte der Böse seinen Sinn verwirrt, dass er beschloss, Damayanti zu verlassen. Sein Verstand suchte sein unruhiges Herz zu beschwichtigen: „Ohne mich!", dachte er „mag Damayanti immerhin nach Widarbha gehen; man wird sie dort besser aufnehmen, als mich Bettelkönig. Ich tauge nur in den wildesten Wald, und mein zartes Weib müsste dort verkommen. Ich darf mein Weib nicht mit ins Elend nehmen!"

Solche überreife Wahrheits- und unreife Lügenfrüchte verwirrten ihn vollends. Er stand auf und schnitt von Damayantis Kleid gar leise die Hälfte ab. Damit verhüllte er seine Blößen und floh aus der Hütte in die Waldesnacht.

Wohl trieb es ihn wieder zurück, wohl graute ihm davor, sein Weib schutzlos den Schrecken der Wildnis preiszugeben, aber Kali flüsterte ihm gute Gründe dafür ins Ohr und drängte so heftig, dass die Morgenröte Nala schon viele Meilen weit von der Hütte fand.

Das war ein böses Erwachen, als Damayanti am Morgen, noch im Halbschlaf, den Gatten an ihrer Seite suchte.

„Mein König, wie kannst Du mich so erschrecken?", rief sie, lief aus der Hütte und suchte Nala in der Umgebung. Aber wie sie auch rief, wohin sie auch lief, er war nicht zu sehen.

„Oh Nala, mein Herr, wie konntest Du die Schuldlose strafen für anderer Fehl?", rief sie ein über das andere Mal. „Oh nein! Du kannst mich nicht verlassen, Du hast mir ja Treue geschworen vor den Welthütern!"

Und ihr Geist begann sich zu verwirren.

„Dort, dort! ich seh' Dich Nala! hinter dem Baum – jetzt unter dem Strauch – oh neck' mich nicht – versteck' Dich nicht! –

Verloren – preisgegeben den wilden Tieren, dem Hunger und Durst, den Schrecken der Nacht – Irrlichtern und bösen Geistern – und mein Nala fern! – Wahrlich, ich erkenne, dass unsere Todesstunde vom Schicksal unabänderlich vorherbestimmt ist, sonst hätt' ich sterben müssen unter seinem Abschiedsblick. –

Oh, ihr Götter! ich jammre und bedaure nur mich – während er, der Herrliche, schutzlos, fast nackt, durch die Wälder irrt, gepeinigt von seinem Gewissen und in heißer Sorge um sein Weib, das er verlassen musste – ja musste – Wie wird er leiden, da ihn sein zerrissenes Herz auch noch des Letzten, der liebenden Gattin, beraubte. – Oh, Fluch über den Feind, der ihm das angetan: zwiefach komme das Leid über den, der das edelste Mannesherz zerfleischt! Wenn das Wort eines reinen Weibes bei den Unsterblichen noch gilt, so treffe den Bösen mein Fluch, wo er auch weile!“

Und weiter irrte sie durch den Urwald, bald links, bald rechts, rufend und suchend, fürchtend und hoffend, taumelnd, stolpernd, sich aus Dornenumstrickung reißend und die Haarflechten aus haschendem Astwerk lösend. Da züngelte ihr eine Riesenschlange entgegen und umschlang die tödlich Erschreckte.

„Oh Nala! jetzt eil' mir zu Hilfe, wenn Du Dein Weib noch lebend sehen willst. Komm! sonst wird der Kummer Dich verzehren, wenn einst der böse Feind von Dir gewichen, und Du in neuem Glück vergeblich nach Deiner Damayanti rufst! Hilf! Nala, hilf!“

Ein Jäger hörte die Schreie, sprang durch den Busch und schoss der Schlange einen Pfeil durch den Kopf. Dann löste er die ihrer Sinne Beraubte aus der Umschlingung der toten Schlange und labte sie mit Wasser und Früchten.

Als Damayanti sich erholt hatte, erzählte sie dem Jäger ihre Geschichte. Und in dem lumpenumhüllten, gramverzehrten, schmutzigen und von Dornen zerrissenen Leib, war noch so viel Liebreiz, dass der Jäger seiner Begierde erlag, und voll Ungestüm seinen Schützling zum Weibe begehrte. Damayanti stieß ihn zurück und sprang ins Dickicht, der Wilde ihr nach. Als die Erschöpfte in ihrer Bedrängnis verzweifeln wollte, suchte sie Hilfe bei den Göttern und flehte: „So wahr keiner meiner Gedanken je einem andern als Nala gehören soll, so rasch befreit mich von diesem Frevler, ihr Götter!"

Da fuhr Indras Blitz aus heiterem Himmel und schlug den Jäger zu Boden.

Entsetzt floh Damayanti von der Stätte des Gerichtes. Floh durch den dichtesten Wald, über mannshohe Wurzeln, durch das zugreifende Dorngestrüpp, über Sumpf und Steine, Berg und Tal, durch Schluchten und Schrunden, Nala rufend, Nala ersehnend, Nala liebkosend im Geist, als den heldenstarken, edlen und weisen Gemahl. Alle Schrecken der Wildnis: Löwengebrüll, Schlangengezisch, Brausen des Sturmes, Heulen der Wölfe, Kläffen des Schakals, Krächzen der Geier – sie riefen ihr eines nur zu: Nala in Not!

Erschöpft sank sie endlich in die Knie und flehte, die Hände erhoben:

„Tiger, starker König des Waldes, sag' mir, wo ist Nala! Damayanti bin ich, des Widarbherkönigs einzige Tochter, und such' meinen Gatten! Rastlos Schweifender, Herr des Getieres, sahst Du ihn nicht? Nala such' ich, den Nischaderkönig, hilf mir starkzahniger Tiger! Streif' durch die Wälder, zieh durch die Schluchten, such' meinen Herrn! Suche ihn, rufe ihn, bring' ihn zu mir, oder zerfleische mich arme Verlassene!

Und Du, hochragender Riese, König der Berge, mit dem silberglänzenden Haupte! Siehst Du meinen Nala nicht? Du siehst doch so weit ins Land! Winke ihm, ruf ihn, bring' ihn zu mir, oder stürz' ein und begrab' mich! mich, des Nischaders unglückliches Weib!"

Und dann sah sich die ruhelos Wandernde in einem friedlichen Hain, wo mächtige Bäume standen und die sauberen Hütten der Einsiedler. Würdige Greise sah sie da, mit freundlichem Antlitz, den Körper in Ziegenfelle gehüllt. Weißbärtig, mit lieben Augen, so saßen sie vor den Hütten oder spielten mit den Tieren des Waldes, die sie nicht scheuten. Papageien und Affen schaukelten in den Ästen, Hirsch und Gazelle sprangen auf der Wiese und die heiligen Männer sangen fromme Lieder. Alles fand Damayanti so, wie es in den heiligen Schriften zu lesen stand.

Da trat sie vor und frug schüchtern, wie es die Sitte erheischte, ob es ihnen allen wohlergehe, ob sie reichlich Nahrung und Wasser hätten und viele Schätze an Buße.

Die heiligen Männer dankten mit freundlichen Worten und fragten die Verirrte, wer sie sei. Da erzählte die Leidgeprüfte ihre Geschichte und weinte bitterlich. Der älteste der Büßer aber tröstete sie und sprach:

„Sieh, für unser frommes und strenges Leben ist uns vom Himmel beschert, dass wir in die Zukunft sehen. Dich, Holde, seh' ich dort glücklich! Der Wahn wird von dem Nischader weichen, er kehrt zurück in sein Reich als König, und Glück, Ehre und Reichtum wirst Du mit ihm teilen!"

Dankbar neigte sich Damayanti zur Erde, in stillem, erlösendem Weinen. Leiser und leiser, ferner und ferner klang das fromme Lied der Büßer, und als die Getröstete erwachte, lag sie allein im hellen Licht der Morgensonne unter einem mächtigen Asokabaum. ‚Asoka' aber heißt auf Deutsch so viel als ‚Sorgenbrecher'.

Neugestärkt erhob sich Damayanti, küsste den hohen Stamm des Sorgenbrechers und umwandelte dreimal den heiligen Baum, ihn mit der Rechten berührend. An seinen Zweigen aber brachen alle Blüten auf und dufteten weit durch den Wald, denn so ist es dem Asoka von den Himmlischen gesetzt, dass er blühe, wenn ihn ein reines Weib berührt.

Da sie noch stand und dem Baum dafür dankte, dass er ihr wirklich ein Sorgenbrecher war, hörte sie die Schellen von Kamelen und die Stimmen von Elefantentreibern. Sie bat noch den Wunderbaum, Nala zu grüßen, wenn er vorbeikäme, und lief dann schnell nach den Tönen, die ihr eine Karawane anzeigten.

Talwärts lief sie und sah unten, längs eines schilfumwachsenen Flusses, einen langen Zug von Menschen auf Elefanten und Kamelen, zu Ross und zu Wagen.

Als die Leute Damayanti erblickten, schrien sie durcheinander und wussten nicht, was sie aus ihr machen sollten.

Sie sah auch aus wie eine Tolle: schmutzig, von Dornen zerkratzt, bleich, mit wirrem Haar und den glänzenden, großen Augen, nichts am Leib als den halben, zerrissenen Mantel.

„Ach! wer bist Du?" „Seht eine Hexe!" „Bist Du eine Elfin oder die Flussnixe?" „Oh, dafür ist sie zu schmutzig!" „Aber seht nur die Schönheit unter dem Schmutz!", so rief es durcheinander, bis die Kaufleute, denen der Warenzug gehörte, in ihrem Elefantenturm daherkamen.

Denen erzählte Damayanti ihre Geschichte, und sie erlaubten ihr, sich anzuschließen. Sie wollten nach Tschedi, einer großen Stadt am Rande des wilden Waldes.

So zog Damayanti mit der Karawane, still und zufrieden, auf die Worte des greisen Sehers hoffend.

Aber das Maß ihres Leidens war noch nicht voll.

Einen halben Tagmarsch vor Tschedi hielt die Karawane an einem großen Weiher Nachtrast. Als alles schlief, kam eine Herde wilder Elefanten zur Tränke. Sie witterten die zahmen Brüder und stürzten sich kampflustig auf sie, alles zermalmend, was ihnen im Weg war: Mensch und Tier, Zelt und Wagen.

Wilder Schrecken erfasste alle, die am Leben blieben und das Stampfen und Trompeten der Rüsselträger, das Ächzen der Sterbenden hörten. Zucht und Ordnung ward gelöst: hier liefen ein paar entsetzt ins Wasser, dort raubten andere Kostbarkeiten, die aus den zertrümmerten Kasten quollen, gaben auch wohl dem Verteidiger einen Messerstich und fielen im nächsten Augenblick unter dem Rüsselschlag eines Elefanten.

Damayanti saß zitternd im Strauchwerk und glaubte alle Dämonen seien los.

Rasch, wie sie gekommen waren, liefen die Elefanten nach der Zerstörung wieder in den Wald.

Am Morgen sammelten sich die wenigen, die noch lebten, und klagten laut über den Verlust an Freunden und Brüdern, an Geld und Gut. Hatte sich doch die Fahrt so gut angelassen, die Opfer richtig gebrannt, alle Vorzeichen Segen verheißen, und nun, kurz vor dem Ziel, dies schreckliche Ende.

„Das war die Tolle, die alles verhext hat!", flüsterten sie und warfen finstere Blicke auf Damayanti.

Und als sie nach Tschedi wanderten, wagte die Gramerfüllte ihnen nur von weitem zu folgen. Still weinend dachte die Gute, dass sie wohl wirklich in einem früheren Leben viel Böses begangen haben müsse, weil ihr Unglück sich über die ganze Karawane ausgedehnt habe.

Als sie gegen Abend todmüde nach Tschedi kam, liefen die Kinder auf der Straße zusammen und begleiteten diese traurige Königin in ihrem närrischen Kleid der

Liebe unter Gespött und Geschrei bis vor den Palast der Königin-Mutter.

Diese sah vom Fenster den fröhlichen Aufzug und sandte nach seiner trauernden Führerin.

Damayanti klagte der edlen Fürstin ihr schreckliches Los, doch ohne sich zu erkennen zu geben, und bat die Gute, sie in ihren Dienst zu nehmen, bis die Götter sie wieder mit ihrem Gatten vereinten. Die Königin-Mutter sah durch all den Jammer das edle und schöne Weib und gab es ihrer Tochter zur Gespielin. Der ward die Leiderfahrene bald zur Freundin.

König Nala hatte sein Weib verlassen und wäre am liebsten vor sich selber geflohen. Er irrte durch den Wald, quälte sich mit Vorwürfen und schämte sich seines Tuns vor sich und der Welt. Wie im Traume bahnte er sich seinen Weg durchs dickste Dickicht, ohne Ziel und Zweck.

Mitten im Walde stieß er auf einen lodernden Ringwall von Flammen.

Daraus klang eine Stimme und rief: „Komm! König Nala! komm, erlöse mich!", und wieder: „Komm, König Nala! komm, erlöse mich!"

„Ich komme!", rief Nala und drang mutig durch Feuer und Rauch in den Ring.

Dort fand er eine große Schlange auf einem Steine zusammengerollt. Die sprach, demütig bittend, mit menschlicher Stimme:

„Wisse, edler König der Nischader, dass ich Karkotaka bin, ein König der Schlangen! Vor vielen Jahren habe ich einen Heiligen belogen, um Eine meines Volkes vor gerechter Strafe zu schützen. Da verfluchte mich der Heilige und bannte mich in diesen Feuerring: bis König Nala mich befreien würde! – Schnell trage mich aus dem Feuer, und ich will Dir den Weg weisen zu *Deiner* Erlösung. Klug ist das Schlangenvolk! und ich bin sein Meister!". Darauf machte er sich klein, kaum spannenlang, und schlang sich um Nalas Daumen. „Nun laufe durch das Feuer und zähle Deine Schritte!"

Nala sprang durch Feuer und Rauch, und als er in frischer Luft hielt, rief er: „Zehn!"

Da schlug Karkotaka seine Zähne in Nalas Daumen, fuhr aus seiner Haut und erschien vor dem Nischader in seiner Gestalt als Schlangenkönig: ein goldschimmernder Schlangenleib mit einem Menschenhaupt!

Nala aber fühlte einen Ruck durch seinen Leib gehen, und als er an sich hinuntersah, merkte er, dass ihn das Schlangengift in eine Missgestalt verwandelt hatte.

„Edler Nischader!", sprach Karkotaka, „verschwunden ist die Gestalt, die Dir zum Abscheu geworden war, und die alle als die des Königs Nala kannten. Darum, und um Kali durch das ätzende Gift zu peinigen, musste ich Dich beißen. Der Spielteufel hat ohne Dein Wissen in Dir Wohnung genommen. Dich wird mein Gift nicht quälen, denn Du bist von heut' an der beste Freund des Schlangenvolkes und seines dankbaren Königs. Den Bösen aber wollen wir aus Dir treiben und ihn bestrafen. Dazu musst Du den Zahlenzauber erwerben, denn der gibt Macht über alle Spielteufel. Rituparna, der König der Kosaler, kennt den Zauber. Gehe nach Ajodhia, und verdinge Dich ihm als Fuhrmann. Deine Kunst, die Rosse zu lenken und sie 100 Meilen in einem Tage zu treiben, wird Dir bald Gelegenheit bieten, Deinem Herrn einen wichtigen Dienst zu leisten. Dann biete ihm Deine Kunst im Rosselenken gegen den Zahlenzauber. Hast Du den Zauber, so beherrschest Du Kali und wirst Reich und Glück wiedererwerben. Willst Du wieder in Deiner alten Gestalt einhergehen, so ziehe dieses, mein abgestreiftes Kleid, über den Daumen, und du bist wieder Nala, der Makellose, vor aller Welt."

Damit verschwand der Schlangenkönig, und Nala, oder *Vahuka*, wie er sich in Knechtsgestalt nennen wollte, schlug den Weg nach Ajodhia ein und kam nach zehn Tagen zum Kosalerkönig Rituparna. Dem verdingte er sich als Stallknecht unter dem Wagenlenker Warschneja.

Bhima hatte seine beiden Enkelkinder gut aufgenommen und harrte nun schon lange des landlosen Königs und seiner treuen Gattin. Da sie sich nicht in Kundina einfanden, sandte er viele Brahmanen aus, um sie zu suchen.

Die Brahmanen zogen oft als geistliche Sänger und Lehrer von Stadt zu Stadt, von Hof zu Hof, durch alle Lande. Da mochte wohl einer Gelegenheit haben, die Ersehnten zu finden.

Der Großkönig versprach reichen Lohn an Vieh und Land dem, der die Flüchtigen brächte oder doch wenigstens ihren Aufenthalt erkunden könnte.

Die geweihten Boten Bhimas durchzogen viele Länder, aber alle mussten unverrichteter Dinge wieder heimkehren, bis auf Sudeva, den sein Weg nach Tschedi geführt hatte.

Als er dort einer Feier im Palaste des Königs beiwohnte, sprach ihn eine tief verhüllte Gestalt an und fragte nach König Nala. Es war Damayanti, die bei allen Fahrenden nach ihrem unglücklichen Gatten zu forschen pflegte. Bei dieser Frage erkannte Sudeva die Tochter seines Herrn an Haltung und Stimme und grüßte sie im Namen ihrer Eltern und Kinder. Weinend fragte Damayanti, wie es allen ergehe, ob die Kinder gewachsen seien, und was eine Mutter wohl sonst noch wissen will.

Als die Königin-Mutter hinzutrat, musste Sudeva erzählen, wer Damayanti sei, und da erkannte ihre Beschützerin sie, als das Kind ihrer fernen Schwester.

Nun wollte sie der lieben Verwandten würdigere Gastfreundschaft bieten, doch Damayanti dankte ihr für die viele Liebe, die sie schon als Unbekannte bei ihr gefunden hatte, und, da Sudevas Grüße die Sehnsucht nach den Ihrigen wachgerufen hatten, bat sie um Reisegelegenheit nach Kundina.

Unter Tränen der Liebe nahmen die königlichen Frauen Abschied von Damayanti und ließen sie in einer Sänfte unter sicherem Schutz nach Kundina bringen.

Dort herrschte große Freude über die Wiedergefundene, und Bhima schenkte dem glücklichen Sudeva tausend Rinder und ein großes Dorf mit fruchtbaren Ackern und weiten Wiesengründen.

Am Tage nach ihrer Ankunft aber sagte Damayanti ihren Eltern, dass sie nicht leben könne ohne Nala!

Da rief Bhima wieder die Brahmanen zusammen, um sie noch einmal auf die Suche zu senden.

Und Damayanti lehrte sie das

LIED IHRER SCHLAFLOSEN NÄCHTE:

Wo weilst, besessner Spieler, Du
Mit meinem halben Kleide?
Bring der im Wald verlassnen Ruh
In tiefstem Herzeleide!
O mögen Götter, treu verehrt,
Dein Schweifen heimwärts lenken,
Zu der, die Glück und Gram verzehrt,
In ew'gem Deingedenken!

„Dieses singet", sprach sie zu den Gottgeweihten „in allen Städten und Weilern, an Höfen und auf Märkten und wo sonst das Volk zusammenläuft! Und wenn euch einer auch nur ein rechtes Wort darauf erwidert, so merket seine Rede gut und hinterbringt sie mir eilig! Aber verratet nicht, dass ihr von mir gesandt seid! Die Götter mögen euer Wandern segnen!"

86

Nach vielen Monden ließ sich der Weihbrahmane Parnada vor Damayanti führen und berichtete also:

„An allen Orten habe ich Dein Lied vergeblich gesungen. Auch zu Ajodhia, als ich in des Königs Halle sang, blieb ich ohne Antwort. Doch als ich gehen wollte, hielt mich im Dunkel des Hofes eine Missgestalt an und sang mit ergreifenden Tönen:

> *Zürne nicht! Du Herzenstreue,*
> *Paar' nicht Fluch der tiefsten Reue!*
> *Narr hat seinem Glück vertraut,*
> *Weil's für ewig schien gebaut.*
> *Schwert verloren – Ehr' verloren!*
> *Steht im Schicksalsbuch des Toren.*
> *Neid raubt ihm das letzte Kleid*
> *Und den letzten Trost das Leid!*

Mit Tränen im Auge schlich der Sänger hinweg und verschwand in des Königs Marstall.

Ich aber forschte bei den Leuten im Hause, wer der missgestaltete Sänger sei.

Da hörte ich, es sei ein Knecht des Königs, namens Vahuka, der sich sehr gut aufs Fahren verstünde, und auch treffliche Speisen bereite. Er hält sich fern von allen Leuten und scheint schweren Kummer zu haben, von dem er des Nachts öfter singt."

„O Nala ist's, mein makelloser Held, den der Böse nun auch noch missgestaltet hat!", rief Damayanti weinend und entließ den Brahmanen mit reichen Geschenken.

In heimlicher Beratung mit der Mutter hatte Damayanti eine List erdacht, um den missgestalteten Sänger nach Kundina zu locken und zu prüfen, ob er König Nala sei.

Sudeva, der gute Brahmane, welcher sie selbst nach Hause gebracht hatte, sollte nun nach Ajodhia reisen und dort vor König Rituparna, wie zufällig, erwähnen, dass Damayanti am anderen Tage eine neue Gattenwahl halte, weil Nala wohl tot sei. Nur König Nala könne die hundert Meilen von dort her in einem Tage fahren. Wenn also Vahuka den Kosalerkönig rechtzeitig nach Kundina bringe, so spräche schon vieles dafür, dass König Nala sich in dieser Missgestalt verberge. Andere Beweise würden sich dann wohl noch finden lassen.

So reiste denn Sudeva ab.

Und Rituparna wollte auch wirklich nicht fehlen, wenn die holde Bhimatochter Gattenwahl hielt.

Warschneja getraute sich nicht, die große Wegstrecke in so kurzer Zeit zu bewältigen, doch Vahuka setzte sein Leben zum Pfand, dass er den König noch rechtzeitig nach Kundina bringen würde. Die Botschaft Sudevas, den er kannte, hatte ihn zuerst niedergeschmettert, aber als er der endlosen Liebe seines Weibes gedachte, verstand er die List und bot dem König seinen Dienst an.

Vier unscheinbare, aber edle Rosse wählte er im Stall, die jedes die zehn Haarwirbel als Zeichen ihrer Schnelligkeit trugen. Der König zweifelte an ihrer Güte, aber Vahuka forderte volles Vertrauen, wenn die schnelle Fahrt gelingen sollte, und so bestieg Rituparna mit Warschneja hinter dem Kühnen den Wagen.

Fort ging's in wirbelnder Schnelle an Häusern und Bäumen vorbei!

Als Warschneja sah, wie Vahuka seine Rosse lenkte, da kamen ihm allerlei Gedanken:

„Der fährt ja wie Matali, der Wagenlenker Indras, oder wie Waju, der wehende Wind … doch nein! –'s ist König Nala, wie er die Zügel führt! – aber die Missgestalt. Ob ihm die Götter zürnen? – die haben schon manchen verwandelt!"

So dachte der Wackere hin und her und schwieg in
Erwartung einer kommenden Lösung.

Auch Rituparna freute sich über Vahukas Kunst, denn er
war ein Freund aller kriegerischen Übungen. Als ihm der
Fahrtwind den Mantel entriss, wollte er halten lassen, um
ihn aufzuheben.

„Lass ihn," lachte Vahuka „der liegt schon eine Meile hinter uns!". Die kühne Fahrt hatte auch ihn freudig gestimmt.

„Herrlich fährst Du, Vahuka!", sprach der König „und
ich möchte die Kunst wohl von Dir lernen. Sieh, ich habe
ein anderes Wissen: den Zahlenzauber! den möchte ich
Dir dafür geben. Dort, der Eckernbaum hat am untersten
Ast zweihundertundsieben Eckern und eintausendsieben-
hundertdreiunddreißig Blätter. Das sagt mir mein Wissen!"

Jäh hielt Vahuka sein Gespann an und sprang vom Wagen.

„Wir werden zu spät kommen!", rief ängstlich der König.

„Ich bringe die versäumte Zeit wieder ein", sprach
Vahuka „doch Deinen Zauber will ich prüfen."

Und er zählte Blätter und Früchte genau und fand alles
so, wie es der König angegeben hatte.

Vahuka staunte über das geheimnisvolle Wissen des
Königs und versprach dem Kosaler, ihn seine Fahrkunst zu
lehren, wenn der ihm den Zauber verrate.

Da neigte sich Rituparna vom Wagen und flüsterte dem
Vahuka die Zauberformel ins Ohr.

Wie der Blitz fuhr nun Kali aus dem Opfer seiner Scheel-
sucht und stand demütig vor seinem neuen Herrscher.

Schon wollte Nala ihn verfluchen, da winselte der
Elende:

„Bezähme Deinen Zorn, o Großmächtiger König der
Nischader! und fluche mir nicht. Denn schwer hatte ich
zu leiden, seitdem mich der Fluch Deiner reinen Gattin
getroffen, und mir das Zweifache Deiner Leiden aufer-
legt hat; bitterer noch schmerzte mich Karkotakas Gift.

Dein Reich will ich Dir wiedergewinnen und nie mehr einen Deiner Lieben quälen, aber fluche mir nicht, edler Dulder!"

Da bannte ihn Nala in den Eckernbaum.

Das gemeine Volk würfelt seither mit Eckern, und der Baum ist verachtet im ganzen Land.

Vahuka aber sprang auf den Wagen zu Rituparna und Warschneja, die Kali weder gesehen noch gehört hatten, und griff nach den Zügeln.

Mit doppelter Schnelle raste das Gefährt dahin, und ehe noch die Sonne sank, rollte der Wagen durch die Straßen Kundinas.

Es war ein Donnern und Tosen, als die windschnellen Rosse die letzten Meilen liefen, dass Pfauen und Elefanten freudig aufschrien, denn sie glaubten ein erfrischendes Gewitter im Anziehen.

Damayanti aber hörte am Fenster das Rollen und rief: „So weiß nur Nala die Rosse zu jagen! Kommt er heut' nicht, so will ich den Scheiterhaufen besteigen und als seine Getreue den Flammentod erleiden!"

Aber dem Wagen, der vor dem Palaste hielt, entstiegen nur der Kosalerkönig Rituparna, der Rosselenker Warschneja und eine Missgestalt, die Damayanti nicht kannte.

Bhima schritt dem Kosalerherrn entgegen.

Dieser hatte mit Staunen bemerkt, dass hier von dem Gedränge und Gepränge, das alle Feste Indiens zu begleiten pflegte, nichts zu sehen war. Sogleich vermutete er, dass Sudeva ihn irregeführt habe, und, um nicht zum Schaden noch Spott zu ernten, verschwieg der Kluge, warum er gekommen sei. Er begrüßte den edlen Bhima und fragte nach seinem Befinden.

Wohl erriet auch der Widarbher, dem die Frauen die List verhehlt hatten, dass Rituparna nicht deshalb allein die hundert Meilen gefahren sei, doch beschloss er zu warten, bis der Gast ihm sein Anliegen vorbringen wolle, und führte ihn freundlich nach dem Ehrensitz in der Halle.

Damayanti aber sandte die kluge Kesini hinab, zu erforschen, wer auf der Fahrt die Zügel geführt habe, und dem kühnen Lenker näher zu treten, so das sie erkunden konnte, ob sich nicht König Nala hinter ihm verberge.

Kesini ging zu Vahuka, der die Pferde abgeschirrt hatte und nun auf dem Wagen saß um zu ruhen. Sie fragte ihn allerlei und wusste bald, dass der Krüppel der schnelle Lenker sei und dem Kosaler als Fuhrmann und Koch diene. Auch das Leidlied Damayantis sprach sie vor Vahuka, und er gab dieselbe Antwort, die er dem Brahmanen gegeben hatte. Dann verfiel er in Schweigen und weinte still vor sich hin.

Als Kesini dies alles ihrer Herrin berichtete, ward diese in ihrem Glauben noch stärker. Aber um sicher zu sein, dass König Nala sich in Vahuka verberge, wollte sie noch die Hochzeitsgaben der Götter bei dem Krüppel finden. Sie befahl deshalb Kesini, ihn auf allen seinen Wegen zu beobachten.

Bald kam Kesini und erzählte, wie vor dem Geheimnisvollen sich das Kellerloch erweitert habe, so dass er aufrecht durchschreiten konnte, um Fleisch für seines Herrn Abendtisch zu holen; wie er die leeren Töpfe voll Wasser gezaubert habe und das Abendrot auf den Herd als Feuer; und wie er dann köstlich duftende Speisen bereitete. Von diesen brachte sie ihrer Herrin ein wenig. Sie hatte es dem Geschickten abgeschwatzt.

Damayanti kostete davon und erkannte die Kunst Nalas, das Göttergeschenk Yamas.

Nun sandte sie Kesini mit den beiden Kindern zu Vahuka, dass er sich in seiner Vaterliebe verrate.

Vahuka küsste die Kinder oft und weinte. Sie glichen so sehr den seinen, sagte er unter Tränen.

Nun ließ Damayanti den Bekümmerten vor sich führen.

Und als der Dulder vor der armen Verlassenen stand, da fiel ein Blütenregen vom Himmel und die himmlischen Spielleute ließen ihre Weisen erklingen.

Jetzt erkannte Vahuka, dass seine Leidenszeit zu Ende sei, und zog die Haut des Schlangenkönigs über den Daumen.

Als Nala, der Makellose, schloss er seine treue Gattin in die Arme.

Nach langer Trauer war heller Jubel im Königspalast von Widarbha.

Einige Wochen blieben die Wiedervereinten noch in Kundina, und Nala lehrte Rituparna die Rosse hundert Meilen im Tag zu treiben, wie er es vor dem Eckernbaume versprochen hatte.

Dann fuhr er mit einer kleinen Heldenschar nach Nischada, erinnerte Puschkara, dass er Damayanti als letzten Einsatz geheischt hatte, und forderte den Bruder nun zum Kampfe mit Würfeln oder Waffen.

Puschkara wählte die Würfel und verlor alles an den zauberkundigen Nala.

Dieser aber schenkte ihm seinen alten Fürstensitz und noch manche kostbare Gabe dazu, denn nicht der Bruder hatte ihm so schweres Leid gebracht, sondern Kali, der Böse.

Das Volk von Nischada jubelte seinem geliebten Herrscherpaare zu, und dieses lebte in Glück und Liebe noch viele Jahre.

Durch alle Zeiten aber klingt das Lied vom makellosen König Nala und seinem treuen Weibe Damayanti!

Bharatas Heldenstamm

*B*rahma, das unerforschliche Haupt der geheimnisvollen Dreieinigkeit ‚Schöpfung – Erhaltung – Zerstörung' sah seine Erde übervölkert.

Auf sein Geheiß spaltete der Gott des Rechtes den Stamm Bharatas, des ersten Großkönigs von Indien. Treue und Trug, Macht und List, Sieg und Tod mussten sein Astwerk unlöslich verwirren, und lohender Hass, dem Liebe und Eifersucht in die Flammen blies, verzehrte alles bis auf ein winziges Samenkorn, aus dem den gelichteten Völkern ein neuer Herrscherstamm erwuchs.

Bhischma

Als der greise König Pratipa, aus dem Geschlechte des Bharata, seinem Sohne Schantanu die Herrschaft übergeben hatte, sprach er zu dem neugeweihten ‚Herrn der Erde':

„Mein Sohn, nach dem Willen der Götter sollst Du ein Weib am Ufer der Ganga finden. Frage die Herrliche nie nach ihrer Herkunft und billige schweigend, was sie auch täte! Das musst Du der Geheimnisvollen geloben, denn es soll zu Deinem Glücke führen!"

Darauf legte er alle Zeichen seiner königlichen Würde von sich und schritt im Büßerkleid in den Wald: nordwärts gegen den eisstarrenden Himawat, aufwärts, immer aufwärts, bis ihn der leuchtende Himmel aufnahm. Denn so musste ein Held sterben, den der Tod auf dem Schlachtfeld gemieden hatte.

König Schantanu aber durchstreifte die Wälder an der Ganga, jagend, harrend, hoffend, das sehnende Glück im ahnungsvollen Herzen.

Und als er eines Morgens am Ufer stand und freudigen Sinnes die Schönheit des stolzen Stromes pries, da trat ein wunderschönes Weib zu ihm und grüßte mit holdseligem Lächeln: „Heil König Schantanu, mein Herr und Gemahl!"

„Du? – Du bist mir bestimmt?", stammelte Schantanu und schloss die Errötende in seine Arme.

„Stamme von Göttern oder Teufeln, von Riesen oder Menschen! ich will's nicht wissen; bring Glück oder Elend,

Leben oder Tod in mein Haus! ich will's nicht wehren. Doch sei mein Weib!"

„Ich will es sein und bleiben, solange Du dieses Wortes gedenkst!", sprach die Göttliche.

Und vereint zogen sie nach Hastinapura, wo des Königs Palast stand, und hielten Hochzeit vor dem heiligen Feuer, indem sie es, Hand in Hand, mit sieben feierlichen Schritten rechtshin umwandelten.

Viele Jahre lebten sie im Glück der innigsten Liebe, und der König gedachte schweigend seines Versprechens, wenn er mit geheimem Schauder sah, wie seine Gattin jedes ihrer Kinder, gleich nach der Geburt, in den Strom warf und dazu raunte:

„Menschliche Liebe rief Dich ins Leben,
Göttliche Liebe schenkt Dir den Tod!"

Sieben schöne Kindlein hatte die Mutter ertränkt, doch als sie das achte in ihre Arme nahm, da ward Schantanu vom Grauen überwältigt, und er vergaß sein Gelöbnis.

„Halt ein! Wer bist Du, Schreckliche, die ihre Kinder mordet? Lass mir den letzten Sohn!", so schrie er, angsterfüllt.

„Er bleibt Dir, Schantanu, doch ich muss Dich verlassen!", sprach die Göttliche mit Tränen im Auge. „Höre denn, wie alles gekommen ist:

Ich bin Ganga, die Stromgöttin! und der Ratschluss der Götter, wie meine Liebe, hat mich zu Deiner Gattin gemacht.

Die acht Erdgötter, die Du als Wasu verehrst und deren Vornehmster Djau heißt, hatten einst die Einsiedelei des Heiligen Wasischta betreten und seine Wunderkuh, die göttliche Nandini, geraubt. Denn die Milch dieser Edlen verleiht zehntausendjährige Jugend, und Djaus Gattin hatte eine Freundin auf Erden, die sie damit beglücken wollte. Als der Heilige den Raub entdeckte, ließ er seine sündlosen Augen über die ganze Erde schweifen und sah in weiter Ferne die acht Wasugötter mit seiner Nandini.

Da verhängte der Büßer, in furchtbarem Fluch, über sie, dass diese räuberischen Götter zur Strafe als Menschen geboren werden sollten.

Traurig kamen die acht zu mir, denn einer, der reich an Buße ist, hat auch Macht über die Götter. Sie baten mich, dass ich sie als Menschenkindlein zur Welt bringen und gleich im Strom ertränken solle.

Und als sie nun Dich, Schantanu, als den edelsten der Menschen, zu ihrem Vater erkoren, da schlug ich freudig ein. Und sie gelobten mir, jeder ein Achtel seines göttlichen Wesens im achten Kind ein ganzes Menschenleben durchlaufen zu lassen, auf dass Du in Deinem göttergleichen Sohn den Lohn fändest.

Alles ist gekommen, wie es kommen musste! Dir bleibt ein Sohn, doch ich muss scheiden! – Lebe wohl!"

Darauf verschwand die Göttin und ließ das Knäblein Bhischma in des Vaters Armen zurück.

Während Schantanu in treuer Sorge um sein Reich langsam den Schmerz um die verlorene Gattin verwand, wuchs Bhischma zum unüberwindlichen Helden heran.

Einst fand der Jüngling seinen Vater betrübt und schweren Herzens und fragte, was ihn so sehr bekümmere. Und als der Gramgebeugte schwieg, erforschte er die königlichen Räte und erkannte gar bald das Leid des Bekümmerten.

An der Iamuna hatte Schantanu des Fischerkönigs Tochter, Satjawati, gesehen, die dort die Wanderer in einem Nachen über den Strom setzte. Und er hatte die Liebliche gebeten, ihn zu ihrem Vater zu bringen. Vom Fischerkönig hatte er die schöne Tochter zum Weib erbeten, doch dieser hatte Unerfüllbares verlangt:

„Ein König, der Satjawati freit, muss schwören, den Sohn, welchen sie ihm schenken wird, zu seinem Nachfolger zu weihen!"

Da musste Schantanu auf die liebliche Maid verzichten, weil er Bhischmas älteres Recht nicht kränken wollte.

Als Bhischma das Leid seines Vaters erkannt hatte, ließ er anschirren und fuhr zum Fischerkönig. Dem gelobte er auf seine Thronrechte zu verzichten und unvermählt zu bleiben, so dass sein Geschlecht mit ihm erlösche.

Der Fischerkönig nahm sein Versprechen voll Freude an und übergab ihm die Tochter. Satjawati bestieg Bhischmas Wagen und im Triumph führte der Sohn dem Vater sein Glück zu.

Doch waren Schantanu nur wenige Jahre des neuen Gattenglückes beschieden. Satjawati hatte ihm zwei schöne Knaben geschenkt: Tschitrangada und Witschitrawiria, doch sie waren beide noch Kinder, als Schantanu starb.

Seinem Versprechen getreu, weihte Bhischma den älteren zum ‚Herrn der Erde' und erzog beide zu tapferen Helden.

Aber Tschitrangada griff in toller Kampflust Menschen und Götter an und fiel, noch jung an Jahren, im Kampf gegen den Gandharwerkönig, den Herrn der himmlischen Spielleute.

Nun weihte Bhischma Satjawatis jüngeren Sohn, den Witschitrawiria, zum König und beschloss ihn alsbald zu vermählen.

Amba-Schikhandin

Zu jener Zeit lud der König von Kaschi alle Fürsten Indiens an seinen Hof, denn seine drei Töchter: Amba, Ambika und Ambalika, waren zu holdseligen Jungfrauen herangereift und sollten unter den Helden ihre Gatten wählen.

Zum Fest in der Kaschistadt fuhr Bhischma in voller Wehr, und als er die drei Lieblichen erblickte, hieß er sie auf seinen Streitwagen steigen und rief:

„Ich, Bhischma, des Schantanu Sohn und der Ganga, raube die bräutlichen Schönen. Tapferkeit sei ihr Kaufpreis! Heran, speergewaltige Helden! Wer wagt es, sie mir zu entreißen?"

Da fuhren die Edlen auf, riefen nach ihren Rossen, Wagen und Elefanten, umringten den tapfern Gangasohn und drangen auf ihn ein. Doch der schoss Pfeil um Pfeil auf die Heranstürmenden, tötete ihre Tiere und schoss die goldgestickten Banner in Brand. Bald flohen die Bedränger vor diesem Pfeilhagel.

Bhischma ließ die Rosse wenden und fuhr mit seiner schönen Beute nach Hastinapura. Die jungfräulichen Königskinder brachte er zu Mutter Satjawati, auf dass sie die Frauen des jungen Königs Witschitrawiria würden.

Als das Hochzeitsfest gerüstet wurde, trat Amba vor Bhischma hin und sprach: „Sage mir, Edler, der Du alle Gesetze der Götter und auch die des Menschenherzens kennst: darf ich das Weib Witschitrawirias werden, wenn ich das Bild des schönen Königs von Schalwa im Herzen trage und mich ihm in süßer Heimlichkeit verlobt habe? – Oh, unüberwindlicher Gangasohn, edelster Bharataspross, lasst mich zu dem Geliebten ziehen!"

Gerührt von Ambas Treue und Aufrichtigkeit und im Sinne einer Sitte, welche Gattentreue bis zum letzten Gedanken fordert, sandte Bhischma die Jungfrau in angemessener Begleitung nach Schalwa.

Doch der König von Schalwa, voll Eifersucht und in Furcht vor dem gewaltigen Bhischma, empfing die Getreue gar schlecht.

„Geh wohin Du willst!", rief er. „Nicht ziemt mir, zum Weibe zu nehmen, was ein anderer geraubt und im Überdruss von sich getan hat! geh hin zu dem Verhassten! Ich mag Dich nicht mehr, denn allzu willig folgtest Du dem Entführer!"

„Du täuschest Dich, Edler!", sprach die Liebende unter Tränen. „Mit Gewalt ward ich hinweggeführt und bitterlich weinend. Wende Dich nicht von mir, die in steter Treue die Deine sein will!"

Doch der Schalwakönig verließ sie, wie eine Schlange ihre alte Haut.

Traurig zog Amba aus der Stadt und verfluchte ihr Geschick. Durch fleißige Bußübung hoffte sie des Himmels Rache auf Bhischma herabzuziehen, denn in ihm sah sie den Schöpfer ihres Leides. Im Walde fand sie eine Siedelei von Büßern, klagte den guten Alten ihr Leid und bat, sie in ihre Gemeinschaft aufzunehmen.

Unter diesen Sündenreinen lebte auch Ambas Großvater. Der hob die Trauernde auf und versprach ihr Hilfe: Sein Freund war Rama, der Sohn Dschamadagnis, ein edler Brahmane und Meister des Waffenhandwerks. Kein Kschattrija – so heißen die Söhne der Kriegerkaste – hatte ihn noch besiegen können.

Diesem Priesterrecken sollte sie ihr Leid klagen, und der würde Bhischma zwingen, ihre Ehre durch Vermählung mit Witschitrawiria wieder herzustellen, oder sie an dem Verhassten rächen.

Während der ehrwürdige Alte so freundlich und tröstend mit seinem Enkelkind sprach, kam ein Gefährte Ramas und meldete dessen Ankunft.

Als der Abend sich über den Wald legte, kam der edle Rama: im Büßerkleid, mit Axt und Schwert, den starken Bogen auf der Schulter und eine Schar von Schülern im Gefolge.

Amba fiel vor dem tapfern Priester auf die Knie, und während sie mit ihren zarten Händen seine staubigen Füße berührte, klagte sie weinend ihr Leid und bat um die Hilfe des Starken.

Vor den tränenerfüllten Augen der schönen Verstoßenen konnte der Priester mit dem Kriegerherzen seine Hilfe nicht versagen, obwohl er Bhischma als den besten seiner Schüler vor allen ehrte. Er versprach Worte und Waffen daran zu setzen, dass die Schmach der Unglücklichen getilgt, ihre Makellosigkeit aller Welt kund werde.

Am nächsten Morgen zog er mit Amba und allen Waldsiedlern gegen Hastinapura und sandte einen Boten mit seiner Forderung voraus.

Bhischma eilte seinem Lehrer bis zur Landesgrenze entgegen und begrüßte ihn dort voll Ehrfurcht. Die Forderung, Amba seinem Bruder Witschitrawiria zu vermählen, wies er zurück:

„Wer lässt ein Weib, das einen andern im Herzen trägt, wie eine Natter, in seinem Hause wohnen?", sprach er.

Und als Rama drohte, die Erfüllung seiner Forderung mit den Waffen zu erzwingen, rief der tapfere Bhischma:

„Dich ehre ich, edler Lehrer, doch Dein Unrecht muss ich bekämpfen! Ich will keinen Brahmanen töten, denn die größte Sünde ist Priestermord; doch des waffentragenden Gegners darf ich mich erwehren, was auch daraus werde! Auf zum Kurufeld, dort wollen wir uns messen!"

Und auf dem Kurufeld trafen die Gewaltigen einander; in schimmernder Wehr, auf goldgeschmückten Wagen, die mit Tigerdecken belegt und von kundigen Rosselenkern geführt wurden.

Beim schmetternden Klang der Kriegsmuscheln fuhren sie aufeinander los, die starken Waffen in Händen.

Amba sah zu und die Büßer aus dem Wald. Die Himmlischen verließen ihre Göttersitze, um die stärksten Recken im Kampf zu sehen, und die Menschen drängten, soweit nur ein Auge reichen kann.

So dicht wie Schlossen sausten von beiden Seiten die Pfeile, und Rama tötete dem Bhischma vier herrliche Falben. Doch der hatte ihn mit Pfeilen übergossen, dass er aus hundert Wunden blutete und stand wie ein Strauch voll roter Blüten. Ein gewaltiger Schuss spaltete den Bogen Ramas. Nun griff der Brahmane zu den Speeren und schleuderte einen nach dem andern auf Bhischma. Ohne zu wanken stand dieser und fing sie mit dem starken Schild oder schoss auch manche mit breiten, vorne halbmondförmig geschliffenen, Pfeilen in Stücke, ehe sie ihn erreichen konnten.

Vierundzwanzig Tage kämpften sie so, vom Sonnenaufgang bis zur Dämmerung, die das Götterauge schließt. Weithin erscholl der Lärm, wenn Erz auf Erz schlug. Götter liehen den Starken ihre Waffen, und konnte doch keiner des anderen Herr werden. Wohl wankte Rama, als Bhischma ihm mit goldfiedrigen Rohren das Haupt spickte, dass er strahlte wie ein Berg in der Morgensonne, doch senkte der Gangasohn in Ehrfurcht vor dem Lehrer die Waffen, bis der Wagenlenker den Wunden gelabt und gestärkt hatte. Wohl wankte auch Bhischma, als ein Speer des Gewaltigen seinen Wagenlenker durchbohrte und ihn in die Lende traf; doch als er vom Wagen stürzen wollte, standen die acht Wasugötter, denen er seine Stärke verdankte, um ihn, glänzend wie die Sonne oder das opferfressende Feuer und duftend wie die Gärten am Götterberg Kailasa. Die stützten und stärkten den Wankenden. Als Bhischma wieder aufrecht stand, sah er die Mutter, die göttliche Ganga, neben sich auf dem Wagen, den Stachelstock schwingend und die Zügel in kräftiger Hand.

Nun sausten sie über das Kampffeld hin und Bhischma schwang in seiner Rechten den goldbeschlagenen Speer des Schöpfers Pratschapati, den der Götterschmied einstens geschmiedet hatte.

Als Rama die furchtbare Waffe sah, rief er, die Lanze senkend:

„Genug! ich bin besiegt, denn Du bist unbesieglich, Bhischma!"

Nun sprangen beide Kämpfer vom Wagen, erwiesen einander alle Ehrerbietung, und schlossen Frieden.

Rama gestand Amba, dass niemand ihr helfen könnte, denn Bhischma sei unbezwinglich.

Die Unglückliche zog darauf in die Wildnis und suchte vom neuen durch fromme Buße den Zorn der Himmlischen auf Bhischma zu lenken. Nach langem Fasten, Beten, Dürsten, Zehenstehen und anderen qualvollen Übungen, erschien ihr Schiwa, der Zerstörer, den goldenen Dreizack in Händen, und ließ sie eine Gnade erbitten. Da bat Amba: „Sterben soll Bhischma, der Räuber, durch mich, die Geraubte, o Herr!"

„Gewährt!", sprach der Gott.

„Doch wie kann ich schwaches Weib den Heldenbezwinger fällen?", fragte die Verzückte, zitternd vor Furcht und Freude.

„Nach Deinem Tode wirst Du an Drupadas Hofe wiedergeboren werden, und dann soll der Starke durch Deine Schwäche sterben!"

Damit verschwand der Strahlende.

Amba schichtete Holz zu einem mächtigen Haufen und legte Feuer daran. Dann sprang sie in die lohenden Flammen und starb mit dem Schrei: „Zu Bhischmas Verderben!"

Zur selben Stunde aber wurde dem König Drupada von Pantschala ein Kind geboren.

Drupada, der längst einen Sohn ersehnte, hatte die Götter in reichen Opfern um diese Gnade angefleht und seiner Gattin die köstlichsten Schätze für einen Prinzen versprochen. Als diese nun ein Mädchen zur Welt brachte, erschrak sie gar sehr, und um ihrem Gatten den Kummer zu ersparen, gab sie das Kind vor aller Welt für einen Knaben aus. Drupada ließ die üblichen Sohnopfer feiern, und das Kind wuchs als Prinz Schikhandin heran. Nur die Mutter wusste, dass es ein Mädchen sei.

Als der mächtige Dascharnerherr später mit Drupada ein Bündnis schloss, vermählte der Pantschalerkönig seinen vermeintlichen Sohn mit der lieblichen Tochter des Königs von Dascharna, um dem Bunde der beiden Reiche starken Halt zu verleihen.

Doch wehe: die Prinzessin von Dascharna erkannte in Schikhandin das Weib und jagte die Verkleidete unter dem Gelächter ihrer Sklavinnen davon.

Als sie das ihrem Vater erzählte, rüstete der Ergrimmte sein Heer, um den Schimpf an Drupada zu rächen.

Der Pantschalerkönig war in Sorge um seine Herrschaft, als ihm die Gattin die Täuschung gestand, und seine Furcht wuchs, als ein Herold das Nahen des rächenden Dascharnerheeres meldete.

Schikhandini, die sich für die Ursache des drohenden Unterganges hielt, lief voll Verzweiflung in den Wald, um dort zu sterben.

Im Walde aber hauste ein guter Geist, namens Sthuna, ein Diener Kuberas, des Schatzgottes. Der sah das arme, weinende Mädchen und versuchte es freundlich zu trösten. Und als die Tränenreiche vor Schluchzen keine Worte finden konnte, versprach er, vermöge seiner Zauberkraft jeden ihrer Wünsche zu erfüllen, wenn sie sich nur endlich beruhigen wolle!

Nun erzählte Schikhandini, wie dem Reiche und Leben ihres Vaters Gefahr drohe, und bat Sthuna, sie in einen Mann zu verwandeln.

Soweit reichte nun die Macht des Waldgeistes nicht, doch um sein Versprechen zu halten, bot er ihr an, ein

Jahr lang für sie als Weib im Walde zu leben. Sie könne derweil als Mann nach der Stadt gehen und den erzürnten Dascharnerherrn beruhigen. Nur müsste sie versprechen, nach Ablauf der Frist in den Wald zurückzukehren und das erborgte Manneswesen wieder mit ihrem weiblichen zu vertauschen. Dessen ward Schikhandini froh und gelobte auch pünktlich übers Jahr zum Tausche zu kommen.

So war sie nun wirklich Prinz Schikhandin geworden und wanderte in die Stadt. Der gute Sthuna aber verbarg sich als Weib im tiefsten Dickicht.

Der König von Dascharna schloss Frieden, sobald er Schikhandin als Mann sah, glaubte sich von seiner Tochter und deren Dienerinnen getäuscht und schalt sie ob ihres dummen Geschwätzes. Die Prinzessin aber tröstete sich bei ihrem schönen Gemahl.

Nun kam zu jener Zeit Kubera, der Beherrscher der Genien und Geister, vor Sthunas Behausung und erwartete von seinem Diener gastlich begrüßt zu werden. Als der sich aber nicht sehen ließ, fragte der Gott die Tiere des Waldes nach ihm. Diese erzählten lachend und spottend, wie Sthuna ein Weib geworden sei und sich jetzt vor seinem Herrn schäme. Da ergrimmte der mächtige Gebieter der Geister und verfluchte den gutmütigen Toren, der aller Welt zum Gespött diente, so lange als Weib zu leben, bis Schikhandin als Mann auf dem Schlachtfelde sterbe.

Als der Prinz, seinem Versprechen getreu, nach einem Jahr zu Sthuna kam, durfte dieser nicht in den Tausch willigen, und glücklich zog Schikhandin, in dem sich die Seele Ambas regte, zur Stadt zurück und übte sich im Waffenhandwerk, um einst an Bhischma Rache zu nehmen.

Pandu und Dhritaraschtra

Nachdem Amba Hastinapura verlassen hatte, um zum König von Schalwa zu ziehen, wurden ihre Schwestern dem jungen König Witschitrawiria feierlich vermählt. Und der Jüngling liebte die holden Töchter des Kaschikönigs so sehr, dass er das Frauenhaus kaum noch verließ und alle Sorgen der Regierung seinem älteren Bruder Bhischma aufbürdete. Ein tückisches Leiden, die Schwindsucht, raffte den König in all seinem Glück hinweg, und erst nach seinem Tode schenkte ihm Ambika den Dhritaraschtra, Ambalika den Pandu und eine Sklavenfrau den Vidura.

Da Dhritaraschtra, der Erstgeborne, blind war, das Gesetz aber verbot, einen Bresthaften zum König zu weihen, so erteilte Bhischma, als Haupt der Sippe, dem jüngeren, Pandu, die Weihe zum ‚Herrn der Erde‘ und zog die drei Knaben mit aller Liebe eines echten Vaters auf.

Später vermählte er den Ältesten mit Gandhari, der Tochter des Gandharakönigs, und diese trug, aus Mitleid mit ihrem blinden Gatten, vom Hochzeitstage an, ein Tuch über ihren klaren Augen. Ihr Bruder Schakuni hatte sie nach Hastinapura begleitet und lebte nun dort am Hofe des Großkönigs.

König Pandu wurde von Kunti, der edlen Tochter des Herrschers von Kuntibodscha, in feierlicher Wahl vor allen Fürsten Indiens zum Gatten erkoren. Für Madri, die Schwester des Königs Schalya von Madras, erlegte Bhischma, nach der alten Sitte des Brautkaufes, einen hohen Preis und vermählte die liebliche Jungfrau dem König Pandu als zweite Gattin. Vidura, der sich schon frühzeitig durch hohe Weisheit auszeichnete, lebte, alle liebend und von allen geliebt, am Hof als Berater seines königlichen Halbbruders.

Viele kühne Taten vollführte König Pandu und unterwarf sich manchen trotzigen Vasallen aufs Neue.

Aus Unvorsichtigkeit durchbohrte er einst auf einer Gazellenjagd mit seinem Pfeil einen Brahmanen und dessen Gattin. Sterbend verfluchte ihn der Priesters Da übergab Pandu die Herrschaft seinem blinden Bruder Dhritaraschtra und zog mit seinen beiden Frauen in die Wildnis, um durch ein bußereiches Leben den Fluch von sich und den Seinen zu wenden.

Und nach Gebet und Opfer schenkten ihm die Götter Leibeserben, denn der Gottesdienst des Sohnes muss die Sünden des Vaters tilgen.

Dharma, der Gott des Rechtes, schenkte der Kunti den Iudhischthira, Waju, der Sturmgott, den Bhima und Indra, der Götterkönig, Donnerer und Gott des Krieges, den Ardschuna. Der Madri aber schenkten die Aswinas, die schönen Jünglinge, welche vor der Morgenröte reiten, die Zwillinge Nakula und Sahadewa.

Zu Hastinapura hatte Gandhari dem Dhritaraschtra einen Kürbis geboren, aus dessen Kernen nach und nach hundert Söhne und das Töchterlein Duchschala erwuchsen.

Der älteste Sohn ward Durjodhana genannt und trat ein Jahr nach seinem Vetter Iudhischthira ins Leben.

Als Pandu die Madri nach Geburt der Zwillinge voll Dankbarkeit küsste, ereilte ihn der Fluch des getöteten Brahmanen: er fiel um und war tot! Die treue Madri ließ sich mit der Leiche des geliebten Gatten verbrennen. Kunti aber nahm die fünf Knaben und brachte sie nach Hastinapura.

Dort wuchsen sie als Pandusöhne oder Pandava heran, zusammen mit den Söhnen Dhritaraschtras, die man, nach dem Kuruvolk, welches in und um Hastinapura siedelte, Kurusöhne oder Kaurava nannte.

Pandava und Kaurava

Jugend

Bhischma, der nach Pandus Tod für den blinden König das Reich verwaltete, erzog in treuer Liebe auch diese Schar von Kindern und galt ihnen allen als Großvater.

Bhima, der Zweitgeborene der Pandava, den einst der Sturmgott der Kunti geschenkt hatte, war der stärkste und wildeste unter den vielen Knaben. Er schüttelte Brüder und Vettern von den Bäumen, wenn sie nach Früchten hinaufgeklettert waren, und zauste sie unsanft an den Haaren oder warf sie wohl auch in den Schlossteich, wenn es zu kindlichen Balgereien kam.

Durjodhana, der älteste der Kaurava, welcher sehr herrschsüchtig veranlagt war, nahm dem Vetter diese kindischen Derbheiten umso übler, als er zu schwach war, den gleichaltrigen, auch nur im Spiel, unter seine Botmäßigkeit zu zwingen. Diese Missgunst des Knaben wuchs sich im Jüngling zum Hass aus.

Einst lud er die Pandava in eine Laube, die er auf einem Floß über dem Strom anmutig und kunstvoll erbaut hatte. Dort setzte er dem Verhassten vergiftete Früchte vor. Bhima aß davon und taumelte betäubt ins Wasser.

Und wie er tiefer und tiefer sank, kam er in das Reich der Naga: der Schlangen und Schlangengeister. Die freuten sich sehr über den schönen und starken Jüngling. Sie brachten ihn vor ihren König Wasuki. Der erkannte die Vergiftung gleich und biss den Betäubten in den Arm, so das Gift durch Gegengift vertreibend. Als Bhimas Sinne sich zu regen begannen, ließ er ihm köstlichen Soma reichen. Der Pandava trank davon acht Krüge und sank berauscht zurück. Nun ließ Wasuki den Trunkenen von seinen Schlangen über das Wasser tragen und am Ufer niederlegen. Dort schlief Bhima acht Tage und Nächte, stand dann völlig genesen auf und ging heim zu Mutter und Brüdern. Die waren um ihn in großer Sorge gewesen.

Auf den Rat des weisen Oheims Vidura verschwiegen die Pandava Durjodhanas rachsüchtigen Angriff, um nicht zwischen den nahverwandten Häusern eine unüberbrückbare Kluft aufzureißen.

Nachdem die erste Kindheit vorbei war, lernten die Prinzen bei zwei tüchtigen Waffenmeistern, dem Brahmanen Drona und seinem Schwager Kripa, das Waffenhandwerk und ritterliches Wesen.

Die kriegerischen Übungen waren ein üppiger Boden für Eifersüchteleien zwischen den Prinzen aus den beiden Häusern des Bharatageschlechtes:

Iudhischthira übertraf im Wagenrennen alle seine Gefährten. Durjodhana und Bhima stritten stets um die Palme im Keulenkampf. Der unbesieglichen Kraft des Pandava setzte der Kaurava eine schlangenhafte Beweglichkeit entgegen. Nakula und Sahadewa, die Madrizwillinge, zeichneten sich im Schwertkampf vor allen aus, und Ardschuna, der Indraspross, war der Liebling des ehrwürdigen Waffenmeisters Drona und sein bester Schüler. Der schwere Streitbogen war seine Hauptwaffe. Unermüdliche Ausdauer hielt ihn den ganzen Tag auf dem Schießstand, und selbst bei Nacht schlich er sich hin, brannte eine große Öllampe an, und schoss Pfeil auf Pfeil nach dem Ziel. Als Drona ihn einst bei solch einer einsamen Übung ertappte, nahm er die Lampe weg, um den Allzueifrigen vor Übertreibung zu bewahren. Doch Ardschuna übte von nun an im Dunkeln und lernte so bald auch bei Nacht jedes Ziel treffen.

Als der Bogenkundige einst in einer Lehrstunde alle Brüder und Vettern beschämte, denn er allein hatte alle hölzernen Zielvögel von den Stangen geschossen, sprang ein schöner Jüngling, in goldenem Panzer, mit prächtigem Ohrenschmuck, in die Arena, ergriff den Bogen und spaltete Schuss um Schuss die Stangen, auf welchen die Ziele gesteckt hatten. Alle staunten über die Kunst des Schützen.

„Prächtig!", jubelte Durjodhana. „Ardschuna, der sich für unübertrefflich hielt, hat seinen Meister gefunden! Wie heißt Du, edler Krieger, und über welches Volk herrscht Dein Vater?"

„Karna heiße ich!", sprach der Goldschimmernde errötend „doch bin ich nicht königlichen Geblütes!"

„So sollst Du die Provinz Anga von mir zum Geschenk erhalten und dort als König herrschen!", rief Durjodhana, der einen Krieger, welcher selbst seinen Vetter Ardschuna im Bogenschießen übertraf, um jeden Preis an sich fesseln wollte.

Da trat der alte Rosselenker Adhiratha aus der Zuschauermenge, umarmte Karna, vor Freude schluchzend, und rief ein über das andere Mal: „Mein Sohn, mein tapferer Sohn, wie stolz bin ich auf Dich!"

Die Pandava hatten während Karnas Schießen voll Staunen, beim Ausbruch von Durjodhanas Schadenfreude voll Grimm, geschwiegen.

Nun aber schrie der heißblütige Bhima: „Fuhrmannsohn! Kutschersprössling!"

„Schweig!", rief Karna, sich stolz aufrichtend. „Ich liebe und ehre meinen Vater, und doch soll mich Dein Wort verletzen! aber die Zeit wird kommen, da die Taten entscheiden, wer von uns adliger ist!". Dann wandte er sich und verließ mit seinem Vater die Arena.

Von nun an nahm Karna an den Waffenspielen der Prinzen teil und schloss sich in Dankbarkeit und inniger Freundschaft an Durjodhana.

Das Fest der Waffenweihe kam heran, und die Prinzen machten ihren Lehrern alle Ehre. Außer Aswatthama, dem starken Sohn des Waffenmeisters Drona und Karna, dem neuen König von Anga, konnte man ihnen keinen vergleichen.

Beim festlichen Wettkampf wäre es fast zu Mord und Totschlag gekommen: Der starke Bhima hatte Durjodhana im Keulenkampf an die Wand gedrängt, und dieser schlug nun, vor Scham und Hass fiebernd, mitten im Scheinkampf, ein paar wuchtige Hiebe. Da ergrimmte der zornmütige Sohn des Sturmgottes und hob seine Keule zu tödlichem Schlag. Mit schwerer Mühe nur konnten die beiden Waffenmeister die Erbitterten trennen.

Der Schluss des Wettkampfes war ein Bogenschießen der erlesenen Kämpfer Ardschuna und Karna. Es galt ein kaum sichtbares, hochhängendes Ziel mit glattschaftigem Pfeil herunterzuholen. Als die beiden Bogenschützen auf den Schießstand traten, sprach der Waffenmeister Drona:

„Nennt mir, nach alter Sitte, die Helden, vor deren Augen ihr glänzen wollt!"

Karna rief:

„Bhischma seh' ich hier, den unbezwinglichen Gangasohn, der möge mich als Sieger schauen, und der blinde König Dhritaraschtra soll von meinem Ruhme hören!"

„Und Du, Ardschuna? auf wen siehst Du voll Stolz?"

„Ich schau aufs Ziel! – und nur aufs Ziel!", rief der Pandava, hob den Bogen und schoss den hölzernen Vogel in Stücke.

„Heil Ardschuna! hoch die Pandava!", jubelte das Volk und umdrängte den blinden Herrscher. „Weih einen der Pandava zum Thronfolger!" „Heil Pandu! und seinen tapferen Söhnen!", rief es rings in der Menge.

Da entschloss sich Dhritaraschtra, den ältesten Prinzen vom Bharatastamm, den rechtlich denkenden Iudhischthira, vor allem Volke zu seinem Nachfolger, zum künftigen ,Herrn der Erde' zu weihen.

Durjodhana aber schlich sich mit Karna und dem Oheim Schakuni beiseite, und die Zornigen berieten, wie sie die Pandava verderben könnten.

Drona forderte von seinen Schülern das halbe Reich des Königs Drupada von Pantschala als Sold und Probe ihrer Kriegstüchtigkeit. Ardschuna zog mit seinen Brüdern aus. Sie bezwangen das Heer der Pantschaler und der Indraspross fing den König Drupada und brachte ihn seinem Waffenmeister.

Bhima hatte sich in der Schlacht besonders ausgezeichnet und unter den Pantschalern gewütet wie Feuer in dürrem Holz. Fast hätte er auch den gefangenen König erschlagen. Der besonnene Ardschuna und Iudhischthira in seinem hohen Rechtsgefühl hatten Mühe, die Kampfwut des Unbändigen zu zügeln.

Drona freute sich dieser kühnen Waffentat seiner Schüler, und, nachdem Drupada ihm sein halbes Reich abgetreten hatte, entließ er den Gefangenen in seine Heimat.

Das Ansehen der Pandava aber wuchs von Tag zu Tag weit über die Grenzen des Landes.

Feindschaft

Neid, Furcht und Hass glommen in Durjodhanas Herzen, als er die Pandava so hoch in Ehren sah. Sein wilder Bruder Duchschasana und sein ränkevoller Oheim Schakuni schürten die Glut mit Bildern, wie die starken Pandava einst den schwachen Kaurava den Fuß auf den Nacken setzen würden und mit Plänen, wie man sich ihrer entledigen könnte. Der tapfere Karna predigte offene Feindschaft. Da trat Durjodhana vor den blinden König. Er sprach ihm von der Volksgunst, die sich die Pandava erschlichen hätten, von der drohenden Gefahr für seine Söhne, wenn die Söhne Pandus durch Iudhischthira zur Herrschaft im Reiche gelangten, und vom Untergang seines Hauses, wenn die Starken sich's einfielen ließen zu ertrotzen, was ihnen nie gewährt werden könnte. Er weinte und drohte, schrie und schalt Dhritaraschtra einen kindischen Greis, der es nicht verstünde, den drohenden Sturm von seinem Hause zu wenden.

Und dem guten alten König bangte um die Seinen. Ängstlich, wie er infolge seines Gebrechens war, lieh er den Klagen des herrschsüchtigen Sohnes, den Plänen des listigen Schwagers sein Ohr und entschlüpfte vor den friedfertigen Ratschlägen des weisen Vidura, vor der ahnungsvollen Warnung seiner treuen Gattin Gandhari.

Er verbannte Iudhischthira und seine Brüder nach dem Wald Waranawata und Kunti zog mit den Söhnen ins Elend.

So geschah es nach dem Willen Durjodhanas: In der Einsamkeit hatte er von seinen Sklaven ein Holzhaus bauen lassen, dessen Doppelwände mit Stroh, Harz und ähnlichen Brandstoffen gefüllt waren. Einer seiner Haussklaven sollte die Verbannten im Walde erwarten, ihnen diese einzige Zuflucht in der Wildnis zur Wohnung anbieten, und bei Gelegenheit Feuer an das Haus legen.

Die Pandava kamen und brachten eine alte Pariafrau samt ihren fünf Söhnen zur Bedienung mit. Vidura, der Durjodhana durchschaute, hatte Kunti vor ihrem Auszug gewarnt. So waren die Pandava auf ihrer Hut und gruben gleich nach ihrer Ankunft einen Gang durch die Erde, dass man vom Wohnraum ungesehen in den Wald gelangen konnte.

Und als sie damit fertig waren, als die Nacht über dem Walde lag, zündete Bhima das Haus an und alle sechs flohen in den Gang.

Doch wehe: in dem dichten, giftigen Rauch des Harzes taumelten sie wie Trunkene, fanden sich nicht zurecht, fielen eines über das andere und wären sicher jämmerlich erstickt, wenn nicht Bhima alle fünf in seine starken Arme genommen und ins Freie getragen hätte. Auch hier musste er noch gewaltig kämpfen, denn weit um das Haus hatte sich eine dichte Rauchhaube gelegt. Doch wie sein Vater, der Sturmgott, brach er mit seiner schweren Last durch das Unterholz, bis er endlich in frischer Luft anhielt. Im ersten Dämmern des Morgens sah er sich vor einem riesenhaften Banyanenbaum.

Der Banyanenbaum ist eines der vielen Wunder Indiens: von jedem seiner waagrechten Äste sendet er Ranken zur Erde, die dort wieder Wurzel schlagen, zu Stämmen erstarken und so das Astwerk weithinaus tragen. Hunderte und Tausende von Stämmen hat so ein einziger alter Baum, und in seinem Schatten können ganze Heere lagern.

Solch einen Baumriesen hatte Bhima gefunden, und unterdessen Blätterdach bettete er die betäubte Mutter mit seinen Brüdern und lief um Wasser.

In dem Harzhaus aber verkohlte die Paria mit ihren fünf Söhnen und Durjodhanas gewissenloser Haushälter.

Als sein Herr nach Wochen in den Wald kam, um zu sehen, ob sein Befehl pünktlich befolgt worden sei, fand er unter den Trümmern des verbrannten Hauses sieben verkohlte Leichen. Da glaubte Durjodhana seinen Streich vollauf geglückt, und, Jubel im Herzen, Trauer im Antlitz, ließ er die vermeintlichen Reste der Pandava nach Hastinapura schaffen, und der blinde König musste zu Ehren der ‚Verunglückten‘ eine prächtige Totenfeier abhalten.

Bhimas Abenteuer

Als Bhima, nachdem er sich erfrischt hatte, mit einem Helm voll Wasser zurückkehrte, fand er Mutter und Brüder in ruhigem tiefem Schlaf.

Ungestüm wallte sein Blut durch die Adern, da er vor den Unglücklichen stand.

In heißem Zorn bist er die Zähne zusammen und klagte dem Himmel das Elend der Seinen: Hier ruhten die Edlen, die im Prunk der Paläste erwuchsen, auf rauer Erde, in Wind und Wetter, inmitten der Wildnis. Ärmer als die Ärmsten waren die Herrscher des Landes!

Er gelobte über ihrem Schlaf, dem einzigen Geschenk eines zürnenden Schicksals, in steter Treue und ohne Ermatten zu wachen.

Nicht weit vom Lager der Pandava hauste unter einem mächtigen Feigenbaum der Riese Hidimbas mit seiner Schwester Hidimbaa.

Gar schrecklich war dieser Waldgeist anzusehen, als er sich im Erwachen auf seinem Laublager wälzte: wohl doppelt so lang und so breit als ein Mensch, rothaarig und -bärtig, mit kleinen, tückischen schwarzen Augen in seinem braunen, hässlichen Gesicht, aus dessen breiten Maul acht weiße, spitzige Zähne gierig hervorlugten. Denn Hidimbas war ein Menschenfresser und der leise Morgenwind hatte ihm den Geruch der lagernden Pandava zugeweht.

Er gähnte langhin, juckte sich im Haar, und weckte die Schwester mit einem freundlichen Fausthieb:

„He! Hidimbaa, mein gutes Schwesterlein, ich rieche Menschenfleisch! Sieh Dich doch ein wenig um und bring die Leckerbissen her! dann wollen wir ein köstliches Mahl halten und lustig sein!“

Hidimbaa erhob sich mürrisch und ging, dem feinen Geruch nach, durch den Wald, während ihr Bruder sich wohlig auf seinem weichen Lager räkelte und von dem leckeren Gericht träumte.

Doch kaum sah Hidimbaa den wachenden Bhima von weitem, so wandelte sich ihr Sinn, und heiße Liebe zu dem schönen und starken Helden fiel in ihr ungefüges Herz.

Rasch flüsterte sie ein Zaubersprüchlein, das sie in ein schönes Menschenweib verwandelte, und schritt aus dem Dunkel der Bäume auf den Geliebten zu.

Bhima ging der Schönen verwundert entgegen.

Hidimbaa neigte sich errötend und flüsterte: „Wer bist Du, schöner Jüngling, den ich lieben muss, und wer sind die, die dort schlafen, ohne die schreckliche Gefahr zu ahnen? Wisse, ein menschenfressender Riese, mein Bruder Hidimbas, haust hier im Wald. Er hat mich nach Euch gesandt, denn er will Euch fressen. Doch ich liebe Dich und begehr' Dich zum Gatten, braunäugiger Held! Flieh mit mir! meine Zauberkraft trägt Dich durch die Lüfte, und wir wollen auf unnahbaren Bergesgipfeln glücklich sein!“

„Wie sollt' ich die Schlafenden verlassen, die mir vertrauen!“, sprach Bhima, die Verführerin erschreckt von sich schiebend.

„Wecke sie,“ flüsterte Hidimbaa „ich rette Euch alle!“

„Nein, nein! sie schlafen zu gut!“, sprach Bhima kopfschüttelnd. „Ich kann mit dem Kerl allein fertig werden! – führe mich nur zu ihm – ich fürchte nicht Tod und nicht Teufel, und ein Riese ist mir gerade recht –“

Während Bhima noch sprach, stürzte Hidimbas, dem das Warten zu lange geworden war, aus dem Wald, griff mit harter Faust nach der Schwester und begann die Verliebte zu schelten. Doch Bhima umfasste den vorgestreckten Arm des Riesen und, wie der Löwe einen Büffel, schleifte er ihn über den Boden, acht Bogenschüsse weit.

„Ruhig!", murmelte der Treue dabei, „wirst Du ruhig sein! dort schlafen meine Mutter und die Brüder! Willst Du sie wecken um nichts?"

Da ermannte sich der Riese und fasste Bhima laut brüllend um den Leib.

„Lärme nicht! die Schläfer ruhen so sanft!", flüsterte Bhima und schleppte den Schreienden wieder ein Stück weiter fort.

Nun ergrimmte Hidimbas und riss sich los. Ein gewaltiger Kampf begann, bei welchem die beiden Bäume entwurzelten und Felsen aufeinander warfen.

Beim Toben des Kampfes erwachten die Pandava. Hidimbaa sprach den Lauschenden voll Angst von der Gefahr, in der sie schwebten, und führte sie zitternd nach dem Kampfplatz.

Da wüteten die beiden Kämpfer gegeneinander, wie sechzigjährige Elefanten. Wie dichter Rauch wirbelten die Staubwolken empor.

Ardschuna rief dem Bruder Mut zu, als er die zwei Starken wie Löwen ineinander verkrampft sah, und griff nach seinem Bogen. Doch Bhima wies jede Hilfe zurück.

Mit Sturmeskraft umfing er den Leib des Riesen, und unter dem eisernen Druck der gewaltigen Arme wurde Hidimbas Brüllen zum Röcheln, die Augen quollen aus ihren Höhlen – ein Krachen – und mit gebrochenem Rückgrat fiel die Leiche des Riesen zu Boden.

„Und nun die Riesenschwester!", rief Bhima, mit rotfunkelnden Augen, und stürzte auf Hidimbaa los. Doch Ardschuna trat dazwischen und der rechtlich denkende Iudhischthira, und sie beruhigten die Kampfwut des Unbändigen. Der wischte sich Staub und Schweiß aus den Augen und sah verlegen die Riesenschwester als schöne Menschenjungfrau vor sich stehen. Schüchtern fasste er nach ihrer Hand und führte sie still unter den Banyanenbaum. Die Schöne gelobte, ein Jahr lang Bhimas getreues Weib zu sein und ihm, kraft ihrer Zauberkunst, die Wonnen aller Göttergärten auf den Bergeshöhen zu zeigen. Dann müsse sie ihn verlassen und ins Riesenreich zurückkehren.

Und fröhlich zog Bhima nun tagsüber mit Hidimbaa durch die Lüfte, von Gipfel zu Gipfel; bei Nacht aber wachte er getreulich am Lager der Seinen, unter dem Banyanenbaum.

Als das Jahr um war, schenkte ihm die Gattin einen starken Sohn, den Ghatotkatscha, und der erwuchs noch in der Stunde seiner Geburt zum fertigen Mann.

Mit ihm schlug Hidimbaa, nach freundlichem Abschied, den Weg gegen Norden ein und entschwand den traurigen Blicken Bhimas für immer. Ghatotkatscha aber hat den Pandava später noch manchen guten Dienst geleistet.

Um Bhimas Leid zu mildern, gaben die Verbannten, bald nach Hidimbaas Abschied, das Lager unter der Banyane auf und zogen weiter durch den Wald. Als sie nach langem Wandern in eine Stadt kamen, gaben sie sich für Büßer aus und fanden bei einer Brahmanenfamilie freundliche Aufnahme. Tagsüber zogen sie einzeln von Tür zu Tür und erbettelten nach alter Büßersitte ihre Nahrung. Abends teilte Kunti alles Erbettelte in zwei gleiche Teile und gab die eine Hälfte dem ewig hungernden Bhima, von der anderen sättigte sie sich selbst und ihre vier übrigen Söhne.

Eines Abends hörte Kunti im Zimmer des gastfreundlichen Brahmanen lautes Wehklagen. Und da sie sich tief in der Schuld der Guten wusste, lauschte sie, in der Hoffnung, ihnen ihre Hilfe anbieten zu können.

Sie hörte den Hausvater klagen:

„Wie ist das Schicksal hart, das mich in den besten Jahren von Euch ruft, ihr Lieben! – denn wie könnte ich weiterleben, wenn ich eines der Meinen dafür opfern müsste? – Dich, gütige Mutter meiner Kinder, oder die sündenreine

Tochter oder den Sohn, das unschuldige Kind, dessen Gebet mir einst den Himmel aufschließen soll!"

„Mich lasset sterben vor allen!", rief die Mutter." „Was wäre eine Familie, der der Ernährer fehlt? Betteln müssten wir gehen! und wer schützte die vaterlose Tochter, wer lehrte den Sohn die Weisheit eines Brahmanen?"

„Ich sterbe gerne für Euch!", sprach die Tochter. „Mann und Weib sind eins, die mag auch der Tod nicht trennen! – Der Sohn versöhnt mit den Göttern, getreu seinem Namen – die Tochter aber heißt Sorge und hilfloser Jammer!"

Gerade als Kunti eintrat, um von den Sorgen der gütigen Wirte ihren Anteil zu fordern, zog das kleine Büblein des Brahmanen einen Halm aus der Bodenmatte und lallte: „Bitte, bitte! nicht weinen! mit dem da schlägt Bubi böse Menschenfresser tot."

Mit Tränen in den Augen lachten die Bekümmerten über das kindliche Gestammel und herzten den tapferen Kleinen.

Als Kunti nach der Ursache von Kummer und Klage gefragt hatte, hörte sie folgende Erklärung:

Ein menschenfressender Riese, namens Vaka, hatte die Stadt gezwungen, ihm nach jeder Vollmondnacht einen Büffel, eine Wagenladung Reis und einen lebenden Menschen zu senden. Diesmal hatte das Los die Familie des guten Brahmanen getroffen, und Vater, Mutter und Tochter, jedes von ihnen, wollte sein Leben für die anderen opfern.

Da konnte die Mutter der Pandava Hilfe versprechen: Ihr Sohn Bhima sollte zu dem Riesen gesandt werden!

Aber der Brahmane verschwor sich, er könnte den Gastfreund nicht für sich sterben lassen. Kunti gestand nun, wer sie und die Ihren seien, und bat ihr Geheimnis zu hüten. Held Bhima aber, das wisse sie, würde den Riesen töten!

Am nächsten Morgen zog Bhima mit einem Wagen voll Reis und einem feisten Büffel durch das Stadttor gegen den Wald, in welchem der Riese hauste.

Draußen angekommen, erschlug er den Büffel, riss ein paar junge Bäume aus und brannte ein mächtiges Feuer an. Während der Büffel, an eine junge Tanne gesteckt, braun briet, machte sich Bhima über den Reis, glücklich, dass er einmal satt zu essen habe. Doch mitten in der Mahlzeit kam der Riese und schalt, dass ein Mensch sich in seinem Gehege breit mache. Aber Bhima, der noch nicht satt war, ließ sich nicht stören und aß mit sichtlichem Wohlbehagen von dem braungebratenen Rind. Vaka warf kopfgroße Felstrümmer nach ihm. Die wehrte Bhima mit der Linken von sich, mit der Rechten hielt er das letzte Viertel des Büffels und aß es schmatzend zu Ende. Dann sprang er auf, wischte sich die Hände am Moos ab, und griff nach einem Felsblock. Geschickt wich Vaka dem schweren Geschoss aus. Nun begann ein Ringen wie einst mit Hidimbas: bald Leib an Leib, in mächtigem Stampfen die Erde aufwühlend, bald Felsen gegeneinander schleudernd oder entwurzelte Stämme wie Keulen schwingend, bekämpften sich die Starken. Es endete damit, dass Bhima den Leib des Riesen über seinem Knie entzweibrach.

Die Leiche führte er auf dem leeren Wagen in die Stadt. Dort ward er vom Jubel des Volkes als Befreier empfangen, und ihm zu Ehren im Rathaus ein prächtiges Siegesmahl gefeiert.

Der gute Brahmane aber hielt sein Wort, so dass die Pandava unerkannt blieben.

Draupadi

Nicht lange nach Bhimas Sieg über den Riesen zog ein Brahmane aus Pantschala durch die Stadt. Er war auf einer Botenreise, um die Fürsten des Landes zu Draupadis Gattenwahl einzuladen.

Als der fromme Priester bei den Pandava übernachtete, erzählte er ihnen von der wunderbaren Geburt dieser schönen Jungfrau:

Drupada, der König von Pantschala, hatte Hastinapura mit Rachegedanken im Herzen verlassen. So sehr er den heldenkühnen Ardschuna bewunderte, so sehr hasste er den Waffenmeister Drona, dem er sein halbes Reich hatte geben müssen.

Zwei fromme Brahmanen, die im ganzen Land als Heilige galten, rüsteten auf des Königs inständige Bitte ein prunkvolles Opfer, und Drupada erflehte von den Göttern einen starken Sohn, der ihn an Drona räche. Da sprang ein glänzend gewappneter Jüngling und eine lotusduftende Jungfrau aus den Opferflammen, als Zwillingspaar, welches die Götter, in ihrer Freude am Opfer, dem greisen König und seiner Gattin schenkten. Der Jüngling ward Dhrischtadjumna genannt und die schöne, schwarzlockige Jungfrau Draupadi.

Als die Pandava die Erzählung des Brahmanen gehört hatten, beschlossen sie unerkannt, in ihren Büßerkleidern, an dem Feste am Hofe Drupadas teilzunehmen.

Am nächsten Morgen nahmen sie freundlichen Abschied von ihren dankbaren Wirten und schlugen den Weg nach Pantschala ein.

An der Ganga hatte Ardschuna einen schweren Kampf zu bestehen: Tschitrasena, der König der Gandharva, wollte die Pandava am Überschreiten des Stromes verhindern. Doch Ardschuna besiegte ihn nach langem Kampf mit dem Bogen Agneya, den der Lieblingsschüler Dronas einst von seinem Waffenmeister erhalten hatte.

Der edle Bharataprinz schonte den Besiegten, die Schwester Tschitrasenas riet dem Bruder zur Versöhnung, und so schlossen die beiden Gegner nun ein aufrichtiges Freundschaftsbündnis. Ein frommer Brahmane, namens Dhaumia, der an Tschitrasenas Hof lebte, schloss sich dort den fünf tapferen Brüdern an und ward der Hauspriester der Pandava.

Beim Abschied schenkte Ardschuna dem Tschitrasena die Waffe Agneya, und die fünf Brüder erhielten als Gastgeschenk hundert der herrlichen, milchweißen Gandharverrosse. Sie ließen sie vorläufig in ihrem Stall, denn sie setzten ihre Reise als Büßer fort.

In Drupadas Residenz nahmen die Pandava im Hause eines redlichen Töpfermeisters Wohnung und heischten, als büßende Brahmanen von Haus zu Haus gehend, milde Gaben für ihren Unterhalt. Auch auf dem Festplatz erschienen sie nur in ihrer Verkleidung.

Der Tag der Gattenwahl kam heran und die Edelsten Indiens zogen in die langgestreckte Arena.

Dhrischtadjumna, mit Draupadi an der Hand, trat in ihre Mitte und rief:

„Seid gegrüßt, ihr Herren der Erde, die ihr um die Schwester steht, wie Speichen um eine Nabe: keiner der Erste, keiner der Letzte! Durjodhana, Prinz von Kuru, mit Deinen Brüdern: sei uns gegrüßt! Und Du Schischupala, mächtiger Herrscher von Tschedi, Schalya, König von Madras, Iarasandha und ihr anderen Herren und Fürsten: Heil Euch und Gruß! und höret wie Draupadi wählt:

Hier liegt ein mächtiger Bogen aus der Zeit unsrer Väter, drei Menschenalter entspannt schon! Wer ihn besehnt und fünf glatte Rohrpfeile durch das Auge des silbernen Fisches am Ende der Bahn zu jagen vermag, den kürt die Schwester zum Gatten und folgt ihm noch heute nach Hause. – Auf, edelgeborene Krieger! der Preis ist des Sieges wert!"

Da trat Durjodhana vor, ergriff den Bogen, setzte das eine Ende, an welchem die Sehne hing, auf den Boden und hing sich mit aller Kraft an das andere, um es durch die Öse am freien Ende der Sehne zu zwingen. Doch wie er auch zog und mit dem Knie gegen die Wölbung des Bogens drückte, es fehlte immer noch eine gute Spanne zum Gelingen. Mit hochrotem Kopf stolperte er endlich bei seiner ruckweisen Arbeit und fiel, unter dem lauten Gelächter des Volkes und manches schadenfrohen Preiswerbers, der Länge nach hin.

Doch die Nebenbuhler hatten zu früh gelacht: Was dem starken Kuruprinzen misslang, das konnte auch ihnen nicht gelingen. Schalya plagte sich vergeblich und der starke Schischupala von Tschedi, sowie jeder andere. Mancher fiel noch unter dem Hohn der Menge in den Staub.

Als letzter tritt Karna vor, der König von Anga: Ein Druck – der Bogen ist gespannt – schon liegt der erste Pfeil auf der Sehne –.

„Halt!", ruft Draupadi. „Dem Fuhrmannssohn wird' ich nie als Gattin folgen!"

Mit einem unsäglich traurigen Blick auf die trotzige Schöne lässt Karna die Arme sinken. Im krampfhaften Spiel der Hände entspannt er den Bogen und wirft ihn zu Boden. Dann hebt er, ohne mit der Wimper zu zucken, sein Auge zum strahlenden Gestirn des Tages und eilt mit einem geltenden Lachen schmerzvollen Hohnes aus den Schranken.

Wo die Sitze der ehrwürdigen Brahmanen stehen, erhebt sich ein Mann und springt über die Brüstung in die Arena.

Ardschuna ist es, von niemand erkannt! So rasch wie Karna besehnt er den Bogen, sein Pfeil fliegt, und klirrend fällt das silberne Ziel zur Erde.

Draupadi legt ihm den Kranz um das Haupt und ruft:
„Dich, starker Held, wählt mein Herz! und das sei der einzige Richter!". Laut jubelte das Volk, als nun Ardschuna, Draupadi an der Hand, mit der Familie des Königs die Arena verlassen wollte. Doch am Tor standen die ahgefallenen Freier und schalten den König, dass er die Tochter einem Brahmanen geben wolle, da doch die Sitte der Gattenwahl nur in der Kriegerkaste Geltung habe. Sie drohten mit Worten und Fäusten und erhoben ihre Waffen. Da griff Ardschuna nach dem Bogen, mit welchem er eben die Braut gewonnen hatte. Bhima brach durch die Menge, mit einem Baum, den er irgendwo ausgerissen hatte, und stellte sich neben den Bruder. Schalya, der König von Madras, stürzte mit Durjodhana gegen die beiden Kämpfer, doch Bhima vertrieb sie lachend mit seinem Baum. Karna sprang vor, aber als er auf Ardschunas Schulter die weiße Schnur des Brahmanen sah, neigte er sich voll Ehrfurcht und senkte die Waffen. Da gaben auch die anderen den Widerstand auf. Die fünf Brüder, die sich einstweilen zusammengefunden hatten, neigten sich vor dem König und gingen mit Draupadi nach dem Hause des Töpfers. Als sie in die Stube traten, sprach Ardschuna:

„Sieh, Mutter, was wir heute Köstliches bringen!"

Ohne aufzusehen sprach Kunti: „Genießet es alle miteinander, und der Himmel wird es Euch segnen!", denn sie dachte, die Söhne kämen von ihrem täglichen Bußgang und brächten die Almosen mit.

Während sie sprach war Krischna eingetreten, ein Fürst der Iadava und Brudersohn Kuntis. Er hatte seine Vettern auf dem Festplatz erkannt und war ihnen heimlich nachgegangen. Der begrüßte sie alle und sagte, dass man der Mutter Wort strenge befolgen müsse: Draupadi sollte die Gattin aller fünf Pandava werden, der leuchtende Mittelpunkt der Familie, deren ganze Macht die Einigkeit war!

Damit waren alle einverstanden und nach Krischnas Abschied gingen sie zur Ruhe: Sahadeva, der Jüngste, breitete die Felle am Boden aus. Darauf schliefen die fünf Brüder, zu Häupten die Mutter, zu Füßen die Braut.

Am nächsten Morgen, als die Freier die Stadt verlassen hatten, erschienen die Pandava vor Drupada und gaben sich ihm zu erkennen. Da herrschte große Freude in Pantschala, denn die tapferen Brüder waren dem König und seinen Getreuen willkommene Bundesgenossen.

Zwar zeigte sich Drupada anfangs wenig geneigt, seine Tochter allen fünf Pandava als Gattin zu geben, doch Iudhischthira, der Sohn des Rechtes, berief sich auf die alte Sitte ihrer unteilbaren Familie, und Krischna bekräftigte seine Worte dadurch, dass er ein paar Beispiele solcher Gruppenehen, aus uralter Zeit und edlen Geschlechtern, nannte.

In aller Feierlichkeit traute Dhaumia, der neue Opferpriester der Pandava, allen fünf Brüdern die Braut an, und ließ Draupadi mit jedem das Hausfeuer in sieben Schritten rechtshin umwandeln. Der Brautvater aber und die Hochzeitsgäste, vor allen Krischna, beschenkten die Neuvermählten mit Gold und Edelsteinen, Blumen und köstlichen Spezereien.

Wie ein Lauffeuer verbreitete sich die Kunde, dass die Pandava lebten. Sie kam auch in den Palast von Hastinapura, und der alte, blinde König freute sich laut, dass das Haus seines Bruders nicht untergegangen sei. Doch Durjodhana schalt darob den Vater vor dem ganzen Hof, und der kindische Greis stammelte verlegen von List und Verstellung, um den erzürnten Sohn zu beschwichtigen.

Durjodhana brachte alte und neue Pläne vor, um sich der gefährlichen Thronbewerber zu entledigen, aber der redliche Bhischma und der tapfere Drona bewogen den blinden König, den Ansprüchen der Pandava durch eine Teilung des Reiches gerecht zu werden.

Der weise Vidura musste nach Pantschala reisen, und er brachte die fünf Brüder samt ihrer Gattin, ihrer Mutter und dem Iadaverfürsten Krischna, der sich in inniger Freundschaft an Ardschuna geschlossen hatte, nach Hastinapura zurück.

Dort geschah die Teilung des Reiches. Der neidige Durjodhana und der ränkevolle Schakuni hatten es so zu wenden gewusst, dass der den Pandava zufallende Teil, die wüste Landschaft Kandavaprastha war. Doch die tapferen Prinzen focht das nicht an. Mit vielem, den Starken stets zulaufendem, Volk zogen sie in ihr Reich und bauten dort eine große Stadt, die sie, dem Götterkönig zu Ehren, Indraprastha nannten.

Ardschuna

In der schönen Residenz, die sie ihrer Kraft und Einigkeit verdankten, lebten die Pandava unter der weisen Herrschaft Iudhischthiras glücklich und in Frieden. Und als sie dessen voll Freude inne warden, schworen sie einander, dass derjenige in langjährige Verbannung ziehen solle, der diese Einigkeit störte.

Eines Abends erging sich Ardschuna im weiten Garten des königlichen Palastes. Da kam ein ehrwürdiger Brahmane und klagte, dass ihm soeben seine letzte Kuh geraubt worden sei. Rasch war Ardschuna bereit die Räuber zu verfolgen und ihnen die Beute abzujagen. Er sprang ins Haus um seine Waffen zu holen. Doch wehe: auf der Schwelle saß Iudhischthira in traulichem Kosen mit Draupadi. Ardschuna stieß an den königlichen Bruder – es kam zum Wortwechsel, der, bei Ardschunas Eifer, dem bittenden Brahmanen rasch zu helfen, bald zum heftigen Streit ausartete, und damit endete, dass der Hilfsbereite, mit scharfem

Spott auf den verliebten König, seinen Bogen ergriff und den Kuhdieben in den Wald nachlief.

Nachdem er diese bestraft und dem ehrwürdigen Brahmanen sein Eigentum ins Haus gebracht hatte, trat er vor die Brüder und erklärte in die Verbannung ziehen zu wollen, da er in blindem Eifer Feindschaft ins Haus getragen hatte. Vergeblich entbanden die Brüder den Bereuenden von der harten Verpflichtung, umsonst reichte der edle Iudhischthira dem Bruder versöhnt die Hand und bat ihn zu bleiben; Ardschuna wollte an einem Gelöbnis nicht gedeutet sehen und zog mit den freundlichsten Wünschen der Seinen in die Ferne.

An der Ganga besuchte er viele Wallfahrtsorte und badete dort nach religiösem Brauch in dem heiligen Strom. Da zog einst Ulupi, eine Schlangenprinzessin, den kühnen Schwimmer in die Tiefe und brachte den schönen Menschensohn in ihren Palast.

Oh! über die zauberhafte Pracht, auf die Ardschuna da stieß:

Auf schlanken Säulen aus Jaspis, die sich oben in köstlichem Schnitzwerk teilten und wieder wirr ineinander verschlangen, ruhte eine mächtige Kuppel aus einem einzigen Smaragd geschnitten. Die Wände schienen aus tausend und aber tausend wasserhellen Kristallen geformt und funkelten in grüngoldnem Licht, dass ringsum alles zu leben schien. Dicke, weiche Teppiche waren gebreitet, und wo sie den Boden sehen ließen, da war Steinchen an Steinchen zu wunderbarem Bildwerk gefügt, oder Perlen, Gold- und Silberküglein, wie Kies auf einen Gartenweg, gestreut. Liebliche Töne, die fernher zu klingen schienen, erfüllten den Raum und einten sich zu Weisen aus längst vergangenen Zeiten.

Weich schlangen sich die Arme der wunderschönen Prinzessin um Ardschunas Hals. Kosend wallte ihr reiches Haar über seine Haut. Es war ein Locken und Halten, ein Fühlen und Sehnen – Ardschuna blieb und nahm die Schlangenprinzessin zum Weib.

Ein Jahr schien dem Glücklichen vergangen, als Ulupi ihm ein schönes Knäblein schenkte, das sie Iravat nannte. Da gedachte Ardschuna der Seinen: Immer tiefer verlor er sich in Sinnen – leise, leise klangen die gewohnten Weisen wie Stromrauschen an sein Ohr – ein kühler Wind strich über seine Glieder, und Ardschuna erwachte. Im ersten Schimmer des Morgens sah er sich am Ufer der Ganga, neben seinen Kleidern und Waffen. Er lief ins Dorf und hörte dort, dass seit seinem Verschwinden nur eine Nacht vergangen sei.

Des schönen Erlebens froh, zog er weiter und kam nach Manipura. Hier sah er die Tochter des Königs, die schöne Tschitrangadaa, und warb um sie, in schnell erwachter Liebe. Doch der König gab ihm die Tochter erst zur Gattin, nachdem Ardschuna gelobt hatte, sie als Putrika von des Vaters Hand zu empfangen.

Die altindische Sitte hielt es für sündhaft, ein Geschlecht erlöschen zu lassen, denn Opfer und Gebet der Söhne und Enkel entsühnte die Verstorbenen, öffnete das Tor des Totenreiches und bereitete einen Platz in Indras lichtem Himmel. Wo die Natur einen Sohn versagte, schuf Rechtsbrauch und Sitte vollwertigen Ersatz. Der König von Manipura hatte ein einziges Kind: die schöne Tschitrangadaa. Er hatte sie von seinem Hauspriester zur Putrika, das heißt Sohntochter, weihen lassen.

Eine Sohntochter durfte ihrem Gatten nicht in sein Heim folgen. Sie blieb im Hause des Vaters, ihre Söhne brachten die Manenopfer für das Geschlecht der Mutter dar und setzten es in gerader Linie fort.

Unter solchen Bedingungen empfing Ardschuna seine Gattin vor dem heiligen Hausfeuer und lebte mit ihr drei Jahre in vollstem Glück zu Manipura. Dann gebar Tschitrangadaa den Babruvahana und der Vater ließ, getreu seinem Gelöbnis, Mutter und Kind beim König von Manipura und zog neuen Abenteuern entgegen.

Zu Naritirtha befreite er fünf Apsaras.

Diese losen Göttermädchen aus Indras und Varunas Gefolge störten gar gerne fromme Büßer in ihrer Andacht durch allerlei Possen, die sie den ehrwürdigen Einsiedlern spielten. Ein heißblütiges Opfer ihrer Scherze hatte sie verflucht, als Krokodile in den heiligen Weihern von Naritirtha zu leben, bis ein Starker sie mutig ans Land zöge.

Der tapfere Indrasohn hatte den Fluch gelöst, als er sich beim Baden der fressgierigen Bestien erwehrte, und so den heißen Dank der himmlischen Schönen erworben.

Auf einer seiner Fahrten stieß Ardschuna auf Krischna, den Vetter und Freund, und zog mit ihm nach dessen Residenz Dwaraka.

Dort kamen sie gerade zu einem großen Fest: Bodscha, Wrischnier und Andhaka, drei Stämme vom Volk der Iadava, feierten ihre Verbrüderung.

Scharen blumengeschmückten Volkes zogen am Morgen aus der Stadt nach dem nahen Festplatz Voran Lymbal- und Paukenschläger, Lauten- und Flötenspieler, Sackpfeifer und die alles übertönenden Muschelbläser. Stabtänzer, Gaukler und Schauspieler folgten, dann kam das Volk in bunten Festkleidern, jauchzend und singend; dann Krieger, Fürsten und der König mit seinen Gästen, umgeben von großem Gefolge.

Auf dem Festplatz fanden Wagenrennen und andere Wettkämpfe statt, Gaukler und Tänzer zeigten ihre Kunst, Gesang und Musik erfreuten das Volk, Soma und Sura, feurig berauschende Getränke, letzten die durstigen Kehlen. An allen Ecken und Enden sah man Würfelspieler vor ihrem Brett sitzen und hörte auch oft ihre heiseren Stimmen im Streit. Auf dem Anger schwang sich die Jugend in anmutigem Tanz nach den Weisen des Lymbals oder auch nur den Rhythmus durch Händeklatschen betonend.

Durch die bunte Menge schritten Ardschuna und Krischna nach den Zeiten des Königs und seiner Gäste. Dort wurde im Freien getafelt. Der König der Wrischnier saß da mit seinen tausend Frauen beim Soma und viele andere Fürsten mit ihrem Hofstaat. Baladeva, der Bruder Krischnas, sang im halben Rausch ein Lied vom männererfreuenden Soma, das diesen Trank mit seinen geheimnisvollen Kräften als des Götterkönigs Freude pries, als Helfer der Sänger, als Balsam der Müden und Feuer der Starken.

In all dem Jubel des Festes sah Ardschuna ein schönes, stilles Mädchen neben Wasudeva, dem greisen Vater Krischnas, sitzen, und schon brannte Kamas blütenspitziger Pfeil in seinem heißen Herzen. Subhadra war die Holde, Krischnas junges Schwesterlein. Voll glühender Sehnsucht nach der Blütenzarten, bat Ardschuna seinen Freund, ihm zu dieser lieblichen Gattin zu verhelfen, und Krischna riet zum Raub, nach alter kriegerischer Sitte.

Boten eilten zu Iudhischthira, dem Haupt der Sippe, und als die ungeduldig Erwarteten mit freundlichen Grüßen und der erbetenen Erlaubnis wiederkehrten, ergriff Ardschuna die Geliebte bei einem ihrer Waldgänge und entführte sie auf seinem Streitwagen nach einem im Dickicht verborgenen Haus.

Nun herrschte wilder Zornmut im Lager der Iadavafürsten. Baladeva wollte diesen Bruch der Gastfreundschaft blutig rächen und rief nach seinen Rossen und Waffen. Da trat Krischna unter die Erregten und beruhigte sie mit wenigen Worten:

„Ist meine Schwester ein Stück Vieh, dass der Gatte sie den Ihrigen abkaufen soll? – Sind wir so arm? oder so geizig, dass wir den Kaufpreis nicht missen mögen? – Tapfer ist Ardschuna und edel sein Geschlecht, das Reichste an Ehren! Ich geh' und reich' ihm als Bruder die Hand!"

Und also tat er!

Ardschunas Waffenruhm versöhnte die kriegerischen Söhne der Berge, und als Krischna das Brautpaar zurückbrachte, wurde in Dwaraka feierlich Hochzeit gehalten. Dann zog Ardschuna mit seiner Subhadra heim nach Indraprastha und wurde von seinen Brüdern voll Freude aufgenommen. Draupadi zürnte anfangs der neuen Gattin Ardschunas, doch die sanfte Subhadra, die sich in verehrender Liebe an die Stolze hing, wie Efeu an die Eiche, unterwarf sich der Älteren als Magd und gewann dadurch bald ihre schwesterliche Freundschaft.

Subhadra schenkte dem Ardschuna einen Knaben namens Abhimanju.

Die schöne Draupadi gebar jedem der Gatten einen Sohn: die fünf Draupadeyas.

In brüderlicher Eintracht lebten die Pandava nun wieder zusammen in ihrem Reich, unter der weisen Herrschaft des redlichen Iudhischthira.

Ardschuna und Krischna, der Freund und Schwester nach der Heimat begleitet hatte, ergötzten sich oft an den Ufern der Iamuna an der Jagd und an manchem fröhlichen Fest. Einst ergingen sie sich dort in einem geheiligten Hain, als plötzlich ein ehrwürdiger Brahmane vor ihnen stand. Demütig falteten sie die Hände vor der Brust und hoben sie, ehrfürchtig grüßend, bis an die Stirne. Der Brahmane dankte den beiden Prinzen und bat die mit Glücksgütern gesegneten, sie mögen ihm dazu verhelfen, seinen nagenden Hunger zu stillen. Kaum hatten die Frommen seiner Bitte Gewährung verheißen, so zeigte sich der Bittende in seiner wahren Gestalt:

Rothaarig und -bärtig, mit sieben beweglichen Zungen, stand Agni, der schwarzpfadige Feuergott, vor ihnen und schwang in der Rechten sein drönendes Banner, die schwarzen Schwaden auf sonnenhellem Grund.

„Der Kandavawald ist's allein, was mich sättigen kann!", rief er. „Lasst mich ihn fressen!"

„Nimm ihn, hehrer Beschützer des Hauses!", sprach Ardschuna und umwandelte rechtshin den Erhabenen.

„Ihr müsst mir helfen, Tapferste der Tapferen!", sprach der Gott. „Indra verschlägt mir mit seinen Regengüssen den Atem, sooft ich mich auch an die Mahlzeit mache, weil sein Freund Takschaka, der König der Nattern, im Walde haust. Und auch andere Götter und Geister verhelfen den waldbewohnenden Tieren zur Flucht und kürzen mein Mahl!"

„Gerne verhülfen wir Dir zur Sättigung, leuchtender Burgenzerstörer", sprach Krischna darauf, „doch unsere Waffen taugen nichts im Kampf mit Himmlischen!"

Da führte sie Agni vor Varuna, den geheimnisvollen Gott der Gewässer, und bat diesen, die beiden tapferen Prinzen mit Götterwaffen aus seiner reichen Schatzkammer zu beschenken.

Varuna schenkte dem Pandava den klingenden Bogen Gandiva, samt zwei unerschöpflichen Köchern, und einen prächtigen Streitwagen. Es war der, auf welchem der Mondgott Soma einst die Dämonen der Luft besiegt hatte. Tausend goldene Möndchen verzierten sein schneeweißes Holz und hundert silberne Schellen erklangen fröhlich bei jedem Schritt der milchweißen Gandharverhengste. Der himmlische Meister Wischwakarman hatte das Kunstwerk gebaut.

Die weithin sichtbare Standarte, ein Affe auf einem gekrümmten Löwenschweif, ward später, als Ardschunas Feldzeichen, ein Schrecken seiner Feinde.

Krischna erhielt aus des gütigen Gottes unerschöpflichem Schatz den niefehlenden Diskus Vadschranabha und die schwere Keule Kaumodaki.

So gerüstet stellten sich die Helden zu beiden Seiten des Waldes auf, und Agni begann ihn zu verzehren.

Fauchend, brüllend, blökend, zischend, heulend und winselnd brachen die Tiere des Kandavahaines durch das Unterholz, um sich zu retten. Doch unaufhörlich schwirrte Gandiva in Ardschunas Hand, Schlag um Schlag traf die Keule Krischnas, und entsetzt flohen die Tiere zurück in den Rachen des sengenden Gottes.

Da donnert Indras Streitwagen über die Erde. Der König der Götter naht, um die Recken im Kampf zu bestehen.

Unnahbar bleiben die Tapferen mit ihren göttlichen Waffen. Steine, Felsen, Berge wälzen sich ihnen entgegen. Waldgeister stürzen aus ihrem brennenden Heim und müssen vor den Unbezwinglichen wieder zurück in Rauch und Flammen und elenden Tod. Ohne zu wanken stehen die Unvergleichlichen gegen eine Welt des Zaubers.

Da tönt eine Stimme aus den Wolken und überdröhnt den Kampflärm:

„Zurück! Vergeblich ist der Kampf gegen Ardschuna und Krischna, denn sie erfüllen, was Brahma verhängte, den Ratschluss des Schicksals: der Kandavahain muss verbrennen!“

Da beugte sich alles dem Willen der Allmacht, und auch der tapfere Götterkönig stand ab von aussichtslosem Kampf. Fünfzehn Tage lang brannte der Wald, dann war der hungrige Gott gesättigt: Baum und Busch, Gras und Blatt, Wild und Schlange, ja die kleinste Mücke hatte er verschlungen. Die Geister, die das alles gehütet hatten, waren verendet vor dem glühenden Atem des Gottes. Nur Maya, der kunstreiche Bildner der Geisterwelt, war dem Verhängnis entronnen. Ardschuna hatte ihn um seiner Kunst willen durchschlüpfen lassen, und der Dankbare versprach es ihm reichlich zu lohnen.

Und Maya hielt Wort:

Nach wenigen Wochen brachte er auf vielen Wagen seinen Schatz nach Indraprastha gefahren, und nachdem er
dem Ardschuna das helltönende Muschelhorn Dewadatta
und dem Bhima einen prächtig geschmückten Streitkolben
geschenkt hatte, begann er dem König Iudhischthira einen
Palast zu erbauen, der alle Bauwerke der Welt an Pracht
übertreffen sollte.

Großkönig Iudhischthira

Das Geschlecht der Bharata hatte stets alle Fürsten Indiens
überragt und der indischen Welt den Herrscher, den Großkönig, den Maharadscha gegeben.

Nun wollte auch Iudischthira, als der älteste regierende
König dieses Geschlechtes, die Fürsten Indiens zum großen Königsweihopfer laden und die Zögernden mit Waf-
fengewalt zur Huldigung vor seinen Thron zwingen.

Iarasandha, der König von Magadha, musste vor allem
bezwungen werden. Der war von übermenschlicher Stärke
und hielt viele Könige und Fürsten Indiens gefangen,
um sie in einem feierlichen Opfer dem Gotte Schiwa zu
weihen.

Die beiden Gattinnen von Iarasandhas Vater hatten einst
jede ein halbes Knäblein zur Welt gebracht und diese Miss-
geburten im Walde ausgesetzt. Eine Hexe hatte sie gefunden und die beiden Hälften unter mächtigem Zauberbann
zusammengefügt. So war das starke Kind Iarasandha ins
Leben getreten und wuchs am Hof von Magadha zum
grausamen und gewalttätigen Herrscher heran. Schischupala, der König von Tschedi, war sein Feldherr und williges
Werkzeug.

Krischna, Ardschuna und Bhima zogen als Brahmanen verkleidet nach Magadha, forderten Iarasandha auf,

seine Gefangenen freizulassen und luden ihn zum Königsweihopfer nach Indraprastha.

Iarasandha lachte sie aus. Er hatte die Verkleideten als
Krieger erkannt, denn jeder von ihnen trug am Unter-
arm eine mächtige Narbe, wie sie die Sehne des schweren
Streitbogens den Schützen schlägt.

Im Übermut forderte er Bhima, den Stärksten, zum
Faustkampf heraus. Es begann ein furchtbares Ringen, das
vierzehn Tage lang unentschieden blieb. Dann gelang es
Bhima den schrecklichen Gegner am Fuße zu packen. Wie
einen Fangstrick wirbelte er den Hilflosen durch die Luft,
bis er mitten entzwei riss.

Damit war der Zauber der Hexe gebrochen, der Gewaltige tot.

Die gefangenen Könige wurden befreit und versprachen
mit den anderen Fürsten Magadhas, zur Huldigung bei
Iudhischthiras Königsweihopfer zu erscheinen.

Nun sandte der Großkönig seine Brüder nach den vier
Weltgegenden aus.

Ardschuna unterwarf den Norden, Bhima den Osten,
Nakula und Sahadewa Westen und Süden in gewaltigen
Kämpfen.

Mit reichen Geschenken ausgerüstet, folgten die tributpflichtigen Könige Indiens den vier Brüdern vor den Thron
Iudhischthiras.

Zu Indraprastha waren einstweilen alle Vorbereitungen
für das Opfer getroffen worden, und Maya, der dankbare
Künstler aus der Geisterwelt, hatte den Königspalast vollendet. Ein Wunder der Baukunst war das geworden:

Auf tausend goldenen Säulen ruhte ein Dach aus erzenen Platten, deren jede ein Bild aus dem Leben der Götter und Helden zeigte. Der Boden der Haupthalle war ein
einziger geschliffener Kristall, der wie ein Wasserspiegel
glänzte. Kunstvoll geschnittene Edelsteine waren, wie

Lotusblumen auf einem Teich, in die Kristallfläche einge-
fügt. Kostbare Schnitzereien aus Ebenholz und Elfenbein
zierten jedes Hausgerät. Seidene Kissen, bunte Teppiche
und schöne Stickereien vollendeten die Ausschmückung.
Rings um den Palast war ein Garten voll duftender Blumen
in allen Farben. Verschwiegene Weiher und abgezirkelte
Teiche waren angelegt und kühlten mit sprühenden Was-
serkünsten die heiße Luft des Südens.

In diesem Wunderwerk Mayas empfing der Großkönig
seine erlauchten Gäste und tributpflichtigen Vasallen.

Unter den Geladenen war auch König Durjodhana mit
vielen aus dem Hause der Kaurava.

Mit bitterem Neid sah er die voll aufgeblühte Macht
der verhassten Vettern. In Mayas Wunderbau fand er sich
kaum zurecht: glaubte sich in der Halle mit dem Kristall-
boden vor einem Teich und legte, unter dem dröhnenden
Lachen Bhimas, die Kleider ab um zu baden; im Schatten
des Gartens fiel er gar in einen der stillen Weiher.

Heißen Hass im Herzen, wohnte er der prunkvollen
Opferzeremonie und der feierlichen Huldigung vor dem
Großkönig bei. Die Gäste wurden mit Ehrengaben ausgezeichnet. Die erste sollte, auf Vorschlag des ehrwürdigen
Bischma, Krischna bekommen. Schischupala, König von
Tschedi, der wilde Feldherr Iarasandhas, bestritt, dass Krischna auf diese Ehre Anspruch hätte. Da berichtete Krischna den versammelten Königen von den Schandtaten,
die Schischupala unter Iarasandha vollführt hatte, und als
der Tschedier Schmähung auf Schmähung gegen den tapferen Iadava schrie und dessen Mahnung zur Wahrung des
gastlichen Friedens als feige verhöhnte, warf der Erzürnte
seinen niefehlenden Diskus und enthauptete so den hämi-
schen Neiding.

Die Gastgeschenke wurden nun verteilt, die Gäste
ehrenvoll verabschiedet, die Vasallen huldvoll entlassen.

Als Durjodhana mit seinem Oheim Schakuni auf der Heimreise war, quoll ihm sein Neid über die Lippen.

„Oh!", rief er aus „wer kann das Leben noch ertragen, wenn er seine Feinde im tollsten Taumel des Glückes sieht! – Nein! was auch daraus werde! nicht länger lass ich ihnen die Freude an ihrem Besitz! Krieg, Oheim! Krieg! Die Pandava sollen ihr Reich verlieren!"

„Ei, mein königlicher Neffe, was soll der Krieg? –Der ist unsicher und gefährlich! Wir bringen den Großkönig leichter um sein Reich! – Weißt Du noch, wie kunstvoll Iudhischthira schon als Jüngling die Würfel auf dem Brett zu ziehen wusste?"

„Ja, ja! das war seine Leidenschaft!", sprach Durjodhana nachdenklich.

„Nun! weiß er gut zu ziehen, so weiß ich gut zu werfen!", lachte Schakuni mit schlauem Zwinkern. „Lad' ihn nur ein, nach Hastinapura – Du willst seine blendende Gastfreundschaft erwidern – und lass mich im Spiel die Würfel werfen, so sollst Du bald sein Reich und all sein Eigen haben!"

Damit war Durjodhana gerne einverstanden, und heimgekommen bestürmte er den blinden Vater mit Ausbrüchen seines Hasses und legte ihm den Plan des Oheims vor.

Der schwachmütige Greis hatte es längst verlernt, dem herrschsüchtigen Sohn zu widersprechen.

Trotz der Warnungen Wohlgesinnter, trotz eigener böser Ahnungen, sandte er seinen Halbbruder, den weisen Vidura, nach Indraprastha und lud das ganze Haus der Pandava nach Hastinapura.

Das Spiel

Mit allen Ehren ward Iudhischthira und seine Brüder, Draupadi, Kunti, Subhadra und das gesamte Gefolge des Großkönigs, in Hastinapura empfangen.

Am nächsten Tag, als alle Männer in der Halle bei einem festlichen Gelage versammelt waren, nahm das Spiel zwischen Iudhischthira und Schakuni seinen Anfang.

Das Würfelspiel war damals nicht so einfach wie heute. Es galt, in wechselnder Folge von Wurf und Zug, bestimmte Zahlengruppierungen auf dem Würfelbrett zu erzielen. Iudhischthira war ein Meister in diesem Spiel und hatte Durjodhanas Herausforderung gerne angenommen. Dass Schakuni diesem die Würfel führte, ward von dem arglosen Sohn des Rechtsgottes kaum beachtet.

Nun nahm das Unheil seinen Lauf.

Satz um Satz verlor Iudhischthira, Gold und Edelsteine, Wagen und Rosse, Sklaven und Sklavinnen. Er erhitzte sich im Spiel und Durjodhana blies mit Spott in die Flammen.

Vidura warnte: „Hüte Dich, Durjodhana! zähme Deine Gier! Kennst Du die Fabel von den Gold speienden Vöglein, die ihr Herr in seiner Gier erschlagen hat?"

„Lass nur!", lachte Durjodhana „ich will dem Vetter nicht ans Leben, aber setzen soll er, wenn sein gepriesener Reichtum nicht schon alle ist!"

Iudhischthira fährt auf! seinen Palast, mit allem was darinnen ist, setzt er aufs Spiel. Schakunis nächster Wurf bringt ihn darum. Nun folgt das Reich mit allem Volk, die Priester ausgenommen!

Vidura warnt: „Auf, Dhritaraschtra, verstoße den unnatürlichen Sohn, der Hass und Rachsucht beschwört, in seiner unstillbaren Gier! Durch ihn muss Dein ganzes Haus untergehen!"

„Hör nicht auf den giftigen Schwätzer, Vater!“, ruft Durjodhana. „Er ist die Natter, welche im Hause der Kaurava nistet. Stets hält er es mit den Pandava!“

Schakuni hat geworfen – Iudhischthira hat sein Reich verloren!

Und Wurf um Wurf bringt nun Nakula in die Sklaverei, Sahadewa, Ardschuna, Bhima und zum Schluss den sinnlosen Spieler.

Ins bange Schweigen höhnt Schakuni: „Vorwärts, kühner Spieler! Dein letzter Einsatz steht noch aus! Spiel’ um die schöne Draupadi, wenn Du Dich aus der Sklaverei lösen willst!“

„Es gilt!“, knirscht Iudhischthira. Und Entsetzen über den frevelhaften Versuch malt sich in den Gesichtern Bhischmas, Dronas und des guten Vidura.

Da fallen die Würfel –. „Gewonnen!“, lacht Schakuni. – Iudhischthira schweigt.

Durjodhana sendet seinen Wagenlenker ins Frauenhaus, um die neue Sklavin in die Halle zu bringen. Draupadi weist den Boten erzürnt zurück. Nun sendet der Übermütige seinen Bruder Duchschasana, und der Wilde schleppt die sich Sträubende an ihren Haaren in die Halle.

Der greise Bhischma hebt bei dem Anblick entsetzt die Hände zum Himmel und fleht: „Heilige Götter, straft den ruchlosen Frevel nicht am ganzen Hause Bharatas!“

Auf ihre Gatten wirft Draupadi einen Blick voll Zorn und Scham, der die Unglücklichen mehr schmerzt, als der Verlust der eigenen Freiheit.

Bhima braust auf: „Verbrennen möcht’ ich die Hände, die Draupadi verspielt haben. Oh! fass ich Dich, Bruder Iudhischthira, so sollst Du das büßen!“

„Schweig!“, herrscht ihn Ardschuna an. „Er ist das Haupt unsrer Sippe, der König und Herr auch als Sklave. Willst Du das Elend durch Uneinigkeit mehren?“

Und der unbändige Bhima neigt sich ehrerbietig vor dem Bruder und schweigt.

Draupadi spricht mit stolzer Stimme:

„Dein grober Bote, Durjodhana, sagte, dass alle Pandava Sklaven seien. Nun frage ich Dich: war Iudhischthira noch frei, als er um mich spielte?"

„Sie hat recht!", jubelte Vikarna, der jüngste der Kauravaprinzen, ein anmutiger Jüngling. „Die schöne Muhme ist frei, denn Iudhischthira war ein recht- und eigenloser Sklave, als er um sie würfelte!"

„Und ich sage: Sklavin ist sie!", rief Karna zornig. „Sklavin und Sklavengattin, die den König von Anga verschmäht hat! – Reißt ihr die Prachtgewänder vom Leib! sie ziemen der Ehr- und Eigenlosen nicht!"

Der wilde Duchschasana sprang auf sie zu und packte ihr purpurrotes Oberkleid.

Hoch aufgerichtet stand Draupadi, den Blick gen Himmel erhoben, und betete: „Erhabener Wischnu! Du wirst die Wehrlose schützen vor Schmach!"

Und ein Wunder geschah: sooft auch Duchschasana der Betenden den Purpur von der Schulter riss, war dort ein neuer, von königlicher Pracht, zu sehen.

Angstvolle Stille herrschte im Saal, nur Duchschasana setzte keuchend seine Henkersarbeit fort.

Da zitterte Bhimas Stimme durch die Halle:

„Nie will ich mit den Ahnen an Indras Tafel Soma trinken, wenn ich nicht halte, was ich jetzt schwöre: Aufreißen werd' ich im Kampf Duchschasanas Brust und trinken das Herzblut dieses törichten Auswürflings der Bharata!"

Alle erstarrten vor Entsetzen, nur Durjodhana höhnte:

„Nun, Vetter Iudhischthira, König des Rechtes, wie denkst Du über den Rechtsfall: Herrin oder Sklavin?"

Bleich vor Scham und Entsetzen, schwieg der Unglückliche und wies mit der Hand auf den ehrwürdigen Großvater.

Da erhob sich Bhischma und sprach:

„Versöhnt und vertragt Euch, Enkel des Bharata, denn hier ist das Recht nicht zu finden! Iudhischthira durfte als Sklave nicht würfeln, er hatte kein Eigentum, doch muss die Gattin dem Gatten folgen in Elend und Not!"

„Hört Ihr?", jubelte Durjodhana „meine Sklavin ist die Stolze!"

Da tastete Gandhari nach der Hand des blinden Königs und flehte:

„Hilf mir von diesem Sohn, mein Gatte, verbann' ihn, verstoß' ihn, er ist der Untergang unseres Hauses!"

Dhritaraschtra raffte sich auf und rief: „Halt! Draupadi ist frei, und für die Schmach, die sie erlitten, darf sie drei Wünsche tun!"

„So will ich, dass meine Gatten auch des Sklavenloses ledig sind!"

„Gewährt!", nickte Dhritaraschtra. „Was noch?"

„Was noch?", lachte Draupadi unheilverkündend. „Nichts! Die freien Pandava schwingen das Schwert und legen mir die Welt zu Füßen! – Hütet Euch!"

„Nein, nein!", rief Durjodhana voll Sorge, „das gilt nicht! Sklaven sind die Pandava, Sklavin ist die Stolze! Hier, Draupadi, salbe meine Füße, wie es der Sklavin geziemt!", und aus dem Kleid streckte er sein nacktes Bein, um die Edle zu schmähen!

Wieder hörte man Bhimas Stimme in verhaltenem Zorne erzittern: „Nie soll Bhima mit seinen Vätern vereinigt werden, wenn er nicht dem Frevler im Kampfe dies Bein zerschmettert!"

In das eisige Schweigen des Schreckens scholl auf einmal das klägliche Heulen eines Schakals.

Entsetzt sprang Dhritaraschtra von seinem Stuhle auf:

„Der Unheilkünder! das böse Zeichen des Unterganges!", murmelte er zitternd.

„Geht, geht!", stammelte er, „Söhne meines Bruders –
ihr seid frei – fort – fort – in Euer Reich – niemand soll
Euch kränken – und Ihr niemanden – geht – geht!"

Erschöpft sank der Greis in seinen Stuhl zurück.

Die Pandava riefen nach ihren Wagen und brachen
eiligst nach Indraprastha auf.

Bald aber holte ein Bote Dhritaraschtras die Heimkeh-
renden ein und lud sie aufs Neue nach Hastinapura.

Der Neiding Durjodhana, der wilde Duchschasana und
der ränkesüchtige Schakuni hatten den schwachen König
umgestimmt. In düsteren Farben hatten sie die Gefahr
geschildert, dass die zürnenden Helden an der Spitze ihres
Heeres wiederkehren könnten, dass das Geschlecht der
Bharata sich in blutigem Bruderzwist selbst vernichten
würde. Einen einzigen Weg, den Krieg zwischen den nahverwandten Häusern zu meiden, wiesen sie dem Blinden:
Ein letzter Gang mit den Würfeln! und der Verlierer sollte
mit seiner ganzen Sippe widerstandslos in lange Verbannung ziehen.

Der schwachmütige Vater sah hier eine Hoffnung, den
blutigen Zusammenstoß zu verhindern, und sandte den
Pandava jenen Eilboten nach.

Die kamen zurück und hörten die Bedingungen des
Spieles; dem Sieger die Krone beider Reiche, die Sippe des
Unterlegenen geht in die Verbannung: zwölf Jahre frei im
Wald, als entthronte Fürsten hausend, zwölf Monde uner-
kannt in einer Stadt, das Joch der Knechtschaft tragend!

Iudhischthira nahm die Bedingungen an, und –dank
Schakunis Gewandtheit – fielen die Würfel zugunsten der
Kaurava.

Unter dem Hohnlachen der Sieger legten die Pandava
ihre königlichen Gewänder ab und bekleideten sich mit
Fellen. Die greise Mutter Kunti ward der Obhut des guten
Vidura empfohlen; Draupadi ging mit ihren Gatten. Als

sie die Halle verließen, hob Bhima die Faust und schwor Durjodhana zu töten; Ardschuna sah auf Draupadi und schrie dann Karna seinen tödlichen Hass ins Antlitz; Sahadewa aber schlug an sein Schwert und rief: „Dieses soll einst den Schuldigen treffen! Dich, Schakuni! der im Spiel betrogen hat!"

Und begleitet von vielem Volk, das die Tapferen immer geliebt hatte, zogen die Verbannten nach dem Norden.

Am nächsten Morgen erschien der Götterbote Narada vor Dhritaraschtra und verkündigte ihm den Untergang seines Geschlechtes.

Die zwölf Jahre

Die verbannten Pandava wanderten bis an die Sarasvati und siedelten sich im Kamjakawalde an.

Viele Brahmanen waren bei ihrem König geblieben, denn der fromme Sohn des Rechtsgottes hatte mit aller Ehrerbietung den ganzen Priesterstand ausgenommen, als er um Reich und Volk würfelte. Nun quälten ihn Sorgen um die Ernährung der großen Schar, deren natürliches Haupt er als Ältester der Pandava war.

Ehrfürchtig neigte er sich in demütigem Opferdienst vor Surya, dem Sonnengott, dessen freundlicher Blick allem Lebenden die Nahrung bereitet. Der Tausendstrahlige erhörte sein Flehen und schenkte ihm einen kupfernen Kochtopf, der sich unter den sorgenden Händen Draupadis zu jeder Mahlzeitstunde mit Früchten, Wurzeln, Fleisch und Gemüse füllen sollte. Mochten auch tausend und aber tausend zur Mahlzeit kommen, es brauchte doch keiner hungrig vom Tische zu gehen.

Und die Schar um die Verbannten wuchs von Tag zu Tag: Die Fürsten der Wrischnier, der Bodscha, der Andhaka kamen, Dhrischtadjumna mit den Pantschalerrecken, Dhrischtaketu, der neue König von Tschedi, die Fürsten von Kaikeya und andere Freunde und Verwandte der Pandava.

Endlich erschien auch Krischna und bat sein langes Fernbleiben zu entschuldigen:

Schalwa, der Herr der fliegenden Stadt, hatte seine Residenz Dwaraka belagert. In kühnen Ausfällen war der Feind zurückgeschlagen worden, Schalwa musste fliehen – weiter, immer weiter, verfolgt von Krischnas Streitwagen. Endlich, die Stadt schwebte schon über dem Ozean, hat ein Wurf mit dem göttlichen Diskus sie zertrümmert ins Meer geschleudert und Schalwa getötet.

Nun sei der Freund der Pandava da, um mit ihnen gegen die Kaurava zu ziehen!

„Gut so, Krischna!", jubelte Bhima „sage es dem Lämmlein Iudhischthira, dass wir endlich zu den Waffen greifen wollen. Beim Indra! man würde hier sterben vor Langweile, gäbe es nicht manchmal einen Menschenfresser zu erwürgen, wie unlängst den Riesen Kirmira, den Bruder der groben Vaka, der mich einst beim Essen störte!"

„Ich habe gelobt, dreizehn Jahre in Verbannung zu leben, ich will es auch redlich halten!", sprach Iudhischthira ernst.

„Ach, dreizehn Jahre!", schalt Bhima. „Ein Tag im Elend, gilt für ein Jahr im Glück, sagt ein frommer Spruch! – Wir sind schon hundert Jahre in Verbannung!"

„Recht muss Recht bleiben!", sprach Iudhischthira.

„Ich habe gespielt und verloren, ich zahle den Einsatz!"

„Ja!", rief Draupadi. „Du hast gespielt, blind wütend gespielt, und alles verloren! alles – sogar den Mut, den Du jetzt, als Herr der Sippe, doppelt brauchtest! –Sind das meine Gatten – die Stärksten der Erde – die Schimpf und Elend auf mir wuchten lassen wollen, durch dreizehn lange Jahre?"

„Mich schmerzt Dein Gram und Zorn, teure Gattin, doch man nennt mich den Dharmaradscha, den König der Gerechtigkeit: Nie will ich dagegen sündigen! Recht schützt den König, der das Recht schützt! – Soll ich den Brand ins eigene Haus werfen? –Harret geduldig des Endes, Brüder und Freunde, und stählt Eure Kraft im Elend! Bhischma, der unbezwingliche Gangasohn, steht vor dem Thron, dem er sein Leben lang Treue gehalten hat. So auch Drona, unser aller Waffenmeister, und Kripa und der starke König von Anga!

Zieh in die Ferne, Ardschuna, so riet mir ein Weiser, und diene den Göttern. Du wirst von ihnen gewappnet und belehrt werden, denn Du sollst unser Hort sein, in der blutigen Schlacht, die ein unabwendbares Schicksal der Menschheit verhängt hat!", Diesen Worten prophetischer Weisheit fügten sich auch die Kampffreudigsten. Die Freunde versprachen im vierzehnten Jahre Heerfolge zu leisten und zogen in ihre Heimat.

Ardschuna wanderte allein nach dem Himawat und lebte dort in strenger Buße, den Göttern nahe.

Vidura kam nach dem Kamjakawald.

Durjodhana und Schakuni hatten neue Pläne geschmiedet, um die Pandava aus der Welt zu schaffen; Karna riet stets zu offenem Überfall, und Dhritaraschtra war, vor Schmerz um den bevorstehenden Untergang seines Hauses, schwächer und wankelmütiger als je. Als er, Vidura, um des Himmels willen zu Friede und Versöhnung geraten habe, war der Blinde zornig geworden, hatte ihn Verräter gescholten, und zuletzt aus der Stadt jagen lassen.

Doch Vidura blieb nicht lange im Wald: Bald kam Sandschaja, der Wagenlenker Dhritaraschtras, und brachte den edlen Greis in allen Ehren nach Hastinapura zurück. Dort fielen die Brüder einander in die Arme und versöhnten sich vor allem Volk.

Ardschuna hatte am Fuße des Himawat in strenger Bußübung gelebt und in heißem Gebet und frommem Opferdienst die Gnade der Götter gewonnen.

Als ihn einst in der Wildnis ein großer Eber anrannte,
brachte er den Wütenden mit einem guten Bogenschuss
zur Strecke. Während der blutigen Arbeit des Ausweidens
trat ein riesiger Waldmensch, nur mit einer Wildschur
bekleidet, aus dem Dickicht, und forderte rauen Tones den
erlegten Eber als seine Beute. Lachend wies Ardschuna ihn
zurück. Der Waldmensch drohte, heiße Worte des Streites
fielen, dann schwirrte Gandiva und Pfeil auf Pfeil flog auf
den Riesen. Doch Wunder: als wären es Reiskörner gewesen oder Steinchen, von eines Kindes Hand geschleudert,
so prallten die leichten und schweren Geschosse des göttlichen Bogens von Haut und Wildschur des Waldmenschen
ab. Da griff Ardschuna zum Schwert und sprang den Pfeil-
festen an. Er hätte eher den schwersten Amboss spalten
können, als seinem Gegner die Haut ritzen. Wie auf Erz
geschlagen, schollen die wuchtigen Hiebe durch den Wald.
Wütend zischte Ardschuna: „Bist Du schuss- und hiebfest,
so soll meine Faust Dich bezwingen!". Dann sprang er dem
Riesen an die Gurgel und suchte ihn zu erwürgen.

Plötzlich fühlte der Pandava sich von eisernen Armen
umschlungen. Vergeblich wehrte er sich dagegen, mit
all seiner fast übermenschlichen Stärke. Schon ward das
Atmen schwerer und schwerer, schon trübte sich sein
Blick, heißes Blut würgte durch die Kehle und quoll zwischen den krampfhaft nach Luft schnappenden Kiefern
heraus – dann schwanden ihm die Sinne.

Als Ardschuna erwachte, stürzte er sich dem Gewaltigen zu Füßen und verehrte ihn als Gott.

Und da er das Antlitz wieder erhob, stand Schiwa, der
allmächtige Gott der Zerstörung, in strahlendem Glanze
vor dem Verehrenden und lobte seine Tapferkeit und

Stärke. Dann führte er den Kampfmüden vor einen See, voll des Göttertrankes Amrita. Zwei Schlangen tummelten sich darin, und Schiwa hieß Ardschuna sie fangen. Kühn stürzte sich der vom Kampf mit dem Gott Erschöpfte in die Flut und fühlte seine alte Kraft wiederkehren. Rasch ergriff er die anmutig spielenden Tiere und schwamm ans Ufer. Schiwa war verschwunden, doch die Schlangen wurden vor seinen Augen zu Pfeil und Bogen. Er hielt die berühmte Schiwawaffe, Paschupata, in Händen.

Aus dem Walde aber schritten die vier Welthüter und beschenkten den tapferen Bharataspross mit Zauberwaffen aller Art: Yama, der Todesgott, gab ihm den alles durchdringenden Stab, Varuna, der Herr der Gewässer, die starken Fangstricke, und Kubera, der göttliche Schatzhüter, die Waffe Anthardana, die ihren Träger unsichtbar macht und ihm Kraft und Stärke verleiht. Indra, der Götterkönig, lud ihn nach seiner himmlischen Stadt Amaravati ein, um ihn dort im Gebrauch der Zauberwaffen zu unterweisen.

Nachdem die Welthüter verschwunden waren, stieg Ardschuna die steilen Hänge des Gandhamadana hinan, um der Einladung seines göttlichen Vaters zu folgen.

Auf dem Gipfel reinigte er seine Seele durch Buße und gedachte im Gebet der Götter und Ahnen.

Auf der von der Mittagssonne vergoldeten Höhe stand der fromme Held und hob die starken Arme ins endlose Blau. In unendlicher Ferne glaubte er ein kleines Wölkchen zu sehen. Das flog heran, wie vom Sturmwind getragen, und wuchs über den halben Himmel hin. Es waren zehntausend Falben, die Indras Streitwagen zogen. Im weiten Luftmeer wogten Licht und Schatten und glitzernde Goldsäume durcheinander und jagten lautlos daher. Rasselnd berührten die erzenen Radschienen den Boden, als Matali, Indras Wagenlenker und Bote, den prächtigen Streitwagen vor Ardschuna anhielt. Eine goldene Lotusblume auf blauem Rohr kennzeichnete als Standarte den Kriegswagen des Wolkenspalters. Matali sprang herab und neigte sich ehrfürchtig vor dem Pandavafürsten:

„Indra bittet Dich zu Gast, Glückseliger!", sprach er. „Die Götter sollen Kuntis starken Sohn sehen!"

Ardschuna hieß den trefflichen Lenker den Wagen wieder besteigen und die ungeduldigen Rosse zügeln. Dann neigte der fromme Held sich vor dem Geist des Berges Gandhamadana und dankte ihm für die huldvolle Aufnahme. In beredten Worten pries er die Kühle seiner schattigen Haine, das Luft- und Duftmeer seiner sonnigen Triften, die klare Frische seiner Quellen: „Wie ein Kind auf dem Schoße seines Vaters, so weilte ich voll Glück auf Deinem Haupte, Fürst der Berge!", sprach er offenem Herzens und hob zum Abschied die gefalteten Hände an die Stirne.

Dann sprang er zu Matali auf den Wagen, und in windschnellem Rosseslauf ging es durch das ewige Blau. Näher und näher kamen sie den Sternen, und Ardschuna sah nun, dass diese kampferschlagene Helden, Büßer und Weise waren, die in strahlendem Glanze zu Tausenden und aber Tausenden durch den Weltraum wandelten. Matali nannte ihm viele mit Namen und sagte, dass sie alle nur kraft ihrer edlen Taten leuchteten und den Erdenkindern wie kleine Sonnen erschienen.

Vor dem Tore der Götterstadt hielt Airawata, Indras schneeweißer Kriegselefant, die ewige Wache. Wie staunte Ardschuna über das vierzähnige Tier, das wie ein Berg an der Straße stand.

Mit jauchzendem Heilruf begrüßten Götter, himmlische Spielleute, Sonnen und Sterne, Nymphen, Windgenien und Morgenrotreiter, den edlen Sohn der Kunti.

An der großen Sternenheerstraße, unter den ewig blühenden Bäumen, die dem Verlangenden, je nach seinem Wunsche, Früchte aller Art spenden, standen Feen und

Geister zu Tausenden und jubelten dem tapferen Indraspross zu.

Der Götterkönig schritt dem Sohne entgegen, unter dem
goldgelben Baldachin, dem uralten Zeichen der Königs-
würde. Fächer an goldenen Stielen wehten ihm himmlische Düfte zu, und die klingenden Weisen der Gandharva
erfüllten die Luft mit Wohlklang. Nachdem der Donnerer
seinen Sohn umarmt hatte, führte er ihn vor den vielbesungenen Indrathron und ließ ihn an seiner Seite sitzen. Voll
Liebe strich die Hand, die sonst den Donnerkeil gegen
die Götterfeinde schwang, über die starken Arme des Hel-
densohnes. Wie Sonne und Mond strahlten die beiden auf
dem Thron durch den Himmelsraum.

Götter und Genien brachten dem edlen Gaste Ehrenge-
schenke, und zu den frohen Weisen der Gandharva tanzten
die Apsaras einen anmutigen Reigen: allen voran die ewig
junge und schöne Urwasi, die einst als Erdenweib die Gattin eines Bharata gewesen und so eine Ahnfrau des tapferen
Pandava war.

Als das Fest zu Ende war, führten die himmlischen
Jungfrauen den Gast in Indras Palast. Urwasi, die Schönste
von allen und ihre Führerin, bat den starken Pandusohn,
unter holdem Erröten, sie zum Weibe zu nehmen. Im
Innersten bewegt ob der Lieblichkeit der Götterjungfrau,
gedachte der Wedakundige doch der strengen religiösen
Pflicht und musste die Ahnfrau, die im vollen Zauber ihrer
ewigen Jugend vor ihm stand, mit ehrerbietigen Worten
zurückweisen.

Schmerzlich zuckte es da um die schönen Lippen der
göttlichen.

„Weh mir allzu schwachem Weib! und weh Dir allzu
starkem Mann!", rief sie. „Mögest Du als Frauenwächter
dienen und tanzen und springen müssen wie ein Ehrloser,
für diese Kränkung meines liebevollen Herzens!"

Weinend zog sie sich mit ihren Frauen zurück und überließ die Betreuung des Pflichtenkenners den dienenden
Geistern.

Fünf Jahre lang lebte Ardschuna in der Götterstadt
Amaravati und übte sich im Gebrauch der göttlichen Zauberwaffen. Sogar den Donnerkeil hatte ihm Indra anvertraut und den kühnen Kuntisohn in der Führung dieses
Dämonenschreckens unterwiesen.

Tschitrasena, der Gandharwerkönig und Herr der
himmlischen Spielleute, mit dem Ardschuna einst an der
Ganga ein harten Strauß bestanden und sodann innige
Freundschaft geschlossen hatte, lehrte ihn Lautenschlag
und Flötenspiel und den anmutigen Reigen über den
Anger führen.

Götter und Genien wurden ihm gute Freunde und liebe
Gefährten bei Arbeit, Lust und Spiel, wie bei festlichen
Somagelagen.

Oft gedachte er seiner Brüder und Frauen, und als er
die göttlichen Waffen so sicher führte, wie einst seine irdischen, da litt es ihn nicht länger bei den Freuden des Himmels, denn er wollte die Schmach seines Hauses auf Erden
rächen.

Ehrerbietig trat er vor Indra und bat den Gastfreundlichen, ihn zu beurlauben.

Der Götterkönig pries die Kunst und Tapferkeit des
kriegsgewaltigen Sohnes. Er schenkte ihm ein Panzer-
hemd, das aus zartester Morgenluft gewoben und doch für
die schärfsten Waffen undurchdringlich war. Dann gab er
ihm eine unzerreißbare Sehne, für seinen starken Bogen
Gandiva und wand ihm einen goldenen, edelsteinblitzen-
den Reif um die Stirne. Den Sängern heißt der tapfere
Pandava von da an: Kiritin, der Gekrönte!

Dann hieß Indra seinen Wagen mit zehntausend pfaufarbigen Rossen bespannen. Matali sollte den tapferen Kun-

tisohn darin zum Kampf gegen die Niwatakawatscha und die Puloma fahren.

Dies waren götterfeindliche Dämonenvölker, die einst, durch jahrtausendelange Askese, von Brahma die Gnade ersieht hatten, dass kein Gott sie besiegen können sollte. Deshalb sandte der Herr der Gewitter den starken und kühnen Erdensohn gegen diese Götterfeinde.

Unter Heil- und Segenswünschen der Himmelsbewohner bestieg Ardschuna den Wagen und sah in der Stärke seines Leibes und im strahlenden Glanz seiner Waffen so aus wie der Götterkönig, für den er in diesem Kampfe stehen sollte.

Jauchzend hob Matali den goldenen Stachelstock, fröhlich stieß Ardschuna in sein Muschelhorn Dewadatta, und schnaubend flogen die Pfaufarbigen die Sternenheerstraße entlang, hinaus ins weite Blau der Luft.

Die Niwatakawatscha lebten in einer Stadt mitten im Meer. In sausendem Sturz ging es abwärts. Hei – wie das klatschte, als die erzenen Radschienen aufs Wasser schlugen. Wie Berge türmten sich rechts und links vom Wagen die Wellen empor, und wie spielende Delphine flogen die flüchtigen Rosse über das Wasser. Dräuend klang Dewadattas erzheller Ton über die Wogen und schreckte die Niwatakawatscha aus der trägen Ruhe ihrer Unbesieglichkeit.

Als sie den Wagen des Götterkönigs erkannten, schlossen sie die Tore ihrer Stadt und besetzten die Mauern mit Bogenschützen, Speer- und Schwertträgern.

Während Matali die Rosse rund um die Stadt jagte, schoss Ardschuna Pfeil um Pfeil vom Wagen, aus den unerschöpflichen Köchern seines Gandiva. Zu Tausenden fielen nun die tapferen Dämonenkrieger aus der Stadt und überschütteten den kühnen Pandava mit wahren Wolken von Pfeilen, Speeren und Wurfscheiben.

Doch der undurchdringliche Panzer hielt stand. Wütend lenkte Matali die Götterrosse in die Feindesscharen, und zu Hunderten und Tausenden fielen die Dämonen unter den Hufschlägen der Pfaufarbigen, über Berge von Leichen rollten die erzschienigen Räder des Wolkenspalters.

Doch von den Stadtmauern brausten neue Pfeilwolken heran, und Ardschunas Arm drohte nach stundenlangem Spannen des schweren Streitbogens zu erlahmen. Die Dämonen warfen Zaubergeschosse, die die Schleusen des Himmels zu öffnen schienen, und Ardschuna musste mit Pfeilen des Feuergottes den Regenguss zum Vertrocknen bringen.

Das Auge des Himmels blendeten sie mit ihren Pfeilwolken, so dass Ardschuna seine alte Kunst, in Finstern zu treffen, gebrauchen musste. Ein mächtiger Zauber ließ die Niwatakawatschen unsichtbar heranstürmen, doch Ardschunas Schwert mähte die Bedränger dahin. Als sie nun aber Felsen und Berge gegen den Unverwundbaren wälzten, da griff der Gewaltige nach Indras Donnerkeil: knatternd zuckten die leuchtenden Blitze vom Himmel und spalteten die Berge, dass die Trümmer mit aller Wucht auf die Stadt der Götterfeinde fielen und alle Dämonen unter sich begruben.

Jauchzend scholl der Siegesruf Dewadattas zum Himmel, und der kühne Dämonenbezwinger fuhr auf Indras Wagen vom neuen durchs Blaue, um die luftdurchwandelnde Stadt der Puloma zu bekriegen.

Als Matali sie am Horizont auftauchen sah: schimmernd und weithin gedehnt, lenkte er die Rosse dorthin. Und unter dem kampflustigen Schmettern Dewadattas nahten sie sich den edelsteingekrönten Mauern der goldenen Stadt.

Da flogen die vier Ebenholztore auf, und Wagen auf Wagen, mit Streitern in glänzender Rüstung, rollten heraus.

Hei! war das eine Lust für Matali, die flüchtigen Götterrosse durch die Tausende von Wagen zu tummeln. Längst war Dewadatta verstummt, und Gandivas Sehne schwirrte die Weise zu diesem kriegerischen Reigen. Wieder hieß es Pfeilregen mit Pfeilregen, Zauber mit Zauber vergelten, und auch hier brachte der Donnerkeil Ardschuna den Sieg: In Trümmer schlug er die fliegende Stadt, und hochauf schäumte das Meer, als diese darinnen versanken.

In eiligem Rosseslauf brachte Matali den Sieger vor des Götterkönigs Thron. Glückseligen Herzens umarmte Indra den trefflichen Sohn und pries ihn ob der götterbefreienden Tat. Dann entließ er ihn mit der Weissagung, dass durch seines Armes Stärke Iudhischthiras Weltreich wieder aufgerichtet würde.

Noch einmal bestieg Ardschuna den göttlichen Wagen neben dem treuen Matali, und nach kurzer Fahrt landete er auf dem Gipfel des Gandhamadana.

Als die Freunde der Pandava sich von den Verbannten verabschiedet hatten, nahm Krischna seine Schwester Subhadra, Ardschunas Söhnlein Abhimanju und die fünf Draupadeyas mit nach der Heimat. Iudhischthira mit den Brüdern, der Gattin und den guten Brahmanen, die freiwillig ihres Königs Elend teilten, führte in der Wildnis ein frommes Siedlerleben und harrte der Stunde, die ihn wieder in seine Rechte einsetzen sollte.

Der Heilige Lomascha kam in den Wald und erzählte den Brüdern, dass er Ardschuna in Indras Himmel getroffen habe. Sehnsucht nach dem kühnen Bruder, litt da die Pandava nicht länger in ihrer stillen Siedelei, und unter der weisen Führung des Heiligen schlugen sie den Weg nach dem Himawat ein. In frommer Ehrfurcht besuchten sie alle vom indischen glauben geheiligten Wallfahrtsorte an ihrer Straße.

Der gute Heilige kürzte ihnen die Zeit durch Erzählung mancher frommen Legende aus der Vorzeit. Auch die Freuden in Indras Himmel, wo jetzt Ardschuna weilte, schilderte er ihnen und die Herrlichkeit des Berges Meru, wo lichtumflossen die Götter sitzen, von Sonne, Mond und Sternen rechtshin umwandelt. Vom sonnenumspielten Gipfel des Kaïlasa sprach er, wo der Schatzgott Kubera die duftenden Göttergärten pflegt, und von der Liebe der Himmlischen zu guten und starken Menschen.

Am Fuß des Gebirges nahm Lomascha Abschied, und die Pandava stiegen die steilen Hänge hinan. Tagelang ging es aufwärts durch weglosen Wald. Der Mühsal wurde immer mehr, je höher die Wanderer stiegen. Besonders Draupadi litt unter den Beschwerden des Aufstieges, trotzdem der starke Bhima ihr sorgsam die Hindernisse aus dem Wege räumte, und Nakula wie Sahadewa der Ermüdeten viele saftige Beeren und manchen Trunk klaren Quellwassers brachten.

Wenige Wegstunden vom Gipfel überfiel die Schwergeprüften ein Gewittersturm, der den Berg in seinen Grundfesten zu erschüttern schien. Bäume und Felsen stürzten um sie und verlegten jeden gangbaren Pfad, so dass selbst Bhimas übermenschliche Kraft versagte. Da gedachte er des zauberstarken Sohnes, den ihm die Riesin Hidimbaa einst geschenkt hatte, und: „Ghatotkatscha!“, schrie er in den Sturm, dessen Brüllen übertönend.

Gleich stand der zauberkundige Riese vor ihm und begrüßte alle mit freundlichen Worten. Kaum sah Ghatotkatscha die Not der Seinen, so rief er mit gellendem Pfiff vier Freunde aus dem Riesenreich herbei. Behutsam, wie ein gebrechliches Spielzeug, nahm er dann die erschöpfte Draupadi in seine starken Arme, seine Freunde machten es mit den vier Brüdern ebenso, und fort ging's in lustigem Flug durch die Luft, hoch hinaus über die Gewitterwolken, bis nahe zum Gipfel des Kaïlasa. Dort legten die Riesen ihre Schützlinge auf die saftig grüne Matte, und, nachdem Ghatotkatscha die Pandava noch gewarnt hatte, den Waldgürtel rund um den Gipfel zu betreten, stoben die fünf mit freundlichem Abschiedsgrinsen durch die Luft davon.

Draupadi erwachte aus ihrer Erschöpfung und bat Bhima, ihr doch einige von den Lotusblüten zu bringen, deren erquickenden Duft ein sanfter Wind vom Gipfel herabwehte. Rasch sprang Bhima auf und lief nach dem Wald, um Draupadis Wunsch zu erfüllen.

Kaum hatte er den Wald betreten, so hörte er einen wahren Höllenlärm: Löwen und Tiger brüllten, Wölfe heulten, Schlangen zischten und wilde Elefanten stampften trompetend durch das Unterholz.

Bhima war ohne Waffen, so sehr hatte er sich beeilt den Wunsch Draupadis zu erfüllen. Kühn sprang er mitten unter die Bestien, riss eine Löwin an den Hinterbeinen empor und schwang sie, wie eine Keule, wirbelnd ums Haupt. Krachend schlug er damit zu und tötete einen Elefanten und zwei Tiger. Die übrigen flohen voll wilden Entsetzens.

Nur ein mannsgroßer Affe war sitzen geblieben, den langen Schweif quer über den Weg gelegt, die großen Zähne, fast wie in freundlichem Lachen, fletschend.

„Nun, Du hast noch nicht genug gesehen?“, lachte Bhima und warf seine sonderbare Waffe zu Boden.

„O Herr, ich bin krank!“, sprach der Affe mit bekümmertem Blick, aber listigem Zwinkern. „Bitte, heb doch meinen Schweif von der Erde und hilf mir auf die Beine!“

Da bückte sich der gutmütige Bhima, griff nach dem Schweif des Affen und – hob – zog – schob –, der Schweif war wie an den Boden geschmiedet. Kopfschüttelnd richtete der Starke sich auf, wischte den Schweiß von der Stirne und warf einen misstrauischen Blick auf den unschuldig dreinschauenden Affen.

Dann begann er seine Arbeit aufs Neue. Nachdem er sich weidlich geplagt und den Affenschweif auch nicht fingerbreit vom Fleck gebracht hatte, sagte der Affe gar freundlich: „Nun lass es genug sein, Bruder Bhima! hast Du Deine Kraft, so habe ich die Meine, denn beide sind wir Söhne des Sturmgottes! Hanumat heiß' ich und bin der König der Affen, von dem Du wohl manches gehört hast. Ich erkannte Dich gleich, als Du wie der leibhaftige Sturmwind unter das Viehzeug fuhrest!"

Darauf schüttelten die Halbbrüder einander die Hand. Hanumat wies Bhima noch den Weg nach Kuberas Gärten, dann schieden sie als gute Freunde.

Bald darauf stand Bhima mitten in den duftenden Beeten des Göttergartens, an dem geheimnisvollen Lotusteich.

Ein riesenhafter dienender Geist, der als Gärtner hier waltete, schrie ihm zu, dass er den Herrn des Gartens um Blumen bitten solle, wenn er welche wollte. Bhima sagte, dass die Kriegersitte nicht bitten, sondern nehmen heiße. Es kam zum Streit, zum Kampf, und Bhima erschlug den groben Knecht, gerade in dem Augenblick, als der strahlende Gott Kubera den Garten betrat.

Beschämt stand der Eindringling da und erwartete die Strafe des Gottes für seine Raschheit.

Doch freundlich lächelte Kubera ihm zu und sprach: „Ich danke Dir, starker Bhima! Du hast mich von einem schweren Fluch erlöst! Wisse: mein Diener Manimat, den Du soeben erschlagen hast, hat einst auf einer Luftreise, im Übermut, dem großen Heiligen Agastya auf den Kopf gespuckt, und der Fluch des Propheten drückte mich schwer, bis zum Tode dieses leichtfertigen Frevlers!"

Da freute sich Bhima des Gottesdienstes, den seine raschen Fäuste geleistet hatten, neigte sich ehrerbietig vor Kubera und bat ihn um Nachricht über Ardschunas Verbleib.

Kubera riet, die Pandava sollten den Berg Gandhamadana besteigen. Dort werde Ardschuna in kurzer Zeit landen. Dann lud er Bhima und die Seinen ein, nach dem Kaïlasa zurückzukehren und sich's in seinen Gärten wohlsein zu lassen. Damit verschwand der Gott vor Bhimas Augen.

Glückselig raffte dieser einen Arm voll der köstlich duftenden Blüten zusammen, lief durch den Wald zu den Seinen, und schüttelte die Blumen über das Lager der schlafenden Draupadi.

Am nächsten Morgen begannen die Pandava ihre Wanderung nach dem Gandhamadana und erreichten den Gipfel, als eben Matali mit den zehntausend Rossen in der Ferne verschwand, nachdem er den siegreichen Ardschuna gelandet hatte.

Wieder vereint, wanderten die Pandava nach dem Kaïlasa und verlebten vier Menschenjahre, wie eine einzige Nacht des Glückes, in den köstlichen Gärten des Schatzgottes.

Im elften Jahr ihrer Verbannung wanderten sie wieder nach dem Kamjakawald.

Dort besuchte sie Krischna, der tapfere Iadavafürst, und brachte der sorgenden Draupadi Kunde, dass es ihren Söhnen wohlergehe, und dass die starken Knaben schon anfingen, mit den Waffen vertraut zu werden.

Iudhischthira und die Brüder ermahnte er, des kommenden Kampfes zu gedenken, und versprach, die Freunde und Verwandten der Pandava an die Bündnispflichten zu erinnern. Dann zog er wieder heim und überließ die Verbannten ihrem traurigen Waldleben.

Gar eng war die Hütte, in der der ‚Herr der Erde‘ mit den Seinen hauste. Oft verglich die stolze Draupadi, zur Rache mahnend, das Leben in Mayas Palast, wo Tausende von Sklaven ihres Winkes geharrt hatten, mit dem Elend in der Einsiedelei, wo eine getreue Dienerin ihre einzige Hilfe im Haushalt war.

Bettelnde Brahmanen, die das ganze Land durchstreiften, brachten an Dhritaraschtras Hof die Nachricht, dass die Pandava wieder im Kamjakawald seien, und erzählten auch von dem entbehrungsreichen Leben, das besonders die edle Draupadi bedrücke.

Da gedachte Dhritaraschtra mit Trauer im Herzen in freundlichen Worten der Verwandten und gab der Hoffnung Ausdruck, dass die beiden Häuser, nach Ablauf der 13jährigen Frist, versöhnt, vereint und glücklich die Erde beherrschen würden. Das war aber nicht nach dem Sinne Durjodhanas und seiner getreuen gesprochen. Mit Sorge sahen sie die Zeit nahen, da die Pandava wieder zu Macht und Ansehen gelangten.

Und eine heimliche Beratung zwischen Durjodhana, seinem wüsten Bruder Duchschasana, dem ränkevollen Oheim Schakuni und dem kampflüsternen Karna, den die wort- und waffenschnellen Pandusöhne, wie die stolze Draupadi, an seiner Ehre gekränkt hatten, brachte neue Pläne zum Verderben der Verbannten zutage:

So lebte zu jener Zeit ein sonderbarer Heiliger an Durjodhanas Hof, und den ersah der böswillige Duchschasana dazu aus, den Pandava Verderben zu bringen. Es war der heilige Durwasa.

Ein Leben voll strengster Kasteiung, tiefinnerster Buße und stoischer Schmerzerduldung, hätte ihm längst den Weg zu Indras Himmel geebnet. Doch wie der geizige über seinem Golde am liebsten verhungern möchte, so verzichtete Durwasa auf die Freuden des Himmels. Denn er sagte sich, dass diese auch den größten Schatz an Bußfertigkeit nach und nach aufzehren und damit seine Macht über

Götter und Menschen vermindern müssten. Darum blieb er bei seiner asketischen Lebensweise und war gefürchtet von Göttern und Menschen, denn neben der Macht, die ihm die aufgehäufte Buße verlieh, konnte sich auch sein Jähzorn sehen lassen, der ihm die Flüche so locker machte, wie anderen Heiligen die Segenswünsche.

Durwasa hatte eine Schar von zehntausend Schülern um sich versammelt und lebte nun schon einige Wochen in Hastinapura. König Durjodhana hatte den Gefürchteten ehrerbietigst empfangen und, ganz liebedienerisch, selbst die Betreuung des unangenehmen Gastes übernommen. Durwasa war von der Unterwürfigkeit seines königlichen Wirtes entzückt und versprach, ihm beim Abschied eine Gnade zu bewilligen. Auf Rat des Duchschasana bat nun Durjodhana den abziehenden Heiligen, auch seinen vielgeliebten Vetter Iudhischthira in seiner Waldsiedelei mit einem längeren Besuch zu erfreuen.

Die Argen dachten, dass die armen Verbannten wohl nicht einmal den Hunger des Heiligen und seiner zehntausend Jünger stillen könnten, und hofften, dass dann ein kräftiger Fluch des Jähzornigen die Unglücklichen verderben würde. Doch es kam anders:

Draupadis kupferner Kessel, das Geschenk des gütigen Sonnengottes, erwies sich als unerschöpflich. Iudhischthiras weise Reden über Recht und Pflicht erfreuten den frommen Brahmanen, sein Jähzorn wurde nicht geweckt, und mit freundlichen Segenswünschen für die Brüder und vielen Dank für die sorgende Hausfrau schied der Gefürchtete und seine Schar aus der Einsiedelei.

Nun schützte Durjodhana eine wichtige Regierungshandlung in der Gegend des Kamjakawaldes vor: eine Volks- und Viehzählung. Er begab sich in Begleitung Karnas, Schakunis und Duchschasanas dorthin, um die Pandava in ihrem Elend zu verhöhnen. Mochte ein Streit,

ein Kampf darob entbrennen! Den Rechtlosen musste das
eher Verderben bringen, als dem König inmitten seines
zahlreichen Gefolges!

Doch unterwegs gerieten sie, an der Iamuna, unter die
himmlischen Spielleute, die dort auf blumigen Fluren die
Apsaras neue Reigen lehrten. Durjodhana forderte von
dem Führer der Gandharva die Huldigung, die ihm als
König dieses Reiches gebührte. Tschitrasena, der Gandhar-
vakönig, verweigerte sie, und es kam zu blutigem Kampf.

Die Gandharva besiegten Durjodhanas Tross. Karnas
Wagen ward zertrümmert, der Wehrlose musste zu Fuß
in den Wald flüchten. Durjodhana, Schakuni und Duchschasana wurden gefangen genommen. Einige Flüchtlinge
aus Durjodhanas Gefolge fanden die Siedelei der Pandava,
beklagten das Schicksal ihres Herrn und baten die Verbannten um Hilfe.

Bhima jubelte zuerst, dass die bösen Vettern gefangen
seien, doch als Iudhischthira es für Pflicht erklärte, Schutz-
heischenden zu helfen, war er Feuer und Flamme und trieb
zum Kampf gegen die Gandharva. Seiner unwiderstehlichen Kraft und Ardschunas göttlichen Waffen, sowie den
schnellen Schwertern der Madrizwillinge, erlagen viele
der Gandharva. Tschitrasena, der sich unsichtbar gemacht
hatte, kämpfte mit seinem alten Freund Ardschuna und
wurde besiegt. Da ließ er die Gefangenen bringen und lie-
ferte sie den Siegern aus. Der edle Iudhischthira schenkte
ihnen die Freiheit und entließ sie ungekränkt nach
Hastinapura.

Plötzlich erschien Indra am Himmel mit einer goldenen
Schale voll Amrita. Schweigend besprengte er die toten
Gandharva. Die sprangen voll Leben auf und scharten sich
um Tschitrasena. Der Gandharvafürst reichte Ardschuna
die Hand und sagte: „Dies alles geschah auf des Götterkönigs Geheiß. Wir wollen die alten Freunde bleiben!“

Durjodhana aber fühlte sich durch den Edelmut der Pandava tief gedemütigt. Als er nach Hastinapura zurückkehrte, und Karna ihn ahnungslos zur Befreiung beglückwünschte, ward der Hassblinde fast wahnsinnig vor Zorn und wollte sich töten: Das glaubte er nicht ertragen zu können, dass er den Verhassten nun Dank schulden sollte.

Nach und nach gelang es Karna, die Todesgedanken des Ingrimmigen zu zerstreuen. Um dem gebeugten Freund einen Triumph über die Verbannten zu verschaffen, zog der getreue König von Anga mit einem Heer durch die Welt und unterwarf seinem Großkönig viele Völker und Stämme.

Ein feierliches Opfer sollte die Unterjochung der neuen Reiche krönen. Aus dem gesamten Gold, das Karna erbeutet hatte, ward ein Pflug geschmiedet und dem Gott Wischnu, dem Erhalter, geopfert.

Wie vielen Fürsten Indiens, ward auch den Pandavas ein Bote gesandt, der die Verbannten einlud, bei Durjodhanas Fest eine Schale Opferfett zu vergießen.

Doch der unbändige Bhima jagte den Boten aus dem Wald und drohte, am Tage der Schlacht die Schale seines Zornes über die höhnischen Heuchler zu ergießen.

Der Raub der Draupadi

Kurz vor dem Ende ihres Waldlebens, drohte den Pandava noch ein schwerer Verlust:

Dschajadratha, König der Sindhu, Sauwira, Trigarta und Schiwi, ein Schwager Durjodhanas, denn dessen Schwester Duchschala war seine Gattin, ging neuerdings auf Brautschau.

Mit einem glänzenden Gefolge zog er durch den Kamjakawald. Kotika, ein Königssohn, führte die Zügel seiner

Rosse, und zwölf Prinzen des Sauwirastammes trugen
seine Banner. Sechstausend Krieger folgten ihm auf Elefanten, Wagen und Pferden, und in geschlossenen Scharen
zu Fuß.

Als der mächtige König an die Waldwohnung der
Pandava kam, stand die liebliche Draupadi an der Türe
und harrte der Gatten, die am Morgen zu fröhlicher Jagd
ausgezogen waren.

Dschajadratha ließ halten:

„Bei der meerentstiegenen Lakschmi! wer ist die Herrliche, deren Schönheit durch den dunklen Wald glänzt,
wie der Blitz aus schwarzen Wetterwolken? – Kotika, nahe
Dich ihr und frage, ob sie eine der Himmlischen ist oder
eine Blume der Erde!"

Kotika sprang vom Wagen und, wie der Hund einer
Tigerin, nahte er sich der stolzen Schönheit.

„Wer bist Du? einsame Siedlerin!", fragte er beklommen,
„die meines Königs Sinn gefangen nahm! Bist eine Göttin Du? Eine Fee? oder die Gattin des nachtwandelnden
Mondes? – Mich sendet Dschajadratha, mein königlicher
Herr, den Du dort auf goldschimmerndem Wagen ragen
siehst, wie Agni auf dem Scheiterhaufen. Herrscher ist er
über di Sindhu, die Sauwira und manche andere Völker.
Er zieht daher in großem Gefolge, wie Indra von Winden
umschirmt!"

Da antwortete die stolze Pantschalerin:

„Draupadi bin ich, des Königs Drupada Tochter. Bei der
Wahl, nach Sitte des Kriegerstandes, hab' ich fünf Gatten
erkoren: die Söhne des Großkönigs Pandu: Iudhischthira,
Bhima und Ardschuna, Söhne der Kunti, und die Madrizwillinge Nakula und Sahadewa. Sie jagen durch den
Wald, doch naht schon die Stunde ihrer Rückkehr. Seid
in ihrem Namen willkommen geheißen! Lasst die Tiere
abschirren und das Volk lagern! Iudhischthira, mein könig-

licher Gemahl, wird euch bei seiner Heimkehr gastfreund-
lich begrüßen.

Damit trat sie in das Haus und traf Vorbereitungen für
die Bewirtung der Gäste.

Bebend vor Leidenschaft hörte Dschajadratha den
Bericht seines Wagenlenkers.

„Nein!", rief er dann, „mein Weib muss sie werden! Wie
Affen erscheinen mir alle Frauen, seit ich die Schönste
gesehen!"

Selbsiebent trat er in das Haus und begrüßte Draupadi der Sitte gemäß: „Heil Dir, Schöngestaltete! Bist Du
glücklich? sind es Deine Gatten und alle deren Heil Du
wünschest?"

Draupadi antwortete:

„Heil Dir, König! Ist Dein Reich mächtig? Dein Schatz
gefüllt und Dein Heer stark? Herrschest Du nach Recht
und frommer Pflicht über alles was Du besitzest? – Glücklich ist Iudhischthira, mein König und Herr! glücklich auch
ich und seine Brüder und alle nach welchen Du fragtest!
Nimm hier Fußwasser und Sitz, und harre der Mahlzeit,
die ich dem Gaste bereite!"

Nachdem mit diesen Reden der ersten Pflicht der
Gastfreundschaft genüge geleistet worden war, brach sich
Dschajadrathas Leidenschaft wieder Bahn.

„Lass Herd und Speise!", rief er, „und steige auf meinen
Wagen! Wie willst Du bei den Sinn- und Glücklosen hausen? Komm' mit mir zu königlichen Freuden!"

Mit gefurchter Stirne trat Draupadi zurück und rief:
„Schäme Dich!"

Und um die Stunde, von der sie die Heimkehr ihrer starken Gatten erhoffte, zu beflügeln, sprudelte sie Wort um
Wort hervor und fesselte die Aufmerksamkeit des Entführers: „Ein Tor bist Du, der den Zorn der starken Pandava
weckt!

Eh' könntest Du einen wilden Elefanten mit dem Hirtenstab lenken, eh' Du den König der Gerechtigkeit bezwingst!

Wie ein Kind an dem Schnurrbart eines schlafenden Tigers zupft, so spielst Du mit dem Zorn des furchtbaren Bhima.

Dem schlafenden Leuen stößt Du den Fuß in die Flanke, wenn Du den Gandivaspanner zum Kampf reizest.

Besser wäre es fürwahr, Dir zischten die Zungen zweier Nattern entgegen, als dass Dich die schnellen Schwerter der Madrizwillinge umzucken, Wahnsinniger!

Wie die Giftblume zerstäubt und den vernichtet, der sie bricht, so verdirbt die Gattin der Pandava den, der sie raubt!"

„Der Schrecken über Deine Worte, Du Herrliche! besiegt nicht den Reiz Deiner zornfunkelnden Augen!", rief Dschajadratha. „Besteige meinen Wagen, Du Stolze! und teile mein Reich!"

„Zurück!", schrie Draupadi. „Wie das Feuer in dürres Holz, wird sich Ardschuna in Dein Heer fressen, für diese frevlerischen Worte! Nie soll mein Denken einem anderen gelten, als meinen Gatten! O höre mich, Dhaumia!"

Der Hauspriester trat über die Schwelle und mahnte den Leidenschaftlichen an Recht und Pflicht.

Doch das war ein Tropfen in lohenden Brand: rasch sprang Dschajadratha vor und griff nach Draupadis Hand. Die Bedrohte stieß ihn zurück, dass er der Länge nach hinfiel.

Da warfen die anderen sich über sie und schleppten die Schreiende nach Dschajadrathas Wagen. Eilig brach der Heerzug auf, doch der Hauspriester Dhaumia ging unter dem Trosse mit und wachte über die Ehre seiner Königin.

Die Pandava hatten sich nach erfolgreicher Jagd in einer Waldlichtung getroffen. Iudhischthira war von unheilverheißenden Ahnungen erfüllt, als er das ängstliche Laufen, Flattern und Kreischen des von Dschajadrathas Heerzug aufgescheuchten Wildes bemerkte. Er trieb die Brüder zur Eile, denn ihm bangte um Draupadi, das köstlichste Gut der Verbannten. Rasch bestiegen sie die Wagen, die ihrer am Treffpunkt geharrt hatten, und eilten in schnellem Rosseslauf nach dem Waldhaus.

Am Waldrand stürzte ihnen laut weinend die Dienerin der Gattin entgegen. Iudhischthira sprang vom Wagen und rief:

„Weh uns, Weib! spricht welches Unheil hat die Königin betroffen? – Ist sie zum Himmel gegangen? – Wir werden ihr folgen!“

Stockend und stammelnd erzählte die Getreue vom Raub ihrer Herrin und flehte die Starken an, den Frevler, dessen Spuren noch frisch seien, zu verfolgen, ehe tödliche Schmach die Stolze vernichte.

„Genug!“, rief Iudhischthira, „aus unserem Weg, treue Dienerin! Die Räuber sollen die Pandava kennen lernen!“

Und in schnellster Fahrt folgten sie dem Heer, dessen Weg gebrochenes Gezweig und geknickte Blumen kennzeichneten.

Bald sahen sie die Staubwolken, die das Fußvolk aufwirbelte. Dann trafen sie auf Dhaumia, der mitten im Tross dahinschritt, und den Helden weit vorne den Wagen des Entführers zeigte.

Wie Wölfe in eine Schafherde, fuhren die Pandava unter die Krieger Dschajadrathas. Der ließ, erschreckt ob des fürchterlichen Kampflärmes, seine Rosse anhalten und forderte Draupadi auf, ihm diese furchtbaren Streiter zu nennen.

„Bangt Dir vor ihnen, Du Tor?“, rief Draupadi stolz. „Du sollst sie kennen lernen, die Deine Macht zertrümmern und Dich heute noch zu meinem Sklaven machen werden.

Sieh dort den Adlergesichtigen, dessen Banner über
zwei heiligen Trommeln weht! Der ist der König des Rechtes, der gewährt auch dem flehenden Feinde noch Gnade:
Iudhischthira ist es, der Herr der Erde!

Jener Riese an Leib, mit den drohend gewölbten Brauen,
ist Bhima, der Furchtbare. Übermenschliche Taten hat er
vollbracht, und ungern verschont er die Feinde.

Dort, der hochgewachsene Bogenschütze, ist der
Indrasspross Ardschuna. Stark wie Bhima und besonnen
wie Iudischthira. Er führt die göttlichen Waffen, und seine
Muschel heult den Löwenruf zum Schrecken der Feinde.

Jener Schöngestaltete, den die Kuntisöhne umschir-
men, ist Nakula, der Liebling der Brüder! Und der Große,
der ruhig, doch stark, sein Schwert schwingt, ist Sahadewa,
der Wackre.

Sie alle sind meine Gatten! – Bangt Dir, elender Tor? –
Dein Heer wird zerschellen vor diesen Tapferen, wie die
Welle am Felsen. Danke den Göttern, wenn Du das nackte
Leben Dir rettest!"

Die Pandava wüteten indessen unter dem Gefolge
Dschajadrathas:

Allen voran brach Bhima mit seiner Keule sich Bahn zu
dem Wagen des Räubers. Kotika deckte mit vielen Streitern seinen König. Bhima erschlug einen Elefanten und
viele Fußsoldaten. In einem wahren Regen von Pfeilen und
Speeren schritt er vorwärts, ohne zu zittern.

Ardschuna schoss seine Pfeile zu Hunderten unter die
wilden Krieger der Berge, die Dschajadratha umringten.

Iudhischthira flog auf seinem Streitwagen durch die
Reihen und tötete hundert der Besten.

Nakula fuhr hinter ihm, und sein Schwert warf die
Köpfe der Feinde zu Boden, wie der Sämann den Samen.
Sahadewa schoss die Elefantenstreiter von ihren luftigen
Sitzen, wie Pfauen von den Bäumen.

Tapfer wehrten sich die Sindhu und Sauwira: Dem Iudhischthira wurden die Pferde erschlagen, er musste zu Sahadewa auf den Wagen steigen. Dem Nakula warf der starke Trigartafürst den Wagen um. Zu Fuß musste der Schwertschwinger sich bis zu Bhima durchkämpfen.

Unter Ardschunas Pfeilen fielen die zwölf Sauwirafürsten, Kotika unter Bhimas Keule.

Bebend ließ Dschajadratha Draupadi frei und floh in den Wald. Dhaumia übergab die Gerettete ihrem Gatten Nakula, und der brachte sie auf Iudhischthiras Wagen in Sicherheit.

Ardschuna hielt den unbändigen Bhima vom gräulichen Morden in Dschajadrathas geschlagenem Heer zurück und nahm den Zornmütigen mit zur Verfolgung des flüchtigen Frauenräubers.

„Tötet ihn nicht!", rief Iudhischthira den Enteilenden nach. „Schwer ist sein Frevel, doch gedenkt des Kummers Duchschalas und der guten Königin Gandhar!"

„Rächt meine Schmach an ihm!", schrie Draupadi, und schon zogen Ardschunas prächtige Schimmel den silberschelligen Wagen dahin.

Meile um Meile schwand unter den Hufen der windschnellen Gandharvahengste. Endlich sahen sie den Sindhukönig im goldglänzenden Wagen, wie eine Sturmwolke dahinjagen.

Da spannte Ardschuna die Götterwaffe, und auf eine Meile Entfernung tötete er Schuss um Schuss die Rosse des königlichen Wagens.

Als die Verfolger nahten, sprang Dschajadratha flüchtigen Fußes in den Wald.

„Feiger Krieger!", schrie Ardschuna „hast Du nur Mut vor Frauen?"

Bhima sprang vom Wagen und folgte dem Fliehenden in den Wald.

„Töte ihn nicht!“, rief Ardschuna.

Bhima fasste den Laufenden beim Haar und riss ihn zornig zu Boden. Eingedenk der brüderlichen Mahnung, prügelte er den Feigen mit Faust und Fuß, bis er die Besinnung verlor. Dann schor er ihm mit einem scharfen Pfeile das Haar bis auf fünf Büschel. Als der Elende erwachte, schrie Bhima ihn an: „Sage, dass Du ein elender Sklave bist, oder ich schlage Dich tot!“

Stammelnd sprach der Bestrafte: „Ich bin ein Sklave!“

Gebunden schleifte Bhima den Besiegten zum Wagen.

Dann jagten sie zurück vor Iudhischthira.

„Lasst ihn frei!“, sprach der großmütige Sohn des Rechtsgottes, als er den Jämmerling sah.

„Ho!“, sprach Bhima „Draupadi, die er so schändlich gequält, die soll ihm das Urteil sprechen, mein gefühlvoller Bruder! Draupadi komm! sieh hier den geschorenen Sklaven. Fünf Büschel ließ ich ihm stehen, für jeden seiner Herren eines!“

Stolz sah Draupadi auf den Gedemütigten.

„Lass ihn frei!“, sprach sie mit verächtlicher Handbewegung und ging in das Haus. Bhima löste die Fesseln des Besiegten. Der beugte sich vor dem edlen Iudhischthira.

„Schmach Dir! Schändlicher Frauenräuber!“, sprach der König. „Erkenne das Schlechte Deiner Tat: die Verletzung von Recht und Sitte. Sammle die Trümmer Deines Heeres und geh! Möge Dein Sinn für Recht und Pflicht wachsen, Dschajadratha! Ziehe in Frieden!“

Beschämt, mit verhülltem Antlitz, schlich sich der Besiegte hinweg und zog nach einem Heiligtum des Schiwa. Dort büßte er seine Tat, und der Gereinigte flehte zu dem mächtigen Gott um Kraft, zur Rache an seinen Besiegern.

Die zwölf Monde

Um diese Zeit waren zwölf Jahre der Verbannung vorüber, und es galt den zweiten Teil des verspielten Gelübdes einzulösen: Zwölf Monde sollten die Pandava, unerkannt dienend, in einer Stadt verleben.

Sie entschlossen sich an den Hof des Königs Virata von Matsya zu ziehen und, verkleidet und unter fremden Namen, bei ihm Dienste zu suchen.

Der getreue Dhaumia zog mit dem geheiligten Hausfeuer seines königlichen Herrn an den Hof Drupadas, des Vaters der Königin, um es den edlen Dienenden zu behüten, bis es wieder auf eigenem Herde flackern könnte.

Die wenigen Diener und die guten Brahmanen, welche treu bei ihrem verbannten König geblieben waren, fanden am Hofe Krischnas freundliche Aufnahme.

Die fünf tapferen Brüder aber und ihre stolze Gattin zogen in die Knechtschaft.

Iudhischthira fand zuerst Aufnahme in das Gefolge Viratas. Seine edle Erscheinung hatte des Königs Aufmerksamkeit erregt. Er gab sich als Fahrender aus, der besondere Kunde im Würfel- und Brettspiel besitze, und ward so dem Hofstaat zur Unterhaltung des Königs einverleibt.

Bhima verdingte sich als Koch, und seine Angabe, dass er nebenbei auch ein unbezwinglicher Faustkämpfer sei, sicherte ihm die Gunst des königlichen Küchenmeisters.

Nakula fand, als genauer Kenner der Rosse, im Marstall des Königs Dienste und brachte es bald bis zum Marschalk.

Der versonnene Sahadewa nahm den Hirtenstab und trieb die Rinder des Königs auf die Weide.

Ardschuna gedachte des Fluches seiner schönen Ahnin Urwasi! Er suchte und fand Dienst im Frauenhaus des Königs, als Tanzlehrer der schönen Prinzessin Uttaraa.

Draupadi irrte lange durch die Stadt, bis sie endlich vor der Königin stand. Dieser freundlichen Herrin bot sie ihre Dienste als Kammerfrau an, und legte Proben ihrer Geschicklichkeit ab. Die Königin freute sich sehr über die Gewandtheit Draupadis, aber sie sprach ihre Sorge aus, dass die Schönheit der Zofe sie mancher Beunruhigung durch dreiste Werber aussetzen würde. Da vertraute die Schlaue der Königin an, dass fünf von den himmlischen Spielleuten ihr verlobt seien. Diese tapferen Gandharva würden sie vor der Zudringlichkeit jedes Mannes beschützen. So ward Draupadi die Zofe der Königin von Matsya.

Im vierten Monat ward zu Ehren des Brahma ein großes Fest in der Stadt gefeiert. Dabei erwarb sich Bhima die Gunst alles Volkes, als er den Sieger in allen Wettkämpfen, den starken Dschimuta, nach kurzem Faustkampf bezwang.

Doch seiner unbändigen Kraft harrte noch eine ernstere Aufgabe.

Kitschaka, der erste Feldherr des Königs, war in Liebe zu Draupadi entbrannt. Als Bruder der Königin hatte er oft Gelegenheit, sie zu sehen und ihr seine heißen Anträge zuzuflüstern. Vergebens wies Draupadi den Verliebten immer mit größter Kälte zurück, er ruhte nicht und begehrte die kalte Schönheit zum Weibe.

Als sein Drängen immer heftiger und schon eine Gefahr für das Geheimnis der Pandava wurde, gab Draupadi dem Ungestümen endlich ein Stelldichein im Tanzsaal der Königin. Dort erwartete Bhima den gefährlichen Toren und erwürgte ihn in der Stille der Nacht.

Draupadi sagte am nächsten Morgen, einer der sie beschützenden Gandharva habe den oft Gewarnten erwürgt.

König und Königin unterwarfen sich diesem strengen Gericht der Himmlischen, aber der starke Anhang des kühnen Feldherrn murrte und forderte, dass die schöne Zofe mit dem Leichnam des Betörten verbrannt werde.

König und Königin mussten ihre Einwilligung geben, wenn sie es nicht, um der Unbekannten willen, zu blutigem Aufstand kommen lassen wollten.

Schon war der Scheiterhaufen auf dem Friedhof geschlichtet, und die traurige Zeremonie sollte ihren Anfang nehmen, als der vermummte Bhima durch die Büsche brach, eine junge Palme aus dem Boden riss, und damit unter die Trauergäste fuhr.

Über hundert hatte er schon erschlagen, ehe die Entsetzten mit dem Schreckensruf: der Gandharva! entflohen.

Draupadi war gerettet, aber das Volk verlangte, dass der König die gefährliche Gandharvabraut aus dem Lande weise.

Da bat Draupadi nur noch um dreizehn Tage Frist, denn so nahe war einstweilen das Ende der Verbannung gerückt, und die gütige Königin gewährte diese Bitte.

Unterdessen war die Nachricht vom Tode Kitschakas durch alle Lande geeilt, und Suscharman, der König der Trigarta, den der tapfere Feldherr der Matsya einige Male aufs Haupt geschlagen hatte, glaubte die Zeit für seine Rache gekommen. Er sandte Boten zu seinem Freunde Durjodhana und lud das Kuruvolk zu einem Raubzug gegen die Matsya ein.

Kurz nach der Rettung Draupadis traf die Nachricht ein, dass Suscharman mit starkem Aufgebot in das Reich Viratas eingefallen sei und alle Herden der Bewohner wegtreiben lasse.

Rasch rüstete Virata sein Heer und zog gegen die räuberischen Nachbarn zu Felde. Iudhischthira, Bhima, Nakula und Sahadewa zogen mit ihm.

Kaum hatten die Krieger die Stadt verlassen, kam schweißbedeckt ein Hirte und meldete, dass die Kuru im

Norden unter ihrem König Durjodhana die Grenze überschritten hätten und unter der dortigen Hirtenbevölkerung
wie Räuber hausten.

Der junge Prinz Uttara, der einzige aus dem Krieger-
stande, der zum Schutze der Frauen zurückgeblieben war,
wollte den bedrängten Hirten zu Hilfe eilen, doch fand er
niemanden in der Stadt, der seinen Streitwagen hätte lenken können. Da riet die kluge Draupadi der Königin, der
Prinz möge es doch einmal mit dem Tanzmeister der Prinzessin versuchen.

Ardschuna wurde gerufen und bekannte sich zu der
nötigen Geschicklichkeit. Frohen Herzens ob der kriegerischen Übung bestieg er den Wagen, und fort ging's mit
dem jungen Prinzen nach Norden.

Doch wehe: als Uttara von weitem die hundert und aber
hundert Krieger der Kuru sah, entfiel ihm der Mut, und er
sprang vom Wagen um zu fliehen.

Rasch packte Ardschuna ihn an den Haaren und zog ihn
wieder auf den Wagen. Dann wendete er schweigend und
fuhr zurück. Doch nicht nach der Stadt, sondern zu einem
uralten Baum vor den Toren.

Dort hatten die Pandava vor einem Jahr ihre Waffen und
Standarten versteckt, ehe sie in die Knechtschaft gingen.

Schweigend rüstete sich der Starke mit Indras undurch-
dringlichem Panzer, mit dem getreuen Gandiva, Köcher,
Schwert und Streitkolben. Dann pflanzte er das Affen-
banner auf Uttaras Wagen, hing Dewadatta, die göttliche
Drommete, um den Hals und sprach zu dem staunenden
Prinzen: „Ich denke Du wirst gerne die Zügel ergreifen und
mir mutig die Rosse lenken, wenn Du weißt, wer ich bin.
Ein Gelübde verbot mir bis jetzt mich zu nennen, doch
heut' ist das Jahr herum. Ardschuna bin ich, der Sohn des
tapferen Pandu; Gandiva siehst Du hier, den starken Bogen
Varunas. Göttliche Waffen trag' ich und habe gelernt sie

zu führen. Auf mein königlicher Lenker und mutig dem Feinde entgegen!"

Von Ardschunas Worten begeistert, sprang der Jüngling an die Zügel, und fort ging's, was die Rosse laufen konnten, gegen den Feind.

Im Innersten erschreckt, hörte Durjodhana den Löwenruf aus Ardschunas Muschel über das Blachfeld schallen. Er ahnte den starken Arm des Rächers und ordnete seine Scharen zum Angriff.

Als der einzelne Wagen mit dem erlesenen Kämpfer sich dem feindlichen Heerhaufen näherte, taten sich die Wolken auf, und Indra mit den Göttern sah auf das Schlachtfeld:

Schon hat das Schwirren Gandivas das Schmettern Dewadattas abgelöst. Gellende Todesschreie mischen sich in diese Kriegsweise. Durjodhana, Duchschasana, der junge Vikarna, der Greise Kripa, ja selbst der tapfere Karna, müssen heute dem Gandivaspanner das Feld räumen.

Als wenn das Jahr im Frauendienst die Kräfte des Kriegers verdoppelt hätte, so fliegt von dem schweren Bogen Tod um Tod in die Scharen der Feinde, lüftet, lichtet, zerreißt sie, bringt sie ins Wanken, und treibt die Refle in regelloser Flucht von dem Felde der Ehre.

Durjodhana und seine Getreuen wenden sich noch ein letztes Mal gegen den furchtbaren Feind. Ein Schuss mit einem Zauberpfeil streckt sie alle betäubt zu Boden. Uttara muss vom Wagen springen und ihnen die prächtigen Mäntel abnehmen. Die will Ardschuna seiner Prinzessin als Trophäe bringen.

Rasch ging's nun nach der Stadt zurück, um die Nachricht vom Siege dorthin zu bringen.

Mittlerweile war Virata nach Hause zurückgekehrt. Er hatte anfangs mit den tapferen Trigartas einen schweren Strauß zu bestehen gehabt und war sogar in Suscharmans Gefangenschaft geraten. Doch der starke Bhima hatte ihn wieder herausgehauen und den König Suscharman im Zweikampf besiegt. Gebunden brachte er den Friedensstörer vor Virata. Auf Iudhischthiras Rat entließ dieser den Gefangenen ungekränkt in seine Heimat.

Als mit Uttara die Nachricht vom Siege gegen die Kuru vor den König kam, umarmte er seinen jungen Sohn voll Stolz und Freude und nannte ihn Sieger. Doch der edle Jüngling lehnte alles Verdienst ab und sagte, ein Gott sei vom Himmel gestiegen und habe für ihn gekämpft.

Am nächsten Morgen gingen die Pandavas vor die Stadt, rüsteten sich an ihrem hohlen Baum, und erschienen sodann im Glanz ihrer Waffen vor dem König.

Ardschuna, durch Uttaras begeisterte Schlachtschilderung vollauf beglaubigt, stellte dem König seine Brüder vor, und lauter Jubel war im Lande der Matsya, ob dieser tapferen Bundesgenossen.

Virata bot dem Helden Ardschuna seine Tochter Uttaraa an. Dieser nahm die liebliche Jungfrau mit Freuden entgegen und bestimmte sie seinem Sohne Abhimanju als Gattin.

Wenige Wochen darauf war die Hochzeit der schönen Kinder zu Upaplavia, der Residenz König Viratas.

Recht oder Macht?

Das große Familienfest gab den Pandava Gelegenheit, die Getreuen ihres Hauses, die Freunde und Verfechter ihres Rechtes, um sich zu versammeln und in ernstem Rat die schnelle Tat zu erwägen.

Krischna kam, der Treuste, mit seinem tapfern Heerführer Kritawarman, der greise Drupada mit seinen Söhnen Drischtadjumna und Schikhandin, ferner Iujudhana, Fürst der Someker, und viele andere.

Wohl riefen die Speergewaltigen alle nach Krieg und schnellem Schlagen, doch der edle Iudhischthira bebte vor dem Blutbad im eigenen Hause zurück. Der König der Gerechtigkeit gelobte, nichts unversucht zu lassen, was auf friedlichem Wege zum Siege führen könnte, doch auch lieber vom Schwerte zu sterben, als das Recht unterliegen zu sehen.

Der würdige Hauspriester Viratas wurde an den Hof der Kaurava gesandt. Er sollte dort das Elend schildern, welches das verbannte Haus des rechtmäßigen Großkönigs hatte erdulden müssen, und für Iudhischthira diejenige Reichshälfte fordern, die dieser vor Schakunis betrügerischem Spiel beherrscht hatte.

Der Brahmane zog nach Hastinapura, und die fürstlichen Gäste eilten heim, um ihre Heere zu rüsten, denn keiner wollte an Frieden aus den Händen des Neidings Durjodhana glauben.

Krischna war am Abend in Dwaraka angekommen und schlief, von der schnellen Fahrt ermüdet, in den hellen Morgen hinein, als König Durjodhana sich vor ihn führen ließ. Im selben Augenblick trat Ardschuna, der dem Freund in aller Eile gefolgt war, ins Schlafgemach des Iadavas. Der Blick des Erwachenden traf die beiden unversöhnlichen Gegner. Beide brachten ihre Bitte vor: der tapfere Iadavafürst möchte für ihre Sache einstehen! Da sprach Krischna: „Ihr seid meine Gäste! Keinem will ich die Bitte abschlagen, beiden kann ich sie nicht gewähren, so muss mein Schwert in der Scheide bleiben! Doch wählet jeder ein Gastgeschenk: Dem einen gebe ich mein Heer, unter Führung des tapferen Kritawarman, dem anderen mich, als Berater und Freund!"

Ohne sich lange zu besinnen, wählte Ardschuna den klugen Iadavafürsten als Freund und Berater; triumphierend zog Durjodhana ab, mit ihm Krischnas Krieger, die

Erbarmen und Gerechtigkeit sind des Kriegers Tugenden nicht! Flammt auf und brennt, stolze Herzen, im Hass! Besser leuchten und verbrennen, als eine Ewigkeit qualmen im Dunkeln! – Von dessen Taten die Menschheit nicht Wunder erzählt, der hat den Haufen gemehrt, doch niemals gelebt! Zum Kampf! Gedenkt eurer Racheschwüre!“

„Auf! auf!“, jubelte Ardschuna. „Mein Schwert tanzt in der Scheide! – Will Durjodhana den Krieg, wohlan – mein Bogen gähnt!“

„Ja, auf!“, brüllte Bhima. „Hat der Kuru Durst nach dem Tod, so mag er den im eigenen Blute löschen. Ich will über sie kommen: Eh’ tritt der Ozean aus seinen Ufern, Berge sollen eher spalten, eh’ ich meinen Eid vergesse! Wehe Duchschasana!“

„Wehe! wehe!“, dröhnte es durch den Waffenlärm.

Iudhischthiras stolze Handbewegung gebot Ruhe: „Euch geziemt, den Kampf zu lieben, mir, das Recht und den Frieden zu schirmen! Es bleibt bei meinem Königswort! Du! Krischna, kluger Freund, sollst nach Hastinapura eilen. Führ’ unsere Sache mit all’ Deiner Weisheit! – Fünf Dörflein! sie bewahren den Frieden und schützen das Recht!“

Schweigend schritten die Helden auf einen Wink des Königs aus der Halle. Krischna bestieg seinen Wagen und fuhr nach Hastinapura.

Am Hofe Dhritaraschtras wurde der edle Gesandte mit allen Ehren empfangen. Der alte und der junge König boten ihm ihre Gastfreundschaft an, doch Krischna lehnte sie dankend ab und bezog das Haus des Gütigen und weisen Vidura, in welchem auch die greise Mutter der Pandava, die edle Kunti, ihr, seit der Verbannung der tapferen Söhne, so trauriges Dasein verbrachte.

Am nächsten Morgen trat Krischna vor die Versammlung der Kurufürsten, sprach in beredten Worten vom Elend der Pandava, bei all ihrem Adel; pries ihre Geduld, bei all ihrer Kraft; ihre Mäßigkeit im Fordern, bei all ihrem Recht! und verlangte von Durjodhana die friedliche Abtretung des halben Reiches, mit der Hauptstadt Indraprastha.

Alle, die es mit dem Kuruvolk ehrlich meinten, lobten die weise Mäßigung der einst so schwer gekränkten Pandusöhne. Vor Allen die Alten! Bhischma, Drona und Kripa reichten dem klugen Gesandten die Hand und unterstützten seine Worte mit friedfertigen Reden, versöhnlichen Vorschlägen und ahnungsvollen Warnungen vor dem Bruderkrieg.

König Durjodhana hatte einstweilen mit seinen Getreusten gesprochen.

Karna hatte zum Kriege geraten, um seiner Freude am Kampf, um seiner Hoffnung auf Rache willen. Der schlaue Oheim Schakuni, der wüste Bruder Duchschasana pochten auf den starken Anhang, den der Machthaber immer finden kann. Sie freuten sich, alle die Demütigungen der Pandava, durch einen Sieg in offener Schlacht, zu krönen. Durjodhanas Habgier hieß ihn einen Weg meiden, der zu einer Verminderung seiner Habe, seiner Macht führte. –

Er sprang auf und rief in das Durcheinander der Stimmen:

„Schweigt! – schweigt mir von einem Frieden, der erhandelt werden müsste, wie ein Stück Vieh!

Iudhischthira spielt vor aller Welt den, der um des Rechtes willen leidet. Er heuchelt, um mich gefahrlos zu berauben.

Kennt ihr die Fabel von dem gefräßigen Kater, dem kein Tierlein mehr über den Weg traute: Halb verhungert, spielte er den Büßer und Asketen, stand mit zum Himmel erhobenen Pfoten am Ufer der heiligen Ganga und schrie seine Gottesfürchtigkeit in alle Welt. Da kamen die harmlosen Tierlein, die Mäuse und Vögel, und baten ihn, ihnen doch von seiner Heiligkeit mitzuteilen, denn sie wären allesamt Sünder und darum ewig von den Stärkeren verfolgt. Der scheinheilige Kater aber stellte sich ganz ermattet, von der Strenge seiner Bußübungen, und bat, ihn in seine Höhle zu tragen: dort wolle er den Schatz seiner Buße an die unschuldig verfolgten Kleinen verteilen, dass sie hinfort in Frieden leben könnten.

Da drängten sich Vöglein und Mäuschen um den falschen Heiligen, und auf ihren hundert und aber hundert winzigen Schultern trugen sie ihn in seine Höhle. Dort sprang der Ermattete auf, stellte sich an den Eingang und zerriss mit seinen Krallen alle, die seine Frömmigkeit nicht bezweifelt hatten.

Nun ich zweifle an Iudhischthiras Gerechtigkeit!

Nicht eine Hand will ich rühren, um den Kater in seine Höhle zu tragen.

Ich zweifle an dem Recht der Pandava, auf eine Krone des Bharatareiches:

Dhritaraschtra war der älteste Sohn des Großkönigs Witschitrawiria! Ihm hätte die Weihe gebührt! Er hat das Reich auch beherrscht, seit sein Bruder zur Buße in den Wald ging! Von ihm stammt mein Recht, das Diadem um den Turban zu schlingen, unter dem gelben Schirm zu sitzen und Königsschuhe zu tragen! Nur mir ward das Recht das *ganze* Reich zu beherrschen! Mögen die Vettern ruhig im Kamjakawalde bleiben, so will ich vergessen, dass sie nach meinem Thron getrachtet haben. Das ist der Friede, um den nicht gehandelt wird! Von meinem Reiche geb' ich nicht so viel Boden, als eine Nadelspitze bedeckt!"

Einige murrten, die Alten mahnten, doch die Mehrheit jubelte dem König zu, denn Schakuni und Duchschasana unterstützten die Worte Durjodhanas gar eifrig mit großspurigen Reden.

„So höre mein letztes Wort!“, sprach Krischna. „Nur um des Rechtes willen, das dem Sohne des Rechtsgottes ein Heiligtum ist, will Iudhischthira sich begnügen, wenn Du ihm die Herrschaft über fünf Dörflein lässt! Nicht Macht, nicht Reichtum sucht der König der Gerechtigkeit, aber wie sollte er leben, wo das Recht mit Füßen getreten wird!“

„Wackrer Iudhischthira! Braver gesandter!“, klang es von den Sitzen der Alten.

„Schweigt!“, herrschte Durjodhana sie an. „Nicht so viel Land als eine Nadelspitze bedeckt! – Ich hab’s geschworen! – Du, Krischna, sei auf Deiner Hut! Deine Unverletzlichkeit als Gesandter gilt mir nichts, wenn Du Zwietracht an meinem Hofe säst. Ich lasse Dich binden wie einen Sklaven!“

„Du irrst!“, sprach Krischna stolz „wenn Du glaubst, dass ich Dich fürchte! Doch mein Amt ist damit zu Ende!“

„Bleib, edler Iadavafürst!“, sprach der greise Bhischma, sich erhebend. „Ich habe vor vielen Jahren auf die Herrschaft über dieses Reich verzichtet. Ich bin der Diener dieses schnellzüngigen Königs, sein bestes Schwert, sein erster Rat! – Und ich rate zum Frieden! Ich rate zur Versöhnung! ich rate einen Krieg zu vermeiden, der das Blut der Bharata stromweise trinken muss, mag hier oder dort der Sieger stehen! – Hört auf mich! den Alten, der viele Geschlechter leben und sterben sah: Haltet Frieden!“

Als sich bei den Worten des greisen Recken ein Murmeln der Zustimmung hören ließ, sprang der goldschimmernde Karna, der starke König von Anga, von seinem Sitze empor und rief voll Leidenschaft:

„Frieden? Frieden? sind wir nicht Krieger? – Ich achte die Erfahrung des Alters, aber nicht seine kindische Schwäche. Bhischma hat Kriegsruhm aufgehäuft, dass er wohl daran zehren kann bis an sein Ende! Fürchtet der Alte, dass ihn die Jungen nun übertreffen könnten, so mag er zu Hause bleiben und auf den Strohtod warten. Doch wir, die noch Mark in den Knochen und Mut in den Herzen tragen, wir wollen hinaus und den übermütigen Pandava zeigen, wo die besseren Männer stehen!"

„Gemach!", rief Bhischma, sich trotzig aufrichtend „Gemach, Karna! noch bin ich der unbezwungene Gangasohn, der erste Prinz der Bharata, dem wohl das Herz bluten darf, wenn sein edles Geschlecht sich selbst zerfleischen will, um Recht und Unrecht, Hab und Gut! Du freilich ahnst es nicht, wie kostbar mir jeder Tropfen königlichen Blutes ist, denn Du bist und bleibst ein *Fuhrmannssohn!*"

„Wehe!", rief Karna, „auch hier das verhasste Wort! – Höre, Durjodhana: ich bin Dein Freund und getreuer Vasall, doch hier schwöre ich beim strahlenden Gott der Sonne: Nie will ich zugleich mit jenem Alten meine Waffen für Dich gebrauchen! Möge es allen klar werden, wer der bessere Krieger ist: Karna, der Fuhrmannssohn, oder Bhischma, der erlauchte Bharatasprössling! Ficht er, so groll ich im Zelt! fällt er, so führ' ich die Deinen zum Sieg oder sterb' als Dein tapferster Krieger!"

Damit wandte sich der Zornmütige und schritt aus der Halle.

Ein Wink des Königs löste die Versammlung auf, und Krischna ging in das Haus seines Gastfreundes, um der edlen Kunti vom Scheitern seiner Gesandtschaft zu berichten und von ihr Urlaub zu erbitten.

Doch kaum war erzählt, was sich alles in der Halle zugetragen hatte, so bat Kunti ihren Brudersohn seine Abreise zu verschieben und ihr zu folgen.

Krischna gehorchte der edlen Matrone, und rasch trugen einige Sklaven des Hauses die beiden in einem geschlossenen Tragstuhl nach dem Palaste des zürnenden Karna.

Karna empfing die edle Greisin mit Ehrerbietung, den Gesandten mit schweigendem Gruß.

„Höre mich, edler Karna!", begann Kunti. „Ich sehe die gerunzelten Brauen auf Deiner Stirne und weiß was sie bedeuten: Sie haben Dir Deine Abkunft vorgeworfen! – Nun! sieh freudig ins Leben! das kann Dich nicht treffen, denn Du bist eines Gottes Sohn und – der Meine! – Oh! nicht diese Bewegung der Abwehr – der Ungläubigkeit – höre wie alles kam:

Ich war noch ein kleines Mädchen als ein Heiliger zu uns kam und die Gastfreundschaft meines Vaters erbat. Dieser räumte dem frommen Büßer sein Haus ein und bestimmte mich zur Dienerin des Ehrwürdigen. Voll Eifer erfüllte ich meine Pflicht, und der heilige Mann, der ein Jahr lang bei uns geblieben war, gab mir beim Abschiede einen Zauberspruch, der mir jeden Gott vom Himmel herabrufen konnte.

Ich war zur Jungfrau geworden und stand eines Abends auf dem Söller meines Schlafgemaches, als die Sonne voll glutrotem Schein ins Meer tauchte.

„Herrlich!", rief ich „Oh könnt' ich Surpa doch von Angesicht zu Angesicht sehen!"

Da fiel mir der Zauberspruch, das Geschenk des guten Heiligen, ein!

Neugierig – ängstlich – halb im Spiel – murmelte ich die geheimnisvollen Worte und gedachte des Tausend-strahligen voll inniger Sehnsucht. – Schon stand er vor mir, im milden Glanz seines goldschimmernden Panzers, das freundliche Antlitz zwischen dem prächtigen Schmuck seiner Ohren! – Ich zitterte vor dem Erhabenen und bat ihn, ob des kindischen Spieles nicht zu zürnen!

Da umarmte und küsste mich der Gott und versprach, mir einen Sohn zu schenken. Ich bat den Strahlenden, das Söhnlein mit dem undurchdringlichen Panzer aus Gold und dem schimmernden Ohrgeschmeide auszurüsten, auf dass es glänze vor allen Helden der Erde. Freundlich lächelnd nickte der Sonnengott Gewährung und verschwand.

Als das Kindlein zur Welt kam, hatte es einen goldenen Panzer um die junge Brust und die glänzenden Ringe Surpas in den Ohren. Ich fürchtete den Zorn des Vaters, legte das schöne Knäblein, bittere Tränen weinend, in einen mit Wachs überzogenen Weidenkorb und setzte das kleine Fahrzeug mit vielen heißen Segenswünschen auf den Fluß.

Der Wagenlenker Adhiratha und seine edle Gattin Radha, die den Sonnengott schon lange um einen Sohn gebeten hatten, fanden das kleine Schifflein, waren voll Freude, und haben Dich, mein Sohn Karna, in aller Liebe erzogen! – Willst Du mir nun die anderen Söhne töten? – Deine Brüder: den edlen Iudhischthira, den starken Bhima, den linksspannenden Schützen Ardschuna –?"

„Halt!", rief Karna „Der Name ruft meine Racheschwüre wach, die eingeschlafen waren bei Deinen süßen Worten! – Was doch eine Mutter alles ersinnt, um ihre Söhne vor sicherem Tod zu bewahren!"

„Oh Karna! ich verdiene Dein Misstrauen, denn ich habe nicht als Mutter an Dir gehandelt – doch meine Worte sind wahr, beim allessehenden Gott!"

Da füllte sich das Gemach mit blendendem Sonnenschein, dass die drei ihre Augen vor der Fülle des Lichtes schließen mussten, und eine Stimme klang in Kamas Ohr und sprach:

„Mein Sohn, das Weib hat wahr gesprochen!". Da neigte Karna sein Haupt in Ehrfurcht vor dem göttlichen Vater und als er sich aufrichtete, war die Fülle des Lichtes verschwunden, das Gemach nicht heller als sonst.

„Höre, edler Karna!“, sprach nun Krischna, „als ältester Kuntisohn bist Du das Haupt der Pandavasippe! Komme mit mir! der rechtliche Iudhischthira lässt Dir die Herrschaft, und wir brennen dies Nest der Neidinge aus!“

„Oh schweige, schlauer Versucher!“, rief Karna. „Soll ich die Treue wechseln, wie einen Mantel, der mir nicht mehr gefällt? – Soll ich Ardschuna lieben, der mir Draupadi genommen, und Durjodhana hassen, der mir Freundschaft und Ehre erwiesen? – Soll ich Radha verleugnen, die nicht meine Mutter ist, aber mir eine Mutter war? – Soll ich Kunti Mutter nennen, die den Sohn des Sonnengottes Fuhrmannssohn schmähen ließ? – Geht – geht! – Deine Söhne, Du ungerechte Mutter, will ich schonen – bis auf Ardschuna – den werde ich tödlich hassen, bis an mein Ende – die Madrizwillinge lass ich Dir für ihn – geh – geh – das ist alles, was Du von dem Fuhrmannssohn fordern kannst – Mutter!“

Mit verhülltem Antlitz wandte er sich ab, als Krischna die weinende Greisin aus dem Hause führte.

Die Schlacht

Bhischmas Ausgang

Auf dem Kurufeld bauten die feindlichen Heere ihre Lager:

Im Osten umzogen die Kuru und ihre Hilfsvölker elf Plätze mit Wall und Graben und siedelten dort ihre Streitmacht an; im Westen umschloss ein einziger starker Gürtel die sieben Heere der Pandava und ihrer Bundesgenossen.

Als die letzten Vorbereitungen getroffen waren, die Brahmanen in brünstigen Opfern und heißem Gebet den

Segen der Götter für die Ihren erfleht hatten, ordneten die Führer auf beiden Seiten ihre Scharen zur Schlacht.

In vier Staffeln standen die Krieger, nach uraltem, geheiligten Brauch der Kaste:

Voran die Edelsten auf ihren schimmernden Streitwagen, weithin an ihren kostbaren Fahnen, Standarten und Wappen zu erkennen. Dann kamen die beweglichen Reiter, welche bedrängten Wagenkämpfern zu Hilfe eilen sollten. Hinter diesen stampften die schwer gerüsteten Kriegselefanten umher: wo die vordersten Kämpfer die feindlichen Reihen ins Wanken brachten, da sollten sie durchbrechen. Ganz hinten stand dichtgedrängt das Fußvolk, mit Keulen und Schwertern bewaffnet.

Nach Krischnas Abreise von Hastinapura, hatte Durjodhana den Sohn eines Spielers, den Uluka, mit der Kriegserklärung und den bei solcher Gelegenheit üblichen Schmähungen zu den Pandava gesandt.

Bhima hatte den ehrlosen Boten empfangen und, nachdem er die Schmähreden aus vollstem Herzen erwidert hatte, seinem Herrn zurückgeschickt.

Nachdem die Führer ihre Krieger in Schlachtordnung gestellt hatten, fuhren sie mit vielen erlesenen Einzelkämpfern auf prächtigen Streitwagen zwischen den Heeren umher und ehrten sich und die Gegner durch Zuruf und Erzählung früherer Heldentaten.

Iudhischthira hatte den tapferen Dhrischtadjumna, den Führer des starken Pantschalerheeres, zum Oberfeldherrn ernannt. Die gesamte Streitmacht der Kaurava stand unter dem Befehl des greisen Bhischma, des unbezwinglichen Gangasohnes.

Die Waffen schlugen hallend aneinander, Muscheln, Flöten, Pauken und Sackpfeifen, spielten kriegerische Weisen, Pferde wieherten kampflustig, und der Schrei der Elefanten mischte sich in das Chaos von Tönen.

Als die Schlachtmusik verklungen war, fuhr Bhischmas
Wagen vor:

Als wandle der eisstarrende Himawat leibhaftig zwischen den feindlichen Heeren, so war das anzusehen: Auf
silbernem Wagen, den vier fleckenlose Schimmel in silbergebuckeltem Geschirr zogen, stand der Heldengreis in
weißem Gewand, mit silbernem Panzer und diamantblitzendem Turban. Bis an den Gürtel wallte sein schneeweißer Bart und seine Augen blitzten in Kraft und Feuer unter
den buschigen Brauen hervor. Hoch ragte neben ihm die
Standarte, ein goldener Palmenstamm mit fünf silbernen
Sternen.

Dhrischtadjumna fuhr ihm entgegen, in Purpur gekleidet, mit goldgeschmücktem Panzer. Vier pechschwarze
Hengste zogen den Wagen aus Ebenholz. Sein Panier war
die Opferflamme auf schwarzem Grund.

Hinter den beiden Oberfeldherrn nahten die Wagen mit
den Königen, Prinzen, Fürsten und Führern, und schlossen
einen Kreis um die beiden Gewaltigen.

Mit weithinschallender Stimme begann Bhischma zu
reden:

„Tapfere Krieger! Das große Tor zu Indras Himmel steht
heute weit offen! Schmählich ist der Strohtod für den Krieger – in der Schlacht zu sterben ist seine Pflicht und sein
Recht!

Hier steht Bischma, des Schantanu und der Ganga unbezwungener Sohn, als Führer der tapferen Kuru und ihrer
Bundesgenossen. Tschina und Kirata kämpfen neben den
Kurus, Bodscha, Andhaka und Kukura; Sindhu, Sauwira,
Kambodscha, Iavana und Schaka. Elf starke viergliedrige
Heere! Recken wie Kripa und Drona, die brahmanischen
Waffenmeister, sind ihre Führer: Schalja, der König von
Madras, Dschajadratha, Herr über Sindhu und Sauwira,
Sudakschina und der tapfere Kritawarman, Asvatthama, der

Dronasohn, Bhurischrawas, der Schubaling Schakuni und endlich Karna, so heißen die Tapfern, die König Durjodhana bestimmt hat, seine elf Heere in der Schlacht zu führen.

Würdige Feinde stehen ihnen gegenüber, die der, weise Iudhischthira unter Deine kluge Leitung gestellt hat, tapferer Drupadasohn Dhrischtadjumna:

Die ungezählten Scharen der Pantschala gehorchen Dir, die Matsya, die tapferen Kekapa und die Wrischnier der Berge, Somakha und Prabhadraka.

Drupada, den König von Pantschala, Virata von Matsya, Iujudhana, Tschekitanu und den unbändigen Bhima, nenne ich als ihre Feldherrn.

Alle will ich im Kampfe bestehen, doch vor dem Führer des siebenten Pandavaheeres, vor Schikhandin, senk' ich die Waffen: Nie wird Bhischma gegen ein Weib kämpfen!

Mahnend erheb' ich noch einmal die Stimme, eh' ich die Waffen erhebe: Kämpft nach der heiligen Sitte der Krieger!

Ebenbürtige nur, mögen einander suchen im Kampf: Wagen gegen Wagen, Reiter gegen Reiter!

Niemand schlage, eh' er den Gegner herausgefordert hat.

Schonet Gefangene, Wunde und Flüchtlinge!

Tötet die Waffenlosen nicht, als da sind: Rosselenker, Spielleute, Waffenträger und Lasttiere!

Ehret die Sitten des Standes, die Sitten der Väter; gedenket der Götter, die über uns walten! Heil!"

Der Ring der Wagen um den Sprecher löste sich, und unter dem Klang der Kriegsmuscheln und kriegerischer Zurufe eilten die Führer vor ihre Scharen, die Helden der Einzelkämpfe vor die Linien ihrer Heere.

In eiligem Lauf jagte Krischna die edlen Gandharvahengste über das Blachfeld.

Finster stand Ardschuna neben ihm, die göttlichen Waffen gesenkt.

„Kann ich?", entrang es sich seiner schweratmenden
Brust. „Kann ich die Waffen erheben, gegen die, die ich
liebe? Töten soll ich den edlen Ahn, der mich auf den
Knien geschaukelt? – Den ehrwürdigen Lehrer schlagen
mit *seiner* Kunst? – Die Vettern vernichten, die meiner
Kindheit Freude– meines Hauses Stolz sind? – Nein! Kri-
schna, wende die Rosse – ich flieh aus der Schlacht in den
Wald!"

„Schweige und kämpfe!", sprach Krischna, und seine
Gestalt schien zu wachsen, ein überirdisches Licht umfing
sie.

„Kennst Du mich, Menschlein?", rief er. „Wischnu bin
ich, der erhabene Schöpfer, Erhalter, Vernichter, der in Krischnas Gestalt zur Erde gekommen ist um zu richten.

Hör'

DES ERHABNEN GESANG:

Tal ist die Pflicht für den, der um Waffen zu tragen geboren!
Erzhart, voll innerer Glut, sä' Tod er, denn Tat heißt die Pflicht ihm!

Himmelhoch raget der Krieger, vor denen, die grübelnd sich quälen,
Wenn er den tötenden Pfeil in ehrlicher Feldschlacht entsendet.
Töte mich! heißt ihm der Feind –" nie Vater, Vetter und Bruder!
Adlerscharfes Gesicht, das späht nach dem Spalt in der Brünne,
Welcher dem Tod sich öffnet, nicht forscht es im feindlichen Antlitz
Nach den verehrten Zügen des längst verstorbenen Ahnherrn.
Sterbe auch Bruder und Freund, von seinen Waffen getroffen –
Seelen steigen empor – des walten die Götter des Lichtes –
Aber Seelen versänken, verließen den Bann ihrer Pflicht sie.
Stark sei der, der es wagt, die Pforten zum Tod zu entriegeln –
Krieger! einzig die Pflicht, entrückt Dich so nahe zur Gottheit:

Da hatte Ardschuna sich gefunden: Dewadatta hob er an die Lippen, und dräuend klang der Löwenruf über das Schlachtfeld.

Krischna-Wischnu hatte die Rosse gegen den Feind gelenkt, und mit gellendem Jauchzen stürzte sich der Indrasohn ins Getümmel.

Bis zum Abend wogte die Schlacht, ohne hier oder dort den Sieg zu verheißen. Der greise Bhischma übertraf die Jüngsten an rascher Kühnheit, die Stärksten an Kraft und Ausdauer, die Entschlossensten an Mut und Besonnenheit.

Wie der Löwe in ein Rudel Hirsche, brach er hier ins ärgste Getümmel der Feinde; wie der Hirte dem Leitwolf, warf er sich dort einem entschlossenen Führer entgegen und brachte so alle Angriffe zum Stehen.

Hunderte und aber Hunderte fielen unter seinen Pfeilen, doch sein edles Herz scheute davor, die starken Vorkämpfer des Feindes, die Söhne seines Geschlechtes zu töten. Hier und dort wechselte er ein paar leichte Pfeile mit dem tapferen Ardschuna, und gab allein durch seine Gegenwart den seinigen neuen Mut, wenn der furchtbare Bhima seinen Schlachtschrei über das ganze Kurufeld brüllte.

Der Sohn des Sturmgottes fuhr unter die Feinde, wie Waju in die Wolken. Die Heerhaufen der Kalinga und Nischada, die sich ihm unter ihren tapferen Fürsten entgegenwarfen, sanken unter seinen Keulenschlägen dahin, wie Gras unter der Sichel.

Zwei tapfere Söhne Viratas, des Königs von Matsya, fielen am ersten Tag der großen Schlacht:

Der Jüngling Uttara, auf einem starken Kriegselefanten, ritt kühn den König von Madras, den tapferen Schalja, an. Wie ein Berg, der ins Rollen gekommen, stürzte sich das erzgepanzerte Tier, unter der klugen Leitung des jugendlichen Reiters, auf das prächtige Gespann des Madrers und zerstampfte die bäumenden Hengste. Schalja, der gefürchtete Wagenkämpfer, konnte nicht vom Fleck. Zornig hob er den Speer und durchbohrte die Brust des Jünglings. Röchelnd glitt der Sterbende von seinem Sitz. Schalja riss das Schwert aus der Scheide, und ein mächtiger Schwung schlug dem Elefanten den Rüssel ab. Das Stöhnen des zusammenbrechenden Tieres übertönte den letzten Seufzer seines Herrn.

Sweta, der ältere Bruder Uttaras, fiel den unnahbaren Gangasohn mit einem Hagel von Pfeilen an. Zwei von den prächtigen Schimmelhengsten erschoss er und umkreiste mit seinem leichten Gefährt den Wagen des Schrecklichen.

Als Bhischma seinen Bogen hob, um den Kühnen zu strafen, traf ein schwerer Pfeil des flüchtigen Schützen die Waffe und schlug sie mitten entzwei. Während der, Gangasohn nach einem neuen Bogen griff, traf ein anderer Pfeil Swetas den Schaft der Standarte und Bhischmas Feldzeichen sank in den Staub.

Aber nun schoss der Gewaltige eines der schweren, vorne halbmondförmig geschliffenen Eisen ab, und das Haupt von Swetas Wagenlenker rollte zu Boden.

Entsetzt sprang der Jüngling von seinem führerlosen Wagen, und in wildem Schwung warf er den Speer nach seinem Gegner. Hellen Auges verfolgte der Greis die Bahn der silberbeschlagenen Waffe, hob den mächtigen Bogen, und im Scheitel traf sein eherner Pfeil den hölzernen

Schaft, dass die Trümmer des Speeres harmlos zur Erde fielen.

Heißblütig riss Sweta das Schwert aus der Scheide, doch kaum hatte er drei Sprünge gegen Bhischma getan, so fuhr ihm dessen Pfeil durch Panzer und Brust, dass er tot auf das Antlitz fiel.

Sanka, Viratas dritter Sohn, sah den Bruder fallen. In seinem Schmerz sprang er vom Wagen, um den Toten noch einmal zu umarmen; doch an der Leiche übermannte ihn der Zorn: er wollte ihn rächen! Pfeil auf Pfeil sandte er nach dem Wagen Bhischmas. Aber der Heldengreis antwortete mit einem wahren Hagel seiner glattschaftigen Rohre, dass Sanka blutüberströmt wankte. Da kam Ardschunas Wagen in vollem Rosselauf vorübergestürmt, und der starke Indrasohn hob den Wunden hinauf und rettete so dem Matsyakönig den letzten Sohn.

Bald darauf sank die Sonne. Die Heere zogen sich in ihre Lager zurück, die Nacht legte sich über das blutige Schlachtfeld und verhüllte die Gräuel der leichenfressenden Dämonen.

Acht Tage schon währte die Schlacht, und doch ließ sich noch keine Entscheidung absehen.

Bhischmas Waffen sandten zwar Tausende nach Indras Himmel, aber sie lichteten nur die Scharen der einfachen Krieger. Die Pandava schonte der greise Bharatafürst, wo er sie in der Schlacht traf, wie auch sie es vermieden, den ehrwürdigen Helden anzugreifen.

Die Pandusöhne hatten dem Yama schon manchen erlesenen Kämpfer aus den Reihen der Kaurava gesandt. Der furchtbare Bhima wütete täglich unter den Söhnen Dhritaraschtras. Von den hundert Gandharisprossen waren schon mehr als die Hälfte unter seiner Keule gefallen.

Iudhischthira hatte den gewaltigen Schrutayus im Wagenkampfe besiegt und getötet, Nakula den betrügerischen Spieler, den Oheim Schakuni, schwer verwundet, Sahadewa den Trigartaprinzen Niramitra erschlagen.

Ardschuna hatte unter den Trigartakriegern gewütet und ihrer tausend vernichtet. Seine Söhne holten sich die ersten Lorbeeren:

Iravat, den die Schlangenprinzessin Ulupi dem Indrasohn geschenkt hatte, besiegte Vinda und Anuvinda. Er tötete fünf Brüder Schakunis in schweren Einzelkämpfen. Aber der tapfere Jüngling freute sich nicht lange seines Kriegsruhmes, denn Alambuscha, ein Bruder des Riesen Vaka, erwürgte den jungen Helden zum Leide der Pandava.

Abhimanju, der Subhadrasohn, kämpfte mehrere Male tapfer mit dem unbezwinglichen Gangasohn. Den starken Magadha hatte er im Zweikampf getötet, als dieser zornmütig in den Heerhaufen der Pandava gewütet hatte.

Überall wo die Krieger der Pandusöhne in Bedrängnis kamen, tauchte der goldene Pfau, des Jünglings Banner, als Erlösung auf.

Die beiden Häupter der feindlichen Häuser waren in großer Sorge:

Iudhischthira sah, wie die Pfeile des greisen Ahnherrn seine Scharen lichteten, und Durjodhana musste Brüder und Freunde unter den Waffen der starken Pandusöhne hinsinken sehen.

In seinem Zelte saß grollend Karna, der einzige, der, wie Bhischma, die starken Vettern im Kampf bestehen konnte.

Da ließ der Kurukönig sich mit den Zeichen seiner Würde schmücken: Das Diadem schlang er um den Turban, hüllte sich in die Prachtgewänder und zog die seidenen Schuhe an. Kämmerer hielten den gelben Seidenschirm über sein Haupt, andere schwangen die mächtigen Pfauenwedel. So schritt er zum Zelt seines zürnenden Freundes.

Voll Freude über diese Ehrung, empfing Karna den König und führte ihn an den Ehrensitz.

„Hilf mir, tapferer König von Anga, Du mein getreuer Freund!", begann Durjodhana. „Schwer zwar lastet Bhischmas eiserne Faust auf dem Heere des Gegners, aber der sieghafte Recke meidet die schrecklichsten meiner Feinde.

Er, der unnahbare Gangasohn, der einzige, der neben Dir, göttlicher Karna, den Gandivaspanner und den furchtbaren Bhima bezwingen könnte, er liebt die Verräter noch, als seines Blutes!

Ha! Fluch den Elenden! – soll ich König sein über ein paar hundert Sklaven und Bauern? – Denn Brüder und Freunde morden sie mir hin, wenn nicht Dein starker Arm ihnen Halt gebietet. – Hilf mir, tapferer König von Anga!

„Gerne, großmächtiger König und Herr!", sprach Karna „Gerne! – ich lebe nur noch für den Tag, der mir Ardschuna in blutiger Schlacht gegenüberstellt. Ich hab' es geschworen. Einer von uns soll sterben in dieser Schlacht! Und Du weißt: Karna hält Wort! –

Darum muss ich Dich bitten, Bhischma einen Tag lang vom Schlachtfelde fern zu halten, denn ich habe gelobt, nie mit ihm gleichzeitig zu fechten!"

„Ich will ihn bitten, morgen zu ruhen! – Töte Du Ardschuna, und ich will den starken Bhima bestehen!", erwiderte Durjodhana und erhob sich; um Bhischma in seinem Zelte aufzusuchen, denn die Nacht lag schon über der Erde und hatte dem Kampfe Einhalt geboten.

Bhischma hörte die Bitte des Königs an und wies sie zurück.

„Geh! König!", sprach er „ich weiß warum ich ruhen soll, aber ich will morgen eine Schlacht schlagen, dass man durch alle Zeiten davon singen wird!

Keinen will ich verschonen! Hörst Du mich? – *Keinen!* – nur den Schikhandin! – denn die Seele Ambas lebt

in dem Mann, der als Weib geboren ward! – ich kämpfe
gegen kein Weib! – Aber Du sollst mich nicht noch einmal
an die Pflichten des Kriegers mahnen müssen. – Geh!“

Der König verließ das Zelt und sandte einen Boten zu
Karna.

Bhischma aber wälzte sich schlaflos auf seinem Lager:
„Schwer ist mein Schicksal!“, so dachte er. „Drei Geschlechter sah ich erwachsen und sterben, und ich trug meine
Waffen vor ihnen in Ehren! – Keiner konnt’ mich besiegen,
keiner kann mich besiegen. – Ach! sie wird mir zu viel, die
sieghafte Kraft, da ich die tapferen Enkel, den Stolz meines
Hauses, nun töten soll!

Erlöse mich, Yama, schweigsamer Völkerversammler! –
des Sieges hab’ ich genug und des Lebens!“

Im Lager der Pandava saßen Krischna und Ardschuna
bei dem König im Zelt und hörten schweigend seine Klagen an: „Hätt’ ich doch nie Euren kriegslüsternen Reden
gelauscht! – Ich, der ruhig denkende Mann, der seinen Ruhm nicht in tollem Dreinschlagen sucht, wie der
unbändige Bhima, sondern in Gerechtigkeit und wahrer
Weisheit, ich – ich hätte ihn kennen müssen – den unbezwinglichen Gangasohn – den seine Treue vor den Thron
zu Hastinapura gestellt hat. Was nützet die Tapferkeit der
Brüder und Freunde! der greise Held allein hat schon mein
halbes Heer erschlagen. – geht doch! wer kann den besiegen, in dem die acht Wasugötter leben!

Beugen wir uns vor Durjodhana, und beschließen wir
unser Leben im Wald – ich habe alle Hoffnung verloren!“

„Mut, König!“, rief Krischna. „Auch Bhischma ist nicht
unbesieglich! Wenn er auch aller Kraft widersteht, vielleicht erliegt er der List! – Kraft und List sind die redlichen
Helfer des Kriegers!

Oh! ich kenne den Gangasohn! – Sieht er den Schikandin
kommen – so senkt er, freundlich lächelnd, die Waffen! –

Darauf baue ich meinen Plan!

Komm, Ardschuna, zur Ruhe! – Morgen wollen wir den Unbezwinglichen bezwingen."

Schweigend verließ Ardschuna mit dem Freunde des Königs Zelt, und Iudhischthira blieb, reicher an Hoffnung, zurück: Er kannte die Klugheit des listenreichen Iadavafürsten!

Mit Bhischmas Fall, hoffte er den schrecklichen Krieg zu Ende, und seine weise und gerechte Regierung sollte die Wunden, die dem Land und dem Volk hier geschlagen wurden, bald wieder heilen.

Karna hatte Durjodhanas Botschaft, die ihn wieder zur Untätigkeit verdammte, voll Unmut vernommen und sich grollend auf sein Lager geworfen.

Heiß brannte in seiner trotzigen Seele die Sehnsucht nach der Stunde, in der er der stolzen Draupadi beweisen konnte, dass sie den besseren Mann verschmäht hatte.

Knirschend biss er die Zähne zusammen, im Gedanken an das göttliche Weib, das ihm – ihm allein – zukam, denn keiner hatte damals die Aufgabe lösen können, die seinen Riesenkräften, seinem Adlerauge ein Spiel war! – Keiner – auch Ardschuna nicht! – Nur die Laune eines Weiberherzens konnte ihn küren!

Oh! wie hätte er die Schwarzlockige mit den Lotusaugen geliebt – sie gehütet vor jedem rauen Wind – ihr die ganze Erde zu Füßen gelegt – und nun –

Langsam schloss die Ermattung, die dem Wiedererwachen des bitteren Schmerzes gefolgt war, dem Heftigen die Augen zu ruhigem Schlaf.

Und er sah im Traume sein Zelt in hellstem Lichte glänzen: der tausendstrahlige Gott stand vor seinem Sohn.

Warnend sprach der Unsterbliche zu dem Krieger, der voll Ehrfurcht die gefalteten Hände in geheiligtem Gruß zur Stirne erhob:

„Tapferer! hör auf die Worte des Allessehenden:

Indra fürchtet für das Leben seines Sohnes! Er will ihm helfen gegen den Einzigen, der dem Helden gefährlich ist. Hüte Dich! – Er weiß, dass Du keinem Brahmanen seine Bitte abschlägst, wenn sie zur Stunde Deines täglichen Sonnenopfers gestellt wird. Hüte Dich!

– Indra wird als Brahmane kommen, wenn Du bei der Andacht bist – er wird den goldenen Panzer und die Ringe erlisten, die Gottesgaben, mit denen Du geboren bist und die Dich unverwundbar machen!

Verweigre ihm die Gabe, sonst ist Dein Leben in Gefahr!"

„Ich kann die Bitte nicht abschlagen!", antwortete Karna. „Ein Gelübde bindet mich: forderte der Brahmane auch mein Leben, ich würde es willig hingeben, denn das Heiligste ist eines Mannes Wort!"

„Du sollst nicht sterben, mein tapferer Sohn!", klagte der Tausendstrahlige. „Du bist noch so jung."

„Besser jung und in Ehren sterben, als ruhmlos zu altern!", sprach Karna.

„Mein edler Sohn!", rief Surya.

„Doch höre meinen letzten Rat! Biete dem Brahmanen, der Deine Brünne fordert, Schätze und Ehren, ein gehäuftes Maß! Lässt er nicht von seiner Forderung –um seines Sohnes willen – so gewähr' ihm die Bitte – um Deines Wortes willen! Aber fordere als Gegengabe den Speer, der niemals sein Ziel verfehlt!"

Damit verschwand Surya, und als Karna erwachte, spielten die ersten Strahlen der Morgensonne durch den Zelteingang.

Um die Mittagsstunde, als der fromme Held seine Sonnenandacht verrichtete, stand ein ehrwürdiger Brahmane vor ihm und bat den sich Neigenden um den Panzer und die goldenen Ohrringe.

Karna lächelte freundlich und sprach:

„Ich höre Deine Bitte, ehrwürdiger Muni, und will sie Dir gewähren! Doch wenn es Dir nur um das Gold der edlen Stücke ist, so will ich Dir Schätze aufhäufen lassen, die hundertmal so viel wert sind. Was soll ein Büßer, wie Du, mit der Brünne? und mir, der ich von den Göttern zum Krieger bestimmt ward, mir ist er angeboren, ja angewachsen!"

„Gib mir den Panzer, frommer Held!", sprach der Büßer „wenn anders Du nicht Dein Gelübde brechen willst!"

„Ich kenne Dich, König der Götter!", sprach Karna und umwandelte den Ehrwürdigen rechtshin. „Ich gebe Dir Panzer und Ringe, doch gib mir dafür die Lanze, die niemals ihr Ziel verfehlt!"

„Du sollst sie haben, tapferer Karna!", sprach der Brahmane. „Aber wisse, die Waffe kehrt nach dem Wurf in meine Hand zurück. Der eine, nach dem Du sie wirfst ist sicher des Todes – aber der *eine* nur!"

Darauf schnitt Karna, ohne mit der Wimper zu zucken, den Panzer von seinem Leib und reichte ihn samt dem strahlenden Ohrgehäng dem Brahmanen. Dieser gab ihm den Stock, an welchem die Priester stets ihr Weihwassergefäß tragen, und der ward in der Hand des Kriegers zu Indras niefehlender Lanze. Der Gott aber war vor den Augen des Sterblichen verschwunden.

Unterdessen tobte auf dem Kurukschetra die Schlacht:

Bhischma wirkte wahre Wunder an Tapferkeit. Hunderte und Tausende warfen sich dem Heldengreis entgegen, aber ohne zu ermüden stand der Alte viele Stunden im Getümmel. Was seinen Pfeilen entging, fiel unter seinen Speeren oder unter den Schlägen seines gewaltigen Krummschwertes. Den starken Tschitrasena, dem es gelungen war, ihm bis auf den Leib zu rücken, zwang er mit Schlägen seines schweren Bogens zur eiligen Flucht, unter dem Hohngelächter der Krieger. Schatanika, den Bruder Viratas, enthauptete er mit einem Bogenschuss. Den wüsten Duchschasana brachte sein Streitwagen vor den Pfeilen Ardschunas in Sicherheit.

Nur wo Schikhandins Banner wehte, da senkte der Unbezwingliche die Waffen und ließ den Pfeilschauer über sich ergehen, wie einen milden Frühlingsregen. Sein starker Panzer widerstand den Schüssen des Schwächlinges leicht.

Neben Bhischma kämpfte Bhurischrawas, der Sohn Somadattas. Wie ein Löwe in ein Rudel Hirschen, war er in einen Heerhaufen der Somakha gebrochen und hatte in blitzschnellem Kampf diese tapferen Bundesgenossen der Pandava zersprengt und zehn Söhne ihres Fürsten Iujudhana erschlagen.

Doch nun nahte der gewaltige Vater und Fürst der Gefallenen.

In stummem Schmerz hob er den Bogen und sandte Pfeil auf Pfeil nach dem grimmigen Mörder seiner Söhne.

Bhurischrawas schoss zurück und rief über das Kampffeld hin: „Habe ich Dich endlich vor meinen Waffen, starker Somakha! Heut' will ich die Weiber derer erfreun, die Du vordem erschlagen hast, Du Tapferer!"

„Prahle nicht wie die Donnerwolke im Herbst, sondern kämpfe!", rief der Somakha.

Da schon zwei seiner Pferde gefallen waren, sprang er vom Wagen und warf den Speer nach dem Gespann Bhurischrawas. Auch dieser verließ seinen Wagen, und mit den Schwertern stürzten die Recken aufeinander los.

Im Zorn des Kampfes standen sie plötzlich Leib an Leib, warfen Schilder und Schwerter zu Boden, und packten einander in wütendem Ringen.

Lange stampften die Helden die Erde, denn sie waren von gleicher Kraft und Gewandtheit. Da stolperte Iujudhana über Bhurischrawas Schwert und fiel zu Boden. Wie der Tiger auf den niedergerissenen Büffel, warf sich Bhurischrawas auf den Wehrlosen. Jetzt tastete er mit der Rechten nach dem weggeworfenen Schwert – ergriff es – die linke fasste das Haar des Gegners – ein Blitzen ging durch die Luft – aber nicht das Haupt des Iujudhana rollte in den Staub, sondern der Schwertarm Bhurischrawas'.

Ardschuna hatte den Freund im letzten Augenblick gerettet – ein Halbmondeisen, von Gandivas Sehne geschnellt, den toddrohenden Arm vom Rumpfe geschnitten.

Taumelnd stand der Wunde auf!

„Pfui, Ardschuna!", rief er. „Hat der schlaue Krischna Deine adligen Sitten schon so verdorben, dass Du Dich in einen Zweikampf mischst?"

„Im Schlachtgetümmel gelten die Regeln des Zweikampfes nicht!", rief Ardschuna finster. „Auch Dir hat manches im Kampfe geholfen: nicht Deine Stärke hat Iujudhana zu Fall gebracht, sondern das Schwert am Boden; nicht Dein Mut hat ihn überwältigt, es war der Schmerz um die gefallenen Söhne –" „Ha! welch Bild rufst Du vor meine Seele!", schrie Iujudhana, riss sein Schwert von der Erde empor und schlug mit gewaltigem Streiche das Haupt Bhurischrawas' vom Rumpfe.

„Pfui, pfui!", scholl es rings im Kreise.

Aber der Somakhafürst lachte wie ein Irrer und schrie: „Sie sind gerächt!". Dann sprang er auf einen der Wagen und fuhr vom Kampfplatz.

Krischna schwang den Stab mit dem goldenen Treibstachel und rief: „Jetzt hinter Schikhandins Wagen gegen den Unbezwinglichen!"

„Noch bin ich nicht entschlossen!", sprach Ardschuna und deutete mit der Hand gegen die langsam sinkende Sonne. „Hörst Du dort Bhimas Schlachtschrei, der das Trompeten eines wunden Elefanten übertönt? – Dorthin lasst uns eilen!"

Schweigend gehorchte Krischna, und in schnellem Rosseslauf flog der Wagen gegen Westen über das Blachfeld.

Dort hatte Bhima den König der Iavana, den kühnen Bhagadatta, angegriffen. Bhagadatta war weit und breit als Elefantenkämpfer gefürchtet. Er ritt eines der mächtigen Tiere aus seinen heimatlichen Bergen, und der Koloss, der in seinem goldschimmernden Kopf- und Brustpanzer dem Aïrawata Indras glich, gehorchte dem edelsteingeschmückten Treibstachel seines Herrn, wie ein gutgerittenes Ross.

Bhima überschüttete ihn mit Pfeilen, aber das trefflich abgerichtete Tier stand im Hagel der Geschosse ruhig, den Rüssel unter den Kopfpanzer gezogen, als fielen nur Sonnenstrahlen auf die schimmernde Wehr.

Da rief Bhima mit gellendem Ruf den König der Dascharna, Kschattradewa, der, seinem Heere voran, auf einem reichgeschmückten Elefanten über das Schlachtfeld ritt.

Dieser trieb sein Tier vorwärts, zum gewaltigen Stoß gegen den Elefanten Bhagadattas. Nun warf der Iavanakönig mit mächtigem Schwung seinen Speer gegen das anstürmende Tier – die glitzernde Wehr zersplitterte und die Waffe drang in den empfindlichen Rüssel.

Heulend wandte der Elefant sich um und achtete nicht mehr auf den Stachel des Lenkers. Mit furchtbarem Schmerzgebrüll fuhr er unter das Fußvolk des Dascharnaheeres, und Kschattradewa musste blutenden Herzens seine Krieger zerstampfen lassen, bis ein Stich ins Genick das rasende Tier tötete.

Bhima hatte unterdessen wieder den Bergelefanten Bhagadattas beschossen. Plötzlich stürzte sich das Ungetüm auf seinen Wagen und zerstampfte Gefährt und Rosse. In größter Not rettete sich Bhima dadurch, dass er sich an den Bauch des Elefanten anklammerte und, als dieser sich wütend zu drehen begann, eiligst entschlüpfte.

Nun nahte Ardschuna, um den gefürchteten Elefantenstreiter zu bekämpfen. Bhagadatta ließ von der Verfolgung
Bhimas ab und hob die Wischnulanze – eine Waffe, die
ihm der Gott einst geschenkt und von deren Besitz seine
Unbezwinglichkeit abhing – gegen den neuen gefährlichen
Gegner. In hohem Bogen warf er die Niefehlende auf Ardschuna. Aber Krischna-Wischnu warf sich zwischen den
Freund und den drohenden Tod, und als die Waffe die
Brust ihres einstigen Herrn berührte, ward sie zum Blumengewinde und schlang sich schmückend um den Hals
des Gottmenschen.

Ardschunas Speer aber fuhr dem Bergelefanten durch
die Augöffnung des Panzers ins Gehirn.

Langsam sank der Koloss: zuerst auf die Knie – dann
stützte er die mächtigen Hauer gegen die Erde – und, als
in diesem Augenblick eine Lanze Ardschunas die Brust
seines Herrn durchbohrte, so dass dessen freundlich mah-
nende Stimme verstummte, fiel er leise röchelnd um und
verschied.

Da wälzte sich von Osten, in der beginnenden Dämmerung, das Heer der Pandava heran, auf der Flucht vor dem
schrecklichen Bhischma. Der Greis allein trieb mit wahren
Schauern von Pfeilen die Scharen vor sich her zum Lager.

„Jetzt Ardschuna, Hort des Pandavaheeres, ist der
Augenblick, den Heldengreis zu überlisten! Dort seh' ich
Schikhandins Banner wehen!", rief Krischna.

„Noch bin ich nicht entschlossen, den Ehrwürdigen zu
töten!", antwortete Ardschuna.

Da griff Krischna nach seinem Diskus, sprang vom
Wagen und rief: „So will ich dem Vernichter Halt gebieten!"

Rasch sprang auch Ardschuna ab, lief dem Freunde nach
und hielt ihn am Arm, voll Sorge die Worte sprechend:
„Du vergisst Deinen Eid! – Du darfst nicht kämpfen in diesem Krieg!"

„Ich muss! wenn Du nicht das Herz hast, den schrecklichen Greis zu töten!"

Da flüsterte der Pandusohn: „Morgen töte ich Bhischma! – Ich schwör es Dir!", setzte er hinzu, als Krischna zauderte. „Nun folge mir zum Lager, denn die Nacht hat die Schlacht zum Stehen gebracht."

Am Morgen des nächsten Tages entbrannte der Kampf aufs Neue.

Der Riese Alambuscha fuhr unter die Scharen der Pandava, wie ein Feuerbrand ins Strohdach. Die fünf Söhne der Draupadi stellten sich dem Ungeheuer mutig entgegen, aber die Jünglinge mussten vor seiner Kraft und seinen Zauberwaffen weichen.

Abhimanju, der kühne Subhadrasohn, brachte den Wütenden endlich zum Stehen. Er überschüttete ihn mit schweren Pfeilen, dass der verdutzte Riese dastand, wie ein Hügel voll roter Blumen. Dann sprang er ihn an und trieb ihn mit Speerstößen zur Flucht.

Aber die Flucht ging nicht weit: Ghatotkatscha kam des Weges, der riesige Bhimasohn. Der sah den feindlichen Riesen, sprang vom Wagen, und umschlang ihn mit seinen mächtigen Armen: Hoch empor hob er den Brüllenden und schmetterte ihn zur Erde, dass mit dem letzten Schrei seine Seele entfloh.

Indessen lenkte Krischna den Wagen Ardschunas stets hinter Schikhandin her, der heute ins Vordertreffen gesandt war.

Mit aller Kraft und geschicklichkeit unterstützte Ardschuna Schikhandin im Kampfe gegen die Helden, die Durjodhana zum Schutze Bhischmas entsandt hatte. Denn der König der Kuru fürchtete Unheil von Schikhandin, vor dem der Heldengreis stets die Waffen senkte.

Der Feldherr Dhrischtadjumna befahl einen allgemeinen Angriff gegen Bhischma. Wie ein Fels in der Brandung stand der greise Held inmitten seiner Gegner, ohne zu wanken. Ardschuna hatte ihm schon zwei Bogen und mehrere Speere zerspellt, aber stets musste der Pandava vor den neuen Waffen des Alten wieder weichen.

Da sah sich Bhischma plötzlich dem Schikhandin allein gegenüber. Lächelnd senkte der Greis seine Waffen und sah nicht Ardschuna, der, unsichtbar durch Kuberas Geschenk – die Waffe Antardhana – toddrohend hinter dem Drupadasohn stand.

Ruhig sah der Greis der Pfeilwolke entgegen, denn er fürchtete nicht die Waffen des Weibmannes.

Doch was war das? – Die Geschosse schlugen durch den starken Panzer wie durch dünne Seide und tranken das Blut des greisen Helden.

„Wehe!", rief er. „Diese Pfeile, die wie Yamas Boten meine Lebensgeister schier vernichten, hat die Hand Schikhandins nicht beflügelt! – Weh! wie gift'ger Schlangen Zähne schlagen sie in meinen Leib sich, alles Leben drin vernichtend! – Schikhandin schoss nicht die Pfeile! – Gandiva hat sie geschleudert – Ardschuna, Du bist der Schütze!"

Mit hundert Pfeilen im Leib, sank der Held vom Wagen, doch berührte sein Körper nirgends die Erde: wie ein Ross trugen ihn die Geschosse, die aus seinen Wunden ragten.

Laut jubelten die Krieger des Pandavaheeres, als der Unbezwingliche endlich gefallen war, und ihrem Jubel antwortete das Wehgeschrei der Kaurava, die ihren besten Helden verloren hatten.

Ein rasch geschlossener Waffenstillstand versammelte die Helden und Führer beider Heere am Pfeilbett des sterbenden Recken:

Ardschuna labt den Wunden mit Wasser, nachdem er sein Haupt mit drei Pfeilen gestützt hat. Jede andere Erleichterung weist der Sterbende, als eines Kriegers unwürdig, zurück.

Klaren Geistes und mit fester Stimme ermahnt er die Enkel, an seinem Totenbett Frieden zu schließen. Doch Durjodhana weist dies schroff von sich.

Der trotzige Karna erscheint am Lager des Sterbenden und bietet ihm die Hand zur Versöhnung. Freudig schlägt der Greis ein und mahnt auch ihn zum Frieden mit den Pandava. Doch Karna will nur seiner Pflicht als Freund und Vasall gehorchen.

Bis in die sinkende Nacht stehen Pandava und Kaurava, einig in Trauer und Bewunderung am Totenbett des adligsten Kriegers, des Ältesten aus dem Geschlechte der Bharata, aber am Morgen werden sie wieder die Waffen gegeneinander heben und der Erde das Blut des eigenen Stammes zu trinken geben.

Dronas Ende

Im Kriegsrat der Kaurava hatte Karna den erfahrenen Drona zum Oberfeldherrn vorgeschlagen. König Durjodhana hatte den vielbesungenen Waffenmeister seinen Heeren als Führer vorgestellt, und lauter Jubel, neue Siegeshoffnung, klang aus den ehrenden Zurufen der Helden, aus dem gellenden Schlachtgeschrei der Krieger.

Drona ordnete die Heere vom neuen zur Schlacht und unternahm einen heftigen Angriff gegen die Scharen der Pandava.

Wie ein Waldbrand wälzten sich die enggeschlossenen Reihen der Kauravakrieger heran und drohten die loser gefügten Heerhaufen der Pandava zu ersticken.

Wo auch die verwegene Tapferkeit einzelner Helden eine Lücke in die starke Kampffront riss, da schloss sich diese schnell unter der geschickten Führung des greisen Waffenmeisters.

Voll Verzweiflung sah Iudhischthira seine Scharen langsam doch stetig zurückweichen.

Doch der kluge Krischna wusste Rat:

„Es gilt das Netz zu zerreißen, das Drona über uns zusammenziehen will. Da ist kein Opfer zu groß. Befiehl dem Heldenjüngling Ahimanju, die feindlichen Reihen zu durchstoßen – andere müssen nachdrängen– und haben die Kaurava erst Feinde im Rücken, so zerfällt ihre ganze Schlachtordnung.

Leuchtenden Auges empfing Ahimanju den ehrenvollen Auftrag, und bald flog das Banner mit dem goldenen Pfauen gegen die Mitte der feindlichen Schlachtlinie:

Ein wahrer Hagel von Pfeilen bricht dem Wagen des kühnen Jünglings Bahn. Über Leichen holpert er, von schnellen Hengsten gezogen, durch die Reihen der Feinde!

Nun ist der Tapfere im Rücken des Angreifers und tummelt sich dort unter den Gegnern, wie der Haifisch im Meer.

Doch wehe! Dschajadratha mit seinen Sindhus tritt in die Lücke, die Abhimanjus Wagen gerissen hat. Wie die Krieger der Pandava auch gegen diese Mauer stürmen, keiner vermag sie zu durchstoßen, ihr tapferer Führer bleibt allein inmitten des feindlichen Heeres.

Wie ein Eber gegen die Hunde, wehrt sich Abhimanju gegen die andrängenden Kauravahelden. Durjodhana drängt er zurück, tötet den Bruder Schaljas und den des Karna; Duchschasana wird zurückgeschlagen und selbst der gewaltige König von Anga kann dem Jüngling nicht gefährlich werden, ehe das Getümmel die beiden Kämpfer wieder trennt.

Lange steht der Tapfere umdrängt von Feinden und führt seine Waffen mit Ruhe und Sicherheit. Aber die Arme erlahmen ihm unter der gewaltigen Anstrengung, seine Köcher sind leer, die Speere verschossen, Keule und Schwert zersplittert.

Mit einem Wagenrad schlägt er in den Schwarm seiner
Feinde, als ihm ein Keulenschlag von Duchschasanas Sohn
auf das Haupt trifft und tot zu Boden streckt.

Das Triumphgeheul der Kuru verkündet den Pandava
den Fall dieses Tapfern. Mit dem Sinken der Sonne stellen
sie den Kampf ein und ziehen zum Lager, um dem Vater
die Nachricht vom Heldentod des Sohnes zu bringen.

Ardschuna war den ganzen Tag auf einem anderen Teil
des Schlachtfeldes festgehalten worden:

Die Trigata, deren Scharen der Held schon einmal
gelichtet hatte, hatten sich verschworen, lieber zu sterben,
als vor Ardschuna zu weichen. Manche stolze Recken aus
anderen Stämmen hatten sich der Verschwörung angeschlossen, und seit dem Morgen war der tapfere Indrasohn
von den Verschworenen umzingelt und musste all seine
Tapferkeit aufbieten, um ihnen nicht zum Opfer zu fallen.

Wie ein Keulenschlag traf den Ermüdeten im Lager die
Nachricht von Abhimanjus Tod. Er schwor, das Dschajadratha, der die Helfer von seinem Sohne abgeschnitten
hatte, morgen vor Sonnenuntergang sterben sollte, von seiner Hand. Voll Trauer und Bekümmernis verbrachte er die
Nacht bis zum Tage der Rache.

Als Ardschuna am andern Morgen seinen Schwur in die
Scharen der Feinde schrie, lief die Drohung von Mund zu
Mund. Und Dschajadratha, der die scharfen Waffen des
Schrecklichen schon gefühlt hatte, als der Pandusohn die
geraubte Gattin aus seiner Hand befreite, ward von Furcht
ergriffen und floh hinter die Linien der Kämpfenden.

Durjodhana sandte ihm zum Schutze sechs der tapfersten Helden, darunter den alten Kripa, Schalja, den Madra-
könig, und den starken Dronasohn Aswatthama.

Ardschuna raste sein Opfer suchend durch die Reihen,
und tötete viele der Recken, die sich ihm in den Weg stellten. Duchschasana führte dem Schrecklichen einen Trupp

Elefanten entgegen, aber der Gandivaspanner tötete viele
der Tiere und trieb die andern mit seinen Pfeilen zur Flucht.

Der gewaltige Drona stellte sich seinem Lieblingsschüler entgegen, aber beide waren in der Führung der Waffen
so erfahren, dass keiner dem andern einen Vorteil abringen
konnte. Das Getümmel trennte sie wieder.

Duchschasana war von seinem Elefanten mit auf die
Flucht gerissen worden, jetzt kam er wieder zur Kampf-
stätte, auf einem goldschimmernden Streitwagen. Als er
sich Ardschuna näherte, schoss dieser mit scharfen Pfeilen die Stränge entzwei, so dass die scheuen Rosse ohne
Wagen davonjagten. Rasch rettete sich Duchschasana
vor dem anstürmenden Jujudhana auf den Wagen eines
Mitkämpfers.

Wie der Wind jagten nun Ardschunas Rosse, unter Krischnas kundiger Lenkung über das Schlachtfeld: Pfeile, die
der Indrasohn nach vorne geschossen hatte, fielen hinter
ihm zu Boden, so flogen die Gandharvahengste dahin.
Dschajadrathas Panier hatte sich in der Ferne gezeigt.

Schauerlich gellte der Löwenruf Dewadattas in des
Sindhukönigs Ohren. Der Schutzwall von streitbaren Helden schloss sich dichter um den Verfolgten:

Nun brauste der Rächer heran!

Aswatthama und Schalja warfen sich ihm entgegen.
Fürchterlich tobte der Kampf: Schalja musste zuerst vor
den Geschossen Gandivas weichen. Sie hatten alle seine
Trutzwaffen zertrümmert. Lange währte der Kampf mit
dem gewaltigen Aswatthama, denn Ardschuna wollte den
Sohn seines ehrwürdigen Lehrers nicht töten. Endlich
gelang es, auch ihn zur Flucht zu zwingen.

Aber Dschajadratha hatte einstweilen mit seinen übrigen Beschützern das Weite gesucht, und die Jagd begann
nun vom neuen. Krischna trieb die Rosse zu überirdischer
Schnelle an, denn die Sonne war schon im Sinken.

In einem Knäuel von Wagen sah Ardschuna Dschajadrathas Banner blitzen, und Krischna lenkte die Rasse dorthin, während Dewadatta, schmetternden Klanges, Hilfe herbeirief.

Bhima hörte den Ruf und eilte dem Bruder zu helfen. Als er das Getümmel um Ardschuna erreichte, sprang er ab, und mit seinen mächtigen Armen stürzte der Sturmgottsohn acht Wagen samt ihren Kämpfern um.

Karna sah den Furchtbaren unter den Seinen wüten und sprang ihm entgegen: Blitzschnell packten sich die Starken und schrien einander Schimpf und Schande ins Antlitz, während sie Brust an Brust in unentschiedenem Ringen standen. Keiner wollte dem andern ans Leben, denn Karna hatte der Mutter Kunti gelobt, Bhima zu schonen, und Bhima dem Ardschuna, ihm diesen persönlichen Feind zu überlassen. – Zornig stießen sie einander zurück. Karna holte von seinem Wagen den Bogen und begann den Pandava mit leichten Rohren zu beschießen. Bhima duckte sich hinter den Leib eines toten Elefanten. Karna eilte hin, berührte den Versteckten mit dem Bogenende und sprach: „Du bist tapfer vor der Schüssel, aber feig in der Schlacht! Geh! verbirg Dich hinter Ardschuna!“

Da sprang Bhima empor, entriss dem Höhnenden den Bogen, und schlug ihn damit auf den Kopf. Wieder packten die Gegner einander im Ringen, wieder stießen sie einander zurück, jeder seines Versprechens eingedenk, da fiel ein Pfeil, von Gandiva geschleudert, zwischen sie. Nun erinnerten sich beide ihrer Pflicht: Karna eilte nach seinem Wagen, und Bhima sprang in das Gewoge, das um Ardschuna tobte.

Dschajadratha hatte das Kampfgetümmel wieder benutzt um zu fliehen. Mit gewaltigen Speer- und Schwertschwung durchbrach nun Ardschuna den Schwarm der Feinde und flog ihm nach, so schnell als die Rosse laufen konnten, denn die Sonne musste in kurzer Zeit hinter dem Berg Asta verschwinden. Plötzlich kam ihm Karnas Streitwagen entgegen. Ein Wort zu Krischna, und der gewandte Rosselenker fuhr so geschickt an des Feindes Wagen, dass dieser im Umstürzen Karna und seinen Lenker weit hinausschleuderte.

Weiter ging die wilde Jagd! Schon war die Hälfte der Sonne hinter dem Berg verschwunden, da waren die Verfolger dem Flüchtigen auf Bogenschussweite genaht.

Ein Halbmondeisen, von Gandivas Sehne geschnellt, enthauptete Dschajadratha, ehe die letzten Strahlen des Gestirnes über die Erde huschten.

Aber die feindlichen Heere hatten sich so sehr ineinander verbissen, dass der Einbruch der Dunkelheit den Kampf nicht beendete. Fackeln wurden herbeigeschleppt, und in diesem gespenstischen Licht und Dunkel wütete Kampflust und Mordgier über das Schlachtfeld.

Karna war in diesem nächtlichen Kampf der Schrecken der Pandavaheere. Er flog durch die Reihen der Feinde und tötete sie scharenweise.

Einige Male wollte Ardschuna dem Furchtbaren entgegentreten, aber Krischna warnte sorglich vor diesem Kampf, denn noch glänzte die niefehlende Lanze Indras auf Karnas Streitwagen.

Endlich riet der listenreiche und skrupellose Iadavafürst, Ghatotkatscha gegen die Stürmenden loszulassen: Die Macht des zauberkundigen Riesen musste im Dunkel der Nacht doppelt wirksam sein.

Bhimas riesiger Sohn freute sich des Auftrages und fuhr unter die Kaurava, wie der Tiger unter die Kühe.

Seine mächtige Keule brach sich Bahn durch Scharen von Feinden. Wenn ein Elefant durch das Röhricht stampft, so fallen nicht mehr Halme, als Kurukrieger unter der Waffe des furchtbaren Riesen.

Voll Entsetzen sandte Durjodhana den Riesen Alajudha, einen Vetter Vakas, gegen den Koloss.

Aber Ghatotkatscha enthauptete den Gegner mit einem Schlag seines Schwertes. Dann ergriff er das blutige Haupt, drang mitten durch die Feinde bis vor Durjodhana, und warf es dem Entsetzten in den Wagen.

„Vor einem König soll man nicht mit leeren Händen erscheinen!", rief er lachend.

Doch in diesem Augenblick kam Karna gefahren und eröffnete den Kampf gegen den Riesen mit einem Pfeilhagel. Lange wehrte sich dieser mit Zauberwaffen, aber dem gewandten Sohn des Sonnengottes konnte er nicht widerstehen. Mit furchtbarem Gebrüll hob er sich in die Lüfte, um zu fliehen.

Da warf Karna die niefehlende Indralanze: Mit durchbohrter Brust stürzte der Riese aus der Luft, im Fall noch einen Heerhaufen der Kaurava erdrückend.

Die Lanze aber stieg leuchtend am dunklen Firmament empor und kehrte in die Hand des Götterkönigs zurück.

Kaurava und Pandava schrien voll Trauer um die schweren Verluste dieses Kampfes, aber Krischna sprach jubelnd zu Ardschuna: „Die todbringende Waffe ist nicht mehr in Karnas Hand: jetzt bist Du ihm gewachsen!"

Die Heerführer gaben nun das Zeichen zu einer kurzen Rast, und die ermüdeten Krieger und ihre Tiere streckten sich auf dem Schlachtfelde zum Schlafe hin.

Am frühen Morgen befahl der Feldherr Dhrischtadjumna einen Massenangriff auf den greisen Drona, dessen geschickte Heerführung die Pandavatruppen so arg bedrängte.

Zwanzig der stärksten Recken umkreisten in ihren Wagen den tapferen Wassenmeister, aber er stand aufrecht und führte die Waffen so ruhig und sicher, wie einst in der Arena vor seinen Schülern.

Bhima hatte sich wieder gegen eine Elefantentruppe gewendet, denn der Kampf mit diesen riesigen Gegnern freute den Sohn des Sturmgottes am meisten. Manchen hatte er schon erlegt, viele zur Flucht in die Heerhaufen der Kuru getrieben, als plötzlich der Malavafürst Indravarman auf einem übermächtigen Bergelefanten gegen ihn antrabte.

„Hallo! Starker Bhima!", rief er. „Da kommt ein Tier, das Dich nicht fürchtet! Mein Asvatthama ist der Stärkste unter seinen Brüdern und scheut vor keiner Waffe!"

„Asvatthama heißt das gute Tierchen?", rief Bhima voll Hohn und überschüttete den gepanzerten Riesen mit Pfeilen. Aber der Elefant kehrte sich nicht an die abprallenden Geschosse und rückte langsam, mit eingerolltem Rüssel, gegen den Wagen Bhimas vor. Bhima warf dem Heranschreitenden seine Speere entgegen, aber auch die konnten den guten Panzer nicht durchschlagen. Schon war der Elefant da, ein Fußtritt zertrümmerte den Wagen, und, wie eine Riesenschlange, fuhr unter dem Panzer der Rüssel hervor, um Bhima zu fassen.

Aber Bhima war schneller: mit starker Hand packte er den Rüssel und riss ihn mit gewaltigem Ruck aus dem Kopf. Stöhnend und blutüberströmt brach der Bergriese zusammen. Jauchzend schlug Bhima den Stürzenden, wie zum Hohn, mit dem blutigen Rüssel auf das Haupt, dann sprang er, seine Trophäe schwingend, davon und jubelte:

„Damit hab' ich den starken Aswatthama erschlagen!"

Krischna, Ardschuna und Iudhischthira hörten den Jubel des Siegestrunkenen. Bhima musste den Hergang erzählen, und der listenreiche Krischna riet: Bhima solle seine jubelnde Rede vor Drona wiederholen.

Sie fuhren alle dorthin, wo Drona noch immer im Kampfe gegen die vielen Gegner stand, und Bhima jubelte dort aus voller Kehle:

„Damit hab' ich den starken Aswatthama erschlagen!“.
Drona erschrak, denn er glaubte, dass sein Sohn Aswatthama von Bhima erschlagen worden sei. Aber er ließ die
Waffen nicht sinken und fragte den schweigenden Iudhischthira: „Ist Aswatthama wirklich gefallen, Du wahr-
heitsliebender König der Gerechtigkeit?“

„Ja, der Schlachtenriese ist tot!“, sprach Iudhischthira
ernst, nachdem Krischna ihm einige Worte zugeflüstert
hatte.

„Wehe!“, rief der Greis und ließ seine Waffen sinken.

Dhrischtadjumna, dem der Gewaltige heute den Vater
getötet hatte, sprang vor:

Mit starkem Schwertschwung schlug er das gebeugte
Haupt des trauernden Greises vom Rumpf und warf es in
die Heerhaufen der entsetzten Kaurava.

Karnas Tod

In wilder Flucht eilten die Haufen zurück, als ihr Feldherr
gefallen war. Aswatthama kam des Weges, und als er von
den Erschreckten hörte, welch' böse List über die sieghafte Kraft seines Vaters triumphiert hatte, da hob er die
Faust zum Himmel und schwor: „Ich will ihn rächen! und
müsste ich so falsch werden wie Krischna!“

Mit trotziger Rede sammelte er die Flüchtlinge um sich
und führte sie wieder gegen den Feind, bis die Sonne hinter dem Berg Asta versank.

Karna ward nun von Durjodhana zum Oberfeldherrn
ernannt, und der Scharen trotziges Schlachtgeschrei
bewies, dass der Mut der Kaurava noch nicht gebrochen
war.

Mehrere Male stießen Karna und Ardschuna am Tage
nach Dronas Tod zusammen, aber der Sohn des Sonnen-

gottes musste stets weichen: nicht vor des Pandava größerer Kraft und Tapferkeit, sondern vor Krischnas unüberwindlicher Wagenführung!

Am nächsten Morgen trat Karna deshalb vor Durjodhana und bat ihn, er möge Schalja, den König von Madras, der weit und breit als der kundigste Wagenlenker galt, für heute zu seinem Kampfgenossen bestimmen.

Der stolze Schalja weigerte sich anfangs, dem ‚emporgekommenen Fuhrmannssohn‘ Dienste zu leisten, doch auf Durjodhanas eindringliche Bitte versprach er, Karnas Wagen im Kampfe zu führen, wenn er, der König und Königsspross, den Niedrigen, dem er heute dienen sollte, nach Herzenslust schmähen dürfe.

Nachdem ihm die vollste Freiheit der Rede zugesagt war, bestieg er mit Karna den Wagen, und sie fuhren auf das Schlachtfeld.

Aber die edlen Rosse stürzten nach den ersten Sprüngen zu Boden, und als Karna vom Wagen sprang und seine Lieblinge unter freundlichem Zuspruch aufrichtete, sah er Tränen in den Augen der treuen Tiere glänzen.

Traurig ob des üblen Vorzeichens, doch fest im Gefühl seiner Pflicht als Krieger, bestieg der Held wieder den Streitwagen und ließ die Rosse gegen den Feind lenken.

Viele siegreiche Kämpfe focht der Sonnensohn an diesem Tage aus. Mancher der starken Recken fand durch seine Waffen den Tod, manchen musste er schonen, um seines Versprechens willen: So den edlen Iudhischthira, den er zur Flucht trieb, und den starken Nakula, welchen er mit seiner Bogensehne fesselte und so ins Pandavalager sandte.

Aber der fieberhaft gesuchte Ardschuna mied den kühnen Helden auf Krischnas Rat, bis die Sonne den Scheitel ihrer Bahn überschritten hatte und langsam gegen den Berg Asta sank.

Bhima wütete wieder unter Durjodhanas Brüdern und erwürgte viele von ihnen. Plötzlich sah er sich dem wüsten Duchschasana gegenüber.

Da tauchte in seinem Innern das schändliche Bild auf, wie der rohe Vetter die edle Draupadi an den Haaren in die Halle schleifte. Blitzartig überfiel ihn die Erinnerung an seinen Eid: Mit mächtigem Schwung seiner Keule schlug er Duchschasana vom Wagen und warf sich wie ein Raubtier über ihn. Mit den Nägeln riss er die Brust des Sterbenden auf und trank sein warmes Herzblut, wie er geschworen hatte!

Die Kuruvölker flohen bei diesem Anblick mit einem Geheul des Entsetzens. Bhima aber taumelte empor wie trunken, griff nach seiner Keule, und, seinen gefürchteten Schlachtschrei brüllend, stürzte er den Fliehenden nach.

Noch zehn der Söhne Dhritaraschtras fielen an diesem Tag unter seiner schrecklichen Keule, aber rastlos tobte der Unbändige über das Schlachtfeld und spähte nach Durjodhana, um auch an diesem seinen Schwur zu erfüllen.

Indessen hatte Karna den Ardschuna und Ardschuna den Karna erblickt, und sie fuhren aufeinander los, um die lange Feindschaft in blutigem Kampfe auszutragen.

Während Krischna seinen Kämpfer mit feuriger Rede und freundlichen Segenswünschen ermutigte, schmähte Schalja den seinigen und zeigte ihm seine Feindschaft.

„He?“, höhnte er, als Karna rief, jetzt wolle er Ardschuna töten.

„He? prahlst Du nicht, elender Fuhrmannssohn? – Du willst den Ardschuna töten? – den besten Krieger aus dem Bharatageschlechte? Oh! – Kennst Du die Fabel von der Krähe im Schwanennest?“

„Schweige, König der Madra!“, stieß Karna zornig hervor.

„Ja! König der Madra!“, lachte Schalja:

„König! – doch Du bleibst ein Fuhrmannssohn, trotz der erbettelten Krone! – die Krähe unter den Schwänen! – Kennst Du die Fabel? – Sie war unter die jungen Schwäne geraten und hatte mit ihnen fliegen gelernt. Nun prahlte sie – wie Du, Karna! – sie flöge am besten von allen. Da strichen die stolzen Schwäne über das Meer hin, die Krähe folgte ihnen voll Eitelkeit, und – als sie vor Ermattung ins Wasser fiel – wäre sie elend ersoffen – wenn die edlen Schwäne sie nicht gerettet hätten! – Prahle Du nur – eitle Krähe – krächze gegen den Schwan Ardschuna – noch weiß ich nicht, ob ich Dich retten werde!“

„Du schmähst mich, König der Madra, als niedrig geboren, aber ich möchte nicht Deines Stammes sein: Verachtet sind die Madra auf der weiten Erde, denn sie lügen und trügen und töten die Kühe, die geheiligten Nährmütter der Menschheit! Überall hört man Schimpflieder auf die Madra, denn sie sind das schlechteste unter den Völkern!“.

Während die furchtbaren Recken sich einander zum letzten Kampfe näherten, öffnete sich der Himmel, und Götter und Genien sahen zur Erde, um die stärksten ihrer Helden miteinander ringen zu sehen.

Indra wünschte seinem Sohne den Sieg und Surja dem seinigen:

Da traten sie beide voll Ehrerbietung vor Brahma und baten ihn, keinem der beiden Menschen zu helfen: Kraft und Kühnheit allein sollten entscheiden! Doch der Allmächtige schüttelte sein Haupt und sprach:

„Mein unabänderlicher Ratschluss hat längst dem Ardschuna Sieg, dem Karna Tod zugewogen. So muss es bleiben!“

Auf dem Kurufeld beginnt der Kampf:

Alle Edlen drängen sich um die erlauchten Kämpfer. Die senden einander so viele Pfeile, dass die Sonne dahinter, wie hinter Gewitterwolken, verschwindet. Ardschuna schießt die Agniwaffe gegen den Feind, und hoch auflodern die Kleider von Karnas Gefolge. Doch Karna gebraucht die Varunawaffe, und die Wasser stürzen vom Himmel, jedes Fünklein verlöschend. Lange beschießen die Helden einander ohne Erfolg.

Asvasena, ein Schlangenfürst, dessen geliebte Mutter im Kandavawalde verbrannt war, als Ardschuna den fressenden Gott mit seinen Waffen beschützte, legte sich heimlich als Pfeil auf Karnas Bogen. Der Wurm hoffte so auf Ardschuna geschossen zu werden und mit seinen fürchterlichen Giftzähnen die Mutter rächen zu können.

Karna schoss, aber der wackere Krischna hatte die schreckliche Gefahr erkannt und mit gewaltigem Ruck riss er die Rosse auf die Knie, so dass das Geschoss vorbeistreifte und nur den Turban samt Indras Diadem von Ardschunas Haupte riss. Das aber zerfiel im Gifte des Schlangendämons zu Asche und Staub.

Rasch kroch Asvasena zu Karna zurück, gab sich ihm zu erkennen, und bat, ihn noch einmal auf Ardschuna abzuschießen.

Doch der Held wies den Giftwurm zurück: „Nie will ich mit Wissen unehrlich kämpfen, und stünden mir zehn Ardschuna gegenüber, statt des Einen!"

Da kroch der Schlangenfürst wieder zu Ardschuna, um allein seine Rache zu nehmen. Doch der wackere Krischna sah die Natter kommen, und der Gandivaspanner zerstückte sie mit fünf Pfeilschüssen.

Im folgenden Gefecht traf ein Pfeil Ardschunas Karna in die Brust, so dass dieser wankend die Waffen sinken ließ. Nach ritterlichem Brauch senkte auch Ardschuna die seinigen, um zu warten, bis sich sein Gegner gefunden hätte.

Aber Krischna trieb zum Kampf: „Schone den Feind nicht, wenn Du ihn geschwächt hast!", rief er. „Auch Indra hat die Dämonen vernichtet ohne Großmut zu üben!"

Doch Karna hatte sich schon erholt, und seine Pfeile schwirrten vom neuen. Einer traf Ardschunas Banner, dass der Affe, sein Wappentier, laut aufheulte.

Doch nun war Karnas Wagen in einen Sumpf geraten, und das rechte Rad steckte tief im Morast.

„Halt!", rief der Edle „lass mich meinen Wagen herausheben, tapferer Ardschuna! Du wirst nicht auf einen Wehrlosen schießen!"

Doch da Ardschuna, auf Krischnas Rat, fortfuhr, Pfeil auf Pfeil zu versenden, ließ auch Karna den Bogen nicht sinken und schoss ein schweres Eisen gegen des Feindes Brust.

Ardschuna schwankte betäubt von dem furchtbaren Schlag, und Karna sprang vom Wagen und legte die starken Hände ans Rad.

Krischna erfrischte den Wankenden, und rasch fand sich Ardschuna wieder. Ein Halbmondeisen, von Gandivas Sehne geschnellt, enthauptete den edlen Karna, der noch immer vergebens an seinem versunkenen Rade zerrte.

Gellendes Triumphgeschrei der Pandava schreckte die Kuru aus der Stille ihres Entsetzens.

Der Leib des getöteten Karna aber strahlte in überirdischem Licht gegen die untergehende Sonne.

Krischna und Ardschuna bliesen Siegesjubel auf ihren Muscheln, und die Krieger schritten ins Lager, um sich für die letzten Kämpfe im Schlafe zu stärken.

Sieg, Rache und Klage

Die letzten Krieger der Kauravaheere sammelten sich am nächsten Morgen unter Schaljas Führung zu ehrenhaftem Untergang in der Schlacht. Schweigend und grimmig rückten sie gegen das Pandavaheer vor und fochten wie Männer, die zu sterben wissen. Schalja, der König der Madra, fiel zuerst im Kampfe gegen Iudhischthira. Der Bodschafürst Kritavarman verlor im Gefecht seinen Wagen und entwich auf flüchtigen Füßen. Durjodhana ward von seinem Wagenlenker, verwundet, aus der Schlacht gefahren. Bhima und Ardschuna wüteten in dem Häuflein von Feinden. Schakuni, der tückische Oheim der Kuruprinzen, fiel unter Sahadewas Schwert. Das Kuruheer war vernichtet, nur wenige Recken entflohen.

Unter der Führung Dhrischtadjumnas zog das Pandavaheer in das Lager zurück. Die fünf Pandusöhne aber, mit Krischna, streiften über das Leichenfeld und suchten lange den König Durjodhana.

Endlich fanden sie ihn, bis an den Hals in einem Teiche liegend und seine Wunden kühlend.

Bhima schmähte den Gebrochenen, dass er, als König, aus der Schlacht geflohen sei. Durjodhana raffte sich auf und forderte Bhima zum Keulenkampfe heraus.

Da freute sich der grimmige Sohn des Sturmgottes.

Als beide Gegner gerüstet waren, schlugen sie los und zerfleischten einander mit den Keulen, wie Elefanten mit den Hauern.

Doch keiner konnte dem andern obsiegen.

War Bhima der Stärkere, so war Durjodhana der Schnellere, und der Kampf hätte nie seine Entscheidung gefunden, wenn nicht Krischna dem Bhima zugerufen hätte: „Denk' an Draupadis Schmach!"

Ardschuna schlug sich auf den Schenkel, um dem Gedächtnis des Schwerfälligen aufzuhelfen, und Bhima verstand:

Als Durjodhana zu neuem Angriff zurücksprang, zerschmetterte ihm der Pandavarecke mit mächtigem Keulenschwung das Bein, welches der Böse einst Draupadi zu niedriger Dienstleistung hingestreckt hatte.

Wohl schalt Baladeva, Krischnas Bruder, der dem Kampfe zugesehen hatte, Bhima einen unehrlichen Kämpfer, denn die Regel des Keulenkampfes verbot es, unter den Gürtel zu schlagen, aber Krischna verteidigte jegliche List, im Kriege gegen Feinde, die durch Lug und Trug den Frieden gebrochen hatten:

„Keiner richte die Menschen, die nur nach dem Willen der Götter handeln!", sprach er und reichte dem beschämten Bhima die Hand.

Sie überließen den schwerverwundeten König Durjodhana seinen Dienern, und, nachdem Iudhischthira Krischna nach Hastinapura entsandt hatte, um Dhritaraschtra und Gandhari zu trösten, begaben sie sich an einen benachbarten Teich und übernachteten dort, denn es war zu spät geworden, um das Lager noch zu erreichen.

Kaum war Durjodhana allein geblieben, so fanden sich drei Helden, die dem Tod auf dem Kurufeld entgangen waren, an seinem Sterbelager ein.

Es war der greise Waffenmeister Kripa, der Dronasohn Aswatthama und Kritavarman, der Bodschafürst.

Voll Trauer hörten sie, wie ihr König besiegt worden war, und Aswatthama schwur, ihn und seinen Vater zu rächen oder zu sterben.

Da nahm der Sterbende von dem Wasser neben seinem Lager und weihte den Treuen zum Führer dieser traurigen Überbleibsel seiner Streitmacht.

Die drei Krieger lagerten sich darauf im Walde, und während Kripa und Kritavarman schliefen, starrte Asvatthama in die Bäume und sann auf Rache.

Mehrere Krähen saßen in den Ästen und schliefen. Da strich lautlos ein Uhu heran und erwürgte die Schlafenden.

Rasch sprang Asvalthama auf und weckte seine Gefährten: „Auf! zu den Wagen und ins Lager der Pandava! wir wollen sie im Schlafe erwürgen!", rief er.

Und als Kripa dies einen groben Verstoß gegen die Sitten der Krieger und ihre Ehre als Helden nannte, hieß er ihn schweigen.

„Längst hat Krischnas Schlauheit Ehre und Recht in den Staub getreten! Wir wollen nicht edler, nicht großmütiger sein als die Sieger!", sprach er und bestieg seinen Wagen.

Im Fluge ging es durch die dunkle Nacht, und am feindlichen Lager angekommen, sandte Asvatthama seine Gefährten an die beiden Tore des Walles, um eine Flucht zu verhindern.

Dann hab er im Dunkel der Nacht die Hände zum Himmel und bat den allmächtigen Zerstörer Schiwa um Kraft und Hilfe für sein Wagnis.

Plötzlich stand der göttliche Dreizackschwinger vor ihm, reichte dem Rächer ein Stirnjuwel, das seine Feinde in den Schrecken der Finsternis verblenden sollte, und verschwand.

Kühn schwang sich der Held über den Wall und drang zuerst ins Zelt des Pantschalaherrn Dhrischtadjumna.

Mit bloßen Händen erwürgte er den Schlaftrunkenen, denn keiner Waffe hielt er den heimtückischen Mörder seines Vaters für würdig.

Dann zog er das breite Schwert mit den tausend silbernen Monden aus der Scheide, die gefürchtete Waffe Dronas und sein einziges Erbe.

Wie der Todesgott in der Seuchenzeit, sprang er von Zelt zu Zelt und mordete Schlafende und Erwachende. Jammern, Stöhnen und Schreie der Todesfurcht weckten das ganze Lager.

Wie der Schnitter durchs wogende Kornfeld, schritt der Rächer durch die von Entsetzten bevölkerten Lagergassen und hielt seine blutige Ernte.

Vor ihm schritt Kali, die fruchtbare Gattin Schiwas, und warf ihre Schlingen nach den Fliehenden.

Die fünf Söhne der Draupadi stellten sich dem Schrecklichen mutig entgegen und fielen, einer nach dem andern, unter dem Schwerte des Rächers. Schikhandin, der letzte Pantschalafürst, ward mitten entzwei gehauen.

Wer von den Kriegern eines der Tore erreichen konnte, fiel unter den Pfeilen Kripas oder Kritavarmans. Nur Dhrischtadjumnas Wagenlenker kletterte über den Wall und entging so dem grausigen Tod im Finstern.

Als kein Lebendiger mehr im Lager war, keine Brust sich im letzten Seufzer noch hob, stieß Asvatthama in seine Muschel und rief die Gefährten herbei. In schnellstem Rosseslauf eilten die drei zu ihrem sterbenden König, und dessen letzter Atemzug war ein Dank für seine Getreuen, ein Jubel, dass die Verhassten ihren Sieg mit allem, was ihnen teuer war, hatten bezahlen müssen. –

Der Heilige Wyasa hatte dem Wagenlenker Dhritaraschtras, Sandschaja, die Gabe verliehen, von seines Königs Palast aus das ferne Schlachtfeld zu übersehen.

Mit beredtem Munde hatte der Barde, Abend für Abend, dem blinden Greis die Kämpfe des Tages geschildert. Schwer lastete der Untergang seines Hauses auf dem Unglücklichen. Krischnas milde Trostworte vermochten ihn nicht aufzurichten. Gestützt von dem guten Bruder Vidura und der treuen Gandhari, bestieg er schmerzversunken den Wagen und fuhr mit Kunti, Draupadi und den übrigen Frauen des Hofes auf das Kurufeld, vor das Antlitz des Siegers, zu den Leichen der gefallenen Söhne.

Eben als Iudischthira die Ehrwürdigen begrüßte, kam der Wagenlenker Dhrischtadjumnas gelaufen und berichtete keuchend und stammelnd von dem Überfall Asvatthamas und dem Heldentod der fünf Draupadeyas.

Entsetzt stand Iudhischthira da, als Draupadi auf ihn zutrat und ihn voll Hohn zu seinem glänzenden Sieg beglückwünschte. In ihrem Mutterschmerz verfluchte sie den Mörder und schwor, nicht eher zu essen, als bis ihre Söhne gerächt wären.

Der unermüdliche Bhima machte sich gleich auf die Verfolgung Asvatthamas: Als er den Flüchtigen eingeholt hatte, besiegte er ihn in fürchterlichem Ringen und brachte sein leuchtendes Stirnjuwel der trostlosen Draupadi.

Krischna-Wischnu aber verfluchte den, der Ruhende erschlagen hatte, dreitausend Jahre rastlos über die Erde zu wandern, aussätzig und gemieden von jedermann!

Der Iadava hatte die Trauernde auf das Schlachtfeld geführt und ließ die Totenfeier für die Gefallenen vorbereiten.

Seiner Beredsamkeit gelang es auch, Dhritaraschtra mit den Siegern zu versöhnen. Einen nach dem andern umarmte der schluchzende Greis. Für Bhima, der auf der Verfolgung Asvatthamas war, schob Krischna dem Blinden dessen eherne Rüstung in die Arme.

Da rief der Trauernde gegen den Himmel: „Ihr heiligen Götter! für eines Atems Länge gebt mir Riesenstärke!", und krachend zersplitterte der leere Panzer in den Armen des blinden Greises. Er hatte den töten wollen, der von seinen hundert Söhnen nicht einen am Leben gelassen hatte. Ahnungsvoll hatte der kluge Iadavafürst die Rache vereitelt.

Über das leichenbesäte Schlachtfeld irrten die Frauen mit aufgelöstem Haar. Gandhari hatte die Binde von den Augen genommen, um die toten Söhne zu sehen. Mit rührenden Klagen eilte sie von einem zum andern, hier die Geier von der Leiche Durjodhanas scheuchend, dort den Kopf ihres Lieblings Vikarna sorgfältig bettend.

Uttaraa kniete vor ihrem toten Gatten, löste den schweren Panzer von den wunden Schultern, ordnete die blutigen Locken, und wusch das trotzige Jünglingsgesicht

Abhimanjus unter leise gesungenen Klagen und langsam fließenden Tränen.

Duchschala und mehrere Sindhufrauen waren um die Leiche ihres Gatten Dschajadratha bemüht.

Kunti kniete vor Karnas strahlendem Leib und gestand den Pandusöhnen, dass sie in ihm ihren Bruder getötet hätten. Voll Trauer umwandelten die Sieger rechtshin den toten Helden.

Iudhischthira ordnete die Totenfeier an:

Weithin leuchteten die vielen Scheiterhaufen auf dem Kurufeld. Aus kostbaren Hölzern waren sie geschichtet, der Rauch von köstlichen Salben und Gewürzen umquoll die Leichen der Helden, als sie mit ihren Waffen und Schmuckstücken verbrannt wurden. Brahmanen vollzogen die Totenopfer nach strengen Gebräuchen, die Frauen sangen Klagelieder und Freunde brachten die heilige Wasserspende aus der Ganga. Im ganzen Land war Trauer um die gefallenen Helden.

Der Pandava Ausgang

Schmerzgebeugt kehrten die Sieger nach Hastinapura zurück.

Iudhischthira weigerte sich den Thron zu besteigen, der mit dem Blute so vieler Freunde, dem Tode des ganzen Geschlechtes und dem Verbrechen des Brudermordes erkauft war.

Krischnas weise Worte blieben so unbeachtet, wie Bhimas ungestümes Schelten. Der Sohn des Rechtsgottes wollte im Wald ein Leben der Buße führen.

Dem frommen Wyasa gelang es endlich, den rechtlich Denkenden zu überzeugen, dass die Sünden ihn vor Göttern und Menschen noch mehr belasten müssten, wenn er den blutig erkämpften Siegespreis, wie ein wertloses Ding, von sich würfe.

Er schlug dem Grübler vor, sich und die Brüder durch das seltene und schwierige Rossopfer zu entsühnen, und durch weise und gerechte Regierung das Volk für alle Leiden zu entschädigen.

Langsam gewann die im Entsetzen versunkene Seele Iudhischthiras wieder Halt, und mit fester Hand ergriff er die Zügel der Herrschaft.

Die Vorbereitungen für das Sühnopfer nahmen ihren Lauf:

Ein makelloser Hengst wurde ausgewählt und sollte nun, nach der strengen Vorschrift, ein Jahr lang ohne jede Fessel im Freien umherstreifen.

Ardschuna wurde zum Wächter des Opferrosses bestimmt und folgte dem mutigen Tier durch alle Lande auf seinem Streitwagen.

Dabei hatte er manchen harten Strauß mit den Gebietern der durchstreiften Länder zu bestehen. Er bezwang sie alle, ohne einen zu töten, und sandte sie nach Hastinapura, auf dass sie dort dem feierlichen Sühnopfer beiwohnen mögen.

Das schweifende Ross führte ihn auch nach Manipura, wo er einst mit seiner Gattin, der Putrika Tschitrangadaa, drei Jahre lang gelebt hatte. Babruvahana, der Sohn der beiden, herrschte nun als König über das Land.

Als dieser vor der Stadt den fremden Krieger hinter dem ledigen Ross herjagen sah, empfing er ihn freundlich und bot ihm seine Dienste an. Ardschuna schalt den Jüngling im Königsschmuck, ob seines unkriegerischen Benehmens. Es kam zu Wortwechsel und Streit, und bald griffen Vater und Sohn zu den Waffen, ohne einander zu kennen.

In furchtbarem Anlauf schlugen die beiden einander schreckliche Wunden, und Ardschuna blieb für tot auf dem Rasen.

Babruvahana wusch seine Wunden in der nahen Ganga,
da kam die Schlangenprinzessin Ulupi daher. Sie hörte von
dem Gefallenen, lief ihn zu sehen, und als sie den geliebten Ardschuna, den Vater ihres Iravat, erkannte, holte sie
schnell aus der Schlangenwelt einen leuchtenden Talis-
man. Kaum hatte sie den auf die Brust des Leblosen gelegt,
so hob sich diese in tiefem Atmen, und Ardschuna kehrte
ins Leben zurück. An der kühnen Führung der Waffen hatten Vater und Sohn einander erkannt und lagen sich nun
versöhnt in den Armen.

Babruvahana versprach zum Opfer nach Hastinapura
zu kommen, und Ardschuna bestieg den Wagen und folgte
dem Rosse weiter durch die Lande.

gegen Ende des Jahres kehrte das Tier nach Hastinapura
zurück, und bald darauf fiel es als Sühnopfer unter den
geweihten Messern der Brahmanen.

Der Rauch seines Fettes entsühnte die Pandavahelden.

Sechsunddreißig Jahre herrschte Iudhischthira voll Weisheit und Milde über die Völker seines weiten Reiches.

Dhritaraschtra war, nachdem er, hochgeehrt, noch fünf-
zehn Jahre am Hofe seines Brudersohnes gelebt hatte, mit
Gandhari, Kunti, dem weisen Vidura und dem wackeren
Wagenlenker Sandschaja in den Wald gezogen.

Die guten Alten führten dort durch zwei Jahre ein fried-
liches Leben der Buße, bis ein Waldbrand sie alle auf einmal dahinraffte.

Krischna ward im Wald von einem Jäger, der ihn im
Halbdunkel für eine Antilope hielt, erschossen. Ardschuna
eilte auf die Nachricht vom Tode seines Freundes nach
Dwaraka und führte die Frauen und Hausgenossen des
Toten nach Hastinapura. Als er die Stadt verlassen hatte,
stürzten die Wässer aus dem Boden und verschlangen die
Residenz des Gottmenschen.

Bald nach diesem Ereignis weihte Iudhischthira den Parikschit, den nachgeborenen Sohn Abhimanjus, zum Herrn der Erde und wanderte mit den vier Brüdern und der greisen Draupadi nach dem Himawat, um dort nach Vätersitte den Tod zu finden.

In Büßerkleidung schritten die Edlen aufwärts zum Himmel Indras:

Draupadi erlag als erste den Anstrengungen und fiel tot zu Boden. Ohne den Blick nach ihr zu wenden, schritten die Gatten weiter. Nakula fiel und Sahadewa, Ardschuna und der gewaltige Bhima.

Iudhischthira allein erreichte lebend den Gipfel und fuhr auf Indras Wagen nach dem Himmel.

Dort forschte er gleich nach den Brüdern und der Gattin.

Aber Indra zeigte ihm den Höllenpfuhl, wo die Bäume statt der Blätter Schwerter und Dolche tragen, und Bäche von Blut durch die düstere Landschaft rieseln.

Dort sah Iudhischthira seine Lieben sich in Schmerzen und Qualen winden.

„Stoß mich hinab!", flehte er zu Indra. „Denn lieber will ich mit den Meinen in der Hölle seufzen, als allein im Himmel die Götter lobpreisen!"

„So gehe mit den Deinen in den Himmel ein!", sprach Indra.

Und auf seinen Wink versank der Spuk, Iudhischthira sah sich mit Gattin, Brüdern und den gefallenen Freunden vereint im lichten Himmel, an der Somatafel unter dem ewigen Feigenbaum.

Freundlich begrüßten die Götter und Ahnen die Helden. Iudhischthiras göttlicher Vater Dharma stand neben ihm und sagte:

„Du, mein Sohn, hast immer dem Rechte gelebt auf Erden, darum hast Du lebendigen Leibes den Himmel erreicht.

Die Deinen haben ihre Sünden in kurzen Qualen ver-
büßt und, dass Du sie mitleidend leiden sehen musstest,
war die Strafe für jene halbe Lüge, die Dronas Leben
gekostet hat! Rein seid ihr nun alle!"

Seither saßen die Helden des Bharatastammes in Indras
lichtem Himmel und teilten die Freuden der Götter.

Parikschit aber herrschte weise über die Völker der
Erde und setzte in seinem Sohne Dschanamedschaja das
Geschlecht der Bharata fort.

Anhang

A.

Abhimanju: Sohn des Ardschuna und der Subhadra.

Adhiratha: Ein Wagenlenker, Ziehvater Karnas.

Aditi: Die Mutter der Götter, Gattin Kaschiapas, Tochter Dakschas.

Aditia: Bezeichnung der Götter nach ihrer Mutter Aditi.

Agasiya: Einer der sieben Heiligen (Seher, Rischi) der Urzeit.

Agneya: Name eines göttlichen Bogens, den Drona seinem Lieblingsschüler Ardschuna schenkte.

Agni: Gott des Feuers. Das Feuer.

Airawata: Indras Elefant.

Ajodhia: Hauptstadt von Kosala.

Akupara: König der Schildkröten.

Alajudha: Ein Riese, der in Durjodhanas Heer kämpft.

Alambuscha: Ein Riese, Bruder Vakas, kämpft im Heere Durjodhanas.

Amaravati: Die Göttersiadt, Residenz Indras.

Amba: Prinzessin von Kaschi, später Schikhandin.

Ambalika: Schwester Ambas und Ambikas und Gattin Witschitrawirias.

Ambika: Schwester Ambas und Ambalikas und Gattin Witschitrawirias.

Amrita: Göttertrank, der Unsterblichkeit verleiht.

Andhaka: Volk. Kämpft auf Seite der Kaurava.

Anga: Provinz des Kurureiches, das Königreich Karnas.

Angiras: Ein Heiliger. Vater des Brihaspati.

Ansuman: Enkel des Königs Sagara.

Anthardana: Eine unsichtbarmachende Waffe (Tarn-kappe), die der Schätzehüter Kubera dem Ardschuna schenkt.

Anuvinda: Ein Recke im Kauravaheer.

Apsaras (Die im Wasser Wandelnden): Nymphen, Götter-jungfrauen in Indras Gefolge.

Ardschuna: Dritter Sohn des Pandu und der Kunti, von Indra geschenkt, daher auch Indrasohn genannt.

Aruna: Sohn des Kaschjapa und der Winata. Wagenlenker des Sonnengottes.

Arundhati: Gattin eines der sieben Rischi.

Asamandscha: Sohn des Königs Sagara.

Asoka (Kummerlos): Name eines vielbesungenen Baumes.

Asta: Der Berg des Unterganges. (Westen.)

Astika: Sohn des Dscharatkaru.

Asuren: Name der Götterfeinde (Dömonen).

Asvasena: Ein Schlangenfürst.

Aswatthama: 1. Sohn des Drona. 2. Name eines Kriegselefanten.

Aswinas: Zwei Halbgötter, Morgenrotreiter, Himmelsärzte.

B.

Babruvahana: Sohn Ardschunas und der Tschitrangadaa. König von Manipura.

Bala: Ein Dämon. Danawafürst.

Baladeva: Ein Bruder Krischnas.

Bana: Ein Dämon. Sohn Balas.

Banhane: Ein Riesenbaum Indiens.

Bhagadatta: König der Iavana, ein gewaltiger Elefanten-kämpfer im Kauravaheer.

230

Bhagiratha: Ein König aus Ikschwakus Geschlecht.

Bharata: Sohn Duschyantas und der Schakuntala, Ahnherr der Pandava und Kaurava.

Bhima: 1. König von Widarbha, Vater Damayantis. 2. Zweiter Sohn des Pandu und der Kunti, ein Geschenk Wajus, daher oft Sohn des Sturmgottes genannt.

Bhischma: Sohn des Schantanu und der Stromgöttin Ganga, oft Großvater der von ihm erzogenen Pandava- und Kauravaprinzen genannt. Oberfeldherr Durjodhanas

Bhrigu: Ein Heiliger. Vater Tschiawanas.

Bhurischrowas: Ein Held des Kauravaheeres. Sohn des Somadatta.

Bodscha: Ein Volksstamm. Kämpft auf der Seite der Kaurava.

Brahma: Das All, der Weltschöpfer, das höchste Wesen, Schicksalslenker, Haupt der Dreieinigkeit: Brahma, Wischnu, Schiwa (Schöpfung, Erhaltung, Zerstörung), das Seiende, Ewige.

Brahmane: Priester, Glied der obersten Kaste (s. d.).

Brihaspati: Name des Himmelspriesters. Er ist ein Sohn Angiras'.

D.

Dadhitscha: Ein Heiliger. Aus seinen Knochen wird der Donnerkeil Indras gemacht.

Daitia: Söhne der Diti. Dämonen.

Daitiasena. Das Dämonenheer. Als jungfräuliche Tochter des Pratschapati verkörpert.

Dakscha: Einer der Schöpfer, der Vater von Kaschjapas Frauen: Diti, Danu, Aditi usw.

Damayanti: Tochter des Königs Bhima von Widarbha, Gattin Nalas.

Danawa: Söhne der Danu. Dämonen.

Danu: Tochter Dakschas, Gattin Kaschjapas, Mutter der Danawa, eines Dämonenstammes.

Dascharna: Ein Reich Indiens.

Dewadajani: Ardschunas Drommete, ein Geschenk Mayas.

Dewajani: Tochter Uschanas', des Danawapriesters.

Dewasena: Das Götterheer. Als jungfräuliche Tochter des Schöpfers Pratschapati verkörpert. Wird die Gattin des Kriegsgottes Skanda, des Feldherrn Indras.

Dharma: Das Recht, der Gott des Rechtes. Schenkte der Kunti den Iudhischthira.

Dharmaradscha: Beiname Iudhischthiras. Heißt: König des Rechtes, der Gerechtigkeit.

Dhaumia: Der Hauspriester der Pandava.

Dhrischtadjumna: Sohn des Königs Drupada von Pantschala, Bruder der Draupadi. Oberfeldherr Iudhischthiras.

Dhrischtaketu: König von Tschedi. Verbündeter der Pandava.

Dhritaraschtra: König der Kuru, Sohn Witschitrawirias. Hat 100 Söhne: Durjodhana, Duchschasana usw. und eine Tochter: Duchschala.

Dilipa: Ein König aus Ikschwakus Geschlecht. Vater Bhagirathas.

Diti: Gattin Kaschjapas, Mutter der Daitia (Dämonen).

Djau: Höchster der Wasu (Erdengötter).

Draupadeya: So nannte man die fünf Söhne, die Draupadi ihren fünf Gatten, den Pandavas, geschenkt hatte.

Draupadi: Tochter des Drupada, Königs von Pantschala; Gemahlin der fünf Pandusöhne.

Drona: Brahmanischer Waffenmeister der Kaurava- und Pandavaprinzen. Kämpft auf der Seite der Kaurava. Vater des Aswatthama.

Drupada: König von Pantschala. Vater Draupadis,

Dhrischtadjumnas und Schikhandins. Kämpft auf der
Seite der Pandava.

Dschajadratha: König der Sindhu, Sauwira usw. Als
Duchschalas Gatte, Schwager und Bundesgenosse
Durjodhanas.

Dschamadagni: Vater des ‚Rama mit dem Beil‘.

Dschanamedschaja: Sohn des Parikschit, Enkel Abhimanjus. König der Kuru.

Dscharatkaru: Büßer und Vater Astikas, Gatte der

Dscharatkaru: Schwester des Schlangenkönigs Wafuki.

Dschimuta: Ein Ringkämpfer des Königs von Matsya.

Duchschala: Einzige Tochter Dhritaraschtras, Gattin
Dschajadrathas.

Duchschasana: Sohn Dhritaraschtras.

Durjodhana: Ältester Sohn Dhritaraschtras. König der
Kuru.

Durwasa: Ein brahmanischer Büßer.

Dwapara: Der Fehlwurf – ein Würfeldämon.

Dwaraka: Krischnas Residenz.

G.

Gandhamadana: Ein Gipfel des Himawat.

Gandham: Ein Reich Indiens.

Gandhari: Die Gattin Dhritaraschtras, Mutter Durjodhanas usw.

Gandharva, Gandharwer: Himmlische Spielleute,
Halbgötter.

Gandiva: Der Bogen Ardschunas, ein Geschenk des Gottes
Varuna.

Ganga: Der Strom Ganges und die Göttin dieses Stromes.
Wegen ihres Laufes am Himmel (Milchstraße), auf
Erden und in der Unterwelt, die Dreipfadige genannt.

Garuda: Der Geierkönig. Vogel des Gottes Wischnu. Ein
    Sohn der Winata und des Kaschiapa.
Ghatotkatscha: Sohn Bhimas und der Riesin Hidimbaa. Er
    ist ein zauberkundiger Riese.

H..

Hanumat: König der Affen. Gleich Bhima ein Sohn Waius.
Hastinapura (Elefantenstadt): Hauptstadt des Kurureiches.
Hidimbaa: Eine zauberkundige Riesin.
Hidimbas: Bruder der Hidimbaa. Riese.
Himawat: Das Himalajagebirge.

I.

Ikschwaku: Stammvater der Könige von Ajodhia.
Indra: Der König der Götter, Donner-Gott. In alter Zeit
    der mächtigste Gott, später zugunsten Brahmas, Misch-
    nus und Schiwas, sowie verschiedener ‚Heiliger‘, mehr
    in den Hintergrund gedrängt.
Indraprastha: Von den Pandava gegründete Hauptstadt
    ihres Reiches.
Indravarman: Ein Malavafürst. Bundesgenosse der
    Kaurava.
Iravat: Sohn Ardschunas und der Schlangenprinzesstn
    Ulupi.
Iadava: Ein Volksstamm, aus welchem der vergötterte Kri-
    schna stammt.
Iajawara: Ein Geschlecht von Heiligen aus der
    Brahmanenkaste.
Iamuna: Ein Fluss.
Iarasandha: König von Magadha.

Iavana: Ein Volk. Bundesgenossen der Kaurava.

Iudhischthira: Ätester Sohn Pandus und der Kunti. Ein Geschenk des Rechtsgottes Dharma, daher oft König des Rechtes (Dharmaradscha) genannt. Er ist Großkönig und Haupt der Pandavasippe.

Iujudhana: Ein Fürst der Somakha (Someker). Bundesgenosse der Pandava.

K.

Kadru: Die Erde als Mutter der Schlangen. Tochter Dakschas, Gattin Kaschjapas.

Kailasa: Ein Berg im Himalaja. Sitz Kuberas.

Kalakeya: Ein Dömonenstamm. Sein Herrscher ist Writra, Indras stärkster Gegner. (Dürre.)

Kali: Verkörperung des Bösen. Ein Würfeldämon.

Kali: Die furchtbare Gattin des Zerstörers Schiwa.

Kalinga: Ein Volk. Bundesgenossen der Kaurava.

Kama: Der indische Liebesgott. (gleicht dem Amor.)

Kambodscha: Ein Volk. Bundesgenossen der Kaurava.

Kamjakawald: Hier siedelten die Pandava während der zweiten Verbannung.

Kandavawald: Ein Hain, der durch Feuer zerstört wurde.

Kandavaprastha: Wüste Landschaft, die den Pandava bei der Teilung des Kurureiches zufiel.

Kapila: Der Gott der Unterwelt. Höllenfürst.

Karkotaka: Ein Schlangenlsönig.

Karna: Sohn des Sonnengottes und der Kunti, Ziehsohn des Wagenlenkers Adhiratha und seiner Gattin Radha. Freund und Vasall des Kurukönigs Durjodhana.

Kaschi: Ein Reich, Heimat Ambas.

Kaschjapa: Der meistgenannte von den Schöpfern.

Kasiap: Ein berühmter brahmanischer Arzt.

Kaste: Stand, Beruf im weiteren Sinn. Im engeren Sinn
  sind darunter die vier durch Geburt bestimmten
  Stände des indischen Volkes zu verstehen. Und zwar:
  Brahmanen (Lehrstand): Priester, Sänger usw. Kschattrija (Wehrstand): Könige, Adel, Krieger. Waischia
  (Nährstand): Bauern, Handel und Gewerbe. (Dies
  sind die drei arischen Kasten.) Schudra: Diener (keine
  Sklaven). (Dies sind nichtarische, unterjochte Völker.)
  Frauen und Kinder gehören zur Kaste, der sie entstam-
  men. Ehen unter Gliedern verschiedener Kasten sind
  verpönt. Kinder solcher Verbindungen waren als Kas-
  tenlose, Paria, Tschandala, verachtet und rechtlos wie
  räudiges Vieh.
Katscha: Sohn des Götterpriesters Brihaspati.
Kaumodaki: Krischnas Keule, Geschenk des Gottes
  Varuna.
Kaurava: So nannte man das Geschlecht und Volk des
  Königs Kuru, eines Vorfahren Dhritaraschtras, beson-
  ders aber das Haus Dhritaraschtras, zum Unterschied
  vom Hause seines Bruders Pandu, der Pandava.
Kekaya: Ein Volk. Bundesgenossen der Pandava.
Keschin: Ein Dämon, Feldherr des Dämonenheeres.
Kesini: Damayantis Gürtelmagd.
Kirata: Ein Volk. Bundesgenossen der Kaurava.
Kiritin: ‚Der Gekrönte‘. Beiname Ardschuna.
Kirmira: Ein Riese. Bruder des Vaka.
Kitschaka: Der Feldherr Viratas von Matsya.
Kosala: Ein Reich und Volk Indiens, (Hauptstadt Ajodhia.)
Kotika: Ein Königssohn. Wagenlenker Dschajadrathas.
Krauntscha: Ein Berg.
Kripa: Ein brahmanischer Waffenmeister. Schwager des
  Drona, Vasall des Durjodhana.
Krischna: Sohn Wasudewas, des Iadavakönigs, Verwandter
  der Kunti, Freund Ardschunas. Eine Menschwerdung

des Gottes Wischnu. Genießt göttliche Verehrung!
Führte den Wagen Ardschunas in der Schlacht.
Krischna: = schwarz, daher sehr häufig als Name gebraucht.
Auch Draupadi heißt Krischna – die Schwarze, ferner
Wyasa usf.
Kritawarman: Feldherr Krischnas, führt dessen Heer auf
der Seite der Kaurava.
Kschattradewa: König vonDascharna. Bundesgenosse der
Pandava.
Kschattrija: Krieger (siehe Kaste).
Kubera: Gott des Reichtums, der Schätze, Herr der Geister.
Kukura: Ein Volk. Bundesgenossen der Kaurava.
Kundina: Hauptstadt von Widarbha.
Kunti: Gattin Pandus, Mutter der drei älteren Pandavas
und Karnas.
Kuru: Ein König aus Bharatas Geschlecht. Nach ihm heißt
das Volk in und um Hastinapura und das dort herr-
schende Königshaus.
Kurukschetra = Kurufeld: Das Schlachtfeld der Sage.

L.

Lakschmi oder Schri: Göttin des Glückes, Verkörperung
der Schönheit. Gattin Wischnus. Sie ist dem Meer
entstiegen.
Lotus: Die indische Wasserrose. In ihrer Herrlichkeit
sagenverklärt.
Lomascha: Ein Heiliger.

M.

Mada: Leidenschaft, als schrecklicher Riese verkörpert.

Madra (Madrer): Reich und Volk. Bundesgenossen ,der
Kaurava.

Madri: Zweite Gemahlin Pandus, Mutter der Zwillinge
Nakula und Sahadewa.

Magadha: 1. Ein Reich. 2. Ein Held im Heere Durjodhanas.

Maharadscha: Großkönig, Kaiser.

Mahisa: Ein Dämonenheld.

Malava: Ein Volk. Bundesgenossen der Kaurava.

Mandara: Der Berg, mit dem das Meer gerührt wird.

Manimat: Ein Geist, Gärtner Kuberas.

Manipura: Ein Reich Indiens.

Manu: Stammvater der Menschen, ein Sohn der Sonne.
Gesetzgeber, Heiliger. Er ist Indiens Adam und Noah in
einer Person.

Maruta: Wind- und Wettergötter in Indras Gefolge.

Matali: Indras Wagenlenker.

Matsya: Ein Volk. Bundesgenossen der Pandava.

Maya: Der Künstler (Bildner) des Geisterreiches.

Meru: Der indische Olymp, Sitz der Götter. Er ist als Mittelpunkt der Erde gedacht.

Muni: Der Schweigsame. Beiname und ehrfürchtige
Anrede für Büßer, Heilige usw.

N.

Naga: Schlange, Schlangendämon.

Nahuscha: Ein König der Erde, der statt des verschollenen
Indra Götterkönig wird.

Nakula: Einer der Zwillinge von Madri und Pandu.
Geschenk der Aswinas.

Nala: König von Nischadha, mit dem Beinamen ,der
Makellose‘.

Nandana: Götterhain, Indras Garten.

Nandini: Eine Wunderkuh, die jeden Wunsch erfüllt.

Narada: Ein Heiliger, der Götterbote.

Naritirtha: Geheiligte Teiche, ein Wallfahrtsort.

Narmada: Ein Fluss.

Naumutschi: Ein Dämonfürst (Dürre).

Niramitra: Ein Trigartafürst. Bundesgenosse der Kaurava.

Nischadha: Reich und Volk. Bundesgenossen der Kaurava.

Niwatakawatscha: Ein von Göttern nicht zu besiegender Dämonenstamm (Lyklon auf dem Meer?).

P.

Pandava: Die Söhne Pandus und ihr Anhang.

Pandu: Ein König aus Bharatas Geschlecht. Gatte Kuntis und der Madri, Vater der fünf Pandava.

Pantschala (Pantschaler): Reich und Volk. Bundesgenossen der Kaurava.

Paria: Verachtete, Ausgestossene (siehe Kaste).

Parikschit: Sohn Adhimanjus, Enkel Ardschunas, Vater des Dschanamedschaja.

Parnada: Ein Brahmane am Hof zu Widarbha.

Paschupata: Der Bogen Schiwas, Geschenk an Ardschuna.

Patala: Die Unterwelt (etwa dem Fegefeuer gleichend).

Pavaka: Der Reiniger, Beiname des Feuergottes.

Prabhadraka: Ein Volk. Bundesgenossen der Pandava.

Pratipa: Ein König des Bharatastammes. Vater des Schantanu.

Pratschapati: Bald ‚Schöpfer‘ im Allgemeinen, bald Name oder Beiname eines Gottes.

Puloma: Ein Dämonenstamm, für Götter unbesieglich, Bewohner einer fliegenden, goldenen Stadt. (Wüstensturm?)

Puloma: Gattin des Sehers Bhrigu.

Puschkara: Bruder des Königs Nala.

Putrika: Sohntochter, eine Tochter, die, in Ermanglung von Söhnen, das väterliche Geschlecht rechtsgültig fortsetzt. (Prinzgemahl.)

R

Radha: Ziehmutter Karnas, Gattin des Wagenlenkers Adhirata.

Rahu: Ein Dämon, dessen abgeschlagenes, unsterbliches Haupt Sonne und Mond verfinstert.

Rama (mit dem Beil): Sohn Dschamadagnis. Ein kriegerischer Brahmane, unbesieglicher Held.

Rati: Die Lust. Gattin des Liebesgottes.

Rischi: Seher, Heiliger, Weiser. Besonders die sieben Rischi der Urzeit! (Sternbild.)

Rituparna: König von Kosala.

Rudra: Wettergötter. Auch ein Beiname Schiwas.

Ruru: Ein Brahmane.

S.

Sagara: Ein König aus Ikschwakus Geschlecht.

Sahadewa: Einer der Zwillinge von Pandu und Madri Geschenk der Aswinas.

Sandschaja: Der Wagenlenker Dhritaraschtras.

Sanka: Sohn Viratas von Matsya.

Sarasvati: Ein Fluss.

Sarasvati: Brahmas Gattin. Göttin der Kunst und Wissenschaft, besonders der Beredsamkeit.

Satjawati: Tochter des Fischerkönigs, Gattin Schantanus.

Sauwira: Volksstamm. Bundesgenossen der Kaurava.

Schaka: Volksstamm. Bundesgenossen der Kaurava.

Schakra: Der Mächtige! Beiname Indras.

Schakuni: Oheim der Kauravaprinzen, Bruder der Gandhari.

Schalja: König von Madras. Bundesgenosse der Kaurava.

Schalwa: 1. Ein Reich. 2. Ein Dämon, Herr einer fliegenden Stadt.

Schamika: Ein büßender Brahmane.

Schantanu: Ein König aus Bharatas Stamm. Der Vater Bhischmas und seiner Brüder.

Scharjati: Ein König. Der Vater Sukanjas.

Schatanika: Ein Bruder des Königs Virata.

Schatschi: Die Macht. Indras Gattin.

Schikhandin: Prinz von Pantschala, eine Wiedergeburt der Prinzessin Amba.

Schikhandini: Schikhandins Name als Weib.

Schischupala: König von Tschedi. Feldherr Iarasandhas von Magadha.

Schiwa: Gott der Zerstörung. Ein Teil der Dreieinigkeit Brahmas. (Schöpfung, Erhaltung, Zerstörung.)

Schiwi: Volksstamm. Bundesgenossen der Kaurava.

Schri: oder Lakschmi (s. d.).

Schringin: Sohn des Brahmanen Schamika.

Schrutayus: Ein Held im Kauravaheer.

Schubaling: Sohn des Schubala. Beiname des Schakuni.

Schudra: Die vierte Kaste (s. Kaste).

Sescha: Eine sagenhafte Schlange, die das Weltall trägt, sich um die Erde schlingt usw.

Sindhu: Volk. Bundesgenossen der Kaurava.

Skanda: Ein Kriegsgott, Indras Feldherr. Sechsköpfig. Sohn Agnis und seiner Gattin Svaha.

Soma: Der Mond, Mondgott.

Soma: Ein berauschendes Getränk aus Bergkräutern. Opfertrank.

Somadatta: Vater Bhurischrawas.

Somakha (Someker): Volk. Bundesgenossen der Pandava.

Sthuna: Ein Waldgeist.

Subhadra: Schwester Krischnas, Gattin Ardschunas, Mutter Abhimanjus.

Sudakschina: Einer von Durjodhanas Heerführern.

Sudeva: Ein Brahmane in Widarbha.

Sukanja: Tochter des Königs Scharjati, Gattin des Heiligen Tschiawana.

Sumucha: Ein Schlangenprinz. Schwiegersohn des Matali.

Sura: Ein berauschendes Volksgetränk (Reisbranntwein?).

Surpa: Der Sonnengott.

Suscharman: König der Trigarta. Freund Durjodhanas.

Svaha: Die Gattin Agnis, Mutter Skandas.

Sveta: Ein sagenhafter Berg.

Sweta: Prinz von Matsya, Sohn Viratas.

T.

Takschaka: König der Giftschlangen.

Taraka: Ein Dämonenkrieger.

Trigarta: Ein Volk. Bundesgenossen der Kaurava.

Tschedi: Hauptstadt von Kosala.

Tschekitanu: Ein Heerführer Iudhischthiras.

Tschiawana: Ein Heiliger. Sohn des Bhrigu.

Tschina: Ein Bergvolk. Bundesgenossen der Kaurava.

Tschitrangada: Sohn des Schantanu

Tschitrangadaa: Sohntochter des Königs von Manipura, Gattin Ardschunas, Mutter des Babruvahana.

Tschitrasena: 1. König der Gandharva. 2. Ein Held im Pandavaheere.

Twaschter (auch Wischwakarman): Der Götterschmied.

U.

Ulupi: Eine Schlangenprinzesfin. Mutter des Iravat.

Upaplavia: Residenz des Königs Virata.

Urwasi: Eine vielbesungene Apsara.

Uschas: Die Morgenröte! Als schönes Weib personifiziert.

Uschanas: Ein zauberkundiger Brahmane. Opferpriester der Dämonen.

Usinara: Ein sagenhafter König.

Utschaisrawa: Das meerentstiegene Götterpferd.

Utanka: Ein Brahmane. Leiter des Schlangenopfers.

Uttara: Prinz von Matsya, Sohn Viratas.

Uttaraa: Prinzessin von Matsya. Tochter Viratas, Gattin Abhimanjus, Mutter Parikschits.

V.

Vadschranabha: Der niefehlende Diskus, den Krischna von Varuna erhielt.

Vahuka: Der Name Nalas als Missgestalt.

Vaka: Ein menschenfressender Riese.

Varuna: Gott der Gewässer. Einer der Welthüter.

Vikarna: Dhritaraschtras jüngster Sohn.

Vinda: Ein Recke des Kauravaheeres.

Virata: König von Matsya. Bundesgenosse der Pandava.

Vidura: Sohn Witschitrawirias und einer Sklavenfrau. Berater seines Halbbruders Dhritaraschtra.

W.

Waischia: Dritte Kaste (s. Kaste).

Wasu: Der Gott des Sturmes.

Waranawata: Ein Urwald. (Erste Verbannung der Pandava.)

Warschneja: Der Wagenlenker Nalas.

Wasischta: Ein Heiliger.

Wasu: Acht niedrige Götter, Erdengötter.

Wasudeva: Der Vater Krischnas. Iadavakönig.

Wasuki: Der König aller Schlangen.

Weda: Vier heilige Bücher der Inder. Offenbarungen Hymnen, Lieder, Vorschriften, Ritualien usw.

Widarbha: Ein Reich.

Winata: Mutter Garudas und Arunas, Gattin des Schöpfers Kaschjapa.

Windhia: Ein Gebirge.

Wirasena: König von Nischadha, Vater Nalas.

Wirini: Ein Fluss.

Wirschaparwan: Ein König der Danawa.

Wischnu: Gott der Erhaltung. Ein Teil der Dreieinigkeit Brahmas (Schöpfung, Erhaltung, Zerstörung).

Wischwakarman (auch Twaschter): Der Götterschmied.

Wischwarupa: Ein dreiköpfiger Dämon.

Witschitrawiria: Ein König aus Bharatas Geschlecht. Sohn Schantanus und der Satjawati. Vater Dhritaraschtras, Pandus und Viduras.

Wrischnier: Volk. Bundesgenossen der Pandava.

Writra: Dämonenfürst. Hauptgegner Indras. (Dürre.)

Wyasa: Ein Heiliger. Der sagenhafte Dichter des Bharataliedes.

<h1 style="text-align:center">Y.</h1>

Yama: Der Gott des Todes und des Rechtes.